FIERY KISS

When she lifted her gray eyes to him, Ace saw the confusion, the uncertainty, in their depths, and he felt compassion for her. Did she think he was going to be rough with her, the way Gibb probably was in bed?

He would have to go slow with her, he thought, sitting down on the edge of the mattress. When she didn't shrink away from him, he lifted his hand and gently stroked it over the softness of her hair, then lifted a curl and brushed his lips across it.

"You smell like my mother's rose garden," he said softly. "And you look like a rose. Your cheeks are like pink blossoms and your lips are like red petals."

He trailed a finger around her lips, then slowly lowered his head and settled his lips on hers.

He meant the kiss to be a light one, to calm any fears she might have. But when he was met with eager passion, his lips took fire and his mouth moved over hers with matching heat.

Lark

NORAH HESS

LEISURE BOOKS   NEW YORK CITY

To my daughter, Jacqueline

A LEISURE BOOK®

June 1999

Published by

Dorchester Publishing Co., Inc.
276 Fifth Avenue
New York, NY 10001

ISBN 0-8439-4522-2

Printed in the United States of America.

Chapter One

A slow drizzle had soaked the three bedraggled people who sat in the wagon pulled by an old horse.

The slender young woman handling the reins glanced often at the old lady who leaned wearily against her shoulder. If they didn't find shelter soon, she was afraid her aunt might not make it to the next day.

Lark Elliot dearly loved her Aunt Lucy and Uncle Ben. To her knowledge they were the only relatives she had.

When she was ten years old, her father and mother had been caught in a cattle stampede caused by a summer lightning storm. She had been devastated by her loss.

The night of their wake, however, new emotions gripped her: fear and panic. She had overheard the neighbor women saying that she would most likely end up in an orphanage. She had heard stories of those places, and none of them good.

The day of the funeral was gloomy and overcast as the neighbors began to congregate in the yard. She prayed that it wouldn't rain. She didn't think she could bear the sound of raindrops pelting her parents' graves.

As she sat off by herself, choking back tears, Reverend Stiger arrived, his much-handled Bible clasped in his hands. She had stared, but not at him. Her gaze was glued to the couple who walked in behind him. Although she hadn't seen the tall, white-haired man in four years, she recognized her father's brother immediately. With a glad cry she jumped to her feet and threw herself into her Uncle Ben's welcoming arms.

"How did you know?" she cried, hugging the smiling man fiercely.

"We ran into a friend of ours a couple days back, and he told us about Jake and Annie's accident. We came as fast as we could."

"I'm so glad you're here." She wiped her eyes. Then turning to the small woman waiting behind Ben, she embraced her, adding, "They were going to send me to an orphanage."

"An orphanage!" Lucy Elliot exclaimed, outraged. "Your Uncle Ben and I will take care of you, child."

And so they had. Her own parents couldn't have been sweeter or kinder to her. They had eased the sharp pain of her loss until only fond memories of her mother and father remained.

But when her uncle took over the running of the farm, she soon realized, even at her tender age, that he didn't plow and raise crops the way her father had. He spent most of his time at a nearby river, passing the day fishing its waters. Either that or he was off in the woods hunting.

Consequently, the bulk of the farm work had fallen to her and Aunt Lucy. They had been unable to handle most of the heavy work, and in less than a year the bank had foreclosed on the farm. The furniture and livestock had been sold and they had taken off in the farm wagon, pulled by two horses that were no longer young.

Lark breathed a weary sigh as she remembered the years of traveling through state after state, settling a few months on some run-down farm, then moving on to another one with the same results.

There was no getting away from it. Her uncle was a dear man, but a shiftless one. He adored his wife and niece, and with all his faults, they loved him in return.

However, after ten years of moving about, mostly living in hovels, her frail aunt had contracted tuberculosis. She grew alarmingly thin, and many times Lark had been awakened in the night by the hard coughs that racked her thin body.

And her uncle, beside himself with the fear of losing his beloved Lucy, decided that she needed pure mountain air to breathe. It would heal her lungs, he said.

Privately, Lark thought that what her aunt really needed was good nourishing food, a soft bed to lie on, and a roof over her that didn't leak.

Lark knew that wasn't likely to happen, though. They had very little money, and even fewer prospects.

It had taken a long time, traveling from eastern

Montana to the foothills of the Rockies. One of the horses had given out and had died beside the road. Lark was afraid that the remaining one was on its last legs.

"Where do we go from here, Uncle Ben?" she asked with a worried look at her aunt, who was barely able to sit up.

"Drive on up the mountain. Maybe we can find a trapper's deserted cabin. They're always moving about."

"Rufus won't make it if he has to climb too far up," Lark said. "And if Aunt Lucy doesn't get somewhere dry, she's not going to make it either."

"Don't say that, Larkie," Ben pleaded.

The old horse had pulled the wagon about a quarter of a mile up the mountain when Ben exclaimed, "Look off to your right. There's a cabin there."

Lark peered through the misty rain, the scrub pine and brush, and spotted a log building. It looked deserted, and although small and rudely constructed, it seemed sturdy enough. If only the roof doesn't leak, she thought, and clucked to Rufus to move on.

The spent horse didn't budge. He stood, head down and sides heaving. Lark's heart went out to him. He had been faithful to them, had pulled the wagon across four states during the past ten years.

"We've got to walk in, Uncle Ben," she said sharply, climbing out of the wagon. "Old Rufus can't go another step until he's rested awhile."

"Poor old fellow." Ben jumped to the ground and gave the bony horse an affectionate pat on the rump. "I hope we can find shelter for him too. I'd hate for him to be set upon by a pack of wolves or a big cat."

Ben held his arms up to the exhausted Lucy.

"Come on, honey," he said gently. "Let's get you out of the rain."

Lucy practically fell into his arms, and clutched his shoulders as he carried her to the little building.

Lark had hurried on ahead of them to make sure the place was empty. After peering through the window and making sure that nothing was stirring, she pushed open the warped door. She saw with relief that the roof didn't leak. The rough floorboards were bone dry. Her sweeping gaze spotted a door to another room. She hurried to open it, praying that she would find a bed inside. It was imperative that her aunt lie down as soon as possible.

Her heart gave a glad leap. In the damp dimness of the small room stood a bed alongside one wall. Its scarred headboard spoke of many years of use. There was a mattress and two pillows on it, but no linens. That was all right though. In the wagon, in a box, were their own sheets and blankets.

A quick glance around the room showed Lark a dresser that looked as old as the bedstead. On an outside wall, next to an uncurtained window, were several pegs to hang clothing on. More than enough for their few threadbare belongings, she thought wryly.

Lark stepped back into the other room just as Ben lowered Lucy into a chair that also had seen better days. Lucy leaned her head back and closed her eyes with a weary sigh.

"There's a bed in there." Lark jerked a thumb toward the open door. "While I go to get linens from the wagon, build a fire in the fireplace, Uncle Ben. From the looks of her white lips, Auntie is half frozen."

Ben had the makings of a fire together even as Lark stepped outside.

As she approached the wagon, she was heartened to see old Rufus cropping the grass that grew at his feet. At least he wasn't too tired to eat. That was a good sign. Now if only Aunt Lucy could eat grass, she thought wryly, they would be in fine shape.

Their rations were the lowest they had ever been. In the larder box beneath the wagon seat was a half slab of salt pork, two days' supply of dried beans, two potatoes and half of a can of coffee beans. None of it was very nourishing for a woman in need of red meat and vegetables.

The box of linens wasn't very heavy. Lark knew that it contained only a couple of threadbare sheets and four pillowcases, two thin blankets, two worn patchwork quilts, four towels, four washcloths and a thin bar of soap.

She gave Ben a bright smile as she reentered the cabin. He had a roaring fire going and was chafing Lucy's hands and wrists to get the blood flowing more rapidly through her veins.

But her forced smile didn't fool Lucy. "Get that worried look off your face, honey," her aunt said. "I'm feeling better already."

Lark saw that there was indeed some pink in the wrinkled cheeks, and this time her smile was genuine when she said, "I can see that, Auntie. And you'll feel better yet when I get the bed made up for you."

As Lark spread a sheet and blanket on the bed, she decided that she would sleep on the floor in her bedroll. If she unrolled it on top of the bedroll her aunt and uncle used, she should be comfortable enough. At least she would be dry. Not like last night, when all three of them had slept beneath the wagon.

When Lark returned to the other room, she found that Ben had made a trip to the wagon for their clothing. He was in the act of settling a gown over Lucy's head. When he had pulled the garment down over her knees, he scooped her up and carried her off to bed.

Lark stood in front of the fire a moment, and as the steam rose from Lucy's wet, discarded clothes spread on the hearth, she let her gaze move over the room.

Beneath the single window was a rudely constructed table with benches flanking the two long sides. A shelf had been fastened to the wall next to the window. It held a few tin plates, four chipped cups, and a glass jar in which odds and ends of flatware had been stored. A blackened skillet and two long-handled pots hung on pegs next to an old, rusty cookstove.

She decided that the place had been occupied not too long ago. It didn't have that musty smell of a dwelling that had been shut up for a long period of time. To strengthen her belief, there was an ample supply of wood stacked in the chimney corner, as well as a full wood box next to the rusty stove.

Lark's gaze shifted to the immediate area around the fireplace. There was the rocker her aunt had occupied, with a small table placed beside it. The chimney of the lamp that sat on its top was so smoke-blackened, she wondered if it shed any light. A straight-backed chair completed the furnishings.

It wasn't much, Lark thought with a sigh, but much better than some cabins they had lived in over the years. She prayed that they could stay here for a while. At least long enough for Aunt Lucy to regain some strength.

"I've got her all tucked in," Ben said as he joined Lark in front of the fire. "She's mighty poorly, Larkie," he added with a catch in his voice.

"She's going to be all right, Uncle Ben." Lark put an assurance she didn't feel into her voice. "She'll feel much better after she's rested awhile. Let's go unload the wagon now and decide what we're going to do about Rufus."

They made three trips between the wagon and the cabin. On the first one Lark carried the box containing their clothing, and Ben struggled with a crate of books that had traveled with them ever since they'd left the Elliot farm ten years ago. Lark had read them so often she knew most of them by heart.

On the second trip, Lark carried Lucy's prized milk-glass kerosene lamp, and Ben carefully held the mantel clock. On the third and last trip they carried between them their meager supply of food, Ben's rifle and ammunition, and two small braided rugs.

They were halfway to the cabin when Ben came to an abrupt stop. "Lark," he said excitedly, "if my eyes ain't deceiving me I see a lean-to shed attached to the back of the cabin."

Lark looked in the direction of Ben's pointing finger and smiled. Half-hidden by a low spreading pine was a small addition to the cabin. It was no more than seven feet tall and eight feet wide, but was roomy enough to accommodate one horse. They had missed seeing it earlier because they were too intent on transferring their goods to the cabin.

"Rufus is going to appreciate a roof over his head. We'll let him rest awhile longer; then maybe he'll be able to pull the wagon to his new quarters."

When the last of their scant belongings had been stowed away, and Aunt Lucy's lamp and clock had been put in places of honor on the table and mantel, they peeked in on Lucy. She was sleeping peacefully, and a tint of pink had returned to her cheeks.

If only we can stay here for a while, Lark thought. *I'll manage somehow to see that she gets some nourishing food into her.*

"She looks better, don't she, Larkie?" Ben whispered.

"Yes, she does. Let's go see if Rufus can make it to the shed now."

Fortunately the old horse made no objection when Lark put an arm around his neck and coaxed him to walk along beside her. His pace was slow, but he managed to pull the wagon the few yards to his new quarters. Ben unhitched him from the wagon and led him inside.

To their surprise and relief there was some hay in the shallow loft a couple feet above Rufus's head. "We'll give him some tomorrow morning," Ben said. "He's got a bellyful of grass now."

"And he'll be quite safe here too," Lark said as she dropped the bars on the heavy door when they stepped outside. "Not even a cougar can get to him."

"I guess we should start thinking about fixing something for supper," Ben said when they walked into the kitchen. "Lucy will be hungry when she wakes up."

"Yes, she will," Lark agreed, and picked up Ben's rifle, which was leaning against the wall next to the door. "I'm going to see if I can shoot some kind of game to make broth. That's what she needs."

Stepping quietly on the wet leaves and pine needles littering the mountain floor, Lark went down to the foothills. She would be more apt to find game in the heavier foliage there.

She had not gone far when she suddenly darted behind a tall, jagged boulder. She had heard two wild turkeys calling to each other. She carefully peered around the stone formation, but couldn't spot them. Just as she prepared to wait for another call, she stiffened, her finger curled around the rifle's trigger. Through the trees she had caught sight of a bright red turkey wattle. A young hen was scratching among the leaves looking for bugs.

Holding her breath, Lark slowly brought the rifle to her shoulder, took a bead on the hen and squeezed the trigger. Its head disappeared and it lay flopping on the ground.

She wanted to whoop her joy as she ran forward to pick up the dead bird. Part of it would be boiled into a rich broth for Aunt Lucy, and the rest would be roasted for their supper tonight.

She swallowed the saliva that formed in her mouth just from thinking about it.

As Lark started back up the mountain with the turkey swinging from her hand, she began to feel a prickling between her shoulder blades. She had a strong premonition that she was being followed. But by an animal or a human?

She heaved a big sigh of relief when the old cabin came into sight. She wondered then if she had imagined it all. Before she opened the door she turned and saw only rocks and trees behind her.

When Lark dragged the warped door shut, Ben looked up from his seat before the fire. His eyes widened at the sight of the turkey when she lifted it onto the table.

"Shot its head clean off, did you?" He grinned at Lark and left the rocker to inspect the bird. "A young hen too. She'll make some fine eating. While you build a fire in the cookstove I'll go get the feathers off this beauty."

It was with some difficulty that Lark finally got a fire going in the aged, rusty stove. Its damper was broken and it didn't want to draw properly. After she had rinsed her hands, she peeked in on her aunt. Lucy was still sleeping soundly. "Poor little thing," she whispered, "you were completely worn out."

As she walked out of the bedroom, Ben walked into the kitchen. "There it is," he said proudly, "plucked clean and dressed out."

Lark nodded her satisfaction, then asked him for his hunting knife. When she had scrubbed the bird inside and out, she picked up the knife and cut off the two wings and one leg and thigh. She placed them in a large pot of water, and set it on the stove to start cooking. The remaining meat she placed in a roaster, which they had brought along, and shoved it into the oven. Within an hour a rich broth was sending its aroma throughout the cabin, mingling with the mouth watering smell of the meat roasting in the oven.

Lark lifted the lid off the pot and sniffed at the steam that floated up. When she forked the meat out of the broth it was so tender it fell apart. She stripped the leg and thigh clean, cut the meat into small pieces and returned it to the pot. She added some salt, then began to fill three cups with the thick liquid.

"Go wake up Aunt Lucy," she said to Ben, who sat at the table watching her. "A cup of this will hold us until the turkey has finished roasting."

Ben hurried from the room and returned almost immediately, leading a sleepy-eyed Lucy. "Here she is," he announced, his face beaming. "She looks better already, don't she, Larkie?"

"You do look ever so much better, Aunt Lucy," Lark said happily. "You've got a color in your cheeks and you look more rested than I've seen you in a long time. Maybe the mountain air is good for you."

"I told you it would be," Ben said as he helped his wife to sit down on a bench, then sat down beside her.

"If only we could stay here." There was a note of worry in Lark's voice as she sat down opposite them.

"I don't see any reason why we can't," Ben replied as he reached for one of the steaming cups. "Nobody has lived here for some time. The trapper who owned this has probably moved on to a better trapping area. They move around all the time."

"I hope you're right, Ben," Lucy said, dipping her spoon into the broth. "I don't know if I could move again, what with winter coming on."

"Now, don't you go worrying, Lucy." Ben patted her hand, then changed the subject. "Eat your meat and broth. It tastes mighty good."

No one talked as hungry appetites were fed. When Ben had emptied his cup he looked longingly at the pot on the stove, but didn't ask for a second helping. The rest of the meaty broth was for Lucy. She could eat it tomorrow and the next day.

When Lark and Lucy had finished eating, Lark gathered up the three cups and took them to a basin of water she had heated. "We'll have some coffee now," she said when she had rinsed out the cups.

"That sounds real good, honey." Ben smiled at her. "Just the thing to round out a good—"

Lark had cut him off by raising a hand for silence. "I thought I heard a noise outside the cabin," she whispered, setting the coffeepot back on the stove. She walked quietly to the door and picked up the rifle before opening it.

Standing just outside, Lark swung a slow look around the area. Nothing stirred. She stood a minute longer, peering into the scrub pine, studying the boulders scattered about. Finally satisfied that she had heard an animal walking about, she went back into the cabin.

Ben and Lucy sighed their relief when she picked up the coffeepot again and said, "I guess I was mistaken. I didn't see anybody lurking around, and Rufus isn't kicking up a ruckus, so I guess there's no wolf or cougar prowling around." She poured the coffee and sat back down.

Ben took a sip of the strong brew and, smacking his lips, said, "Wonderful, just wonderful."

Lark agreed as she took a sip. Then, remembering that her uncle always lived for the moment, she said, "We must think about what we're to eat after the turkey is gone."

She knew by the startled look that came into her uncle's eyes that he hadn't thought that far ahead. He sat a moment, then agreed that she was right. "Have you thought of anything, niece?"

Lark withheld a frustrated sigh. She was so weary of having all the decisions left up to her. She wished that for once her uncle would take hold of a worrisome situation and solve it.

But that wouldn't happen, she knew. She looked into Uncle Ben's hopeful eyes and answered, "Not really, but before I shot the turkey I saw signs of deer around a small, spring-fed pool. If you can keep us supplied with game, I'll see if I can find some kind of employment at that big ranch we passed a few miles back. A place that large must need a lot of help to keep it running. If I can get hired on, I'm sure I'll make enough to buy our other essentials."

"I knew you would think of something, Lark, dear," Aunt Lucy said with a tender smile at her niece. "I know that I will get better if we can only stay on here."

All worry had left Ben's face at Lark's words. As far as he was concerned, their future was assured. "I'll go bag us a deer the first thing in the morning. Maybe I'll find a stream where I can fish. Wouldn't a mess of trout taste good, Lucy?"

"It would indeed, Ben." Lucy beamed at her husband. "I can almost taste them now."

They were just like a pair of carefree children without a worry in the world, Lark was thinking when a knock sounded on the door.

All three gave a startled jerk and stared at the flimsy, warped entrance into the cabin. A moment later the old folks swung their frightened gaze to Lark.

"What are we going to do, Lark?" Lucy said in a quavering voice. "Do you think we'll have to move?"

"Shhh." Lark patted the thin, small hand that had gripped her arm. "Maybe it's just a friendly neighbor," she said as she rose and walked to the door.

Before she opened it, she picked up the rifle leaning there.

Her eyes were almost on a level with those of the fat man who stood smiling brightly at her. "Good afternoon, miss," he said in a soft, congenial voice. "My name is Cletus Gibb. I own the ranch down at the edge of the foothills."

A stirring of excitement made Lark's pulse beat a little faster. Here was the man she intended to ask for employment. I must be friendly to him, she thought as she leaned the rifle back against the wall.

"I think we passed your place on our way here, Mr. Gibb. Please come in." She stepped back to give him passage. "My name is Lark Elliot," she said, closing the door behind him. "And this is my aunt and uncle, Ben and Lucy Elliot."

When Ben stood up and offered his hand, Gibb took it and said, "I'm pleased to meet you, Ben." He smiled gently at Lucy then. "You look like you've been feeling poorly, ma'am."

"Yes, I have." Lucy nodded. "But I'm sure I'll feel much better breathing this pure mountain air."

"There's no better place in the world to cure ailments than the mountains," Gibb agreed.

"Won't you take a seat, Mr. Gibb, and have a cup of coffee with us?" Lark invited.

"Don't mind if I do," Cletus said, and so answering, he pulled the bench that Lark had occupied farther away from the table to accommodate his wide girth.

"Something sure smells good," he said as Lark filled a cup for him. "It's a turkey roasting." Lark sat down beside him. "I shot it down in the foothills a couple of hours ago."

"So it was your shot I heard." Gibb took a sip of his coffee.

"But you weren't hunting too," Lucy said. "You aren't carrying a rifle."

"No, I wasn't hunting. I like to ride around when there's a slow, gentle drizzle like the one today. You see, I own this land, including a mile up the mountain."

"Then you own this cabin." A fine worry line creased Lark's forehead. "We figured it was an abandoned trapper's place."

"No." Gibb smiled and twisted his bulk around to face Lark. "I use it once in a while when I want to be alone. Maybe to hunt or fish a little. Even though I own a big house, I have no wife or children. Sometimes I get so lonesome wandering around in it, I come up here to find peace of mind."

"A person can find that up here," Ben said, then sighed. "We'll move on in the morning. That is, if you don't mind our spending the night."

"No, not at all. Mrs. Elliot looks all tuckered out."

"She is, and we sure appreciate your letting us spend the night." Ben put an arm around Lucy's trembling shoulders.

In the ensuing silence Lark remembered the uneasy feeling she'd had that someone had followed her after she shot the turkey. Had it been the rancher? If so, why hadn't he made himself known to her?

She glanced at Gibb calmly sipping his coffee and dismissed the thought. This big, open-faced, friendly man wasn't the type to stalk a woman. If she had indeed been followed, it had probably been by a wolf.

Gibb set his cup down, fidgeted with it a moment, then began to speak in a shy, uncertain voice. "I've been thinking on something that would benefit all of us."

Ben sat forward, hope flaring in his eyes. "What would that be, Mr. Gibb?" he asked eagerly.

"Well, it's like this, and you'll probably say it's a crazy idea, Lark, and will say no right off. But it came to me as we sat here that I need a wife and you, Ben and Lucy, need security."

He squared around to face Lark and to smile at her shyly. "Miss Elliot, I would feel honored if you would become my wife."

When Lark, shocked, opened her mouth to refuse his proposal outright, he held up his hand. "Think on it a spell, Miss Elliot. I have a fine big house, run three thousand head of cattle, and I have no heirs. Everything would be yours at my death.

"I know that I'm not much to look at, and that I'm twice your age, but I would be good to you, treat you like a lady." He looked at Ben and Lucy, who were watching Lark anxiously, and continued coaxingly, "And your aunt and uncle would never have to worry about what was to become of them. I would see to it that they were well taken care of."

Lark started to protest that she could never marry a man she didn't love, but then her gaze fell on her relatives. There was silent pleading in their eyes.

Could she sacrifice herself for these two old people? she wondered. How much did she owe them? She thought back to the time of her parents' death, how the loving couple had saved her from going to an orphanage. They had given her a home, such as it was, but above all else they had given her an abundance of love. But could she bring herself to marry a stranger to secure them a haven in their old age?

It wasn't as if she was in love with another man, she told herself. Over the years they hadn't been in one place long enough for her to fall in love. And she felt that this big, friendly man would be good to her.

Still she hesitated. It seemed so cold-blooded to marry a man she didn't love. She would, in fact, be selling herself to him.

Gibb saw the indecision on her face and said, "Why don't you think it over. I'll come by in the morning for your answer."

"Yes, do that." Lark stood up, relieved that she didn't have to give the rancher her answer right now. "It is all kinda sudden, your proposal," she said weakly as Gibb stood up beside her.

Lark was thankful that after Gibb left her aunt and uncle didn't bring up the subject of his proposal. She would have been unable to discuss it.

The next morning, however, after a restless night of considering the rancher's offer, she found that her aunt and uncle were very vocal about their thoughts on the subject.

They had barely eaten their breakfast of fried salt pork when Gibb knocked on the door. Ben and Lucy sat forward, watching her closely when she rose to answer the loud rap. They want me to accept him, she said to herself, the thought chasing away her decision to refuse the rancher. She forced a smile to her lips as she opened the door.

"Well, Miss Lark, what have you decided?" Cletus Gibb asked as soon as he stepped inside.

All three faces beamed at her when she said, "I will marry you, Mr. Gibb."

"You won't regret it, Miss . . . Lark. I'll bring the preacher in."

"You mean you want to get married today?" Lark looked at him, shocked.

"I know it seems sudden, but I have a very good reason. I got word day before yesterday that my brother in Denver passed away. I will be leaving soon to attend his funeral. I will be gone for at least a week and I'd like to think of you waiting at the ranch for me, Lark."

"I can't think of any reason to wait, can you, Larkie?" Ben looked at Lark anxiously.

Lark could only shake her head helplessly. There really wasn't any reason to wait. It wasn't as though she had a wedding gown, had plans for a big, fancy wedding. Her main objective was to provide security for her relatives.

When Cletus left with a pleased smile on his face, Ben and Lucy moved to sit on either side of Lark. "You made a good decision, Larkie," Ben said earnestly. "It eases my mind that you are marrying a good man. It's true he's somewhat older than you, but a young man couldn't afford to give you the good life that Mr. Gibb can. You'll never want for anything."

"You do like him, don't you, honey?" Lucy reached for her hand. "You're not afraid of him, are you? I wouldn't want you to marry him if you're the least bit afraid of him. I want you to have a marriage like Ben and I have had over the years."

Lark patted the skeletonlike hand that gripped her. "I'm not afraid of him, Auntie, and yes, I like him fine. He seems to be a very kind man." She looked at her aunt and, seeing the disquiet that lingered in the

27

gentle, faded eyes, laughed softly and joked, "Imagine me, little old Lark Elliot, becoming the mistress of a big, fancy house."

Her levity brought a change over the wrinkled features, and Lucy and Ben chattered away like a pair of magpies. They had put to rest any concern they'd had about her welfare.

Lark took a deep breath and said, "I hope I can find a decent dress to stand up in."

Chapter Two

It didn't take Lark long to pack her few clothes, then change into a dress a little less faded than the one she had on. She wiped the dust off her shoes; then without benefit of a mirror she brushed her long, sun-bleached brown hair until it lay in curls and waves on her shoulders.

"You look beautiful, honey." Pride was in Lucy's eyes as she looked at the niece she loved so deeply.

"Thank you, Aunt Lucy." Lark smiled, then sat down at the table and folded her hands in her lap to hide the nervous trembling of her fingers. Why was she feeling so uneasy at the last minute? she asked herself.

She hadn't long to wait. Not even half an hour passed before Cletus arrived with a tall, lanky man dressed all in black and carrying a Bible in his long, bony hand.

"Folks, meet Rev. Jacob Nelson," Cletus said with a smile that didn't quite reach his eyes. "I caught him on his way to a church meeting in Dogwood and persuaded him to take the time to marry us, Lark. I guess we ought to hurry it up. We don't want to keep him away from church too long."

The preacher wasn't paying any attention to Cletus's babbling. His intent gaze was on the two old people, and on the lovely girl whom Gibb had somehow managed to coax into marriage. He knew that the old run-down cabin belonged to the rancher, and he could see that the small family was on its last legs, so to speak. Was the young woman marrying Gibb so that the two old people would have a home? One thing was for sure: the beautiful woman didn't know what she was getting into, marrying this brutal man.

Lark grew nervous at the reverend's close scrutiny and said in a small voice, "I am Lark Elliot, and this is my Aunt Lucy and Uncle Ben Elliot."

When the two men had shaken hands, Jacob Nelson pinned Lark with somber eyes. "Are you entering this marriage wholeheartedly, child?"

Lark hesitated but a fraction of a second before answering, "Yes, Reverend, I am."

The tall man of the cloth looked into Lark's gray eyes a moment longer, and then said with a soft sigh, "Let's get on with it, then."

To the background sounds of a crackling fire in the old rusty stove and the quiet sobbing of Lucy, Lark Elliot became Mrs. Cletus Gibb. When the marriage certificate had been signed, Cletus pressed a bill into Jacob Nelson's hand and hurried him out of the cabin.

"Well, bride," Cletus said, closing the door and

rubbing his hands together, "we'd better get started for the ranch. I've got a lot of work ahead of me."

Lark embraced her sobbing aunt and kissed Ben on the cheek. "I'll be up tomorrow with some provisions for you," she promised.

She and her new husband were outside then, and he was helping her to mount a big roan stallion. When the animal shied at her long skirts slapping against its sides, Cletus gave the reins a savage jerk that caused the bit to cut into the animal's tender mouth.

"That wasn't necessary," Lark protested sharply. "He evidently isn't used to having a woman on his back."

"A little roughness is what you understand, ain't it, Devil?" Gibb said as he gathered up the reins and started the animal down the narrow trail.

Lark tried to make light conversation as the horse picked its way around boulders and stunted trees. But when her new husband's response was only grunts, she grew silent. He probably had his mind on the work waiting for him at the ranch.

She didn't notice that the drizzly rain had finally stopped as she thought of the big house she was going to be mistress of, how she would care for it, how she would do her best to be a good wife.

Lark was looking forward to the children she would have when Cletus drew the roan in sharply. Startled, she came out of her daydreaming and saw that they had reached the edge of the foothills. Why was he stopping here? she wondered.

She learned soon enough when Cletus fastened his hands on her bodice and ripped it apart. "What are you doing?" she gasped in anger and surprise.

"I'm taking a look at what I bought up there on the mountain," he growled, and twisted her around so that he could see the quivering breasts he had bared.

"Real pretty," he said harshly, breathing fast. "Let's see how they taste."

With a dip of his head, his mouth came down to fasten on one breast.

In indignant reaction Lark brought her hand up, the heel of her palm under his chin. When she shoved to remove his mouth, he bit down hard on her nipple.

She let out a small scream and shoved at his thick shoulders until he lifted his mouth from her. Grabbing her chin, forcing her to look at him, he said quite plainly, "Every time you rebuff me in anything I say or do, you will pay dearly for it. And if you displease me in any way, them old folks won't get a bite from me. They can sit up there and starve to death. So, missy, if you care for them, you'd better mind your manners around me and do as I say in all things. Is that clear?"

Lark could only nod her head dumbly. Dear, Lord, she prayed silently, what have I gotten myself into?

When they arrived at the ranch shortly afterward, Cletus slid out of the saddle and ordered roughly, "Get in the house, pick yourself a bedroom, and strip off your clothes. I'll be with you as soon as I send a man up the mountain with some grub for your no-account relatives."

When Lark saw that she wasn't going to be helped to dismount she slid down off the tall horse, and, holding her torn bodice together, she entered her new home. She walked into the first bedroom she came to down the long hall. With shaking fingers she undressed and crawled onto a bed bare of linens. With her eyes squeezed tightly together, she lay waiting for whatever hell this brute of a man would deal her.

Lark's heart was pounding so loudly she didn't hear her husband enter the room. She became aware of him when he threw his fat, naked body on top of her. The breath whooshed out of her lungs at his heavy weight, and she was unable to cry out when he jerked her onto her back and yanked her arms from across her breasts.

"Come on, bitch, open up for me," he said in a growl, and, grabbing her by the tender flesh of her inner thighs, he yanked them apart.

She shuddered in revulsion when she felt his fat belly pressing against her, felt him trying to enter the core of her. He began to sweat as time and time again he tried to penetrate her, to no avail. For a fleeting moment she was relieved at his failure; then the beating began.

Filthy words she had never heard before spewed out of his mouth as he straddled her and began to rain blows on her face and body.

She was near to fainting when he finally crawled off her. Through eyes that were beginning to swell, she looked up at him, wondering what he was going to do next.

When a few seconds passed and he didn't raise his hand to her, it appeared he was finished with her for the time being. She dared to relax; then she tightened up again when he began to speak.

"You are like all the rest," he said, breathing heavily. "You promise things to a man with your smiles and nice words, but when he takes you to bed your coldness freezes his expectations.

"Well, my fancy miss, one way or the other you are going to pay for stringing me along. If you want that useless old couple to continue living in my cabin and for me to feed them, this is what you're going to do.

"I have six men working for me at the moment. You are going to cook two meals a day for them, scrub their clothes, keep the house spotless and once a week drive into Dogwood for provisions."

He looked at Lark's battered face. "You can take up your duties in a couple of days." He left her then, slamming the door behind him.

Hot tears scorched Lark's face, stinging her split lip and mingling with the blood that trickled from its corner. She feared she would have a lifetime of her husband's brutality. She had discovered that he was impotent. He could not do his husbandly duty in bed. This embarrassed and enraged him. And so he blamed her. She lay curled on her side, staring at the wall. How was she to get out of this hell she found herself in? The welfare of two old people depended on her. If she walked away from this marriage, what would become of them all? Winter was approaching. Where would they go when Cletus kicked them out? The area was new to them, and old Rufus didn't have very many miles left in him.

Lark concluded that there was only one answer. For the time being she must stay here, live by Cletus Gibb's rules. Come spring, when Aunt Lucy was well and old Rufus was stronger, they would take off in the wagon again.

She dragged herself off the bed and picked up the small bag of clothes she had dropped beside the door. She longed to have a bath, to wash away the scent and feel of her husband's disgusting body. But before she even looked into the water pitcher sitting in a matching basin, she knew it would be empty. With a long sigh she picked her underclothing off the floor and pulled it on. She folded the torn dress over the bed's footrail. She would mend it later. Her husband wouldn't be buying her any new ones, of that she was sure.

When she had taken a much worn and faded dress from her small supply, she walked over to a dresser that had a large mirror. Pushing the hair off her forehead, she stared at her face. It was hardly recognizable, it was so bruised and swollen. The area around both eyes was beginning to turn black, there was an angry-looking bruise on one cheek, and her lips were puffy, the bottom one split. She must bathe her face in cold water as quickly as possible.

Lark opened the bedroom door and stepped out into the long hall. She stood a moment, listening for sounds of Cletus moving about. When she heard nothing but the ticking of a clock, she went in search of the kitchen.

When she found it she could only gape in awe. Her gaze swung from a big black cookstove that she was sure had never been used, to a table sitting in the middle of the room, and four matching chairs grouped around it. There was a cupboard full of dishes, and finally her gaze rested on a sink with a small pump attached to it. She hurried across the floor and worked the handle of the pump until cold water rushed out of its spout into a basin beneath it.

Lark stood bent over for several minutes, bringing

hands full of water to her face. It was icy cold, but felt so good to her battered flesh.

Patting her face dry with the bottom of her petticoat, Lark looked out the window, and when she didn't see Cletus around, she decided to make a tour of her prison. Off the kitchen was a large dining room with a long, shiny table in its center and eight chairs around it. There was a large glass-doored cabinet against one wall. It held glassware and a beautiful set of dishes. For company, she guessed, but couldn't imagine anyone coming to eat dinner with Cletus Gibb.

She stepped next into a parlor that took her breath away. There was furniture there that she never knew existed. Was it possible that her crude husband had chosen the sofa and chairs, the gleaming tables, the rich-looking window hangings? One big chair held the imprint of his fat body, but other than that it looked as if none of the other furniture had ever been used.

Lark walked down the long hall then, peering into the bedrooms that opened off it. There were four. Only the bed at the end of the hall had linens on it. This was her husband's room, she knew. She could smell the sweaty scent of him. As she turned to go back to her room, she saw next to Cletus's door a tall, narrow piece of furniture with double doors. Upon opening it she found shelves of bed linens. She lifted out two sheets, a blanket and two pillowcases and returned to her room.

After she had spread the sheets and blanket over the wide, comfortable mattress, Lark walked over to the window that looked out at the barn and stables and other outbuildings. By craning her neck she could see a cookhouse a short distance from the house. Five men and a teenager stood and sat about, waiting to be called to supper, she imagined. No doubt they were the men she would be cooking for in a couple of days. What would happen to the present cook? she wondered. No doubt Cletus would fire him.

She dreaded cooking for so many men. Until now, she had only cooked for her aunt and uncle.

Lark stayed mostly in her room for the next two days, venturing into the other part of the house when she was sure Cletus wasn't around. She dreaded bedtime. Each night when she retired, she lay shivering with dread that he would come to her bed and try to make her his wife in every sense. Her tense body would sag with relief every time his heavy tread continued on down the hall to his own bedroom.

She hadn't spoken to her husband since their wedding night. The young teenager brought her two meals a day. Breakfast and supper. He was a polite young man and always pretended that he didn't see her fading bruises and purple-rimmed eyes. She felt that she might find a friend in him.

She worried about her aunt and uncle. Cletus had lied about needing to go to Denver after the wedding, and she prayed he hadn't lied about sending food up to them as well. She didn't dare slip up the mountain to visit them. It would make them sick to see what her husband had done to her.

Lark heard the men leaving the cookhouse, and she walked over to the window to watch them coming out. She wondered if they would have the same contented looked tomorrow morning when she prepared breakfast for them.

Lark darted away from the window when she saw Cletus walking toward the house. She sat down on the edge of the bed, her hands nervously clenched together. He had never returned to the house before. She gave a start when her door slammed open and he stood glowering at her.

"Well, Mrs. Gibb," he said to her with a sneer, "you've lazed around long enough. Tomorrow morning you start earning your keep. Have breakfast ready for the men at six o'clock sharp. And plenty of it."

Lark nodded, and he continued, "You'll find what you need in the larder room in the cookhouse. When you have fed the men and cleaned the house, you'll need to hitch up the wagon and drive into Dogwood for the provisions we are short of. Get what you need and put it on my tab at the store."

Lark nodded again and relaxed her tense shoulders as she watched him waddle out of the room.

Chapter Three

The rider pulled the travel-worn gelding in to rest a few minutes, and swung out of the saddle.

His facc was strong and handsome in a rugged way, but his eyes were as cold as ice on a slow-moving river. On one hip dangled a holster. It was not fancy, and most men would know that it was not worn for show. He had a superior swiftness and an unerring aim with the Colt.

Ace Brandon, ex-gambler, was lean and leather tough. Woe to the man who called him out to test his strength or the accuracy of his gun.

He couldn't remember how many miles he had traveled the past three months. But they were many, he knew, starting out from a small town in Utah.

Utah, he thought, looking grimly ahead as the tired gelding plodded along. He had buried his wife there.

He and Michelle had been married three months

when he took her there to meet his widowed mother. That had been a mistake, he had thought later. After two weeks spent away from the excitement of the Lady Chance saloon, where he worked, he grew bored and longed to get back there, to handle a deck of cards again.

For a large part of his adult life he had made his living, and a good one, at the poker table. He had been a dealer at the Lady Chance for years.

When he had wanted to cut their visit short and return to Colorado, his new bride had protested, claiming that she wasn't ready to go back to the noise, the drunks, the dancing girls. "To tell the truth," she had added, "I'm tired of singing for those people. I've been thinking that we should leave Denver and go to California. San Franscisco, maybe. They have fancy theaters where a singer would be appreciated."

A hot and bitter argument ensued. Angry words and charges had been flung about, some hurtful. Their quarrel had ended when they both stamped out of the house, slamming the doors behind them. Michelle had left by the kitchen door, walking fast toward the barn and stables, while he had stormed through the house and flung himself onto the gelding hitched to the porch. He galloped the big animal toward town. With any luck, he'd find a game going on.

His ire was still high as he rode down the dusty main street. He and Michelle had been snapping at each other lately, but this was the first time they'd exchanged such harsh words. She had accused him of being self-centered, thinking only of what would please him. She had said that if he really loved her he wouldn't make her live in quarters above the Lady Chance.

He had retorted that their apartment was as luxurious as any house in town, that she was a spoiled young woman, always wanting more.

Ace found a poker game going on in the saloon and was invited to sit in. Back in his element again, he forgot everything but the cards he held in his hands. He was unaware, as the hours passed, that the sun was near setting and that his mother would have supper waiting.

A new hand was being dealt when a teenaged neighbor burst into the saloon and hurried to the poker table. Out of breath, he panted, "Ace, you gotta get home quick."

"What's wrong, boy?" Ace jumped to his feet.

"Your wife has been bit by a rattlesnake."

"Has the doctor been notified?" Ace asked, hurrying toward the bat-wing doors.

"Ain't no use for the doc, Ace," he said; then he blurted out, "She's dead."

Ace had been riding across a seemingly endless plain all day. The sun would be down soon and he could see no place to make camp, unless he built his fire out in the open. He didn't care to do that. He was wondering how much farther he would have to ride when suddenly there before him was a deep, winding valley of grass, pines and aspens. Through the center of it ran a river.

"Rest and water are just ahead, Sam," he said, patting the big Appaloosa's neck.

As he descended to the floor of the valley a sage hen flew off her nest of eggs. Ace drew his Colt and shot her while she was in midair. His supper was assured.

Ace's first act when he drew near the river was to unsaddle the footsore Sam and turn him loose. He had no fear that the gelding would stray too far away from him.

He built his campfire in a clump of aspens whose leaves were turning a soft yellow that stood out against the stark green of the pines. The fowl was quickly plucked of feathers and dressed out. He sparingly rubbed salt over it. He had very little left, or any other grub. He hadn't seen a town in days. A coffeepot filled with water from the stream and a handful of coffee beans was set on the fire where the sage hen roasted on a green-wood spit.

The aroma of roasting meat and brewing coffee made Ace's mouth water as he opened up his bedroll and spread it close to the fire. He went to gather a pile of deadwood he found in plentiful supply beneath the trees. He intended to keep a fire going all night. He suspected there were wolves in the area, as well as cougars up in the foothills of the mountain he could see in the distance.

It was deep twilight when Ace sat down in front of the fire and attacked the tender, roasted meat, washing it down with swallows of coffee. Sam was nearby, cropping his evening meal.

Night had fallen when he ate the last bit of meat off the bones, and in a distant clump of aspens a whippoorwill began its call. Then two owls perched high in the branches began hooting to each other.

The evening air had cooled considerably, and Ace sat hunched close to the campfire. As he stared into the glowing coals and leaping flames, he saw in them a picture, and the haunting words that went with it.

He remembered standing in a lonely cemetery, and a preacher saying solemnly, "I am the resurrection and the life," as Michelle was lowered into the ground.

He'd had a lot of time to think as he'd ridden aimlessly for the past three months. Sitting in front of lonely campfires he had finally admitted to himself that he hadn't truly loved his wife. He knew now what had attracted him to Michelle. She was a cut above the women he was used to, the dancers at the Lady Chance, the girls from Belle's Pleasure House, even the so-called society girls he sometimes courted. Those young ladies only had an eye out for a husband and didn't hesitate to use their bodies in order to trap one.

Michelle, though, had led him a merry chase, and that was what had excited him, made him determined to marry her. That would never happen to him again, he vowed.

He still felt guilty, though, that he had not been able to prevent Michelle's death. The rattler had struck her in the neck, pouring its venom into the jugular vein, taking the life away from her within minutes.

It's time now that I light somewhere for a while. Sam needs a long rest, and I'm about broke. A wry smile twisted his lips. He'd try to hire on at some ranch, punch cattle, which he had sworn years ago never to do again.

A pack of wolves began to howl, and Ace piled more wood on the fire. Removing his boots and holster, he crawled between the blankets. He whistled to Sam to come close to the fire, laid the Colt near at hand, and soon drifted off to sleep.

It was not quite light the next morning, when Ace awakened to the cool dampness of a fine, misty rain on his face. He sat up and swore under his breath when he saw that his campfire was a mass of wet, gray coals. He'd have a hell of a time finding enough dry wood for another fire, and damn it, he had half a pot of coffee left over from last night.

As he pulled on his damp boots he looked around for Sam. The gelding stood a few feet away, in a thick stand of aspens. He looked at Ace when his master rose and strapped on his Colt, which was still dry from being under the blanket.

"Don't look at me like I shot the dog," Ace said affectionately. "Blame old Mother Nature." The gelding's answer was a snort.

Surprisingly, Ace found plenty of dry wood under the thick growth of trees. He built his fire under their thick canopy and soon had a roaring blaze going. When he had placed the pot of coffee near the flames to reheat, he spread the damp blankets around the fire to dry out. By the time he pulled on the slicker that had bulged at the cantle of the saddle, steam was rising from the battered coffeepot.

Ace downed three cups of the strong coffee and had a smoke while the blankets dried. He dumped the coffee grounds on the fire, then walked down to the river to rinse the pot out.

When he was ready to break camp, Ace decided to ride along the river until he came to a fur post. He imagined there were several up and down the river, since the Indians and most of the white trappers brought their furs in by canoe.

There was also the possibility that he might come upon a town. He was acquainted with the mountainous area of eastern Colorado.

The mist became a light, steady rain, and as Ace rode along, a soft patter filled the stillness of aspen and pine. Water was running freely down the slicker when he came to a spot where the trail forked. The one he had been following went on, following the curves of the river. The other one branched off, leading to the open plains. He reined in, thought a minute, then nudged Sam to head out for open country.

Lark had not slept well. She was afraid she wouldn't awaken in time to have breakfast ready for the men by six o'clock. The clock in the parlor had just struck midnight when she'd heard rain slashing against her window.

It was still raining the next morning when Lark awoke. In a panic she'd lit the bedside lamp and carried it into the parlor to check the time. Four-thirty. She had plenty of time to make breakfast. It had taken but a few minutes to get dressed, and, holding her slicker over her head, she'd splashed to the cookhouse.

In the gray darkness she made out the shape of a long table. Walking to it, she fumbled around on its top until her fingers found a box of matches. When she had lit the lamp sitting there she crossed the room to light the big black cookstove. Her gaze ranged around the large room. It was not fancy, but everything was spotlessly clean.

Lark started a large pot of coffee brewing, then

opened the narrow door to the larder room. There were shelves of tinned vegetables and fruit; ham, slabs of salt pork and bacon hung from the rafters. There were eggs and butter in crocks. Lark hoped that Cletus had sent some of this nourishing food to her aunt and uncle.

On further inspection Lark noted that they were low on flour, sugar, coffee and potatoes. A trip into town would indeed be necessary. She carried the eggs and a slab of bacon into the kitchen, added more wood to the fire she had started in the stove, then went back into the larder room to bring back an apronful of potatoes. She poured herself a cup of coffee, drank it, then started to prepare breakfast.

At ten minutes to six she set the table for eight people. By the time she heard the men coming, piping hot food sat on the long table.

Lark stood beside the stove, her eyes cast down. Amid the scraping noises of the benches being pulled away from the table, Cletus said gruffly, "Men, this is my wife, Lark."

She was too embarrassed about her bruised face to answer when the men said "Pleased to meet you, missus."

The men had hearty appetites, but luckily she had cooked plenty. No one would go away hungry. Twice Cletus growled at her to pour coffee. From the corner of her eye she saw the men giving her pitying looks.

When the men had finished, the last to leave was the teenager, Thad. She stayed him with a hand on his arm. "I have to go to Dogwood for provisions," she half whispered. "Can you tell me where it is?"

"Certainly, miss." Thad spoke in low tones also.

"Just follow the wide road out of here. It will take you straight to town. Do you want me to hitch up the wagon?"

"Oh, no. I'll do it." She looked fearfully over his shoulder.

Thad seemed to sense her unease and said before he walked off in the rain, "I'll see you at suppertime then."

It took Lark about an hour to clean the kitchen; then she hurried to the house to sweep and dust. She took off her apron, brushed her hair, then pulled on her old black slicker.

Cletus was waiting for her when she entered the barn. He didn't speak, only sat on a bale of hay watching her harness the workhorses, then hitch them to a large buckboard. When she was finished she climbed into the cumbersome-looking vehicle and said, "I'll be leaving now."

"Take that raggedy-looking slicker off first," Cletus ordered. "You look like a scarecrow. It's not raining that hard."

Lark looked out into the barnyard. It wasn't raining hard; nevertheless, it was falling steadily. She would be soaked by the time she reached town. She looked at the threatening expression on Cletus's face and her protest died on her lips. She shrugged out of the old slicker, picked up the long reins and slapped them against the horses' rumps.

As the buckboard rolled outside, she was surprised to see Cletus riding ahead of her.

It wasn't a long ride to Dogwood, but as Lark had expected, she was wet to the skin when they entered the single street of the small town. The livery was the first place of business they came to. Cletus drew rein there and motioned her to pull the team in.

"Wait here for me," he ordered. "I'll be back shortly."

Lark watched him ride down the street, wondering if she dared go into the long building, where it was warm and dry. She decided she'd better not.

Ace figured he had ridden a couple of hours when in the distance he saw a scattering of buildings that had to be a town. Half a mile later a signpost proclaimed it to be Dogwood.

Like a dozen other cow towns, he thought as he rode down the single street, although a little larger. The gelding plodded past a mercantile, a dress shop, a drugstore, a doctor's office on one side of the street, and on the other side the sheriff's office. There was a restaurant, a hotel, a barbershop, a bank, a post office, and finally a livery stable.

He always found that saloons and barbershops were the best sources of information. He fingered his whisker-stubbled jaw and decided it was Tom's Barbershop he would visit first. The proprietor would know if any ranchers were looking for men.

Judging from the number of men in town, it must be Saturday, Ace thought. On the wooden sidewalk of the muddy street men jostled one another as they walked along, their eager eyes searching for entertainment. There were mountain men clad in buckskin clothing. Shaggy haired, bearded and rough-looking, they watched for any danger that might appear suddenly. He saw a couple of stage drivers, their faces creased from exposure to the elements. There were a few gamblers in their black suits and hats. The rest were cowboys, ranchers and townspeople. He saw very few women about.

Ace pulled up in front of the livery. He narrowed his eyes, peering through the rain at a team hitched to a wagon. What had aroused his curiosity was the woman who sat on the high seat. Her clothing was soaked, her slender body bent against the rain. Her profile was dead white, with strands of hair dripping water down her shoulders and back.

Sam tossed his head, his action drawing her attention. She turned her head and, wiping the rain out of her eyes, stared at him. Her dark gray eyes, haunted and filled with disillusionment, blinked once, then looked away.

"Miss," Ace asked, "why are you sitting in the rain? Why don't you go inside somewhere?"

The young woman gave a nervous look over her shoulder, then shrugged. Maybe she's not right in the head, he thought, and wondered why no one was looking after her.

Mind your own business, Ace told himself and turned Sam's head toward the entrance to the livery. Inside he turned the gelding over to a towheaded teenager. "Give him some grain, but don't get familiar with him. He doesn't much like people."

In the door of the livery Ace paused at the sound of a man's harsh voice. "Bitch, ain't you done shopping yet? Get your lazy ass off the buckboard and get on down to the mercantile."

"You told me to wait here for you," the young woman said in a quavering voice as she climbed over the wagon wheel and stepped to the ground.

"Like hell I did." The fat man raised his hand and slapped her so hard that she staggered and fell to the street. "Get your chores done and go on home." She sat in the mud and water, her head bowed, waiting for the man who stood over her to leave. He finally did, but only after kicking her hard on her thigh.

Swearing under his breath, Ace hurried to help the abused woman to her feet.

"Are you all right?"

The wet, bedraggled woman gave a bitter laugh. "I've been hurt worse than this. Go away now, in case he comes back."

Ace watched her struggle to her feet, turn and walk down the street. "The bastard," he muttered. "Wouldn't even let her drive the wagon to the store. How could a man treat his daughter like that?" When she walked into the mercantile, he left the livery and headed for the barbershop.

As the tall, lanky man lathered his face, then started plying the straight-edged razor, Ace asked, "Any ranchers around here looking to hire a man on?"

"None that I've heard of," Tom answered. "It's a bad time of year to look for a job on a ranch. With winter coming on, a lot of the ranchers have let some of their men go."

"I was afraid of that," Ace said.

"There is one man who is always looking for help," Tom said as he laid a steaming cloth over Ace's face. "He has the biggest spread around here, and it takes a lot of men to run it. Those who work for him detest the man, but he pays more than the other ranchers and they stay on because of that. It's whispered that a couple of his men have taken potshots at him and missed. The bet is that someday somebody isn't going to miss."

"Well"—Ace stood up and felt his smooth-shaven

face—"I need a job right now, so I'll talk to him. What is his name?"

"Cletus Gibb. I saw him in town today. You can't miss him. He's fat and has the face of a mad bull."

Ace paid the man with almost the last of his money and, leaving the shop, went to the Longhorn Saloon.

The big room was packed with humanity. The racket of loud guffaws and the shrill laughter of women were an insult to his eardrums. Had such a clamor gone on in the Lady Chance? Had he been so accustomed to it that he had begun to think the din was normal?

At any rate, I don't like it now, he thought as he started making his way to the bar. *I expect having only the company of Sam the past three months has something to do with it.*

He had squeezed his way through the press of people and was within three feet of the long mahogany bar when a sullen-faced man the size of a barn door jolted up against him, spilling his glass of whiskey down his own shirtfront.

Swearing a vile oath, he swung around, his mean eyes boring into Ace. "You damn saddle tramp, why don't you watch where you're going?"

"I could say the same thing of you, mister." Ace looked at the troublemaker with cold contempt.

"What did you say?" The bully took a step forward as everyone cleared a path around them. "Come on, repeat what you said." A big hand dropped to rest on the butt of his gun.

Ace realized that he would have to fight the blustering bigmouth. Either that or shoot him. But the man might have friends, and if Ace killed him, he'd have other guns to draw against.

51

Ace had no illusions about fair fighting. He fought to win, and without warning, his fist lashed out, catching the man alongside the head. The town bully went down like a poled steer.

Ace stood with clenched fists, his eyes glittering coldly as his gaze swept the men standing in a circle around him. "Do any of you want to take up his fight?"

Various words of denial were spoken. "It's about time he came up against someone who could beat the hell out of him," one man said. "He's got half this town afraid of him."

I should have shot the bastard, Ace thought as he continued on to the bar. *He doesn't seem to have any friends.*

The bartender had a glass of whiskey waiting for him. "It's on the house, mister," the grinning man said. "That one has torn up my place more times than I've got fingers."

Cletus Gibb stood at the end of the bar, a few feet away. He had watched the confrontation with envious eyes. The stranger was everything he was not. The man had grit and nerve. He hadn't been afraid to tackle and beat the man who never missed a chance to shame Cletus in front of everyone. His tormentor made fun of his fat paunch, and his favorite remark was to sneer that Cletus would never get a woman with that ugly mug of his. And when he had learned that his favorite prey had married, he had sneered, "How much did you have to pay the woman to get a ring on her finger? I bet she don't even let you get between her legs."

When Cletus denied the taunt, the bully laughed

loudly and said, "I'll believe that when she gives you a brat."

Remembering that jibe, Gibb became thoughtful. He left his spot and wedged himself in next to Ace. "You handled yourself real good there, mister," he said.

Ace remembered him. It was the man who had treated his daughter so brutally. He shrugged and brought the glass of whiskey to his lips.

"You wouldn't be looking for a job, would you?"

"Are you offering one?" Ace set his glass back on the bar.

"Yes, I am. I run the biggest spread within a hundred miles, and I'm always in need of men."

Ace turned toward Gibb, ready to tell him that he wouldn't work for a man who treated his womenfolk so badly. But his eyes widened slightly when the rancher mentioned the monthly pay he would get. He knew it was almost double what other ranchers paid their men.

Ace raised the glass to his lips again, staring thoughtfully as he sipped its contents. Winter was coming on and jobs would be scarce this time of year. He couldn't see himself riding a grub line in the winter with snow up to his rump. He would save his money, and come spring he would ride away. He would make himself tolerate the despicable man for a few months.

He tipped his head back and let the last of the whiskey flow down his throat, then turned to Gibb. "Where will I find your spread?"

"It's about five miles out of town. I'll take you there."

It was still raining when Ace and Gibb left the saloon. It was a cold rain now as the sun prepared to set. Ace pulled his collar up and tucked his chin as he followed his new boss out of town. He was thankful the man set his horse to a gallop. They wouldn't be able to have a conversation over the noise of the pounding hooves. He didn't want to talk to the man more than necessary.

Cletus had had his house and outbuildings built facing east so that the foothills behind would protect them from the icy winds that blew in the winter. The house was large, painted white. It had a wide porch, and the shutters and trim were painted a light green. A nice place like this shouldn't belong to such a man as Cletus Gibb, Ace thought as they rode past the house to the barn.

No one seemed out and about, and Ace wasn't surprised. Who would want to be out in this weather? He saw her then, Gibb's skinny young daughter. She was unloading the buckboard, struggling with a fifty-pound bag of potatoes. Why had she stopped the wagon here at the barn? Why not at the cookhouse? Ace asked himself. Didn't she realize she was making extra work for herself?

"Why didn't the girl drive the wagon to the cookhouse, make it easier on herself?" he asked as he swung out of the saddle.

"Because she's simple," Cletus said with a growl as he dismounted.

"Well," Ace said, frowning, "let's give her a hand."

"She don't need any help," the rancher said, walking toward the struggling Lark. "Everybody does what he's supposed to do around here. Her job is to cook and to make sure she has everything she needs to put a good meal on the table."

"Good Lord, man, she's your daughter, isn't she? Surely you don't treat her like hired help."

Gibb gave a laugh that grated on Ace's ears. "She ain't my daughter. She's my wife."

Ace looked at the man, thunderstruck. His wife? Why would any woman marry such a brute of a man? What made her stay here and take his abuse?

It was all he could do not to draw his Colt and shoot the man when he said, "Get a move on. The men will be wanting supper soon."

"I'm hurrying as fast as I can," the scared little rabbit replied, panting as she dragged another large bag from the buckboard.

Ace's hand dropped to his gun when Gibb responded, "Like hell you are." Raising his hand he slapped her so hard she fell to her knees. "And don't go crying to any of the men for help." He stared down at her a moment; then without another word he stomped off toward the house.

Swearing under his breath, Ace hurried to help the young wife to her feet.

"No, don't," she begged. "It will go hard for me if he sees you helping me. Please go."

Ace reluctantly turned away. He seriously doubted that he could work for such a man. Remembering then that he had only some change in his pocket, he led Sam toward the barn.

He had just unsaddled and stabled the gelding when a man of middle age came and leaned against the top board of the stall. Ace looked at the gray-haired man, a question in his eyes.

"Yeah, me and the men saw him strike her. But if any of us had tried to defend her he'd probably fire us on the spot. We need our jobs, what with winter coming on. I wouldn't be surprised if the whole bunch don't up and leave, come warm weather."

"I know I sure as hell will. I just hope I can keep from killing the bastard before then."

"He's been shot at out on the range a couple times."

"I wonder why she married him in the first place. Why does she stay on and take his abuse?"

"We've all wondered about that too. Some think she married him for his money; others think that maybe she was sold to Gibb by her father. Whatever the reason, he's got his hooks in her.

"When you've finished with the gelding come on over to the bunkhouse and meet the rest of the men. My handle is Jake Henry."

Chapter Four

The grandfather clock struck five, and Lark put aside
the light blue shawl she had been knitting for the
past eight days. It was for her aunt, and she planned
on finishing it tonight and taking it to her tomorrow.

She hadn't seen her relatives since the day she'd
married the man who had deceived them so thoroughly.

How were the two old people faring? she wondered. She hadn't visited them since her wedding
day. She had been waiting for the bruises on her face
to fade, praying every day that Cletus wouldn't put
fresh ones there, or maybe blacken her eyes again.
The old people would be so upset if they knew that
he abused her almost daily in some fashion. Her
clothing hid the black and blue marks on her arms
and legs, but there was nothing she could do to hide
a battered face. If she could just stay out of his reach

tonight and tomorrow morning, she intended to make a short trip up the mountain to see how they were getting along.

Lark heard the laughter of two male voices and rose to look out the window. She saw the teenager, Thad, and the new man walking from the barn toward the bunkhouse. Ace, she had heard him called.

There was strength as well as grace in the way he moved. Twice he had tried to help her, his eyes full of compassion in his rugged, handsome face. There was something solid about him, something dependable. He was the sort of man she would like to be married to.

That is wishful thinking, she thought with a sigh. As long as her aunt and uncle lived, she was bound to Cletus Gibb. But as unbearable as that was, she hoped her relatives lived a long time.

Lark stayed on at the window after Ace and Thad disappeared into the bunkhouse. As she watched the red ball of the sun moving slowly westward, her thoughts turned to the man she was married to. Her husband hated her, and would do everything he could to make her life miserable. It seemed, though, that he hated everyone . . . the men who worked for him, even the poor stallion he treated so brutally. There was a demon in Cletus Gibb, and she prayed that he wouldn't beat her to death someday.

Lark gave a start when the big clock bonged the half hour. She had half an hour to get supper on the table.

As she hurried the short distance across the yard to the cookhouse she prayed that the stew she was going to serve this evening would please Cletus. If it didn't, she would feel the weight of his hand on her face. A new bruise would delay her trip up the mountain another few days. If she didn't show up soon, Uncle Ben might come looking for her. She did not want that. There was no telling what Cletus might say or do to the old fellow.

Pushing open the cookhouse door, Lark went straight to the big stove and built a fire in it. She next lit the two lamps on the long table, then went back to the stove. She felt its top, and finding it beginning to warm, she pulled a large pot of stew to the front to heat up.

She had cubed the beef and started it simmering at four o'clock this morning. Half an hour before the men came in for breakfast she had added potatoes, onions and carrots. All she had to do now was set the table and slice up a couple loaves of bread.

Once the table was set, Lark passed in front of the mirror the previous cook had hung on the wall to shave by. She stopped and looked into it. She looked a fright. Her hair was still tied up in a kitchen towel, her face was dirt-smudged from cleaning the house, and her old dress was so limp it looked as though it had been pulled from a ragbag.

She burst through the door and sprinted to the house. In her room she hurriedly changed into a worn, flowered-print dress that now hung loosely on her because of the weight she had lost. Taking up her brush, she uncovered her hair and drew the bristles through it until the tresses lay in loose sun-streaked curls on her shoulders and down her back. Satisfied with the way her hair looked, she threw down the brush and ran back to the cookhouse.

Lark had barely gotten into the long house and walked to the stove when she heard the men coming.

She had just placed a gallon-size bowl of stew on the table and added two plates of sourdough bread when they began coming inside.

Cletus led the way, his heavy tread shaking the floor. The five regulars came next, then the new man and the teenager. The first five shot her quick glances as she stood nervously beside the stove, then took their places at the table.

But the new man, as usual, smiled at her and said, "Good evening, ma'am." And as usual Lark felt her husband's beady eyes on her and didn't dare answer the greeting. Thad gave her a wide grin before he sat down beside the man called Ace.

No one talked at the table except to say, "Pass the stew," or "Hand me a piece of bread."

When the clinking of knives and forks finally died down, Lark grew nervous at what was to come next.

"Hey, bitch, pour us some coffee."

Her head bent, her gaze on the floor, Lark picked up a pot holder to protect her hand and carried the big gray-speckled coffeepot to the table, praying that Cletus would not strike her. It was embarrassing to her to hit in front of the help, and it also embarrassed the men.

Although the other men didn't lift their gazes to her, Ace couldn't seem to take his off her as he marveled at her creamy complexion, delicate bone structure and the thick lashes that hid her eyes. His gaze moved over her hair, where the lamplight shot streaks of gold among the curls.

He looked at her husband, who sat at the head of the table, a sullen look on his face. He wondered for the hundredth time why this lovely young woman had ever married such a man.

60

Lark felt Ace's steady gaze on her and grew more nervous. As she raised the pot over her husband's cup, her trembling hand made the coffee flow unsteadily. When some spilled over the side of the cup Cletus said with a growl, "You'd better not splash me, bitch," and raised his hand. It paused in midair. His little, mean-looking eyes had caught the threatening look of a pair of cold gray eyes.

Ace Brandon was watching him, his eyes glittering dangerously. Cletus knew in that instant that if he struck his wife, he would be in for the worst beating of his life. Of course he could fire Ace, he told himself, but he had other plans for the man.

He let his hand drop. He could wait.

Lark had flinched. When the expected blow didn't come, she darted a look at him. He was staring down at his cup, a sulky look on his fat face. She glanced quickly at the new man and saw the remnants of cold contempt in his eyes. Had that look stilled her husband's hand?

Cold sweat broke out on her forehead. If that was the case, she would pay dearly for it.

When everyone's cup was filled, Lark started to return the pot to the stove. "Why don't you leave the pot on the table, Mrs. Gibb?" Ace suggested. "We can help ourselves if we want another cup."

A soft gasp feathered through Lark's lips. Dear Lord, she thought, he is going to cause me to get a terrible beating. It was Cletus's habit to demand she refill the cups at least two times, even though the pot was close to his elbow.

She waited for Cletus to fire the man on the spot. She stood a moment, and when Cletus ignored her, she set the coffeepot on the table and for the first time entered the living quarters of the cookhouse.

Lark softly closed the door behind her and stood a moment before sitting down in a straight-backed chair pulled up to a small table. There was a lamp sitting on it, a box of matches beside it, and a small clay pot filled with river sand to snuff out cigarette butts.

Leaning her tired body back against the chair, she let her gaze travel around the room. Like the kitchen area it was spotless, though sparsely furnished. There was a single bed, neatly made up, a chest of drawers, and several pegs on the wall to hang clothes on. An apron hung on one peg.

She wished she could live here instead of at the big house. Even a cave shared with a cougar would be better than always fearing she might get a beating, she thought wryly.

Why hadn't Cletus slapped her when she was pouring the coffee? she wondered. Ordinarily he would have. He never missed an excuse to strike her. It had to be because of the man, Ace. Her husband was afraid of him.

There was something else about this new hired man. He confused her and made her feel uneasy. Every time she was near him, saw him even at a distance, her pulse increased and a fluttering went all through her body. It was a sensation she had never experienced before. She hoped it wasn't a sexual reaction to the handsome male.

She must fight it, whatever it was, she told herself sternly as she heard the men leaving the cookhouse.

Lark heard the door close and gripped her fingers tightly together. Cletus would come bursting through the door any second, fury in his eyes. He would be in a rage because his fear of the new man had kept him from striking her.

All was quiet in the kitchen, but still she waited. It would be like Cletus to stand back out of sight until she walked in, then pounce on her. When several minutes passed and she could hear nothing but the beating of her heart, she stood up and warily stuck her head through the kitchen door. She saw only the table, covered with dirty dishes. She hurriedly set the big room to rights and, blowing out the lights, left the cookhouse. If she could get to her room before Cletus came back, maybe she could avoid a beating.

Lark barely had time to blow out the light and get into bed when she heard the front door open and Cletus's ponderous footsteps on the parlor floor. Shivering and filled with dread, she lay tensely, the covers pulled tightly around her shoulders. When the footsteps paused outside her door, she squeezed her eyes shut. He was coming in. She braced herself for the nightmare that was to come.

Several seconds went by; then a breath of relief left her weak when her husband continued down the hall to his room and slammed the door behind him.

Chapter Five

It was a cool, bright morning when Lark left the house. Birdsong was all around her as she walked to the barn. She thought sadly that most of the birds would be leaving soon, like the V line of geese whose honking could be heard now as they flew southward.

As she had hoped, there was no one in the barn or around the stables. She quickly saddled a little mare, then tied to the back of the saddle a few things she was taking to her aunt and uncle, including a batch of cookies and some apple turnovers she had baked without Cletus's knowledge.

As she took the mountain path that led to the old cabin, she wished that she could take off with the geese. But the bond that held her to Cletus Gibb was the strongest kind. The two old people depended on her.

Already, though, their dependence was beginning

to take a toll on her. She didn't know how long she could withstand Cletus's cruel treatment, the laborious work he demanded of her. There was hardly a day when she was able to take a moment's rest. There was the big house to be kept spotless, loads of heavy clothes to be scrubbed, and the cooking for the cowhands. And if that wasn't enough, there was the outside work.

Cletus had fired the boy whose job had been taking care of the livestock in the barn. Of course that job had been passed on to her. Every night she fell into bed exhausted.

As the mare continued to climb, Lark smoothed her fingers over her face. There were a few spots that were sore to her touch, but on examining her face in the mirror this morning, she had seen no signs of bruises. Surprisingly, she hadn't received a beating last night.

Lark was still mulling over the unusual events of the previous night when the old, run-down cabin came into view, half-hidden by boulders and scrub pine. It needs a lot of work done to it before winter sets in, she thought, noticing the shutters, some missing, others barely hanging on. The icy wind and snow would slip right into the log building.

As she dismounted and looped the reins over a bush, she saw that the old place was badly in need of new chinking as well. Stepping up on the rotting porch, she wondered if she could find the time to slip up here one day and take care of the repairs that were necessary.

Without knocking, Lark opened the door and stepped inside the cabin. The two old people hugging the fireplace looked up, and their faces took on wide, welcoming smiles. She set the bag of gifts for them on the table, then went to her relatives with outstretched arms. It was so good to see their sweet faces. They rose stiffly, with creaking joints, and she hugged them both in one big embrace.

"We've missed you," Lucy said, kissing Lark's cheek.

"We were beginning to think that you had forgotten us," Ben added.

"I'd forget my name before I'd forget you two," Lark laughingly said as she took off her jacket. "How have you been? Have you been eating well? Is your cough any better, Aunt Lucy?"

There was a slight hesitation before Lucy said, "I seem to cough less often."

Lark frowned when no mention was made of what they had been eating lately. She was about to ask what they'd had for supper last evening when Ben spoke excitedly.

"What you got in the bag, niece? Something sweet, I hope."

"Let's go take a look," Lark answered, amusement in her eyes. She well knew her uncle's sweet tooth.

Ben let out a whoop when the first thing she brought out and placed on the table was a flaky apple turnover. "Ah," he said, licking his lips, "just smell it, Lucy. Did you ever smell anything so good?"

"This will please Auntie more." Lark smiled at Lucy as she lifted out a bag of cookies with white icing.

Like children at Christmas, Lucy and Ben watched eagerly as Lark took out a round bar of shaving soap, a white bar of scented soap, and a tin of tobacco.

As her aunt and uncle exclaimed rapturously over

the treasures, Lark recalled the chances she had taken procuring the items that pleased them so. If Cletus checked off the items when he paid his bill at the store, she was sure to get a beating.

She shook the thought off and said, "Uncle Ben, why don't you put these things in your room while I make some coffee."

As Lark put water in the pot, Lucy tried to surpress a cough, and was unsuccessful. Lark put down the pot and gave her aunt a worried look. "I don't like the sound of that cough, Aunt Lucy, and you look very pale. Are you still drinking meat broth every day?"

"Well," Lucy said haltingly, "Ben ran out of shells for his rifle three days ago, so there hasn't been any meat to make broth out of."

"What about the beef Mr. Gibb sends up to you? You could boil some of it."

"Yes, that is true," Lucy said after a moment.

"Let's put a piece to simmering right now," Lark said.

"We're out of beef just now," Lucy said hurriedly. "Mr. Gibb said he'd send a man up with grub every Friday. He'll be arriving anytime now. As for my cough, I caught a chill the other night. Do you think your husband could send us up a couple of blankets? It gets quite cold up here in the mountains of an evening."

"I'll see to it," Lark promised, thinking to herself that maybe she could sneak a couple of horse blankets from the barn. They would smell horsey, but at least they would provide warmth for old, arthritic joints.

As Ben and Lucy ate their treats, Lark worked hard

to hide the concern she felt for the two old people, especially her aunt. The pure mountain air would be beneficial to her during the summer months, but if this old building wasn't made winterproof, she was afraid her aunt wouldn't make it through the bitterly cold months of winter. There must be some new chinking put between the logs as soon as possible. No matter where she sat or stood, she felt a cold draft.

At the sound of horse hooves Lark looked out the window. Lucy and Ben exchanged an uneasy look before Ben said, "That must be the man bringing us our weekly grub."

Lark stood up. "I'll just step into the other room until he's gone," she said.

Lucy and Ben didn't say anything, but they gave each other a curious look when she left the room.

Lark stood with her ear pressed against the bedroom door. She could hear the murmur of her uncle and the man talking as something was thumped onto the table. She heard the cabin door close then and she waited for the man to make a second trip into the cabin, bringing in the rest of the provisions. When she heard him riding away she thought she must be mistaken. She waited a minute, then walked back into the other room.

She could only lean against the table and stare in disbelief at the cloth bag there. It was not even half full. "Is that it?" she asked.

Ben shrugged. "I guess Mr. Gibb don't think old people eat much."

Tears stung Lark's eyes as she took from the bag a cut of beef that weighed less than two pounds, five potatoes, a small bag of coffee beans, a good-size bag of dried beans and half a slab of salt pork. Not enough here for one nourishing meal, Lark thought in rising anger.

"Oh, dear, he forgot sugar," Lucy complained. "I do like sweetening in my coffee."

When Lark looked up at her aunt and uncle she was so incensed she could hardly speak. "There has to be some mistake. I'll look into it as soon as I get home."

It was time she was getting back down the mountain, Lark thought as she glanced out the window and saw that the sun would soon be overhead. She had ironing to do and bread to make. Then there was the stable to be cleaned out, the horses to be fed and watered. All this before she put a roast in the oven to be served for tonight's supper.

"I've got to go." She smiled at her elderly relatives. When they put up a fuss she promised, "I'll be back in a couple of days."

"Don't forget," they said in unison as they followed her out onto the porch and waved to her until she was out of sight.

As Lark guided the mare down the mountain, she was still fuming at what she had just learned about her aunt and uncle's diet. What was her husband trying to do, starve them to death? And there was the cabin. How was she supposed to get it ready for winter?

These worries were tormenting her mind when Lark heard the clip-clop of a horse coming up the rocky trail. Her fingers tightened on the reins and her heart beat in alarm. Was it Cletus? She had heard him tell the men this morning that he had to go into town. A short time later she saw him ride away. But perhaps he had only pretended to leave the ranch. Maybe he was playing a trick on her. It would be just like him to slip back and spy on her.

Lark was flooded with relief when she rounded a bend in the trail and saw Ace Brandon climbing toward her. He reined in, a slow smile changing the hardness of his face as he said, "Good morning, Mrs. Gibb."

Lark gave him a fleeting smile and said shyly, "Good morning, Mr. Brandon."

Ace gave her a crooked grin. "We're being awfully formal, aren't we?"

"I guess we are." Lark grinned back, relaxing a bit. "My name is Lark, and I know you're called Ace."

"Do you ride up the mountain often, Lark?"

Lark shifted uneasily in the saddle. "I . . . um . . . sometimes."

"You can trust me, Lark," Ace said gently. "I won't mention that I saw you if you don't want me to."

"I'd appreciate it if you didn't." Lark looked away from the understanding in Ace's eyes. "I'm not supposed to ride so far away from the ranch. Cletus says it's too dangerous."

"He looks out for you, does he?"

Lark felt her cheeks growing warm. This stranger knew full well that Cletus cared nothing for her welfare. It would be foolish for her to pretend otherwise. Still not looking at him she said in a low voice, "I've been visiting my aunt and uncle. Cletus told me he doesn't want me to do that more than once a month."

Once a month, my Aunt Nellie, Ace thought. If the bastard had his way, Lark would never see her relatives again. "You'd like to see them more often, wouldn't you?"

"Yes, I would. They are old and I want to know that they're all right."

"When you can't make it, would you like me to look in on them, see if they need anything?"

"Oh, I would appreciate that." Lark lifted her head, her gray eyes showing her thankfulness. "My aunt looks so frail. I'm beginning to fear that the winter up here in that old cabin is not going to agree with her."

"I rode past that cabin the other day. It wouldn't cost Gibb much to fix it up for the cold weather. Couldn't you—"

"No, I couldn't," Lark interrupted, and reining her mare around his gelding she said. "I thank you in advance for looking in on my relatives once in a while."

"There is a mystery here, Sam," Ace said, watching the graceful sway of Lark's back until she reached the timberline and disappeared among the trees. "I think I'll just mosey on up the mountain and drop in on her aunt and uncle. See what light they can shed on the strange marriage of their niece."

When Ace spotted the old cabin he saw an elderly man about to enter it, his arms full of firewood. "Howdy," he called loudly.

The slightly bent, white-haired man turned and peered at him. "Are you lost, young feller?" he asked in a cracked voice.

"No, I'm not." Ace reined Sam in at the porch. "I'm a friend of your niece, Lark. She asked me to look in on you if I was ever up this way. I've been hunting deer, and I thought that since I was in your area I would stop by for a quick visit."

A genial smile replaced Ben's suspicious frown.

"Get down and come in," he invited. "You're the first visitor we've had since moving up here. Me and my Lucy get tired sometimes, only talking to each other. Funny thing, our Larkie left here not more than ten minutes ago."

"Did she, now. I must have just missed her on the trail," Ace said as he swung out of the saddle. "I suppose she comes often to see you."

"No, she doesn't. Today is the first time we've seen her since she got married. She's had a lot of work to do lately. She said she'd be coming more often from now on."

As often as the condition of her face permits, Ace thought as he followed Ben inside.

A small, frail-looking woman with white hair was clearing the table. She looked startled at Ace's entrance. But her face lit up when he removed his hat and smilingly said, "My name is Ace, and I'm a friend of your niece."

"A friend of Larkie's, Ben. Isn't that nice." She set the plates back on the table. "Come sit by the fire and get the chill out of your bones, young man," she said, leading the way to the small fire burning in the grate.

Amusement flickered in Ace's eyes. It had grown quite warm now. He had shed his jacket over an hour ago. But he imagined the blood was thin in these old people's veins, and no doubt the air was cold to them.

"How did you meet our niece?" Lucy asked when Ace sat down in the other rickety chair.

"I work on her husband's ranch."

"You're one of Mr. Gibb's cowhands, then," Ben said, taking a seat on the hearth. "Our niece is lucky to have married such a caring man."

Well, Ace thought, these two old people have no

idea of the hell their niece is living in. It was evident that Lark was keeping her husband's brutality from them.

"I take it he treats you folks pretty good too." Ace looked at Ben.

"Well, yes." Ben was slow to answer. "First off, this is his cabin. Then once a week he sends grub up to us. He told Lark before they got married that he would take care of me and Lucy."

"I imagine he sends you all kinds of goodies for your table."

"Well, not that, exactly. Just plain grub that will stick to your ribs."

"I just bet." Ace swore to himself. *Probably a chunk of beef and a pound of potatoes. Just enough to keep his wife bound to him, the mean bastard.*

Ace felt he understood now why the marriage between the lovely Lark and the brutal Gibb had taken place. Lark had married the man to keep a roof over her aunt and uncle's heads and food on their table.

He could understand why the rancher would want such a lovely woman for a wife, but why did he treat her as if he hated her? He should be treating her like a queen instead of like some trampy woman who didn't deserve respect. That part was still a mystery.

Ace sat on, listening to Ben's tales of how he and his wife and niece had traveled all over the West, the things they had done, the things they had seen. It sounded as though the old man had enjoyed every minute of their wandering around, but he wondered how Lark and the old lady had felt about it. It couldn't have been easy on them, living like gyspies.

As Ben rambled on, Ace's gaze traveled over the drafty cabin. He could see daylight between most of the logs. New chinking would take care of that. The shutters and door were so warped there wasn't much that could be done for them. The only solution there was to install new ones.

Ace was afraid Lark had sacrificed herself for nothing. The old couple would probably die of influenza when the first blast of freezing weather hit the mountains.

After he had silently condemned Cletus Gibb to hell, Ace picked his hat up off the floor. Settling it on his head, he said, "It's been nice talking to you folks, but I've got to get going."

"We'd like for you to drop in again," Ben said as he and Lucy stood up and followed him to the door.

"I'll be back," Ace assured them. "Maybe the next time I'm up here I'll have better luck and bring down a deer. We'll dress it out and you'll have some extra meat for at least a month."

"We sure would appreciate that," Ben said. "Mr. Gibb keeps forgetting to send me up some shells for my rifle."

"I'll just bet he does," Ace muttered under his breath as he mounted the gelding. He doesn't want them to have more meat, he thought as he nudged Sam to move out.

Ace sensed that the lonely old couple was still standing on the porch, gazing after him. He pushed back the compassion he felt. He mustn't get too involved with them and their plight. He would be gone when spring came and would never see them again. He didn't want to take any sad memories with him when he left. It didn't pay to let anyone get too close.

And that was especially true of the lovely, haunted-eyed Lark. He must make it his business to stay as far away from her as possible.

Chapter Six

Lark stood in the hall looking up at a flight of stairs. She wondered what lay beyond the closed door where the steps ended. It can only be an attic, she thought.

She had been curious about the wide, unpainted door but had never found the time to investigate it. Actually she didn't have time today, she reminded herself. There were several hours to be spent in the stables. Cletus had decided this morning that they needed new hay spread around once she had mucked them out.

"Lay down a thickness of six inches," he had ordered on his way out of the cookhouse.

"He's always finding something extra for me to do," she muttered, even though most of the time it was some chore of no importance. Only something that was backbreaking for her.

Lark took a deep breath and started up the uncarpeted, creaking steps. Arriving at the door, she paused a moment before reaching out and grasping the doorknob. What would she find on the other side? she asked herself. Nothing alarming, she decided. Otherwise the door would be locked.

She stepped inside a large, peaked room and gazed at shapes that had no detail in the pale light struggling through three narrow, grimy windows. But in moments her eyes became accustomed to the dimness and she felt like a child at Christmas.

Everywhere she looked, there was furniture. She knew instantly that Cletus had discarded these items to make room for the fancy pieces that now furnished his house.

Lark moved about the room, inspecting the dusty pieces. There was a dresser with an attached mirror, a chest of drawers, an end table, a brown leather sofa, worn, but in good condition, a padded rocking chair, a kitchen table and four chairs. And rolled up and leaning in one corner was a large piece of carpeting.

There was nothing fancy about the pine pieces, but there was a glow, a warmth about the wood that seemed to welcome her. She much preferred this furniture to the fancy furnishings downstairs.

How great these old, unwanted pieces of furniture would look in the mountain cabin, Lark thought. It was if all these things had been made with it in mind.

Lark was suddenly gripped with an idea that was outlandish and probably dangerous. Could she manage to slip these treasures up the mountain? she asked herself. There must be a way. Aunt Lucy would be so pleased to finally have a home with good furniture that wasn't in danger of falling apart.

She looked down at the floor. Only her footprints showed in the heavy dust. No one had been up here in a long time. Possibly not since Cletus had the pieces carried up here. He would probably never know they were gone.

Now to find a way to get it up the mountain, Lark thought as she left the attic to hurry to the barn.

Lark stretched her aching back, then leaned on the handle of the pitchfork she had been using for the past two hours. She had three more stalls to tend to, and it was nearly time to start supper. If she was late getting the meal on the table, even by five minutes, God help her.

Cletus hadn't struck her all week. She had stayed out of reach of his heavy hand and tried not to call attention to herself. But if supper wasn't on the table when the men came in, he would make her pay for it.

That mustn't happen. She forced herself to dig the long tines into the pile of hay she had tossed down from the hayloft. If her face was marked up, she would be unable to visit her aunt and uncle for another week, and she was anxious to get the furniture up to them as soon as possible. How she would do this, she had no idea yet.

Lark was halfway finished with one of the three stalls when a shadow fell over her. She gave a small cry and spun around.

"It's only me, miss." Thad smiled at her. He looked at the pitchfork in her hand, the tired look on her face, and his young features grew hard. *Cletus Gibb should be shot.*

He took the long handle from her grasp and said gently, but firmly, "I think you could use a little help with this. Go sit down somewhere and catch your breath. I'll have this done in no time."

"But Cletus . . ."

"Gibb is in town and won't be back for a couple hours," Thad interrupted her.

"If you're sure . . ." Lark mopped her sweating face with a rag she kept tucked in her bodice. "He wouldn't like it if he caught you helping me."

"You know, miss, me and the other men don't like it at all the way he treats you. We're all willing to do anything we can to help you. You only have to ask."

Did the young man mean it? Lark asked herself as she sat down on a bale of hay. Was it possible that he would help her get the items she had found in the attic up to the old cabin?

When Thad had finished the second stall and started on the third, Lark asked, "Do you know that my aunt and uncle live in Cletus's cabin a short distance up the mountain?"

"Yes, I know." Thad stopped working and looked at her. "Ace told me."

Thad's tone of voice told Lark that Ace had said more than that. She didn't have to wait long to find out what else Ace had had to say.

"He told me that he had dropped in to visit with them for a while and that he didn't like the conditions they were living in. He said the old building was drafty and that he didn't believe Gibb was sending enough grub to the old people.

"He plans on going up there one day soon to see what he can do about fixing the place up a bit before winter arrives."

"He said that?" Surprise and pleasure shone in Lark's eyes. She couldn't believe that the aloof man would take the trouble to do that for two strangers.

"Yeah, he said that." Thad grinned at her. "He told me one day that he mostly only liked old people and younguns. He said they were helpless and would always be truthful with a feller."

Encouraged by all that she had heard, Lark looked at Thad and dared to ask the question that was so important to her. "Did you mean it when you said you'd be willing to help me if you could?"

"Of course I meant it, miss." Thad looked insulted that she would ask. "Do you need help of some kind?"

"Yes, I do, but it would be risky for you. You might lose your job if Cletus finds out."

"Hah," Thad scoffed. "That wouldn't bother me. My folks live on a farm about fifty miles from here. I'd just go home for the winter. Now, what is it you need me to do?"

"Well, like Ace told you, the cabin is in a deplorable state and so are the few sticks of furniture in the place. All of it should have been thrown out years ago."

Lark paused, getting up the nerve to ask her favor.

"Go on, miss," Thad urged. "Do you want me to help Ace fix up the cabin? I'd gladly do it."

Lark shook her head. "It's not that. It's something that must be done in secret."

Thad grinned. "That sounds just like something I'd like to do. What is it you need done? I'll tell you ahead of time, though, I've never tried my hand at making furniture. Maybe a wood box or something simple like that."

Lark laughingly said, "You don't have to be a car-

79

penter. I don't need anything built. The thing is, I was poking around in the attic before, and found a bunch of furniture stored up there. It's all just sitting there, gathering dust, and my aunt would be thrilled to have it in the cabin. Is it possible that you could help me get it to her?"

"That would take some doing without Gibb knowing about it." Thad sat down beside her.

When disappointment clouded Lark's eyes, he said quickly, "But with careful planning it can be done."

"Do you think so, Thad?" Relief was in Lark's voice as she grabbed hold of his arm in excitement. "Do you have any ideas?"

"Of course, it will have to be done when we know for sure that Gibb will be gone from the ranch for a full day. If you don't mind, I'll speak to Ace about it. Between us we'll come up with something."

"Of course you can tell Ace. I think we can trust him. I can't tell you how grateful I'll be, Thad."

"It's nothing, miss," Thad said, touched by her earnest gratitude. She shouldn't have to ask outsiders for help. She should be able to go to her husband for such a simple request. It was on the tip of his tongue to ask her why she put up with a man who treated her so cruelly.

Something told him not to pose the question to Lark. He patted her hand, which still lay on his arm, and said, "I'll have a team and wagon ready when the time is right. Now, why don't you go to the house and rest a bit. I'll finish up here."

"Thank you, Thad." Lark jumped to her feet. "I've got to start thinking about what to make for supper."

As Lark half ran to the cookhouse, her mind was

already considering what meal she could prepare and have on the table in two hours' time.

Thad finished cleaning the stalls in half the time it would have taken Lark. He leaned the fork and shovel in a corner and went to look for Ace.

He found his idol at the water trough waiting patiently while his big gelding quenched his thirst. "What did the fat man have you doing today, Ace?" he asked.

"I've been riding fence since eight o'clock this morning and my rump feels it." Ace looked at the teenager, squinting his eyes against the red ball of sun lying low in the west. "I may have to eat my supper standing up," he joked, then asked, "What did he have you doing today?"

Thad laughed. "I kept out of his sight this morning and he went off without giving me any orders. I've mostly hung around the barn. I gave Lark a hand cleaning out the stalls. The old bastard had her laying down fresh hay in all of them."

"Does she have any new bruises on her face?"

"I didn't see any. But she's going to have plenty if she gets caught at what she's planning to do."

"What's that? Run away from him?"

"No. I don't know why she doesn't, though. She'd have a better chance running than trying what she intends to do."

"Out with it, Thad," Ace said impatiently. "What is she planning to do?"

"She found some furniture in the attic at the big house. She wants to get it moved up to the cabin. She says her aunt needs it, and she wants me to help her get it up there."

Ace lifted Sam's dripping muzzle out of the water. "And what did you answer her?" he asked as he started walking the gelding toward the barn.

"I told her it would take some planning, doing it on the sly, but that I would help her." He grinned sheepishly at Ace and added, "I told her I'd get you to help us."

"You took a lot on yourself, hoss," Ace said gruffly as he led Sam into the barn. "There'll be hell to pay if Gibb finds out. We'll both be fired, and she'll get an awful beating."

"I know; that's why we've got to be real careful."

"We? I haven't said that I'll help you."

"But you will, won't you, Ace?" Thad looked on as Ace unsaddled the gelding, then led him into the stall.

"I don't know." Ace shook his head. "What she should be more concerned about is getting that old cabin weatherproofed. If some new chinking isn't put between the logs, her aunt and uncle will have snowdrifts inside this winter."

"I'm sure Lark knows that. She's probably planning on taking care of that herself. She's used to hard work, you know."

"Yeah. Her low-life husband sees to that. According to what her uncle had to say about their traveling around, she's had to work hard all her life."

"I think she needs a little help now, don't you?"

"All right, damn it, I'll give you a hand to help her."

"Thanks, Ace. How will we get the furniture up the mountain?"

Ace gave an aggravated sigh. He should have known that everything would be laid in his lap. The kid's heart was in the right place, but that was about the end of it. He didn't think beyond his nose. After a thoughtful pause Ace said, "We'll have to get the furniture out piecemeal. Every time Gibb goes to town for a couple hours, we'll bring some of it out and put it in the bunkhouse storage room. When it's all out of the house, we'll have to wait until Gibb is going to be away from the ranch all day before we can haul it up to the cabin."

"That sounds like a good idea," Thad said enthusiastically. "We can trust the other hands to help us. They hate Gibb too, and they all feel sorry for Lark."

When they stepped outside Ace looked toward the cookhouse. Through the window he could see Lark hurrying about, making their supper. Was he being a dammed fool for getting himself involved with the hapless young woman? he asked himself.

Chapter Seven

Lark hurried the little mare down the mountain, a worried frown on her face. Cletus had gone into town this morning, and she had taken the opportunity to make a quick visit to her aunt and uncle. She had stayed longer than she'd planned. But the old folks had been so happy to see her, she had extended the half hour she had planned to an hour.

She had been tempted to tell Aunt Lucy that before long she would have some nice furniture to keep house with. However, not knowing when Thad and Ace could get it up the mountain, she didn't mention it. It would be a nice surprise for Auntie when it eventually arrived.

All the pieces had been carried from the house and now waited in the bunkhouse for the time when Cletus would be gone from the ranch all day. Then they would be carted up to the cabin.

When she reached the lowland she urged the mare into a hard gallop. The ranch lay only a mile away. She sighed her relief when it came into sight.

Lark dismounted in front of the barn and led the mare inside. She quickly tugged the saddle off the sleek back and heaved it up over the top board of the enclosure. Giving the little animal an affectionate pat on the rump, she left the barn, walking swiftly toward the cookhouse.

She lifted a hand to Thad, who was trimming a hedge alongside the house. In her hurry she didn't notice him waving his hands, trying to get her attention. She had only one thing on her mind: to get inside and get started on her ironing.

She opened the cookhouse door and stepped inside. She had barely taken off her jacket when Cletus sprang at her from a shadowed corner.

"Slut!" he said in a hiss as his fist landed on her cheekbone. "You thought you could sneak up the mountain and visit your worthless relatives, didn't you?"

Blinded by tears, Lark opened her mouth to beg him not to hit her again. Before she could get a word out, his fist hit her again and again. She fell to the floor, the sharp tang of blood in her mouth.

Lark was near to fainting. Would he kill her this time? Instead he said, "Get up off the floor and see to your duties."

It took several minutes before Lark could pull herself to her feet with the aid of a chair. She teetered there a minute until the room stopped spinning. With slow steps she walked to the sink and pumped water into a basin. When she had bathed her bruised and battered face in the cold springwater, she staggered into the room in back of the kitchen area. Even if Cletus came back and beat her again, she had to lie down for a while. She would be lucky if she could make the evening meal.

Rage still rode on Cletus Gibb's face as he brought the riding crop down on the stallion's rump. "The bitch," he grated through bared teeth as the animal raced along, blood oozing from its hide. "She'll think twice before she tries to put something over on me again."

Suddenly it was not his wife's face Cletus saw, but that of his mother. Hester Gibb, the woman who had given birth to him forty-five years ago. A woman who looked much like Lark, beautiful of body and face. His mother was sly and cunning, a woman who spread her legs for any man who came along. And there had been many.

"I know what you did with those men, mother, dear," Cletus said now with a sneer. "When you made me look out for Pa so you wouldn't get caught, I used to watch you in bed with them. I saw all the things you did to them and it disgusted me. It sickened me more when Pa almost caught one of the men scooting through the window. Then with the sheets still warm from the other man he climbed in bed with you. I wanted to puke when you did the same things to him.

"But that was when I was ten years old. By the time I was thirteen or fourteen I realized that you hadn't fooled your husband at all. The poor sap was so afraid of losing you, he turned a blind eye to your carrying on with other men. That's when I vowed that no woman would ever put blinders on me."

He had kept that vow. The problem was that he couldn't make love to a woman. Every time he tried, his mother's mocking smile appeared on the woman's face. Furious, he would beat the woman. Word soon got around about his brutality and he was barred from all the pleasure houses within fifty miles of Dogwood.

Then finally, when he was forty-five he met Lark Elliot. It hadn't taken him long to see the hard times she and the old folks were having. His cunning brain had seen how he could get a wife. And maybe this time, married to the woman, he could get an erection.

It had been the same old story on their wedding night. Nothing but anger had stirred him. His bride's resemblance to his dead mother became more pronounced when he tried to make love to her. In a rage he had beaten her. A hatred for the young woman grew inside him, for in order to get the beauty to become his wife he had made promises that would cost him money.

The vow he had made to her he intended to keep. He would flaunt his beautiful wife in front of his neighbors, who looked down on him. And he had another plan that would surprise the hell out of them.

Cletus slowed the weary stallion down as he turned him around and rode back in the direction of the ranch house.

Lark allowed herself ten minutes to rest before she dragged her sore and battered body to the ironing board. She would barely finish the big basket of clothes waiting for her before it would be time to start preparing supper for eight hungry men.

As she lay a moment longer, gathering strength and determination, she heard the soft cooing of a mourning dove. Bitter tears slipped down her cheeks. The sound expressed so perfectly sadness, hopelessness and never-ending grief. How close it was to the reality of her own life.

Lark sighed and dragged her aching body off the bed. Taking slow, painful steps, she limped into the kitchen area, where she had set up the ironing board before going to visit her relatives.

As she walked past the small mirror hanging on the kitchen wall, she caught a glimpse of her face and wanted to cry. It was so battered she wouldn't be able to visit her aunt and uncle for at least a week.

And all the furniture Thad and Ace had struggled to get out of the attic was sitting in the bunkhouse spare room. Would she ever get it up to them? There was also the chinking to be done before the winter winds began to blow. Already it had snowed in the upper elevations of the moutains. It was just a matter of time before the fall rains turned to snow on the bottomland. She couldn't bring herself to think what that would do to her aunt's health.

The ironing was going slow and the small clock on the shelf was ticking fast. It was fast approaching time to start supper. Finally, in desperation, Lark took the basket of unironed clothes into the back room and hid it under the bed. She would try to finish it tomorrow.

Nervous and in a hurry, Lark had cut her thumb as she sliced steaks off a haunch of beef, then had cut her finger peeling potatoes. Although her body ached until she could hardly stand up, she managed to have supper on the table by seven o'clock. When she heard the men approaching the cookhouse, she escaped to the small bedroom. She sat on the edge of the bed, dreading for the men to see her face when Cletus ordered her to come pour the coffee.

Lark noted that the men were quieter than usual, and she wondered why. Probably Cletus wore his surly look tonight, putting a damper on any conversation.

Twenty minutes passed and Cletus did not call out to her. After another ten minutes ticked by she heard the men leaving. She couldn't believe it. Had Cletus allowed them to help themselves to coffee?

Lark waited another couple of minutes, and when it remained quiet in the kitchen, she heaved herself up and ventured out. She breathed a long sigh of relief. Her husband wasn't there, ready to pounce on her. Moving slowly, she cleared the table, washed the dishes, pots and skillet, and set the kitchen to order.

When the cowhands filed out of the kitchen with Gibb following them, Ace found himself walking beside Thad. "I wonder why Lark didn't pour the coffee tonight," he said, letting some distance come between them and the others.

"Gibb found out she visited her aunt and uncle this morning and he beat her bad."

Ace shot him a narrow-eyed look. "Do you know that for a fact?"

"Yes, I do. I was trimming bushes alongside the house when I saw her riding in. Then from the corner of my eye I saw Gibb slipping into the cookhouse. I waved my hands at Lark, trying to get her attention, to warn her he was waiting for her. But she was hurrying along and didn't stop. She went in and a second later I heard her let out a cry.

"I peered through the window. He had her down on the floor, beating her with his fists, cursing her. I was ready to run into the house and attack him with my pruning shears when he got off her and left."

Savage words ripped out of Ace's lips. He ended with, "That man isn't fit to live."

"My sentiments exactly," Thad agreed, a hard note in his young voice.

Later that night, when Gibb was about to enter the house, a shot rang out. His loud, angry swearing told the men in the bunkhouse that again the sniper had missed.

"I wish that gunman, whoever he is, would learn how to shoot straight."

No more was said, but they all knew why their boss had been shot at. The men were unanimous in their hatred of the wife beater.

Ace, sitting on his bunk oiling his Colt, let his gaze roam over the room. Three men were missing: two of the cowhands and young Thad. They had said they were going into town to visit the pleasure house. But had all three gone there? Had one slipped back to take a shot at Gibb? Maybe the kid, Thad.

Chapter Eight

"Thad, have you seen Lark lately?" Ace lifted the saddle onto Sam's back. "I haven't seen her all week," he added, cinching the belly strap and checking the stirrups.

"Not really. I saw her at a distance a couple times. Once when she was hanging up clothes and another time when she came out on the porch to dump out a pail of scrub water. She hasn't been cleaning out the stables lately. I think she still takes care of the chickens, though."

"That no-good Gibb must have marked her face up pretty bad if he doesn't want anyone to see it." Ace looked across the yard at the fat man, loathing glittering in his eyes. "It's too bad that whoever took a shot at him the other night missed."

"They'll try again and eventually get the son of a bitch." There was such assurance in Thad's tone that

Ace looked at him, wondering again if the teenager was the one taking shots at Gibb. The kid was awfully fond of Lark. He'd have to keep an eye on him. He'd hate to see the young man hanged for murder.

"What's in the gunnysack?" Thad eyed the big bag Ace was fastening to the back of the saddle. "Where are you working today?"

"I'm supposed to go up in the foothills and chase out any cattle that are still up there. I think though instead I'll drop in on Lark's aunt and uncle, see how they're coming along. I've got some tools in here." He patted the burlap. "Thought maybe I could tighten things up a little on that old cabin. You want to come with me, give me a hand?"

"Sure," Thad answered eagerly.

Ace and Thad were nearing the vicinity of the cabin when Ace reined in, holding up a hand for Thad to do the same thing. He silently pointed to a stand of pines to his left. Thad looked, and excitement glittered in his eyes. A yearling deer stood there. He reached for his rifle, but Ace had already carefully eased his out of its case and raised it to his shoulder. When he had a bead on the spot between the animal's ears, he slowly squeezed the trigger. It dropped instantly, dead from the bullet that had entered its brain.

"The old folks will be happy to get this fellow." Thad grinned as he dismounted and pulled a long blade from his boot top. "I happen to know the shameful amount of grub Gibb sends up to them each week. It's hardly enough to keep body and soul together."

"Yeah, I'd like to see him on that kind of diet. He'd soon shed some of that fat he carries around."

Within half an hour the deer was gutted and dressed out. It was strapped onto the back of Thad's little quarter horse. The proud, high-strung Sam wouldn't allow it on his back.

Ben and Lucy had spotted the two visitors climbing up the mountain. They were standing on the badly canting porch, smiling eagerly at Ace and Thad when they pulled rein.

"Howdy, Ace," Ben called, his eyes on the deer. "I told Lucy you'd be back."

"I brought you some fresh meat, too." Ace grinned at the old couple as he and Thad dismounted. "This is Thad, a friend of your niece's," he said, jerking his thumb toward Thad, who was lifting the deer off his horse's back.

"We're right glad to meet a friend of Lark's," Ben said with a smile at Thad. "Bring the meat into the cabin. We'll have us some steaks as fast as me and Lucy can fry them up."

Thad carried the kill into the cabin, and as Ben watched him slice four thick steaks off it, Lucy asked Ace for news of her niece.

"How is she, Ace? She's grown so thin lately. Do you think she's happy in her marriage? Cletus seems like a very nice man."

Ace looked into the faded, worried eyes and knew he must lie to the gentle little woman. Frail as she was, the truth might kill her. "I don't know your niece real well, but she seems happy enough. She said to tell you that she'll be up to visit you next week. It's a real busy time at the ranch now."

"Yes"—Lucy nodded—"I can understand that. But me and Ben miss her terribly."

"I'm sure she misses you too. She asked me and

Thad to add more chinking between the logs and to check to see if you have enough firewood cut up."

"Ben mentioned this morning that the woodpile was getting low, and we'll certainly appreciate some of the cracks being sealed up. When the wind blows, it comes right into the cabin."

Ben had fired up the old rusty stove and set a skillet on top of it. Thad laid the steaks in the heavy, black cast iron. As the meat fried, Lucy placed four chipped plates on the table, then added thin, worn knives and forks.

"I wish we had some potatoes to go with the meat." She sighed. "We ate the last one for supper last night," she added as she sliced the end of a dried-out loaf of bread. "I expect someone will be bringing us up some supplies tomorrow."

And I'll see to it that he brings you more than he usually does, Ace thought grimly. The old couple was going to be in for a very pleasant surprise.

When the steaks were cooked to Thad's satisfaction, he forked one onto each plate and said with a grin, "Eat up, folks."

Ace didn't know whether to laugh or cry as he watched Ben and Lucy wolf down the tender venison. Then anger replaced both emotions. If these old people were kept on the meager supply of food Gibb sent them, starvation would kill them before the winter weather did.

When Ben sat back, rubbed his belly and gave a soft burp, and Lucy gave him a chastising look, Ace pushed away from the table. "Thad and I are going to plug up those cracks that are letting the cold air in. Then we're going to see what we can do about the door and shutters. If we have time after that, we'll chop you a supply of firewood."

"Me and Lucy sure appreciate you and the young feller doing all that," Ben said.

Ace and Thad walked outside and Ace removed the gunnysack from Sam's back. He opened it and dumped its contents onto the ground. It held a hammer, some tenpenny nails, a shovel and an ax.

"I see you came prepared." Thad grinned and picked up the shovel. While he dug into the clay and fine gravel, throwing it into a pile, Ace walked to the lean-to behind the cabin. Inside it he rummaged around until he found a couple pails. They were badly dented but had no holes in them.

His next trip was to the spring that provided water for the cabin. He dipped one pail into it and brought it up full of water. When he joined Thad, he found that Ben had followed them outside.

The old man stood quietly watching Ace make up a thick mixture of clay, stone and water. "I think that will do it," Ace said when the three ingredients got firm enough to form a ball.

As he began to apply the chinking, he told Thad, "put it in thick and tight. It will shrink as it dries, and there will be new chinks if enough of the mixture hasn't been shoved into the cracks."

Ben followed Ace and Thad from wall to wall, regaling them with tales of his wife and niece's travels. Ace finally set him to mixing up more caulking just to give his ears a rest for a while.

Three hours passed before all the cracks were filled. But when Ace stepped into the cabin to check the inside walls, he couldn't see a hint of daylight. It was several degrees warmer in the room already and Lucy was very pleased.

Feeling good about a job well done, Ace went back outside to tackle the door and shutters.

He found that job wasn't going to be easy or simple. The shutters were badly in need of work. Never having used a hammer before, Ace hit his thumb so often that Thad laughed and took the heavy tool away from him.

But even though the teenager was well acquainted with a hammer, it took him an hour before he got the thick boards realigned so that they shut securely.

The door was even more troublesome. It was so warped, it took an hour of sweating and swearing to straighten it so that it closed easily. But once they were finished, the bar inside could be dropped into place.

"It doesn't look much better," Ace said, "but the old folks can at least bar it against hungry bears and cougars." He picked up the gunnysack and returned to it all the tools except the ax. "Let's see what we can do about chopping some wood now."

The sun was quite westward when, after he and Thad had taken turns at the chopping block, Ace drew an arm across his sweating forehead and declared he was tired and ready to go home. They carried the wood and stacked it on the porch, then mounted their horses and rode off down the mountain.

Lark was staggering from exhaustion when she walked out onto the porch and sat down on the top step. Besides cleaning the seven-room house and cooking two meals for the cowhands, this had been washday. Her arms and back throbbed from bending over a washboard, scrubbing dirty, rough denims.

A tired sigh feathered though her lips. Starting tomorrow morning, she would resume cleaning out the stables. Cletus had given her the order right after supper.

She could still see him standing there, glowering at her and saying gruffly, "You've lazed around long enough. Tomorrow get your rump down to the barn and start earning your keep again. Don't forget I'm supporting your shiftless aunt and uncle."

Earning my keep, Lark thought wearily, gazing up at the full moon rising behind a hillside of pine and aspen. Every day she used every ounce of her strength earning her and her relatives' keep.

She ran her fingers lightly over her face. Her cheekbone wasn't as sore as it had been a couple of days ago, and the bruises were beginning to fade. Bathing her face in cold water several times a day had helped the healing along. She hoped that tomorrow she could slip up the mountain and visit the old folks.

Lark drew up her knees, rested her elbows on them, and gazed out into the soft darkness. In spite of the pain and misery she endured here, she loved the house and all that surrounded it. She loved such evenings as this, listening to the horses whinny in the corral, watching the fog lift off the river and crawl along the ground.

She gave a start and straightened up when a male figure stepped out of the shadows and came toward her. She was ready to stand up and dart into the house when young Thad said quietly, "How are you this evening, Lark?"

Lark relaxed and smiled at the boyish face that promised to be quite handsome once he reached maturity. "It's a beautiful evening, isn't it?" She invited him to sit down beside her by scooting over to give him room.

"It sure is." Thad stretched out his long legs. "We should take advantage of these mild nights as often as possible. Before long it will be too cold to sit out here of an evening."

"You're right. I dread the thought of winter coming."

"It's the cold weather that I want to speak to you about," Thad said. "Actually it's about your aunt and uncle."

"What about them, Thad?" Concern leaped into Lark's eyes.

"Me and Ace was up at the cabin today. Ace shot a deer for them on the way up. Then we worked the rest of the day chinking between the logs, strengthening the shutters and fixing the door, then chopping wood. Your aunt and uncle were very pleased."

"I'm thankful too," Lark choked out, tears in her eyes. "I must thank Ace."

"You don't have to give us any thanks, Lark. We did it because we like your relatives and feel sorry for them. They're living in awful conditions and aren't getting enough to eat. Ace thinks the winter weather will do them in. Especially your aunt. She has an awful cough."

"Oh, Thad, what am I going to do?" Lark wailed, tears now rolling down her cheeks. "I can't move them somewhere else with winter at our heels. And even if that were possible, we don't have a dime to our names."

98

"Lark," Thad said softly, moved by her tears and words, "Ace thinks you married Gibb to make a home for your aunt and uncle. Is that true?"

"Yes." Lark hiccuped. "The deal was that if I married him, he would take care of Uncle Ben and Auntie."

"Did you take that to mean he would provide good food for them, that they could live comfortably in the cabin?"

"Yes, of course. I never would have married him otherwise."

There were a few moments of silence; then Thad said, "You know, Lark, I just realized that besides being mean, Gibb is stupid. And so are we."

"What do you mean?" Lark looked at him, wiping a hand across her wet eyes.

"It's simple, if you think about it. If he causes your relatives to starve to death, you won't be bound to him any longer. The dumb bastard hasn't figured that out." Thad gave Lark a wide grin and added, "Why don't you point that little gem out to him?"

Lark looked at Thad, stunned. "I can't believe that I didn't figure that out myself. I'll explain that fact to him tonight," she said excitedly.

"Don't be in too much of a hurry," Thad cautioned. "Although your aunt and uncle will eat better, you'll still have to take his abuse. It will probably be worse because of the fact that you'll have him over a barrel."

"I don't care. It will be worth it, knowing that my old aunt and uncle are getting enough food to eat. I'm going to tell him tonight."

"Now wait a minute. He'll mark your face up again, and you'll have to wait another week to visit the old folks. I'm going to talk to Ace when I leave you and see if we can come up with an idea that will get Gibb away from the house all day. If we can get rid of him, we'll move the furniture up to the cabin. You'll want to come with us, won't you?" Thad asked with a smile.

"Oh, Thad, you know I will." Lark grabbed his hand and squeezed it. "I don't know what I'd do without you."

"Aw, that's all right," Thad said, embarrassed, but pleased. "Don't forget Ace. He'll be helping you too." Thad stood up. "I'm gonna go find him now. I'll try to let you know if he comes up with an idea about how to get Gibb away from the ranch." He moved down the steps then and faded into the darkness.

Chapter Nine

Lark was feeding the chickens when she overheard a conversation between her husband and one of the neighbors. "Damn it," Cletus was complaining, "I'll be all day at the blacksmith's getting that axle fixed on the buckboard. I don't know how in the hell that useless Thad managed to break it. He must have been driving over boulders. And on top of breaking it, he didn't tell me about it. I found it after all the men had left to chase cattle."

"You know how it is with them young fellers. They've only got one thing on their minds. That thing between a woman's legs," the neighbor joked.

"Humph." Cletus grunted and stamped off to the crippled vehicle to hitch it to a team of horses.

"Don't drive too fast, Gibb; otherwise your buckboard will break down for good," the man called after him.

Lark peeped through a crack in the henhouse and saw with amusement a tickled smile on the neighbor's face. It appeared to her that it wasn't only the cowhands that didn't like her husband.

She gave a startled exclamation and dropped two eggs when the door behind her opened. What did Cletus want now? She turned slowly around and relaxed. Thad was walking toward her, a wide grin on his face.

"Where did you come from, Thad?" she asked. "I thought you left with the others."

"No. I hid in the hayloft until I saw Gibb ride away."

"Did you break that axle on purpose?" She tried to sound stern, but the twinkle in her eyes gave her away.

"I sure did," Thad admitted unashamedly. "Me and Ace are going to move the furniture today."

When Lark gave a happy little cry, he ordered, "Hurry up and get ready to go. It will take about ten minutes to hitch up the wagon and start putting the pieces in it."

As Lark darted out of the chicken house, a basket of eggs swinging from her arm, she saw Ace walk out from a patch of pines next to the barn. Her eyes sparkled with amusement. Ace had hidden himself also.

Lark entered the house, set the basket on the kitchen table, then hurried to her room. She knelt down beside the bed and dragged from under it a flat package.

A few days ago she had made one last trip to the attic. Rummaging through an old, dusty trunk, she had come upon some curtains and heavy drapes. They were soiled but in good condition. She had chosen two pairs of curtains and one set of drapes. They had looked quite nice when she had washed and ironed them. They now lay folded on top of three framed pictures she had also discovered among the jumble of items on the floor.

The largest one, which would hang over the fireplace, was of a woodland scene. Of the two smaller ones, there was a deer standing in a growth of aspens, and a painting of a handsome horse's head. They, too, would help brighten up the cabin.

Holding the package to her chest, Lark left the house and hurried to the cookhouse. She walked into the small room where the previous cook used to sleep. There, under a small bed, she had stashed away two loaves of bread wrapped in a clean dish towel, an applesauce cake and a bag of cookies. Carrying it all back into the kitchen area, she put the goodies into an oblong woven basket. Before covering them up, she added the package.

Lark jerked her worn shawl off a peg and, settling it around her shoulders, picked up the basket and walked rapidly to the bunkhouse. She stepped inside and found much activity going on. It appeared that two more of Cletus's men had also made themselves scarce until he left the ranch. Laughing and grunting, they were helping to carry the furniture from the bunkhouse to the wagon right outside the door. A pair of sturdy workhorses had been hitched to it.

Breathless with excitement, Lark stood back watching the men. Her gaze was mostly on Ace. She marveled at the muscles in his back and shoulders, which bulged beneath his shirt as he handled the heavy pieces of furniture. How powerful he is, she thought.

She was wondering how it would feel to be held in his arms, pressed against his magnificent body, when suddenly he looked at her and smiled. He lifted his hand in greeting, then went back to work.

You fool, Lark chastised herself. *Mooning over a man you know you can never have. You're a married woman, remember? Besides, he wouldn't be interested in a skinny woman dressed in rags. He could have any beautiful woman he wanted.*

She fell to wondering how many women had been in Ace's life. A lot, she decided, and took no comfort in the thought.

The last piece of furniture had been placed in the wagon, and it was time to go. When Thad climbed up into the wagon, Lark handed him her package, and Ace boosted her onto her mare's back. Thad picked up the reins, popped them over the team's back, and the wagon rolled out. A mule, heavily loaded with supplies, was tied to the tailgate, and Lark and Ace rode behind it.

Although the sun shone brightly, there was a crisp, cool breeze as the wagon made its creaking way up the mountain. Lark didn't feel its chill, though. She was warm with the excitement of anticipating the pleasure that would jump into her relatives' eyes when they saw what she was bringing them. Especially the large bundle of provisions tied to the mule's back. Their near-starvation diet was at an end.

Lark wasn't surprised that Ben and Lucy weren't outside to greet them. They were both hard of hearing and wouldn't have heard the wagon approaching. She dismounted and walked into the cabin. Her aunt and uncle sat in front of the fireplace. Lucy was reading from a book of poetry, and Ben's head was nodding in a half sleep. When she called out a greeting, they gave a start, then rushed to greet her enthusiastically.

"Me and Lucy was just wondering when you'd come to visit us again," her uncle said, giving her shoulder a squeeze.

"We get lonesome for you if you don't come visit every week," Lucy added as she embraced Lark and kissed her on the cheek.

"I've been under the weather a bit the last few days," Lark said. Then, seeing the concern that jumped into her aunt's eyes, she added, "I'm feeling fine now."

Ben's gaze went to the rickety old kitchen table. When he saw no basket there, disappointment clouded his eyes. "I thought maybe you brought us some more cookies. My sweet tooth has been acting up something fierce this week," he half complained.

Lark laughed softly and put an arm around his bony shoulders. "I've brought you something much better than cookies."

"There ain't nothing better than your cookies," Ben retorted as Lark took his and Lucy's arms and led them outside.

"Howdy, Ace and Thad," Ben said in surprise. "I didn't know you two was out here. What you got in the wagon?"

"It looks like furniture, Ben," Lucy whispered in awe.

"That's what it is, Auntie." Lark hugged Lucy around the waist.

"Is it for me and Ben, child?" Lucy took a step forward to peer more closely at the items in the wagon.

"Indeed it is. Let's go back inside now before you catch a chill."

"Oh, dear, I can't believe it," Lucy said over and over as she followed Lark back inside. "I never thought to see the day I'd ever own real furniture. . . ."

It was high noon by the time the old pieces, except for the stove and bedstead, had been replaced with the pieces from Cletus's attic. Lucy had watched in wonder as carpets were laid and tacked down in the two rooms; then Gibb's discarded pieces were brought in and placed where she wanted them.

During this time Lark had brewed a pot of coffee. After Ace and Thad had carried in the food supplies, she insisted they have coffee and a slice of her cake before they left.

Thad wolfed down two pieces, and when it looked to Ace that the teenager was going to ask for a third helping, he said, "We've got to get started back to the ranch, Thad. We've got to put the wagon back in place before Gibb returns home."

"Yeah, I reckon." Thad reluctantly stood up, his eyes still on the cake.

Lark followed them out onto the porch. "I can never thank you two enough," she said earnestly. "You have made my aunt and uncle very happy."

"We were pleased to do it, Lark," Ace said as he swung onto the gelding's back. "They're a fine couple."

"See you at supper," Thad said, whipping up the team.

Lark watched them ride out of sight, the mule trotting along behind them. She turned and walked back into the cabin. She still had some work to do inside.

Ben and Lucy were walking through the two rooms, murmuring their delight over the used, ordinary pieces.

Lark, listening to them as she hung the curtains in the kitchen, then the heavy drapes in the main room, wondered what they'd say if they could see the fancy furniture in her new home. Her prison.

Lark stepped down from the kitchen chair that had served as a ladder, then made her own round of the cabin.

The two rooms bore no resemblance to what they had been. The cabin had a coziness that the old place had never had before. And best of all, Lark thought happily, the rooms were warm now. The carpeting, the window hangings and the chinking had worked wonders. She dreaded going back to Cletus's beautiful, but cold house. Mostly, she dreaded going back to him.

But she must if she was to keep this nice little cabin for her family. When Ben and Lucy finally settled down in front of the fireplace, she reached for her shawl and said with a smile, "I've got to get back down the mountain now. I have a few chores to do."

"Will you be coming back next week?" Lucy asked anxiously.

"I'll certainly try," Lark answered, not sure when she could visit them again. It depended on the outcome of her confrontation with Cletus tonight. If he had somehow learned about some of his discards being taken to her relatives, he would be in a rage. If he marked her face up it could be days, even weeks before she saw them again. "It's a very busy time at the ranch now."

She gave them a teasing smile and settled the old shawl around her shoulders. "You'll be so busy keeping house now, you won't notice my absence."

"Don't you believe that," Lucy denied. "Even if we lived in a palace, we would miss you."

Lark leaned over and kissed each wrinkled cheek. As she walked to the door she said, "There in that basket on the table is something for your sweet tooth, Uncle Ben."

As the mare picked her way down the rocky trail, an anger began to grow inside Lark that became stronger than her fear of facing Cletus tonight. He would rant and rave at what she planned to say, maybe beat her senseless, but she didn't care. It was bad enough that he used her as a slave, but when he endangered the lives of two innocent people, it was too much.

She couldn't wait to face him and point out some facts that he had overlooked.

Lark remained indignant all the while she was preparing supper. She weakened a bit when the men came in to eat and Cletus glared at her as he sat down at the table.

Uneasiness fluttered through her. Had he found out about the furniture?

When she encountered encouraging smiles from Ace and Thad, she relaxed and her courage returned. They wouldn't smile if Cletus were aware of what they had done today.

Lark swayed between wanting the men to rush through supper and wanting them to take longer than usual. Since the men were never quite at ease in Cletus's presence, the meal was short.

When they were walking out of the room, Lark gathered her nerve and courage and called to her husband, who was walking behind the other men. "Cletus, I would like a few words with you before you leave." Gibb turned and glared at her in surprise through his small, slitted eyes. Lark had never before addressed him first. She spoke only when spoken to.

"What do you want?" he demanded. "I don't have any time to waste on you."

"What I have to say won't take much of your time," Lark said, moving quickly to put the long table between them as Gibb took a step toward her. "I visited my aunt and uncle today and saw the meager supplies you send them every week. It's hardly enough to keep a pair of sparrows alive, let alone two people who need nourishing food."

"Is that right? What do you plan on doing about it?" Cletus sneered as he lunged across the table, grabbing at her.

Lark stepped away from his reach. She would be safe from him as long as she kept the table between them.

Evidently Cletus had come to the same realization, for he stood still, glaring his rage at her.

Lark took a deep breath and, clasping her hands behind her so that Cletus wouldn't see how they trembled, made herself speak firmly. "There is one thing you have overlooked in our relationship. Maybe you're not intelligent enough to realize it, but think deeply on what I'm about to say to you."

At her words, Gibb's face turned a mottled red and he lunged at her again. She eluded his grasping hands and continued as though he hadn't interrupted.

"If my relatives die from starvation and neglect this winter, I will divorce you. There will be no reason for me to continue taking your abuse.

"From now on, I'll decide what foods are delivered to them each week. So it is up to you to choose whether you want to lose an unpaid servant."

His teeth bared in a snarl, Cletus glared at Lark, his piglike eyes giving away the knowledge of his defeat. After a moment he grated out, "Have it your own way." Spinning on his heel, he left the cookhouse, slamming the door so hard it rattled the window.

Weak now that the confrontation was over and she had won, Lark sat down and took a long breath. She had escaped his fists tonight, but the gleam in his eyes as he left her promised that she would pay for the barrel she had put him over.

Chapter Ten

There had been a sudden snowfall during the night, which wasn't unexpected in mid-November. It was only a forewarning of what was to come later, Lark thought as she walked over the skimming of white on her way to the cookhouse. She had been told that in this part of Colorado it wasn't unusual for snow to drift eight feet high.

She had won her battle with Cletus just in time, she told herself, noticing the packhorse standing in front of the long building. "Starting today, I choose what is to go to Uncle Ben and Aunt Lucy," she said under her breath as she unlocked the cookhouse door, then stepped inside.

She walked straight to the larder room and stepped inside it just as Newt Alder, the man who made the weekly trip up the mountain, walked into the kitchen.

He said, "Good morning, Lark," and when she answered in kind, he grinned and said, "Thad told me to use a strong horse today. That I would be delivering more supplies than usual."

"That's right," Lark agreed, returning the big man's smile. "Come on in here and I'll show you what I want delivered to my relatives."

Newt was sweating freely by the time he carried out and strapped on the horse all the items Lark had pointed out to him.

There was a quarter side of beef, a twenty-five-pound side of pork, three plucked and cleaned chickens—two for frying and one for stewing. There was a long length of pork sausage, a sugar-cured ham, a slab of bacon and one of salt pork.

Next came a five-pound bag of potatoes, a small one of onions, a large bag of dried beans, a pound of coffee beans, a sack of sugar, a bag of flour and one of cornmeal.

Lark went through the shelves of air-tights then, choosing cans of peaches, tomatoes and condensed milk.

When Newt made his last trip to the packhorse he looked at Lark and grinned. "The old folks' eyes are gonna pop when I carry all this inside the cabin. I was ashamed and embarrassed when I brought in the pitiful supplies Gibb sent them. I knew there was hardly enough to keep body and soul together."

"Those days are over," Lark said grimly.

"Are you gonna ride up with me? I'll saddle your mare for you."

"I wish I could, but I've got to get breakfast ready for the other men. They'll be here before long." She looked up at Newt and added, "I expect you're hun-

112

gry, too, but Aunt Lucy will make you a big breakfast."

Cletus stood a few feet away from the parlor window, growing angrier by the minute as he watched Newt carry out bag after bag of supplies and strap them onto the horse. He vowed revenge on Lark, and he knew just how he would make her pay. He would put his plan into action tonight.

When the men entered the kitchen that evening, it was evident by the strained expressions on their faces that they knew of the increased supplies that had gone up the mountain. They expected her husband to raise hell with her and they didn't want to hear it. When Cletus came stomping into the kitchen, they kept their eyes on their plates.

Lark grew tense and edged closer to the stove when Cletus scraped back his chair and sat down. She could see by the cross look on his face that his mood was bad. But she had expected that it would be. After all, he had lost a battle with her last night. Would he find some excuse to strike her in front of the men?

Not bothering to speak to anyone, Cletus began passing around the platter of pork chops, a bowl of mashed potatoes, string beans and hot biscuits. His sullen face reminded Lark of a puffed-up bullfrog as he bent his head over his plate and began shoveling the food into his mouth.

Lark glanced at Ace sitting next to Thad and noticed that he was keeping an eye on Cletus, as though waiting for him to start in on her. This made her even more nervous. If Ace came to her defense, it was possible that he would be fired on the spot. She did not want that to happen. She hadn't realized it before, but she had been depending on the new man who had recently come into her life.

The meal was eaten without incident. Then the dreaded time for the coffee arrived. As though sensing her gaze upon him, Ace glanced up at Lark. His eyes sent her the message to relax, that everything was going to be all right.

Lark took a deep, relieved breath. She had served the coffee and Cletus hadn't insulted her in any way. But, she thought, Ace didn't know her husband as she did. He wasn't likely to let her off without some kind of retaliation.

I don't care what he does to me, Lark told herself, as long as Aunt Lucy and Uncle Ben get ample food from now on.

When the men began leaving the table, Gibb stood up, wiped his greasy mouth and said, "I think I'll ride along to town with you men. I could use a little relaxation."

Lark noticed that the men weren't too happy about that, but there wasn't much they could say.

Lark washed the dishes and swept the floor. Then, pulling on her jacket she left the cookhouse and walked toward the big house. Instead of going inside right away, she sat down on the top step of the porch.

She had sat there for just a minute, resting her tired body and breathing in the pine-scented air, when a rollicking tune floated up to her. She peered toward the dim shape of the barn and smiled when she saw Thad appear out of the shadows. He is always in such good spirits, she thought, and hoped that growing into adulthood wouldn't harden him too much.

"I thought you might be sitting out here." Thad gave her a wide smile and turned his steps toward the porch.

When he sat down beside her Lark asked, "Why didn't you go to town with the rest of the men?"

"I don't know." Thad shrugged. "I guess it's because I always feel out of place when I go into town with them at night." He leaned his back against the porch railing. "They go to the saloon, where I'm not allowed to enter, or they go to . . ."

"To the pleasure house?" Lark finished for him.

"Yeah," Thad admitted, ducking his head. "Ace told me to stay away from such places. He said that someday I'd meet a nice girl and I'd be glad that I had."

"I think he's right," Lark agreed as she stared out into the darkness. But she wondered if Ace visited the women he had told Thad to stay away from. She didn't like thinking of him in bed with a prostitute, doing things that she could only imagine. She and Aunt Lucy had never talked about what went on between a man and a woman in bed.

When Lark found herself imagining that she was the one lying in bed with Ace, that he was moving his hands over her bare body, she crushed the image immediately. Like it or not, she was bound to Cletus Gibb as long as her aunt and uncle lived.

Still, Lark wanted to know if Ace visited pleasure houses. After a few moments of silence she asked casually, "Do all the men visit the pleasure house?"

"Yeah, they do," Thad answered, and Lark's heart plummeted. Then it jumped back in place when he added, "All but Ace, that is. He said he had never paid a woman to go to bed with him and that he never would."

"Do you know if he has a lady friend somewhere?"

"I don't know about a special woman, but I know he was married once for a short time."

"Only a short time? Did he say why it didn't last?"

"He said a rattler bit his wife in the throat and she lived only a few minutes after that."

"How dreadful," Lark exclaimed, feeling honestly sorry for Ace. "Her death must have been very painful for him."

"I guess. He never said so, though. He just said it was a shame. She was so young, so beautiful. He said she was a singer."

So young, so beautiful. The words kept echoing through Lark's mind after Thad left her. Of course Ace's wife would have been beautiful. That was why he never looked at Lark Gibb with interest in his eyes. How could her rail-thin body attract him?

To the background of a night owl hooting, a full moon rose slowly. Lark went in to bed, but several hours later she was still awake, gazing out the window at the moon. In its light she saw her husband ride up to the barn.

About fifteen minutes later she heard another horse ride up to the barn. Her pulse beat a little faster when she recognized Ace dismounting. She watched him unsaddle the gelding then put him in the corral with four other horses.

When he had gone inside, Lark lay thinking about how Ace had walked to the bunkhouse. His pace had been slow, his head bent as though in deep thought.

Was he thinking about his dead wife? Was he mourning her?

Ace was in a deep study as he walked to the bunkhouse. He was still stunned by the conversation he'd had with Gibb in town.

He and the cowhands had entered the single dirt street of Dogwood and gone straight to the Longhorn Saloon. In high spirits, looking forward to a few hours of relaxation, they bellied up to the bar.

The bartender and owner, Big Red, greeted them with a wide smile and placed a glass in front of each man. "What's new, fellers?" he asked as he uncorked a bottle of whiskey and filled their glasses.

"Nothing much." It was John Henry, the ranch foreman who answered. "Riding fence, keeping an eye on the cattle."

"Yeah, and trying to look busy in case Gibb is around spying on us," another man added with a laugh. "He sure wants his money's worth from us."

"How's that timid little wife of his?"

"Practically worked to death," someone answered. "She works harder than we do."

"That Gibb is a mean bastard," Red said, refilling their empty glasses. "He's bound to get his one of these days," he added before walking to the other end of the bar to serve another customer.

The fresh drinks were downed quickly; then John Henry said with a grin, "Any of you men want to go with me to Meg's place?"

All but Ace followed him out the door, anticipation of a romp with one of Meg's girls glittering in their eyes.

Ace was still nursing his drink, wondering what to

do with the rest of the evening. There was a poker game going on in the back of the room, and he was tempted for a moment to join the men. He hadn't had a deck of cards in his hands for months, and sometimes his fingers itched to shuffle a deck, to riffle the cards, to feel the smooth slide of them as they were dealt. He pushed the urge out of his mind. To sit in a game again would bring back guilty memories. If he hadn't gone off to play poker that morning, his wife might still be alive.

Ace had decided to finish his drink and return to the ranch when the door opened and Gibb entered the saloon. As the rancher walked toward him, he swore under his breath. Another minute and he would have missed the hated man.

"Evening, Ace." Gibb settled his wide girth beside Ace. "Have a drink."

"Thanks, but as soon as I finish this one, I'm riding back to the ranch."

"I'd like a minute of your time before you leave. I want to put a proposition to you."

A warning bell went off in Ace's brain. Something told him that the rancher wanted to discuss Lark. Probably Gibb was going to warn him not to help her anymore, or he would lose his job. He prepared himself to lose his job. He would continue to help the poor lonely, brow beaten woman whenever he could.

He looked at Gibb and said coolly, "Say your piece."

"Let's go sit at that table in the corner. Our conversation is to be strictly private. I don't want anyone to overhear us."

His curiosity aroused, Ace followed Gibb to the table. Was the rancher planning on killing someone and needed his help to do it? He wouldn't put anything past the man.

When they were seated, Gibb clasped his hands on the table, looked at Ace, then looked away. After a moment he brought his gaze back to Ace. Clearing his throat, he began to speak in low tones.

"As you know, I'm a very wealthy man." Ace nodded and he continued. "There is only one thing missing in my life."

When Ace didn't make a response, only sat looking at him, Gibb drew a long breath and said, "I want a son . . . or a daughter, if it should turn out that way. The thing is. I want an heir. I want someone to carry on my name, to inherit everything I have worked so hard to get."

"Why are you telling me this, Gibb?" Ace asked when the rancher paused for a moment. In an attempt at humor, Ace added, "I'm too old for you to adopt me."

Gibb leaned forward and, dropping his tone lower yet, said, "Maybe so, but you're the right age to put a baby in my wife's belly."

Ace was sure he had misunderstood his boss's words. He couldn't have said what it sounded like he had. He gave Gibb a narrow look and said sharply, "Will you repeat that?"

"You heard me," Gibb said. "I want an heir, and I have chosen you to be the means of my getting one."

Ace studied him a moment, thinking that the man was out of his mind. He leaned forward and asked bluntly, "Can't you sire one yourself?"

"No, I can't, damn it," Gibb answered angrily, bitterly. "If I could, I wouldn't be asking you to do it, now, would I?"

"But why me? Any of your men would jump at the chance to do that job for you."

"I chose you the first time I saw you. The time you fought and beat that bully, Ham Landers. You have strength and courage and could be a leader of men if you chose to be. Those are all the qualities I want in my heir."

"You've chosen the wrong man," Ace said with some anger. "I'll not be a stud like your prize horses. You'll have to look somewhere else."

"I'd make it worth your time," Gibb insisted, then named an amount that made Ace blink. "That's enough money to start your own small ranch," Gibb pointed out. "But not in Colorado," he added quickly. "When you've accomplished what I want, I'd expect you to ride a long way from here."

Gibb stood up. "Think on it. You're a smart man. I'm sure you'll come to the right decision."

"What does Lark think about all of this?"

"She doesn't know anything about it. But she'll do whatever I tell her, if she wants that useless aunt and uncle to continue having a roof over their heads and food in their bellies."

Ace watched the rancher walk away, still not sure he hadn't dreamed the whole conversation.

Chapter Eleven

It was the last day of November, cold and blustery, as Lark stood in front of the cookhouse watching Newt ride off toward the mountains. The pack animal trotted along behind him, the supply packs fastened to its back.

She shivered in the cold air and pulled the shawl tighter around her shoulders. The frosted grass crackled under her feet as she started walking toward the house. There, she heaved a tired sigh and sat down in her favorite rocker on the porch. She looked out over the large yard.

The aspens were shedding their leaves, and one of her chores was to rake them up. Cletus had taken his revenge on her by demanding that she keep the yard free of the leaves that fell like rain these late autumn days. It added an extra two hours to her workday. Every time she thought she had raked up and burned the last of them, the next morning there was yellow foliage covering the ground again.

Lark dreaded the coming winter, when the deep snow would fall. No doubt she would be expected to keep all the paths shoveled free of snow. But every aching muscle would be worth it, she told herself. For the second time in a row she had sent Newt off with a good supply of food for her aunt and uncle.

With the coming of winter she would have another burden to contend with, Lark remembered: the washing of the laundry. She hoped that Cletus would allow her to set up the tubs in the kitchen. However, there was still the chore of hanging the wet clothes up in the freezing weather. The garments would freeze stiff almost as soon as she hung them on the line.

Lark sighed and stood up to enter the house. She had work to do.

As Lark made up the two beds, swept the floors and dusted the furniture, her thoughts turned to Ace and lingered. She hadn't talked to him for two weeks. She had the distinct feeling that he was avoiding her. Before, when he happened to see her outside, raking leaves or hanging up clothes, he would stop a minute and chat with her. Lately if he saw her he would lift his hand in greeting but would walk on.

Why? she wondered. Had she done or said something to cause his changed attitude toward her? He still made weekly trips up the mountain to check on her relatives. Thad had mentioned that he and Ace rode up to the cabin every Friday to carry logs from the woodpile and stack the pieces on the porch, handy for Ben to carry into the cabin.

Lark suddenly had the urge to see her aunt and

uncle. Visiting them kept her sanity intact. Days would sometimes go by with her hardly using her voice. When the men came in for their meals they didn't dare strike up a conversation with her. And Ace didn't even look at her anymore, let alone say a few words to her.

Dear Thad. He, as usual, always had something to say to her the few times she saw him.

The mantel clock in the parlor struck ten, and Lark calculated the time it would take her to ride to the cabin, visit with the old folks, then ride back down to the ranch. She should have plenty of time to get back to the house before Cletus returned from town. She had heard him tell the ranch foreman that he would be back in the early afternoon.

The mare's hooves made little noise as they trod the carpet of leaves on the trail. As her mount climbed upward, Lark thought how different the mountain looked with only the green of the pines showing any color. She could see farther through the trees now, see things that had been hidden before. She saw a small waterfall tumbling from a break in the mountain, and she smiled when she saw two deer drinking from the pool it made before disappearing into a jumble of rocks.

Squirrels scampered about, gathering winter food to stow away in some hollowed-out place in a tree, and she caught sight of a handsome gray wolf that stared at her a moment before trotting away. And there was birdsong everywhere.

She had grown to love the mountains, the serenity, the seclusion that let her forget for a while the hell she lived in. She wished she could live here the rest of her life but knew that would never happen. Once her aunt and uncle passed away, she would be gone from Colorado as fast as her mare could take her.

Ben was on the porch, loading his arms with firewood, when Lark rode up. "Larkie," he exclaimed, a wide, pleased smile on his face. "Lucy said this morning that she expected you to come visiting today."

"How have you two been?" she asked, dismounting and kissing her uncle's weathered face.

"Fine as frog hair. Lucy looks the best I've seen her in twenty years."

When Lark followed Ben into the cabin, Lucy gave a squeal of delight and straightened up from shoving a pan into the oven. "I felt it in my bones that you would come visit us today."

"Something smells delicious," Lark said after hugging and kissing her aunt on the cheek.

"Newt brought us a bag of apples this morning and I'm making a cobbler out of some of them."

Lark held the small woman away from her and looked her over. "Aunt Lucy, I do believe you've gained some weight."

"Yes, I have." Lucy's eyes twinkled. "Me and Ben eat real good these days. And I don't have that racking cough that used to shake the meat off my bones."

Lark glanced around at the neat, cheerful-looking room and thought how cozy her aunt had made it. To see her aunt and uncle so well situated was worth every slap and insult Cletus gave her.

Lucy poured coffee for them, then placed a platter of oatmeal-and-raisin cookies on the table. As the three exchanged news of what had gone on since last they saw each other, Lark made up stories of how she loved her new home, how well Cletus treated her.

She pretended not to see the look Lucy scanned over her old, worn clothes.

Was she fooling her aunt? she asked herself.

When Lark refused more coffee, Lucy showed her the sweater she had been knitting for Ben. Then Ben showed her a pair of snowshoes that an old Indian from the nearby village had taught him how to make.

All too soon it was time for Lark to leave, to return to the never-ending chores that filled her days. "I'll stay longer the next time," she promised when Ben and Lucy protested her leaving. "Cletus mentioned that he would like a piece of apple pie with his coffee when he gets back from town today. I've got just enough time to get it baked by the time he rides in."

The old couple followed her outside as usual and watched her until she became hidden in a clump of pines.

Lark's shoulders slumped then. She no longer had to smile and pretend that life was grand.

She had left the foothills and was about a hundred yards from the ranch buildings when she pulled the mare down to a walk. What was all the commotion in the barnyard about? she wondered. Three men, one squatting and two standing, were gathered around a man on the ground. As she drew nearer, she recognized that the downed man was her husband; the other three were ranch hands.

She reined the mare in. What should she do? If she rode in and Cletus saw her, he would punish her for leaving the ranch without his permission. Still, she didn't know how she could avoid riding up to the barn. Whatever had happened to Cletus couldn't be too bad, for she could hear his angry yelling even from this distance.

"I might as well get it over with," she thought out loud, and was about to lift the reins when she saw Thad running toward her.

"What's going on?" she asked when the teenager, out of breath, reached her.

"Someone took a shot at Gibb, and this time he didn't miss," Thad told her, panting. "Got him in the shoulder, and he's bleeding like a stuck pig. Newt rode to town to get the doctor. The men will be carrying him to the house in a minute, and I think it best you be there when they do."

"I agree, but how do I get there without being seen?"

"I've got it all figured out. The back of the house is only a few yards away. And though it's thick with brush back there, you can manage to push through it to the back door. Meantime I'll ride the mare in. Hurry up now."

Lark was out of the saddle and sprinting toward safety almost before Thad had finished speaking. Thad watched her fight her way to the door, then swung onto the mare's back and nonchalantly rode toward the barn.

Lark barely had time to smooth her hair and tie an apron around her waist when she heard the trampling of men lugging Gibb's heavy weight onto the porch. She opened the door and gave a believable performance of surprise.

"What's happened?" she exclaimed. "You're full of blood, Cletus."

"I've been shot, you fool." Gibb snarled between grunts of pain. "Go turn down my bed."

Lark hurried ahead of the men and had the covers pulled back when, struggling and puffing, the men carried Gibb into his bedroom. They laid him down, but not too gently.

"Who shot you, Cletus?" Lark asked, stepping up to the bed, but not too close. It would be like her husband to strike her in his rage.

"How in the hell do I know? The same polecat who's been taking shots at me before. I'll get the bastard if it's the last thing I do. Where in the hell is that doctor? I'm losing blood fast."

"He'll be here any minute," one of the men said. "Try to keep yourself calm."

"Calm, hell. How can I keep calm when I'm bleeding to death?"

If Gibb could have seen through his pain and rage, he'd have seen that the three men looking down at him wished that he was, indeed, bleeding to death.

Dr. Amos Randal arrived about fifteen minutes later. "It's about time you got here," Gibb ranted at the man. "What kept you so long? I expect you were helping some worthless Mexican woman bring another brat into the world. As if we don't have enough of them running around now."

Randal shot him a contemptuous look, then drawled, "No, I was delivering a cow of its calf."

As the men hid tickled grins behind their hands, the doctor said briskly, "Get him undressed."

As her husband's boots, pants and underwear came off, and his shirt was cut away, Lark stood at the window, looking outside. She didn't want to see his repulsive body. She remembered clearly how it had felt on top of her on their wedding night.

When the sheet was pulled up to Gibb's waist, the doctor sat down on the edge of the bed. As he started probing around the wound with his fingers, he said, "I'll need a basin of water, Mrs. Gibb."

Lark rushed to the kitchen. She didn't want her husband to start swearing at her in front of the doctor.

She returned to the bedroom in time to hear Randal say, "The bullet is still in him. I'll have to dig it out." When she set the basin down on the bedside table, the middle-aged doctor looked up and smiled at her. "You can leave the room now," he said. "Your husband is going to do some squealing when I start cutting the bullet out."

"No!" Gibb barked. "I want her to stay."

"I think that it's best that she doesn't," Randal said firmly. "Please leave now, Mrs. Gibb."

Despite Cletus's continued protests Lark walked toward the door. The doctor doesn't like him either, she thought as she closed the door behind her. Wasn't there anyone who liked the man?

As she walked down the hall she heard Randal order, "One of you men hold his shoulder, and you other two sit on his legs."

Lark could hear Cletus yelling his pain and fury all the way into the kitchen. If that was Ace under the knife, she thought, the most she'd hear from him would be a deep groan.

After about fifteen minutes it quieted down in the bedroom, with only groans and complaints coming from the wounded man. Lark was wondering how long Cletus would be laid up and was thinking what a terrible patient he would be when Dr. Randal walked into the kitchen.

"Is everything all right, Doctor?" she asked, standing up from her seat at the table.

"Everything is fine, Mrs. Gibb," Randal answered, his professional eyes seeing how drawn her delicate features were, how haunted her gray eyes. "Would you come back to your husband's room a minute? I have a few instructions about your husband's care I want to speak of."

Lark nodded, then looked at the outside kitchen door when it opened and Thad stepped inside.

"Did you want something, Thad?" she asked.

Thad looked at the doctor. "Newt said that you wanted to see me."

"That's right, young man. Come along with me and Mrs. Gibb."

Lark and Thad exchanged questioning looks as they followed Randal into the big bedroom.

"It's about time you came to see how I'm faring." Gibb glared at Lark as soon as he saw her. "I'm going to need a lot of taking care of. You can start by bringing me a glass of whiskey."

"There will be no spirits for you while you're mending, Mr. Gibb," Randal said as he placed his instruments back into his black bag. "You must eat moderately and drink a lot of broth to build up the blood you have lost."

When Gibb stopped bellowing his displeasure at having no whiskey, he turned his disgruntled gaze on Lark. "You heard what he said about building up my blood. Get your lazy self into the kitchen and start making some broth."

"She'll go in a minute." Randal frowned, his expression showing his dislike for his patient. "I have a few more instructions to give.

"Mr. Gibb's bandage is to be changed twice a day, and I have left some medicine to help his wound heal. He's to have a spoonful after each meal."

"What about my pain?" Cletus whined. "Ain't you going to leave anything for that?"

"If you lie still and keep a rein on your temper, the pain will ease by tomorrow."

"Tomorrow? How in the hell am I supposed to sleep tonight?"

Randal ignored Gibb's outburst, and looking at Thad, asked, "Did you hear my instructions, young man?"

"Why, yes, sir," Thad answered, confusion in his eyes.

"Good. You'll be nursing your boss until he can be up and around."

"What are you talking about? That kid won't be taking care of me!" Gibb roared. "I've got a wife to do that."

"Your wife is not physically able to tend to the needs of a man as heavy as you are. Besides, her presence seems to upset you. Young Thad will take good care of you."

A stream of oaths fell from Gibb's mouth as Randal took Lark by the arm and led her out of the room.

Thad stared after them in bewilderment. He was to be nursemaid to this roaring devil?

Chapter Twelve

"That mean bastard, I'm gonna kill him," Thad said as he took his usual seat beside Ace. "I'll choke him to death with my bare hands."

"What's he been up to now?" Ace took the bowl of string beans passed to him from the man on his left.

"Nothing more than usual. But I didn't have a minute's rest from waiting on him. It's 'Get me a cup of coffee.' 'Bring me a piece of pie, if that bitch has any more left.' 'I need the chamber pot.'

"It goes on and on. Thank God Doc is gonna let him get up in a couple days. He can go down to the barn then and aggravate the other men for a change."

"I guess his being laid up has been hell on Lark too," Ace said, picking up his knife and fork and slicing into a beefsteak.

Amusement shone in Thad's eyes. "That's the one

131

blessing in the whole miserable thing," he said, passing the beans on to the next man. "Doc gave orders, in front of Gibb, that she's not to go near his room. He said that her presence upset her husband.

"But I'm not sure that's the reason he said it. I saw humor in his eyes when he gave the order. I think he was having sport with Gibb. I believe that he saw right off how Gibb treats Lark and he figured she would suffer, tending the mean varmint. I bet anything that's why he gave that order."

The men acted very different at their meals now. Without Gibb's sour face at the head of the table, there was laughter and bantering going on. The cowhands even gently teased Lark a little.

She was different also. Her eyes sparkled and her face was alive. It no longer looked dead, as it had when her husband was around.

Ace didn't join the easy tomfoolery among the men, nor did he make eye contact with Lark. He knew, though, that she looked at him often. He was afraid of what she might read in his eyes. Maybe she could see that he was considering doing something shameful to her. He knew beyond a doubt that Gibb was going to ask him for his decision any day.

And he hadn't reached one yet. He had mulled the rancher's proposal over and over. One hour he would tell himself that he absolutely wouldn't do it. The next hour he'd tell himself that with the money promised he could start his own ranch. He could stop wandering around, leading a useless life.

And it wouldn't be hard, making love to Lark.

But what if she's against such a cold-blooded mating? he asked himself every time he considered acquiescing to Gibb's request. *She might feel like a whore, sleeping with a man without any commitment between us.*

But I wouldn't treat her like a whore, he told himself. *I would naturally take the time to arouse her, to make her want me.*

Ace smiled smugly. He'd never had a woman complain about his performance in bed.

The men were leaving the table, complimenting Lark on a good supper. Ace stood up and walked outside with them. He hadn't made up his mind yet what he would answer Gibb when the time came. He probably wouldn't know until he actually said yes or no to Cletus Gibb.

When the cowhands had gone, Lark sat down to her own meal. She had learned early on to prepare a plate for herself and to keep it in the warming oven for when she had time to eat it. The men usually left very little in the bowls by the time their appetites were sated.

She was enjoying a cup of coffee when Thad, stiff-lipped and grim, opened the door and stepped inside. "What's wrong?" she asked as the teenager flung himself into a chair across from her. "What has Cletus done now?"

"Damn him to hell." Thad kicked out at a chair. "I saw him deliberately knock his bottle of medicine off the table. It broke into smithereens, spilling out all its contents. Now he's insisting that I ride into town and get more from Doc. He's a mean, scheming devil."

"What do you think he's planning in that sick mind of his?"

"Can't you figure that out, Lark?" Thad asked impatiently. "After I leave the ranch, he plans on coming here and raising hell with you. Ever since Doc banned you from his room he's been like a mad dog, practically foaming at the mouth."

"Oh, dear, what am I going to do, Thad?" Lark wrung her hands together.

"I'll tell you what to do. When I leave here, you put out the light and bar the door behind me. Then you go into the back room and don't make a sound until I get back."

Lark was weak with fear and dread as she followed Thad to the door and dropped the thick, heavy bar into place when he left. She blew out the light then and hurried into the bedroom. With her heartbeat loud in her ears, she sat down and waited for her husband to come pounding on the door.

She hadn't long to wait. The sound of Thad's horse riding away had barely died when she heard the kitchen doorknob rattle. She jumped at the noise of a loud knocking on the door. Then Gibb shouted, "You'd better open this door, bitch! I know you're in there. Let me in right now if you know what's good for you."

Lark sat on the edge of the bed, praying that the enraged man wouldn't be able to break the door down.

The pounding continued and Gibb's voice rose higher and higher as he demanded to be let inside. Lark was ready to put her hands over her ears when suddenly the hammering stopped.

She sat forward and listened. Had he given up and returned to the house? Then she recognized Ace's voice speaking to Cletus.

"What are you doing out of bed, Gibb?" he was asking.

Lark slipped into the kitchen and stood where she could see out but remained invisible herself in the darkness of the kitchen. She could plainly hear Gibb's raised voice.

"I'm trying to have a few words with my wife and the damn door is barred."

"Lark has probably gone to bed and she doesn't hear you," Ace pointed out.

"She can hear me, and she'd better damn well get her lazy rump out of bed and let me in. That arrogant doctor won't let her come around me. I want to see if she's been doing her chores and cooking the men decent meals."

It was all Ace could do to keep from hauling off and smashing Cletus's fat face with his fist. He knew why the man wanted to see his wife, and it had nothing to do with her housekeeping or cooking meals. He wanted to knock her around, to remind her that he held the welfare of her relatives in his hands.

Ace unclenched his fingers and said as calmly as he could, "She's been doing her work as usual, and the meals are good as usual. Come on now, get back in bed before you reopen your wound."

"No, by God, I'm gonna have a word with her right now," Lark heard Cletus growl and she stepped back as he lifted his fist to strike the door again. Would Ace stop him before he broke the door down? she wondered uneasily.

She saw Ace step forward to stop him. Then a shot rang out. She gasped when she heard a bullet strike the door frame. In the light of the moon she saw the color drain out of her husband's face as intense fear jumped into his bulging eyes. Her gaze darted to the stand of pines next to the barn.

She saw only gunsmoke floating up among the trees. There was no sign of the sniper who had once again tried, unsuccessfully, to gun down her husband.

Lark heard Ace tell Gibb he had better get back to the house, and she smiled wryly. The fat man was already halfway to the house. "The coward," she muttered when the door slammed behind him. Had it been Ace who was shot at, he would have run after the man, not scuttled for cover like a frightened rabbit, she thought.

When she saw Ace walk back toward the bunkhouse, Lark decided to have another cup of coffee to settle her nerves. Besides, she didn't trust Cletus not to wait a few minutes and then try to get into the cookhouse again.

She had finished her coffee and had relaxed somewhat when she saw Thad return from town, a small package in his hand. Cletus's medicine. She rose and walked into the back room. By the moonlight coming through the kitchen window she disrobed and pulled on the gown she had folded under the pillow.

The mattress wasn't wide, and it wasn't too soft, but for the last three nights she had slept more soundly than ever before since becoming Cletus's wife.

Lark sighed softly. Those peaceful nights were coming to an end. Tomorrow night would be the last one. The doctor would allow her husband to get up tomorrow.

I'd better go visit Uncle Ben and Aunt Lucy tomor-

row, she thought. *There's no telling what Cletus will do to me once he is allowed to leave the bed.*

As Ace walked back to the bunkhouse, he wondered who had taken another shot at the rancher. There were two men missing from the ranch tonight: young Thad and Newt Alder. He doubted that it was Thad; otherwise the kid wouldn't have called him out of the bunkhouse and alerted him to keep an eye on the cookhouse while he was gone to town.

As for Newt, he couldn't believe the lazy, easygoing man would go to the trouble of standing out in the dark and waiting for the chance to take a shot at his boss.

"But who then?" Ace asked himself as he lay in bed later. When no answer came he thought of Lark. He would feel sorry for her when Gibb resumed his normal activities.

Chapter Thirteen

Lark stood on the porch, looking toward the distant foothills. It was late morning and black clouds were building in the north. The cold air stabbed through her thin jacket, and she wondered if she dared ask Cletus for a new, heavier one. She knew in her heart it would be a waste of words.

Today was December first, and a long overdue storm was threatening. I hope I can visit Aunt and Uncle and get back down the mountain before it hits, Lark worried as she walked down the steps. The sharp air was so cold it brought tears to her eyes.

Half blinded, Lark walked full-tilt into a hard masculine body. The man grunted at the impact and his hands came out automatically to steady her. She blinked away the moisture in her eyes and gave a small laugh when she recognized Ace.

He started to laugh too, then cut it off. His eyes

sober, and somehow aloof, he asked as he released her, "Are you all right?"

"I'm fine." Lark smiled up at him, ready for a little chat. But before she could say more, Ace tipped his hat and walked off.

Lark stared after him in hurt confusion. What had changed his manner toward her? She racked her brain, trying to think what she might have said or done to have changed him so.

Nothing came to mind.

Cletus must have given him orders not to talk to me, she decided as she saddled the little mare and led her out of the barn.

Lark was about to swing into the saddle when she paused, one foot in the stirrup. Ace had gone to the house and was stepping up on the porch. She watched him knock on the door, then saw Thad open it to him. They spoke to each other a moment; then Thad stepped outside and Ace entered the house and shut the door behind him.

"What's that all about?" she asked herself. When she saw Thad walking toward the barn, she lowered her foot and waited for him. Thad knew just about everything that went on around the ranch. She would ask him if he knew anything about Ace's early visit to her husband.

"I'm just as mystified as you are, Lark," Thad answered when she put the question to him. "All I know is that last night Gibb told me to tell Ace he wanted to see him this morning. He's been edgy and crabbier than usual ever since he got up. He had me looking out the window every ten minutes to see if Ace was coming. When finally I reported that Ace was coming, he told me that as soon as I let Ace in, I was to make myself scarce. Said he wanted to talk business with Ace."

"I can't imagine what kind of business Cletus would have with Ace." Lark's teeth worried at her bottom lip.

"Maybe he wants Ace to be his bodyguard." Thad grinned crookedly. "Maybe he's tired of being shot at."

"You joke about it, but it could be that," Lark said, and this time she swung onto the mare's back.

"Where are you off to?" Thad asked.

"I'm going to visit my aunt and uncle while the weather permits." Lark picked up the reins and, with a wave of her hand, rode off toward the mountain.

Ace found Gibb propped up on pillows, his obese body bare to the waist except for the bandage on his shoulder. Ace cringed inside, thinking how Lark must have suffered beneath his heavy weight as he tried, unsuccessfully, to sire a baby on her. It was all he could do to keep from putting his fist in the hated man's thick lips when they parted over tobacco-stained teeth in a grimace that was meant to be a smile.

He had made his decision the night before. He would accept Gibb's offer, but with some reservations known only to him and Lark. He could never bring himself to make love to an unwilling woman. Especially to browbeaten Lark. She was too fine a person.

I will let her know right away that we will only make a pretense of making love. That will relieve her mind.

They could continue this deception all through the winter months. He would be assured of a job through the cold season. Also he would see to it that Gibb kept his fists off Lark. When the weather warmed up, they would tell the mean bastard that Lark was expecting his heir and Ace would take his promised money and ride away.

Ace's smile was almost evil. It would give him much pleasure to pull such a trick on the fat man.

"Have a seat." Gibb motioned to a chair pulled up close to the bed.

When Ace had seated himself, Gibb said, "Let's get right to it. Your time is up. What have you decided?"

"It's going to be a hard thing to do." Ace made his tone sound reluctant. "I've never lain with a woman that I didn't care for . . . not counting whores, of course."

Gibb waved his hand as if that were of no importance. "Just pretend she's a whore. In the dark she'll be just another woman ready to pleasure you. I don't expect you to have any romantic notions about that bag of bones. Just keep in mind the money you're gonna get every time you spill your seed inside her."

Ace dropped his gaze to the floor. If that leering bastard saw the murderous look in his eyes, the deal would be all over. And he wanted that ranch.

Lately he had thought more and more of the Lady Chance in Denver. The saloon was luring him back, and he didn't want to return to that life. Now that he was away from it, he felt it was like a sickness that got into a man's blood.

His gaze jumped back to Gibb when the man said, "You may have to slap her around a little before you can bed her. She's a cold bitch."

"I have never abused a woman," Ace said sharply. "I've always found that gentleness is best."

"Gentleness, bah." Gibb snorted. "The only thing they respond to is fear. If you don't knock them around once in a while they'll think you're weak. The first thing you'll know they'll be going to bed with any man who comes along."

"All I can say is that you must have been around the wrong kind of women."

"Think what you want to, but I know what I know," Gibb said in a growl, tired of the subject. "Now, back to business. Come to the house tonight around eight o'clock, after the men are in the bunkhouse or gone to town. Lark will be waiting for you in her bedroom."

"No, no." Ace shook his head. "I couldn't perform in the house knowing that you're nearby."

"The noise you'll make won't bother me." Gibb barked a laugh. "I'm gonna enjoy the sound of you two making the bedsprings squeak. I'll know I'm on the way to getting an heir."

"It's out of the question," Ace said firmly.

The rancher sighed in exasperation. "What about the cookhouse then? There's a narrow cotlike thing in the back room where the cook used to sleep. It's hardly wide enough for two, though." He gave a sneering laugh and added, "Of course, it's wide enough if one is on top of the other. I expect that's the way it's gonna be, huh?"

Ace knew he couldn't take much more of the vile man without attacking him. He stood up and said shortly, "I'll be at the cookhouse around eight." He started toward the door, then turned around. "If you've marked up her face in the meantime, I won't touch her until she heals."

Gibb's only answer was a grunt as Ace walked out of the room.

The air was stinging cold when Lark stepped outside the cabin. "Don't come out with me," she said to Lucy and Ben. "You'll get a chill and come down with a bad cold."

"We're gonna get snow before tomorrow morning," Ben said, peering over Lark's shoulder at the dark sky. "After holding off for so long it will be a humdinger when it gets here."

"I hope the snow won't be too deep," Lark worried. "I'm afraid Newt won't be able to get supplies to you."

"Don't worry about that, Larkie," Ben said cheerily. "That packhorse and the one Newt rides are mountain bred and very strong. They're used to making their way through deep snow. And don't forget my snowshoes." Ben laughed. "If me and Lucy get too hungry, I'll strap them on and walk to Dogwood for a few supplies."

"I don't like to think of you doing that." The worry lines deepened in Lark's forehead. "The mountain will be full of hungry cougars."

"You forget that I'm a crack shot with a rifle," Ben said, then added, "most times."

"I must get going." Lark stepped off the porch. "Take care of yourselves, because if the snow piles up, I don't know when I'll be able to come up and check on you."

"Don't worry about us, honey," Lucy urged. "Just take care of yourself. I don't like the way you've lost so much weight."

Maybe I am being too anxious about them, Lark

thought as the mare started down the mountain.

She had gone into the larder room at the cabin and found it well stocked with provisions. And Ace and Thad had stacked so much wood on the porch, there was only a narrow path to the door.

I'd better start worrying about myself, she thought as she reached the low-lying foothills. *Cletus will be up tomorrow and that will be the end of the peace I've been enjoying.*

As she rode out onto the range Lark shivered at the thought of having to watch every move she made, of being the meek little wife who never lifted her gaze to anyone. Cletus always looked for the slightest excuse to strike her or abuse her vocally.

Her dread of her husband increased when she rode past the house and Thad ran out to hail her. "Gibb wants to talk to you after supper tonight, Lark."

"What about?" Alarm shot into her eyes.

"I don't know." Thad gave her a pitying look. "He's been in a good mood all day, if that means anything."

"I doubt that his good mood has anything to do with me," Lark said, and she rode on to the barn.

After turning the mare loose in the corral, Lark hurried to the cookhouse. As she fixed Cletus a tray with a beef sandwich and a cup of coffee, a question kept running through her mind: What meanness had her husband thought up now? Surely there was nothing more he could do to add to her misery.

After Thad picked up the tray to take it to his boss, Lark scrubbed the kitchen floor, then began ironing the basket of clothes that was waiting for her. When the ironing was folded and put away, the clock struck five. She shoved more wood into the firebox and put a pot of stew to simmering on the stove.

At seven o'clock as usual, the meat and vegetables were on the table, along with a mound of hot biscuits on a platter.

When the men came trailing in, it was as if they knew this would be the last meal when they could laugh, joke around and tease Lark a bit.

The kitchen had never rung with such lighthearted hilarity. But it was hard for Lark to join their tomfoolery. Uppermost in her mind was the meeting with Cletus, which was drawing nearer and nearer.

Lark gave a start when Thad entered the kitchen and sat down beside Ace. "Aren't you going to take Cletus's supper to him?" she asked as he helped himself to the stew.

"He said that you should bring it when the men are finished eating. He's getting up tomorrow, so I guess I'm finally finished waiting on him. Thank God."

Ace saw her hands begin to tremble, and pity for her stirred inside him. He knew she was fearful of being knocked around again. But poor woman, she was unaware that what her husband was going to demand of her would seem worse than a beating.

He felt like a dirty, low-down cur for the part he was going to play in it.

Chapter Fourteen

When the men had left the kitchen, Lark stood at the table, looking at the dirty dishes. Should she wash them before taking Cletus his meal, or find out what he wanted of her?

She decided to go to the house and get it over with. She was becoming a nervous wreck, wondering if she was to get a beating.

She placed a bowl of stew on the wooden tray and added several biscuits. With uneasiness gripping her entire body, she walked across the yard and entered the house.

It seemed eerily quiet inside, almost ominous somehow, Lark thought. She told herself not to be ridiculous, but she was still cautious as she entered her husband's bedroom.

She gasped and almost dropped the tray when Cletus stepped from behind the door. "You're up," she said in a squeak, her heart pounding at the malignancy in his slitted eyes. "Shouldn't you still be in bed?"

Gibb ignored her question. "Put the tray on the table and sit down," he ordered. "I want you to listen closely to what I'm going to say to you."

Lark placed his supper on the table, then perched on the edge of the chair. What did he have in mind for her now? she asked herself, gripping her hands together to stop their trembling.

Gibb lowered his heavy bulk onto the bed, his knees almost touching Lark's. "Now," he began, fixing her with a cold, baleful glare, "the only reason I married you was to get an heir. I even agreed to support that worthless family of yours because I wanted an heir so badly. But as you know, I was unable to get you bigged. So another man will have to do the job for me."

"What do you mean?" Lark exclaimed, horrified. "Surely not what I'm thinking."

"If you're thinking that I intend to have another man bed you, you're right. Ace Brandon is going to put a baby in your belly."

Lark stared at him in disbelief. "Ace would never be a party to something like that," she cried.

"Wouldn't he though?" Gibb sneered. "If you offer a man enough money, he'll do most anything. Ace Brandon is no different."

Lark's fear turned to anger. "I won't do it," she almost shouted, and started to stand up.

Cletus jumped to his feet and slammed her back into the chair. Standing over her he grated out, "You'll do it or tomorrow morning your aunt and

147

uncle will be turned out of the cabin, and you'll get your no-account self out of the house.

"It will probably snow tonight, might even be a blizzard. How long do you think those two old people would survive in freezing weather without a roof over their heads?"

Lark stared back at his anger-twisted face. He would do as he threatened, she knew, and her two relatives wouldn't last any time at all in a blizzard. And there was no place nearby she could take them for shelter.

Her shoulders slumped, and defeat clouded her clear gray eyes.

"That's more like it," Cletus gloated, reading her surrender. "You're to meet Brandon in the cookhouse at eight o'clock. Be undressed and waiting for him in bed."

He picked up the fork and started eating. When Lark continued to sit in a daze of disbelief, he waved a hand at the door and snapped, "Get going."

With tears streaming down her cheeks, Lark stumbled out of the house and across the yard to the cookhouse. The tears continued to fall as she washed the dishes and put the kitchen in order. What pained her almost as much as having to commit adultery was the loss of her belief that Ace was above most men. For the right price he would sire a child on her.

A glance at the clock on the wall alerted Lark that she had five minutes to get into bed. With a gulping sigh she blew out the lamp and moved like a sleepwalker into the back room. Fully clothed, her heart hammering, she lay down and waited for the worst thing that could ever happen to her.

* * *

When the clock in the bunkhouse showed a minute to eight Ace stood up, stretched, then said to the men playing cards, "I'm gonna take a walk, breathe some fresh air into my lungs, rid them of the stink of dirty socks."

As he took his jacket down from a row of pegs that held similar garments, several high-heeled boots were tossed at him in a laughing, good-natured way.

He closed the door behind him and stood a moment, looking toward the black bulk of the cookhouse. No light shone from its window. Had Lark gotten up the nerve to refuse Gibb's demand? he wondered.

He half hoped that she had. His heart certainly wasn't in this rendezvous.

Ace told himself he'd better check to make sure she wasn't huddling in the dark, dreading the invasion of her body.

Condemning Cletus Gibb to hell, Ace crossed the distance to the cookhouse.

The doorknob turned readily in his hand, and Ace stepped inside. All was quiet in the rustic building, but he sensed Lark's presence. He closed the door and shot the bolt. He wouldn't put it past Gibb to sneak into the kitchen and spy on them.

After a little while he could make out the dark opening of the door to the back room. He hung his jacket on the doorknob and made his way to the room which was in total darkness.

"Lark," he whispered softly. "It's me, Ace. I'm going to light the lamp before I bump into something and break my neck."

When there was no response from Lark, he took a match from his shirt pocket and scratched his thumb across its sulfur end. By its flame he found the lamp on a small table. He removed the glass chimney and touched the flame to the wick. He saw Lark then, huddled on the bed, the covers pulled up around her ears. As he tugged off his boots, he was filled with pity for her. How helpless, how ashamed she must feel to be degraded in such a manner.

"Lark," he said gently, sitting down on the edge of the bed, "I'm not going to hurt you. We're not going to do anything but talk."

Lark turned her head and looked at him from red-rimmed eyes. "That's all?" she whispered, her tone saying that she wasn't fully convinced.

"That's all. I promise. Did you really think that I would go along with Gibb's dastardly plan?"

"I didn't want to think that, but why are you here?"

"I'll tell you why," Ace said as lay down beside her, "but first you've got to scoot over a little, give me some room before I fall on the floor."

Lark gave a small laugh and slid across the mattress until her back was pressed against the wall.

"Now," Ace began, facing her because there still wasn't enough room for him to lie on his back, "a little over two weeks ago Gibb came to me with a proposal that set me back on my heels. He said that because he was unable to get you with child, he would pay me handsomely to do the job for him. I refused him outright, but he insisted I think it over for a couple weeks.

"I did mull it over, and to my shame I was tempted. He had offered me enough money to start my own small ranch.

"I'm thirty-five years old, Lark, and have never owned anything except a deck of cards, a Colt and my gelding. The money I would get from him would give me a chance at a more secure life than I have now. So, in the two weeks that I thought about it, I came up with this idea."

Lark listened closely as Ace laid out his plan of how they could put something over on the rancher.

Lark was quiet for a while, thinking through what Ace had said. What he planned wouldn't do her any good, she decided, but if she could help put something over on Cletus Gibb, she was all for it.

Before she could make a response to Ace, he said, "Of course, before I leave I'll give you enough of the money so you can take your aunt and uncle and get away from the monster."

Ace's offer so stunned Lark, she couldn't speak for a moment. She sensed then that he was waiting for an answer from her, and she gazed up at him and said earnestly, "I'll be ever so grateful if you do that. Sometimes I think that I can't go on much longer with things the way they are."

Ace lifted his hand and smoothed her tangled curls. "It's settled then. The mean bastard doesn't know it, but his money will be helping both of us."

"Happy day, hurry up and come," Lark said, almost as a prayer.

Ace positioned her head to rest on his shoulder. "Now," he said, "let's get acquainted. Tell me about yourself, your aunt and uncle."

Speaking in low tones Lark went back to when she was ten years old and had lost her parents. There was no bitterness in her voice when she spoke of her Uncle Ben's dislike of hard work, of how they'd lost the homestead. They had been forced to go on the road then.

She skimmed over the states and many towns they had been through, she and Ben looking for work when she became old enough to apply for a job. Gradually, unintentionally, it came out that she had been the main provider for the little family since she was fourteen years old.

She told how in desperation one rainy day they had taken cover in Gibb's old cabin. "He found us there and tricked me into marrying him." Lark sighed. "You know how that turned out."

"You and I are going to make him pay for the pain he has caused you," Ace said grimly.

"Yes, we will," Lark agreed, then said, "Tell me about yourself now."

Ace didn't speak of how he became a dealer in his cousin's saloon. He only said that he had dealt poker at the Lady Chance saloon, and that handling cards was what he had done all his adult life.

He mentioned briefly that he had been married once and that his wife had died from snakebite a few months after their marriage. He said that he felt guilty about her death. That if he hadn't been playing cards, she would probably be alive today.

"I haven't had a deck of cards in my hands since," Ace said, finishing his story.

As Lark lay wondering if he still mourned his wife, Ace began bouncing his body on the mattress, making the bedsprings squeak rhythmically.

Lark leaned over and asked, "What are you doing, Ace?"

"I heard a noise outside the window," Ace whispered. "I'm pretty sure that Gibb is out there listening for telltale noises that we're doing his bidding."

Ace continued to bounce his hips, even giving a couple of loud groans before lying still.

He looked at Lark and laughed softly at the bewildered look in her eyes as she leaned over him. "You're quite an innocent, aren't you, Lark?"

"I guess I am," Lark agreed, and lay back down.

Ace reached across her and parted the heavy drapes wide enough for him to peer outside. "I was right," he said with amusement. "Gibb is running toward the house right now." He sat up and reached for his boots. "I'd better get back to the bunkhouse before my shadow Thad comes looking for me."

When he had stamped on his boots, he smiled down at Lark and said, "I expect I'll see you tomorrow night at the same time."

"I expect so." Lark smiled back.

Lark continued to lie in bed a couple of minutes after she heard Ace softly close the kitchen door behind him. She wasn't looking forward to facing Cletus. She knew he would be waiting for her. He would say condemning words to her, even though it was his doing that she and Ace were sleeping together. He would call her every vile name he could think of; worse, she feared he would beat her.

Thinking that if she stayed here any longer Cletus might come looking for her, she sighed and slid off the bed. In the kitchen she shrugged into her jacket and stepped outside.

The breath was drawn out of her lungs. A furious wind was blowing out of the north, driving before it a blinding snow. Driven back against the door by the icy blast, Lark peered through the white curtain until she could make out the kitchen light from the house.

The flakes were small and hard, stinging her face

like hailstones as Lark made her way toward the dark shape of the house. As she had known he would be, Gibb was sitting before the fire in the fancy parlor he was so proud of. When she walked inside the room, her body a knot of tense muscles, he looked up at her. The glint in his eyes was unnerving.

"Well, whore," he said, sneering, "I expect you're all worn out from the pounding you've been enjoying."

When Lark shook her head negatively, Cletus said in a snarl, "Don't go shaking your head at me. I heard the bedsprings popping and Brandon groaning."

He stood up and stalked toward her. "You liked it, didn't you, slut?"

Lark caught herself just in time. She had been about to deny that she and Ace had done anything but talk to each other. Cletus was wily. If he suspected that he was being played for a fool, Ace could kiss his dream of owning a ranch good-bye, and she would be a prisoner here until her relatives died.

She stood quietly with bowed head, waiting for his fist to lash out at her face.

The blow didn't land there. It hit her hard in the stomach, bending her over. As she gasped for breath through her pain, Cletus threw her on the floor and kicked her hard on the thigh two times before lumbering off to his room.

When Lark heard his door slam shut, she dragged herself off the floor and limped into her room. She undressed in the darkness, pulled a gown over her head and crawled painfully into bed. She lay on her back, wondering if she would have to go through this kind of treatment every time she met Ace in the little back room.

She consoled herself with the thought that every blow was worth the freedom she would have, come spring.

Chapter Fifteen

When Lark awakened there was a thick silence outside. The wind had died away. She slid out of bed and, shivering when her bare feet hit the floor, walked to the window and parted the heavy drapes. Though the sky was still gray and cloudy, she saw that it had stopped snowing. "Thank God," she said softly, for already there were snowdrifts three feet high around the cookhouse and a foot of the white stuff on the ground.

She took her heaviest petticoat and midthigh underpanties from the dresser. As she hurried into them, she worried about her aunt and uncle and how they were faring in this frigid weather. Pulling a worn, faded blue dress over her head, she fretted that the wind might have drifted snow against their door, making it impossible for Uncle Ben to get it open.

She must somehow talk to Thad or Ace and ask

156

them if they would try to get to the old cabin and see that her relatives were all right.

When Lark had pulled on a pair of black woolen stockings and slid garters past her knees to keep them up, she lifted the lid of the battered trunk at the foot of the bed.

She took from it a black-and-red-plaid mackinaw that had seen her through five winters. She dug beneath the few remaining clothes and lifted out a pair of shoes equally as old. She remembered that the soles of both shoes were cracked straight across. She picked up a newspaper that was three weeks old and folded pieces of it to pad the inside of the black footwear.

As she laced them up, well past her ankles, she thought with a wry twist of her lips that her feet would be wet before she got to the cookhouse. She dreaded to think what condition they would be in by the time she finished shoveling the paths that led to all the outbuildings. She had no doubt in her mind that Cletus would force her to do that as soon as breakfast was over.

As she passed through the kitchen, Lark wondered at the grating sound coming from outside. When she opened the door, two smiling faces looked up at her.

"Good morning, Lark," Thad said, leaning on the handle of a shovel. "Me and Ace figured we'd better clear a path to the cookhouse if we wanted to have breakfast this morning."

"And we're starved." Ace grinned at her, puffs of white vapor floating from his mouth with each word.

"Thank you both so much." Lark smiled down at them, her teeth chattering. "But Cletus won't like you doing it. I'm sure he'll want me to do it."

"I don't think he'll say anything," Ace said, and jerking his thumb toward the barn, added, "He'd have to take on the whole crew."

When Lark looked toward the barn, her mouth opened in surprise. All five cowhands were wielding shovels. Cletus wouldn't dare tackle all of them.

With a relieved smile she stepped off the porch and walked down the path to the cookhouse.

Ace and Thad resumed removing the snow, then stopped again when Gibb came through the kitchen door, his face as stormy-looking as the overcast sky.

"Good morning, boss," Ace greeted him coolly. "Me and the men decided we'd start clearing paths before you had to tell us to."

"Hell and damnation," Gib roared. "I wasn't going to tell you men to do it. That's one of my wife's chores."

Ace looked at Thad and said, "I'd like a private word with him."

Thad nodded and walked a few yards away.

"Now—" Ace fastened cold eyes on Gibb—"you're not a very smart man, are you?"

"What in the hell are you trying to say?" Gibb blustered.

"Let me put it in a way you might understand. When you put one of your bulls to a prize cow, do you keep her in a healthy condition so that she can breed?"

"Hell, you know how I pamper those special cows."

"That's right. Don't you think that your wife should get the same attention if you want her to conceive? She'll never do it if you continue to work her like a slave. Her body will be too weak to nurture my seed.

"And I'll tell you straight out, every time she miscarries I'm going to charge you an extra fee."

Gibb gave Ace a look of anger and defeat, and without another word clomped down the steps and waddled down the path to the cookhouse.

"Wow! What did you say to him?" Thad asked as he rejoined Ace.

Ace shrugged. "I just told him some home truths. Gave him something to think about."

"From the looks of his face, he's not liking what he's thinking." Thad chuckled.

"Probably not," Ace said dryly.

When Gibb stormed into the big kitchen, Lark pretended not to see the anger on his face as she stirred the ingredients for flapjacks. She left the batter long enough to bring him a cup of coffee, expecting a slap on the face or a kick on the leg. She couldn't believe that neither happened.

She heaved a sigh of relief when Gibb wordlessly drank the strong brew then left, slamming the door behind him. She could only think that he must be ill.

Half an hour later Lark had two platters of steaming flapjacks on the table. She stepped outside and called that breakfast was ready. The men, their cheeks and noses red from the cold, threw down their shovels in anticipation of a hot meal.

When they came in, they had stamped the snow off their boots, all except Gibb.

With Gibb's glowering face at the head of the table, the meal was a fast one. When each man had drunk two cups of coffee, they returned outside and picked up their shovels again.

Lark and Ace were aware that Gibb watched them, and not once did they look at each other.

159

Thad, however, stayed to have a third cup of coffee. When the door slammed shut behind the frowning Gibb, he said, "As soon as we can slip away, me and Ace are gonna see about getting through the snow to check on your aunt and uncle."

"I was just going to ask you if you'd do that. I worry about the snow drifting against the door. Do you think you can get through to them?"

"I think we can do it. We'll ride sturdy little mountain horses to begin with, and there will be stretches of windswept range where it won't be any problem at all. It's gonna take a while, though, to make the trip there and back, so don't expect to hear from us real soon."

When Thad finished his coffee and left, Lark, humming a little tune, cleaned the kitchen, then went into the back room to make up the little cot. As she smoothed the covers she unconsciously let her hand linger on the side of the pillow where Ace's head had lain. Would they share the pillow tonight also? she wondered and hoped.

When Lark went to the house to tidy up the rooms, her mind dwelled on the many subjects she would like to discuss with Ace, matters that her aunt and uncle knew nothing about.

She wanted to know about the lives other people led. She was curious about the young women she had observed from their wagon as they passed through the many towns. She had longed for their pretty dresses, to be one with them as they walked along, smiling and chatting with friends.

She had never known any young girls her own age. Uncle Ben had never stopped in one place long enough for her to become acquainted with any. Not that any of them would have cared to be friendly with one such as she in faded, worn clothes and scuffed shoes that said she was no more than a squatter.

Maybe someday, Lark thought, and continued moving a dustcloth over the furniture.

When she came to the dresser in her room, Lark took a long look at her reflection in the mirror. Her features looked drawn and her eyes were too big for her face.

But it was her hair that claimed most of her attention. It was lifeless-looking and hung in greasy strands to her shoulders. She remembered that she hadn't washed it in over two weeks. She hadn't had the time or the inclination to do so. She asked herself how Ace had borne the sweaty stench of it as they lay close together.

Lark decided that if she didn't do anything else today, even if she got slapped for it, her hair was going to get a good scrubbing. She opened the top dresser drawer and took from it a bar of rose-scented soap. A friendly old woman who owned a mercantile in one of the towns they had passed through had given it to her. She took it and several towels into the kitchen and spent the next half hour in the ritual of soaping and rinsing.

That evening when she served supper to the men nothing was said by them, but she received many admiring looks at her hair, which lay in soft curls around her shoulders.

She dreaded the moment when the men would leave and she would be left alone with Cletus. He would accuse her of prettying herself up for the hired help.

Forty-five minutes later that moment had arrived. She waited for him to begin on her. When he stood up, though, the only thing he said to her was, "Be ready for Brandon at eight o'clock."

Lark fought not to let her excitement show in her eyes. "Again?" she said, her tone sounding as though she didn't like the idea.

"Yes, again," Cletus said in a growl, his eyes gloating at her reluctance. "You'll meet him every night until you're bigged. Get used to the idea."

Lark slumped her shoulders and made her features look downcast until her husband closed the door behind him. Then her lips curled into a wide smile and her eyes shone like stars. She couldn't wait for eight o'clock to come.

Lark had brewed a fresh pot of coffee and was slicing into a dried-apple pie when she heard Ace outside stamping the snow off his boots. She smoothed her hands over her hair just before he opened the door and stepped inside.

"It's getting colder by the minute out there," Ace said, shrugging out of his mackinaw and hanging it up. "I feel sorry for the man or beast who has to be out there tonight," he added, hanging his hat beside his jacket.

"I know," Lark agreed. "I've been thinking about the poor cattle out on the range. Do you think they'll survive?"

"All but a few will make it. Most of them will head for the foothills where the snow won't be so deep, and where they'll be protected from the wind," Ace said.

He looked at the table and a smile lit up his face. "I hope I get a piece of that pie."

"You do." Lark smiled back at him. "And a cup of coffee to go with it," she added as she lifted the black pot off the stove.

"That sounds right fine." Ace pulled a chair away from the table and sat down. As Lark filled two cups with the steaming brew he said, "What more could a man want if he has a warm room, with coffee and pie served by a pretty woman?"

Lark's cheeks flushed pink with her pleasure. It had been a long time since she had been called pretty. And that had come from Uncle Ben and Aunt Lucy. And they said it because they loved her, she thought wryly.

"Did you and Thad make it up to the cabin?" she asked as she placed pie and coffee in front of Ace.

"We did, and it wasn't too difficult getting there. You were right to worry about the drifting snow, though. It was piled three feet deep against the door. Old Ben had worn himself out trying to get it open. He was sure glad when we showed up. He had put his last log on the fire an hour earlier."

"Is that going to happen every time we get a blizzard?" Worry lines etched across Lark's forehead.

Ace shook his head. "You don't have to worry about that happening again. Thad and I stacked wood four feet high on the north side of the door. The snow will drift against that, leaving the rest of the porch mostly clear."

Ace picked up his fork and sliced into the pie. "Your uncle is raring to try out his snowshoes."

"Do you think they'll work?" Lark asked, a little doubtful. "They look so awkward."

"Sure they will. Indians use them all the time in the winter."

Not much more was said between them as they ate the pie. Then as they sipped their coffee, Lark said, "I know so little about the way other people live. I wonder if you could tell me a bit about it?"

"I'll try. What do you want to know?"

"Well, for instance, I'd like to know about the pretty young women I see on the streets. Are they as nice as they appear?"

"Some are," Ace answered as he rolled himself a cigarette. "But I've known older women who are much nicer."

"You mean married women," Lark prompted.

"No, I don't mean that. Most of them are very nice, though. I guess I'm referring to dancers and women who work in saloons."

"Dancers, saloon women?" Lark looked at Ace, confusion in her eyes. "I wouldn't think they would be very nice."

"That's where you're wrong, Lark. Those women have a kindness in them that some of the so-called respectable women will never have."

"Are these women pretty?"

"Yes, I'd say they're pretty in a harsh sort of way. The life they lead isn't easy."

"Have you ever been . . . ever been in love with a woman like that?"

Ace thought of his dead wife a moment, then said, "No, but I've been good friends with a lot of them."

"I guess you've always been around pretty women then."

"Pretty much, I guess. But one of the women I'm fondest of is a homesteader's homely wife. She's a big, rawboned woman who dresses like a man, and works like one. Bertha Sheldon has an inner beauty that is wonderful to behold."

Ace gave Lark a teasing grin. "What about you? I bet a pretty girl like you has had a lot of young men courting you."

Lark shot him a sharp look. Was he poking fun at her? When she saw only sincerity in his eyes, she decided that he really did think that she'd had a lot of suitors.

"Other than Cletus, there have been no other men in my life, handsome or otherwise. As you know, my relatives and I were always on the road. We never stayed in one place long enough for me to make friends with anyone, male or female."

Pity for the young girl swept through Ace. How she must have longed to be with people her own age. It was a shame that she had never attended a party, a dance, had never walked with a young man.

"Those times will come for you, Lark." Ace squeezed her hand. "Remember the money I'll give you when Gibb pays me. You'll be able to get away from him and have this normal life you're so curious about."

"I can't wait for the day," Lark said, returning the pressure of his hand.

Ace released her hand and said, "I guess it's time we went into the back room and started making some noise. Gibb will be sneaking around pretty soon, listening at the window. I wish that bed was a little wider, though."

"Me too. I keep thinking of the two discarded mattresses up in the attic. If we had one of those in the back room, we wouldn't have to practically lie on top of each other."

"I wonder if that's possible," Ace said, as though to himself.

"What's possible?" Lark asked as she stood up.

"If it's possible that we could sneak one of them into the cookhouse," Ace answered, following her into the small room.

"It would be chancy." Lark sat down on the edge of the cot and removed her shoes. "We'd have to be very careful, choose the right time," Lark pointed out as she lay down and scooted as far she could across the narrow cot.

"Yeah," Ace agreed as he pulled off his boots and stretched out beside her. "We not only have to be careful that Gibb doesn't catch us, but the men as well."

"If we're successful, how can we keep it hidden from Cletus? He comes in here sometimes to check on the larder room."

"That is a poser," Ace said thoughtfully. "How could we hide something that big?"

Lark suddenly inched away from the cold wall pressing against her back. "I think I have an idea," she said. "We could roll it up each night and push it under the cot before we leave. We'd have to make sure it was well out of sight."

"You're a right smart filly, Lark, girl." Ace chuckled. "Now all we have to do is get it in here."

"I'll leave that up to you. I'm the last person to know when Cletus will be away from the ranch."

"He'll have to—" Ace began, then stiffened and raised his head to listen to a noise outside.

"Is Cletus out there?" Lark whispered.

"Yes, the fat bastard is out there. It's time we start making the noise he wants to hear," Ace whispered back. He lifted himself up enough for Lark to shift herself beneath his hard, long body.

When Ace eased himself down on Lark's soft feminine curves, he grew still for a moment. The heady perfume of her rose-scented hair brought a stirring in his loins that he hadn't felt in a long time.

When he found himself wishing that there were no clothes between them, he firmly reminded himself that he wasn't supposed to think such thoughts, that he wasn't supposed to feel that way about Lark.

His body didn't know this, however, and as he started moving against her rounded hips and full breasts, making the appropriate sounds Gibb waited to hear, he found himself growing harder and harder. He wanted to slide his hand up Lark's skirt, unbutton her bodice, to feel, to taste the glory of her breasts.

Even in his aroused state, though, Ace knew better than to do either thing. But he couldn't stop his body from simulating the real thing. He forgot to wonder what Lark might think of his rocking movement on her as his body demanded release.

Without conscious thought, he gripped her hips and bucked his body harder and faster against her. When the climax washed over him the deep groans that came from his lips were not shams.

As Ace went limp on top of her, Lark stirred and whispered anxiously, "Are you all right, Ace? Have you hurt yourself somehow?"

Ace laughed softly at Lark's naivete, her innocence and, taking his weight off her, he said, "It's nothing, just a crick in my back. I'll be fine in a minute or so."

"We've got to get that mattress in here as soon as possible," Lark said. "You can't do this to your back every night. You could do permanent damage to it."

Something will be permanently damaged, Ace thought wryly, feeling sticky in his denims as he sat up and reached for his boots. He doubted that a wider mattress would solve his problem. He had at least three months ahead of him in which he had to keep up the pretense of making love to Lark. He repressed a sigh. It was going to be hard not to make it the real thing.

When he was ready to leave Lark, he whispered, "I'll see you tomorrow night." He couldn't resist trailing his fingers down her smooth cheek before leaving the room.

As he opened the kitchen door and stepped outside, he saw Gibb scuttling into the big house. "You poor excuse for a man," he swore as he set off for the bunkhouse. "You've put me in a fine fix."

It was cold and windy when Lark left the house. Ice flashed like rainbows on the pines as the rising sun shed its red light on them.

She hugged herself against the cold air that penetrated her thin jacket as she made her way to the cookhouse. She dreaded the first half hour in the big room. It would be freezing cold until she built a fire in the kitchen stove and its heat reached throughout the large kitchen.

But when she stepped inside the cookhouse, Lark found to her surprise and pleasure that it was nice and warm. Who had built the fire? she wondered, hearing the cheery crackle of flames in the firebox of the big black range.

She hung her jacket on its usual peg, and as she walked to the stove to put on the apron hanging near it, she spied a slip of paper on the table. She picked it up and read, *Lark, I hope you enjoy the fire I built for you, Thad.*

How kind and thoughtful you are, she thought. *You are going to make some lucky young lady a fine husband one of these days, Thad.*

As Lark busied herself slicing bacon from a long slab, she thought of the hour she had lain sleepless in bed after retiring last night. She had gone over and over in her mind how Ace's movements on her body had seemed different somehow. Not like the night before, when they lay together for the first time in the narrow cot. Last night there had seemed to be an urgent rhythm in his bucking hips. And unlike the first time, at the end of their pretense his body had stiffened and his breathing had come fast and harsh. Also his groans didn't come just from his mouth. They were deep, as though they came from his chest. And when he let his full weight fall on top of her, his face was so hot where it rested between her throat and shoulder.

As Lark laid the strips of bacon into a large black skillet, she gave herself a mental shake. In the cool light of morning she decided that she had imagined it all.

By the time the wall clock showed five minutes to seven, Lark had a mound of fried bacon on the table and a dozen and half scrambled eggs keeping warm at the back of the stove. She had just taken two pans of biscuits from the oven when Cletus walked into the kitchen. He sat down at the table and gruffly ordered her to pour him a cup of coffee. When she placed it before him, he said in the same rough tone, "I took a good look at the rooms in the house. They're filthy. The furniture is so coated with dust, I could write my name on it. Everything needs to be scrubbed and waxed. You've been getting lazy on me, and I'll not have it. By the time I get back here this afternoon, the place had better be shining."

Lark knew that everything in the house was spotless. Cletus was just being spiteful. Since she no longer did any outside work, he wanted her to work harder in the house.

But overshadowing her annoyance at Cletus's pettiness was the excitement of learning he would be away from the ranch today—long enough for Ace to bring the mattress down from the attic. That was, if the men weren't around.

When the cowhands started coming in, Lark was careful not to look at Ace. She wouldn't be able to keep her excitement from showing in her eyes.

It was toward the end of the meal when Gibb announced that he would be going into town. "I want every last man of you to be out on the range today. I want the fences inspected for breaks and snow drifts."

He looked at his foreman. "Jake, send a couple men out to scatter hay for the animals. If you see any cattle in bad shape, drive them in close to the ranch, where they can be looked after.

"That's it," he said, standing up. "Finish your coffee and get going."

When the door slammed behind Gibb, the men, amid much grumbling, gulped down their coffee and followed him. As Ace went through the door he looked at Lark and gave her a wink.

She understood what it meant. The mattress would be brought to the cookhouse today.

Chapter Sixteen

Lark stood at the kitchen window. She watched the barn to make sure her husband left the ranch. He did shortly, his rotund body bobbing up and down on the mountain-bred horse. The animal's hooves sent plumes of snow flying as Gibb brought his riding crop down on its flanks, putting it to a gallop.

He is so cruel, Lark thought angrily. *Why does he make that poor animal gallop in snow so deep?* With a shake of her head she moved her gaze to see if the men would ride out as Gibb had ordered.

The cowhands were taking their time, but eventually they led their horses out of the barn. They mounted and rode off on little quarter horses, but they carried no whips, and their mounts were kept at a walk. The last to leave was Newt, driving a wagon heaped high with hay.

Lark's brows knitted when she saw Ace ride away

with the men. Had she misread his wink? "Drat," she muttered, and began clearing the breakfast dishes off the table. She couldn't believe that Ace wasn't taking advantage of this perfect time to carry out their plan.

She was sliding a stack of dirty plates into a basin of hot, sudsy water when the kitchen door opened. She turned her head and saw Ace smiling at her.

"I bet you thought I wouldn't be bringing the new bedding to the back room today." His eyes twinkled teasingly.

"Well"—Lark dried her hands on her apron—"I wasn't sure when I saw you ride off with the others. How did you get away from Thad?"

"I told him my horse was about to throw a shoe and that I had to return to the barn. I told him that I'd catch up with him later."

"I guess we'd better get started then. If you don't join him when he thinks you should, he'll come looking for you." Lark laughed lightly.

"That's no lie," Ace agreed as he followed Lark out the door.

The mattress wasn't heavy, but it was unwieldy. Lark helped Ace carry it across the attic floor and down the stairs. Ace wanted to drag it by himself but Lark disagreed. The dust on the floor was thick, and the mattress would get filthy. After all, they would be lying on it every evening. There would be no sheet on the mattress, only a blanket to cover up with. Ace would be rolling it up and shoving it under the cot before he left her each night.

Lark had looked directly at Ace only a couple of times since his arrival. She was afraid that if he looked closely into her eyes he would read her thoughts, that she was looking forward to what their next meeting might bring.

She didn't look at him after the new bedding was carried inside and shoved under the cot. Instead she asked, "Would you like a cup of coffee before you leave?"

Ace had noticed that Lark had avoided eye contact with him, and he smiled to himself at her shyness. It was probably on her mind, as it was on his, that tonight they would take their relationship one step farther.

He knew it wasn't the wise thing to do, but he doubted that he could stop himself from making love to her. He had never slept with a married woman before, but Lark was not a married woman in the real sense. There was no love in her marriage. She was treated like slave. Who would they hurt if they found some pleasure in each other?

Ace looked at Lark, who was waiting for his answer. "I'd better not take the time," he said, pulling the mackinaw's collar up around his ears. His white teeth flashed in a crooked smile. "I'll more than likely meet Thad riding in to see what's keeping me."

"I wouldn't be surprised." Lark smiled too. She followed Ace to the door and closed it behind him when he stepped outside.

When she went back to the basin of dishwater she found that it had grown cold. As she added hot water from the big kettle steaming on the stove, she found herself humming a tune from a song her father used to sing. She hadn't felt like doing that in a long time. There hadn't been anything to sing about.

So what was different now? she asked herself as

she rinsed a plate. She was still married to Cletus, was still his slave.

She refused to believe that Ace Brandon had anything to do with her rise in spirits. It couldn't be because she would be spending a couple of hours with him after supper and . . .

Nevertheless Lark's happy mood persisted as she finished doing the dishes, then set a batch of sourdough to rise. If Ace popped into her mind occasionally, she firmly pushed him away. To dwell on him meant only heartache in the end. He would be leaving once the weather broke, when they lied to Cletus that she was expecting.

Later, when Lark went to the house to do the unnecessary cleaning that Gibb had ordered, her mind continued to dwell on Ace. Would he really give her enough money to get away from Cletus? If he broke his word, life wouldn't be worth living when her husband discovered they had lied to him. He might even beat her to death in his rage. What would become of her aunt and uncle then?

"I've got to believe in Ace," she thought out loud when the sun was ready to set and it was time to start supper.

The men looked tired and half frozen when they straggled into the cookhouse. Lark had figured they would appreciate a bowl of hot soup to start the meal, and thankful sighs sounded as she ladled chicken-and-noodle soup into their bowls.

The two roasted chickens she had cut up were eaten in record time, along with side dishes of vegetables. Wide smiles greeted the appearance of her apple pie to go along with the coffee.

Lark knew the men wanted to express their thanks but didn't dare with Cletus wearing his usual glowering look. A couple of the hands, however, dared to give her a quick smile as they filed out of the cookhouse.

When Gibb remained at the table, Lark's nerves tightened. What was he up to now? she asked herself as she started clearing the table, staying clear of his reach.

"I expect you can't wait to get in bed with Brandon tonight," Gibb said with a sneer as she walked to the sink with a stack of dishes. "You're gonna miss lying with him once he's got you bigged, ain't you?"

When Lark made no response, Gibb, irritated, said in a harsh, threatening voice, "If I see you making up to some of the other cowhands to replace him when he's gone, I'll make you sorry you were ever born."

Lark made no reply to this remark either. If she said one word he might jump on her.

A glass almost slipped out of her hand when Gibb said, "I think it's best if Brandon don't mount you tonight. I don't want you getting too used to it."

When she heard his chair scrape against the floor, and the door slam, Lark wanted to cry her disappointment. She had so looked forward to lying beside Ace, talking to him, smelling the clean outdoor scent of him.

She had just finished the dishes and was about to go to the house to spend the lonely evening in her room when the door opened and Ace walked in. "Ace," she exclaimed, alarm in her voice, "you're not supposed to be here tonight."

176

"Who said?" Ace asked as he removed his coat and hat and hung them up.

"Cletus said, not half an hour ago."

"That's strange. I just saw him outside and he growled that I was late."

Lark shook her head in confusion as she took a broom from behind the stove. "There's no figuring that man out. I think he says and does things just to keep me in a muddle."

As she started sweeping the floor she said, "Why don't you pull the mattress out while I finish up in here. I'll just be a minute."

"I was just thinking to do that," Ace said, but he continued to stand there watching Lark swing the broom. The way her hips moved with the sweep of the broom had his pulse racing and his blood hot. When Lark gave him a questioning look, he walked into the back room.

Hunkering down beside the cot, he tugged at the mattress until it lay flat in the middle of the floor. "Get control of yourself," he ordered under his breath as he took the pillow and blanket from the bed and arranged them on the new bedding.

When Ace had taken off his boots and stretched out on his back, he thought of how his eyes had stripped away Lark's clothing as he watched her, how he had envisioned her lying naked beneath him, her long legs wrapped around his waist.

When Lark crawled under the blanket a moment later he was hurting bad. It was all he could do to keep from reaching for her when she stretched out beside him.

"I guess I'd better sneak a pillow from the house,"

Lark remarked as her head settled next to his. "This one is pretty short."

"We'll get used to it." Ace nestled his head against hers. He wanted the closeness the single pillow provided.

"So what part of Cletus's orders did you carry out today?" Lark asked, making herself comfortable on the new bed.

The full weight of her side pressing against Ace, the slight pressure of a soft, firm breast nudging his arm, made Ace repress a groan. His voice was thick when he answered, "Thad and I went looking for cattle that might be weak, need some care. Cows, unlike horses, are dumb. They don't have enough sense to dig down under the snow and find the dry grass there. They'll just stand in one spot and starve to death."

"And a horse won't?"

"Naw. They paw away at the snow and find enough summer growth to sustain them through the winter. Their ribs might show come spring, but they'll be alive."

After a moment of silence Lark said, "If cattle are so stupid, I'm surprised you want to raise them. Why not have a horse ranch, if those animals are so intelligent?"

Ace was silent for a full minute; then he laughed softly. "Lark," he said, "you've just given me an idea. Until Gibb offered me all that money, I'd never given much thought to my future. When he pointed out that I'd be able to start my own small spread, I just naturally thought of cattle. But you've made me think differently now. There's some handsome horseflesh out there on the range running wild. All a man has to do is catch them, tame them and sell them."

In his excitement Ace raised himself up and smiled down at Lark. "I can't wait to get started."

Seeing her hair fanned out on the pillow, her soft lips smiling up at him, he leaned down. He was a hairbreadth from kissing her when a bumbling noise outside the window alerted them that Gibb was there.

The sound brought Ace back to his senses. Kissing Lark wasn't in the bargain either.

But try to tell his throbbing body that, he thought wryly. For sure Lark was going to feel his stiffness tonight. He was hard as a rock. What was she going to think?

She going to think I'm a rutting bull, he told himself.

His voice was thick when he whispered, "I guess it's time we start giving him what he's waiting to hear."

Lark muffled a giggle. "Why don't we wait awhile, let him get real cold."

"I'd like that fine," Ace agreed as he positioned his long body on Lark's softness. "But it would be just like him to come bursting in here, demanding why I'm not doing what I'm supposed to."

"He's brash enough to do that." Lark's voice was a little weak as she felt Ace settle on her. Although she hadn't realized it yet, the weight of his body was intensely pleasurable to her.

She noticed immediately the long hardness pressing against her stomach as Ace began to move on her. She wasn't so naive not to know what it meant. After all, she had seen bulls mount cows. Ace was aroused. She couldn't believe that she could do that to worldly Ace Brandon.

As Ace continued to thrust against her, Lark felt a stirring in her breasts that reached all the way down to the core of her. She wanted to fling off her clothes, to tear Ace's off. She wanted to feel his hardness inside her, thrusting and thrusting.

When she unconsciously arched her back beneath him, Ace grew still a moment. Then, breathing fast, he slid his hands under her small bottom and raised it off the mattress. He spread his legs so that he could pull her up between his thighs, his erection throbbing against her soft mound as he increased his thrusts.

A moment later he was whispering her name as he bucked furiously against her eager body.

The deep, throaty groan that escaped him when he let his weight fall on Lark was not for Gibb, lurking outside, but the real thing.

When his breathing settled down, Ace lifted himself off Lark. Gazing down at her, he said softly, "I'm sorry, honey. What must you be thinking about me?"

"I think you're wonderful." Lark lifted a hand and smoothed the hair from his brow.

"You're not angry?" he asked, surprised.

Lark shook her head. "No, I'm not. I'm glad if I brought you some pleasure."

Ace stroked her cheek, then her hair. "Tomorrow night we're going to talk more about this, all right?"

"I think we should." Lark smiled up at him.

Chapter Seventeen

Lark was hardly aware of what she was doing. She did everything by rote as she made up the two beds, swept the floors and dusted the furniture.

Her mind was on Ace and the talk they would have tonight. She had a good idea what the main topic would be, but she hoped they would also discuss her future—a life that Cletus Gibb would have no part in.

She wondered what it would be like, being made love to by Ace. She had no doubt that it would be wonderful. He had known many women and had probably slept with a lot of them. He was very experienced, she suspected, and would be disappointed with one who knew nothing about the art of making love. One night with her would probably be all he'd want.

Lark remembered the one glance Ace had shot her

this morning as he followed the men out of the cookhouse. His eyes had a knowing sparkle in them that had sent a hot, tingling rush through her body. She couldn't wait for night to come.

The day seemed endless to Lark, but at last it was time to start the evening meal. At seven o'clock sharp she had the meal on the table. She had just put a small tub of butter out when she heard the men stamping the snow off their boots on the little porch. With the exception of Cletus, all the men were careful to track as little dirt on her floor as possible. Cletus brought in as much snow and mud as he could, and expected it to be gone the next morning.

As the men took their places at the table, Lark pretended to be busy at the stove. She didn't dare face them tonight. She knew there was no way she could keep her gaze from wandering to Ace. Cletus must not suspect the tender feelings that were growing between her and his hired hand. She wouldn't put it past him to cut down their time together to ten or fifteen minutes.

Her fingers clenched into tight, angry fists. As far as her husband was concerned, she and Ace were like animals. In his mind he was putting one of his bulls to a cow that was in heat. Cletus Gibb was a man without any sense of morality.

After Lark poured the coffee, which Gibb had barked at her to do, she went and stood in front of the window, staring outside. A full moon shining on the white landscape gave a light almost as bright as day. All the outbuildings stood out in clear relief, as did a pair of owls roosting in a pine tree next to the toolshed.

She wondered how her aunt and uncle were making out as she wiped away the film her breath had made on the panes. She had overheard Newt telling one of the men that he was going to try getting some provisions to them tomorrow.

Maybe I can slip away and go with him, she thought. *I miss them so much.*

The scraping of chair legs alerted Lark that the men were leaving. As they walked past her she heard Gibb say, "I'd like a word with you, Ace."

What is he up to now? Lark wondered uneasily. A sudden thought made her grip the windowsill. What if he was going to tell Ace that he had changed his mind, that their deal was off?

Her heart seemed to stop beating. How could she bear going back to the time when Cletus slapped her around anytime the notion struck him? When she would have to resume mucking out the stables and no doubt do all the snow shoveling? And she couldn't bear to think of losing those hours with Ace.

She pulled the heavy drapes together, except for an inch of space, and fastened her gaze there. She had no problem seeing Ace and Cletus standing midway between the bunkhouse and the cookhouse. It appeared that Cletus was doing most of the talking, with Ace nodding his head occasionally. When they started walking away, she turned from the window.

Her mind in a turmoil, she cleared the table and started washing the dishes. When she realized she had washed the same plate three times, she gave herself a mental shake.

She had to get a grip on herself. She would know soon enough what the devil had thought up in that devious mind of his.

Lark put her thoughts on what she was doing and soon had the kitchen put to order. She looked at the clock. Five minutes to eight. She sat down at the table and waited.

Eight o'clock came, then nine, then nine-thirty, and still no sign of Ace. She wanted to put her head down on the table and cry. She knew that her worst fears had come to pass.

It's a shame how that bastard is ruining a fine piece of horseflesh, Ace thought grimly, his eyes narrowed on the laboring stallion that Gibb was forcing to gallop through snow that was over a foot deep in places. This cold night ride was hard enough on the little quarter horse he was keeping at a walk. It could withstand the cold. It had been bred to it. But not the stallion. It was not meant to be abused.

A wry smile twisted Ace's lips. Gibb hadn't realized yet that his cowhand was a good fifty yards behind him. Not very good protection if someone wanted to take a potshot at his head. But no man in his right mind would be out in such a night unless he had to be.

Protecting the fat man's back was the reason he was freezing his rump tonight. By rights he should be in the warm cookhouse, snuggled up to Lark, making love to her for the first time.

When Gibb had said he wanted a word with him, the last thing Ace had expected to hear was that the man wanted him to ride at his back, to be on the lookout for anyone who might want to shoot him.

Ace pulled his bandanna up over his mouth and nose. He was so cold he doubted that he would go

184

after anyone if they did put a bullet in Cletus Gibb. The man wasn't fit to live anyway.

What kind of business did Gibb have in Dogwood that couldn't wait until tomorrow morning? he asked himself. The only places open would be the Longhorn Saloon and Meg's whorehouse. He knew they wouldn't be visiting Meg's girls. There wasn't a woman alive that could do the fat man any good. As for the saloon, Gibb wasn't much of a drinker, and he wasn't the sort to seek out the companionship of men.

Ace dismissed from his mind the reason for the strange night ride and fell to thinking of Lark. She was probably wondering why he hadn't shown up at the cookhouse. He'd had no way to get word to her that he wouldn't be seeing her tonight. He and Gibb had walked straight to the barn, saddled up and struck off toward town.

Ever since last night he had given a lot of thought to what was growing between him and Lark. He wanted her badly, and the way she had responded to him, agreed that they must talk, told him that she had the same feelings.

But were their feelings really the same? Lark was vulnerable now, hungry for affection and kindness. What if she fell in love with him? He didn't want that to happen, but could he tell her straight out that the only thing he would share with her was his body? Could he tell her that she had no future with him?

Ace was thinking that would sound too cold-blooded when two dim lights shone in the distance. At last they were about to reach Dogwood and some heat.

When they rode onto the single street, where the

snow had been trampled down and frozen solid, Gibb turned the stallion's head toward the livery. "Maybe"—he looked at Ace—"you'd like to stop in the saloon and have a drink while I conduct business."

What kind of business? Ace wondered, looking down the street where no light shone from any window. He shrugged and swung out of the saddle. "That's a good idea," he said. "I'll just bring the horse into the livery."

"Do you think that's necessary?" Gibb asked, turning his head and looking down the row of stables. "It won't hurt him to stand outside the saloon for a while."

"It won't help him either," Ace said sharply, and led the sturdy little animal into the warmth of the livery.

As he looped the reins over a post, he heard the lowing of cattle in the farthest stalls. *That's strange,* he thought. *I've never known cattle to be housed in a livery before.*

When he saw Gibb riding toward the complaining animals, he began to suspect what the night ride was about. Gibb was going to take possession of these cattle.

But why in the dead of winter, when he already had at least a thousand head scattered over the range?

Ace stood in the shadows, out of sight, until he saw Gibb dismount near the last two stalls of the row. Then, still keeping in the shadows, he moved quietly after the rancher, stopping when he heard the sound of voices.

He quickly stepped behind a three-foot stack of

baled hay and listened to the conversation between Gibb and a rough-speaking man.

"They look pretty worn out," Gibb was complaining.

"You'd look worn out too if you'd just finished walking a hundred miles, and part of it through a blizzard," the man answered gruffly. "A few days rest and some feed, they'll look fine. Durhams are strong, sturdy animals."

So that's it. Ace swore softly. *Gibb wants to breed them with his longhorns to produce more meat.* But why was he buying them at night? Why hadn't the animals been delivered to the ranch?

Ace knew suddenly that the cattle had been stolen. The man his boss was dealing with was a lousy cattle rustler. That explained why the new cattle would be driven to the ranch under the cover of darkness.

Damn, Ace thought, I hope that rustler isn't being followed by a posse. Durhams were very expensive, and he felt sure that the rightful owner would want them back. It would be just his luck to get caught herding them back to the ranch. He knew now the real reason he had been asked to accompany Gibb to town.

When he heard Gibb ask, "How much do I owe you? I want to get the hell out of here," Ace slipped out of the livery and hotfooted it to the saloon.

He drank one glass of whiskey and was about to order another one when Gibb tapped impatiently on the saloon window—a signal that he was ready to leave. Ace put some silver on the bar and said good night to the bartender and the two men who had also braved the weather.

"I've just bought myself four Durham bulls," Gibb

gloated, leading the way to the livery. "They're tired now and we won't have any trouble herding them to the ranch."

"How did you get hold of Durhams?" Ace played dumb. "I didn't think that breed was in these parts."

"They're not. I'll be the first to have them," Gibb bragged. "I bought them from a rancher in Wyoming."

"Yeah, like hell you did," Ace muttered under his breath, "and I've got half a mind to turn you in."

They had to move at a slow pace to guide the new short-legged Durhams through the snow. The bulls were already about dead on their feet. Ace had grave doubts that the Durhams could survive the winters here.

It was close to midnight when the ranch was reached and the bulls were stabled. Ace led his horse into a stall and unsaddled him. After he had pitched some hay into the wooden trough, he spread a blanket over him and without a word left the barn before Gibb could tell him to feed the four tired bulls.

Before he entered the bunkhouse Ace looked longingly at the long, low building a few yards away. He hoped, but doubted that maybe a light still shone in the window, that maybe Lark still waited for him.

Only darkness greeted him. He sighed and pushed open the bunkhouse door.

Chapter Eighteen

The next morning when Ace walked into the barn, the other men were gathered around the stabled bulls. His gaze lit on Gibb, strutting around like a fat bantam rooster as the hands talked excitedly about the new breed. Ace glanced at the bulls and saw that they looked much better after a night's rest out of the elements. Someone had forked a plentiful supply of hay for them, and they were placidly munching away.

Gibb, full of himself, was answering the men's questions: Where did the animals come from? How did he come to hear about their being for sale?

Talk on, you stupid bastard, Ace thought with a sardonic twist of his lips. *Spill your guts. The more you run off at the mouth, the faster the owner will know where to look for them.*

Ace turned and left the barn before he was spotted

by the men. He didn't want to be drawn into the conversation about the Durhams, and he couldn't stand any more of Gibb's lies.

Besides, he wanted a private word with Lark before the others came tramping into the cookhouse.

Lark saw Ace coming, his tall, lean body moving gracefully as he walked up the path cut in the snow. Her heart gave a jump and her pulse raced. He was so handsome; every time she happened to see him unexpectedly her bones felt as if they had dissolved into water.

When he walked into the kitchen, a wide smile on his face and smelling of the outdoors, she could only stand and stare at him, unaware that her eyes were devouring him.

"No 'Good morning, Ace'?" he teased. "Are you angry with me because I didn't show up last night?"

"Of course not," Lark managed after swallowing a couple of times. "I figured you had a reason for staying away."

Ace hung up his jacket and hat. Sitting down at the table, he said, "You were right. Gibb wanted me to ride into town with him."

"On such a cold night? What business did he have in Dogwood that couldn't wait until today?"

"Bad business is what, Lark," Ace answered, and proceeded to tell her about the secret ride at night.

When he had finished, the expression on Lark's face was one of incredulousness. "Doesn't Cletus realize that he's just as guilty as the man who rustled those expensive bulls? Doesn't he think that sooner or later the sheriff will track them here?"

"I would say that come spring the law will arrive at the Gibb ranch."

"Will you be involved, Ace?" Alarm grew in Lark's eyes. "You know, helping to drive the animals here?"

"Naw." Ace shook his head. "I'm only a hired hand who did what he was ordered to do," Ace said for Lark's benefit. The truth was, he intended to be gone from the area for good once spring arrived.

"I guess you're right," Lark answered, but doubt lingered in her voice.

"Are you looking forward to tonight?" Ace asked, dropping the subject of Gibb and the bulls.

A shy smile lifted the corners of Lark's lips. "Are you?"

"You know that I am." Ace gave her a crooked grin that said he couldn't wait.

A fluttering grew in the pit of Lark's stomach as she looked into his eyes and read the message in them, his intent. When she heard the men coming toward the cookhouse then, panic pushed everything else out of her mind. Breakfast was ready, but it wasn't on the table.

Ace saw the fear and dread in her eyes, and, swearing softly at her distress, he stood up and swiftly helped her get everything on the table. Seconds later Gibb tromped into the kitchen, the men following him.

Gibb was in a rare good mood. He was still basking in the men's praise of his new bulls. Lark wondered if now would be a good time to ask permission to visit her aunt and uncle. He wasn't often this mellow.

She was a nervous wreck by the time the men finished eating and drinking their coffee. As they prepared to leave, she sent Ace an imploring look and was relieved when he remained seated.

When Gibb stood up, ready to follow his men, Lark

gathered her courage and said in a voice so low it was almost inaudible, "I would like to go with Newt when he takes the supplies to my aunt and uncle." When Gibb made no response, only stared at her, she rushed on, "It may be the last time I'll be able to see them for a while. Another blizzard might make it impossible to get to them."

Lark looked at her husband hopefully. When she saw the malignant expression that came over his fat face, the hatred in his small eyes, she knew he was going to refuse her request.

The clatter of a spoon hitting the floor drew Lark's and Gibb's attention. When Gibb encountered the threatening look in Ace's eyes, he froze. The smirk of pleasure he felt at telling his wife she was to stay home where she belonged was wiped from his face.

He dragged his gaze away from Ace and said gruffly, "I hope you freeze your rump off on the way there."

Lark was too stunned to thank her husband. Besides, she was pretty sure that he had agreed only because he was afraid of Ace. She didn't dare look at Ace, though, to let her eyes thank him.

She would do that tonight.

She had just finished sweeping the floor and was propping the broom in a corner when she glanced out the window and saw Newt riding up. This time instead of one packhorse, he was leading two.

"Why two animals, Newt?" she asked when the genial man walked inside with two rolled-up gunnysacks under his arm.

"I figured I'd better bring extra provisions to the old folks this time. You never know what the weather will bring in the next few days. If we get a lot more

LARK

snow dumped on us, I might not be able to get up the mountain for some time."

"I've been thinking that too," Lark said, leading the way to the larder room. "That's why I'm riding up with you today. It may be my last chance to see my aunt and uncle for a while."

By the time the two large bags were filled, the ranch supplies had dwindled considerably. Newt would have to drive the wagon into Dogwood tomorrow to replenish their stores. Lark hoped it could be done without Cletus's knowledge. He begrudged every mouthful her relatives ate.

"It's cold out there, Lark," Newt said when they were ready to leave. "You'd better bundle up good."

Lark walked to the row of pegs to take down her scarf and thin jacket. How, she wondered bitterly, was she to bundle up when she had only a raggedy jacket and a moth-eaten scarf?

"I have an idea, Lark," Newt said gruffly. "Why don't you take my sheepskin instead of taking the time to go back to the house for another jacket. I've got another one in the bunkhouse. I'll pick it up on my way to the barn to saddle your mare."

Lark started to object, but Newt had already shed his jacket and was holding it for her to slide her arms into the sleeves. "It's a little big on you"—he laughed at the sleeves that came well past her hands—"but it will keep you warm."

"Thank you, Newt," Lark said softly.

The day was still and cold when they rode away from the ranch. Lark was thankful for the sheepskin, which smelled of man and tobacco. She shivered, thinking how cold she would be right now if it weren't for Newt's thoughtfulness.

Riding side by side, Lark and Newt broke a trail through the snow, the two heavily loaded packhorses bringing up the rear. Clouds of white vapor floated from the nostrils of both humans and beasts.

They were halfway to the foothills when a few hundred yards away Lark and Newt spotted two figures moving easily over the ice-crusted snow. When they grew nearer to the pair, Lark gave a startled grunt. She recognized one figure. Her Uncle Ben. She watched in amazement at how swiftly he moved in the cumbersome-looking snowshoes.

Her gaze moved to the man walking beside him. She looked at Newt and asked in surprise, "An Indian?"

"He's an Indian all right," Newt answered, taking in the man's buckskin trousers and heavy moccasins that reached to the knees. A colorful blanket was wrapped around the man's bony shoulders, and a dilapidated felt hat rested on top of long white hair that hung down the man's back. "Looks like your uncle has made himself a friend."

When Ben and the Indian came up to them, Lark and Newt reined in their horses. "Uncle Ben, what are you doing out so early on such a raw day?" Lark asked in concern. "You are going to catch your death."

"Naw." Ben shook his head. "I'm feeling fine. Me and my friend have been tracking a deer. His village is low on meat." He looked at the old Indian. "Ragged Feather, meet my niece, Lark," he said proudly, "and her friend, Newt."

Ragged Feather nodded solemnly at Lark. She stirred, a little nervous as his sharp black eyes studied her. She asked herself if he could read her mind, that she wasn't sure she trusted her uncle's friend.

She sighed a silent breath of relief when Ben said, "We've got to get going. Your aunt will be happy to see you, Larkie."

"You won't be gone too long, will you, Uncle Ben?" Lark called after him. "I'd like to visit with you too."

"I'll be along shortly. Have the coffeepot hot."

As the two old men went sliding along, Lark said with a frown, "I'm not sure I like the fact that my uncle's new friend is an Indian. Do you think Ragged Feather can be trusted?"

"Sure he can. Indians aren't all alike. They're just like white men. Some are good; some are bad. I'd say Ragged Feather is one of the good ones."

Newt lifted the reins and they moved on.

After about half an hour of traveling over the snow, Ben called a halt in a grove of pines. "I don't know about you, friend, but I need to catch my breath and rest my bones a minute."

The Indian sat down on a snow-covered log. "It's been many moons since my bones felt like they did in my youth. When I was a young brave I could run all day, sometimes covering ten miles or so. Today I do well to *walk* two miles."

"I guess if we don't come on a deer pretty soon we might as well go home," Ben said.

"Yes. My old flesh would welcome the heat from my son's fire pit."

A companionable silence grew between the two old men and lasted a couple of minutes before Ragged Feather broke it.

"I had a vision last night," he said. Ben nodded encouragingly for him to go on. "I saw a lone man standing on a knoll. He was watching with much interest a large building where many men were gathered. Four men sat on horses and the others stood on the ground. One man on the ground was shouting and waving his hands at a tall man on horseback. This man talked loudly also. Then the man standing pulled a gun from his pocket and aimed it. The horseman did the same. There was flame, powder smoke and gunshot. The man on the ground went down. He was shot between the eyes."

Ragged Feather paused for a thoughtful moment, then said, "It was the man on the knoll who shot him. Nobody knew this and the man rode away."

When Ragged Feather paused again, and it appeared that he wasn't going to say more on the subject, Ben asked, "What do you make of your vision?"

"Someday, maybe not this cold season, my vision will be acted out. A man is going to be shot and killed."

"And no one will know who did it?"

"Not for some time. Maybe when the willows put on new leaves."

There was another short silence; then Ben said, "I expect it's time we got home."

Chapter Nineteen

That night Lark tugged the mattress from under the cot. She wanted to be lying on it when Ace came. She wanted to avoid the lamplight of the kitchen, where he would be able to see how nervous and unsure she was of herself.

As she lay waiting she was filled with a mixture of anxiety and anticipation. She knew nothing about what went on between a man and woman caught up in desire for each other. What if she was a big disappointment to him? Again she asked herself if tonight would be her first and last chance to have Ace make love to her.

She had dreamed all day about tonight. She had managed to bathe and wash her hair with the rose-scented soap. She had kept the shiny softness of her hair hidden under a scarf so that Cletus wouldn't notice that she had spent time on her looks. He must not know of the feelings that were growing between her and Ace. That wasn't part of the deal he had made with his ranch hand.

Lark left off thinking of Cletus's anger and what he might do when she heard the cookhouse door open. Ace had arrived.

She had no idea how beautiful she looked to Ace when he entered the small room and gazed down at her. The soft glow of the lamplight reaching from the kitchen shone on her hair, making a halo around her beautiful face. He had never seen a woman, not even his cousin Roxy, who was lovelier. Nor had he ever wanted a woman as much as he did this one.

But when she lifted her gray gaze to him, Ace saw the confusion, the uncertainty, in their depths, and he felt compassion for her. Did she think he was going to be rough with her, the way Gibb probably was in bed?

He would have to go slow with her, he thought, sitting down on the edge of the mattress. When she didn't shrink away from him, he lifted his hand and gently stroked it over the softness of her hair, then lifted a curl and brushed his lips across it.

"You smell like my mother's rose garden," he said softly. "And you look like a rose. Your cheeks are like pink blossoms and your lips are like red petals."

He trailed a finger around her lips, then slowly lowered his head and settled his lips on hers.

He meant the kiss to be a light one, to calm any fears she might have. But when he was met with eager passion, his lips took fire and his mouth moved over hers with matching heat.

When Lark's arms came up to wind around his shoulders, Ace lifted her to lie across his lap. He slipped his tongue into her mouth, and when she readily accepted it, he began undoing the buttons on her bodice. When she made no effort to stop him, he slid his hand inside her camisole and freed a firm breast that fit perfectly in his palm. He left her lips then and settled his mouth over the puckered nipple.

"Ah, Ace," Lark cried when he began to nibble and suckle her.

The desire in her voice drove him on, and in seconds he had uncovered the other breast and was giving it the same attention he had given the first one.

Lark could only moan her pleasure as desire shot from her breasts to the very core of her.

And Ace, his face hot, his breath coming fast, knew that if he didn't have her soon, he would surely burst.

He lifted his head and murmured in a choked voice, "I want you, Lark. Right now."

"Oh, yes," she agreed breathlessly.

"Let's get out of our clothes then."

Boots hit the floor; male and female clothing was flung about. In only seconds Lark lay waiting for the moment she had been dreaming about all day.

Ace took the time to run his gaze over her shapely curves, then crawled between her satiny smooth legs. He hung over her a moment; then, settling himself between her thighs, he slid his hands beneath her small rear. Taking his hard, throbbing member in his hand, he slid inside her waiting heat. With a shove of his hips he drove himself deep inside her.

Lark's small cry of pain so shocked him, all his desire drained away. "I'm sorry, Lark," he said softly, stroking her cheek. "I had no idea that you were still a virgin. I somehow got the idea that Gibb was only infertile."

Lark stroked the space between his concerned eyes. "He may be, but he's not able to get aroused either. He tried to consummate our marriage on our wedding night, but he couldn't.

"For which I was very thankful," Lark added. "If I had to bear his fat, smelly body on mine regularly, I would go out of my mind. I gladly take his abuse as long as I don't have to sleep with him."

Ace was thankful too. The thought of that obese man on Lark's lovely body was unbearable.

He toyed with a thick tress of Lark's hair. "Do you hurt a lot?" The question came huskily.

"No." Lark reached up and pulled him back to her. "I would like to continue . . . that is, if you want to."

Ace chuckled softly. "I'd like that better than anything else in the world," he murmured, and lifted her hips into the well of his own again.

He wanted to thrust hard and fast, but he made himself go slowly and carefully, keeping in mind that Lark must be sore inside.

He soon wondered about that, though, considering the way she was eagerly lifting her hips to receive him. He wanted to make it good for her, and held himself back.

Lark had different ideas. She wanted a deeper, faster thrust of his hips. She relayed the message to him by reaching down and grasping his hips, urging him to a faster pace.

With a throaty groan he began moving against her, driving his hardness as fast and as deep as he could inside her. When he felt the walls of her femininity tighten around him, he knew she was reaching her peak and would shatter.

When she cried out his name and arched her back

he grew tense, gave one last, deep thrust and let his shuddering body go limp on top of her.

As his head lay on her shoulder Lark stroked his damp back until his breathing returned to normal.

When he lifted himself from her, Lark asked shyly, "Did I please you? Did I do everything right?"

"Lark"—Ace laughed softly—"if you'd done anything more right I don't know if I could recover from it. I've had a few women . . . a lot of them actually, but I've never before made love to a virgin." He dropped a kiss on her forehead. "It was a wonderful experience."

"I'm glad." Lark snuggled up to him. "I was afraid I would disappoint you."

"Well, you didn't. But what about you? Did you find pleasure in your introduction to making love?"

"It was wonderful, Ace. I never dreamed that making love could be so beautiful."

Ace thought about her statement a moment and decided that their mating had been beautiful. He sighed and sat up. "I wish we could do it again, but you can be sure that Gibb is sitting out there waiting for me to leave."

"I guess so," Lark agreed, disappointment in her voice.

When Ace had climbed into his clothes and helped Lark to dress, he shoved the mattress back under the cot. He pulled Lark into his arms then, and after giving her a deep, lingering kiss, he walked out into the night.

Lark blew out the lamp and followed him. She hurried up the snow-packed path. She was sore, but had never felt so happy and complete in her life. For the first time since her marriage she felt that freedom from Cletus would somehow happen.

Later, curled up in bed, she relieved every moment of her time with Ace that night. When she fell asleep she dreamed of what tomorrow night would bring.

The sky was dark and threatening when Lark awakened the next morning. She felt sure another blizzard would visit them before the day was over.

Would her aunt and uncle be all right? she worried as she got dressed. She was thankful that she had visited them yesterday. If the new snow was as deep as the last one, it would be a while before Newt and his packhorse could get up the mountain again.

Lark consoled herself with the knowledge that their larder was well stocked. There was enough food to last a month, if need be. And thanks to Ace and Thad, there was enough wood chopped to last them through the winter. They should be fine, providing her uncle stayed off those fool snowshoes and didn't break a leg.

The only sound in the cold air was the crunch of snow under Lark's feet as she walked to the cookhouse. When she pushed the door open she was greeted with cheery warmth and the aroma of fresh-brewed coffee.

"It's cold out there, isn't it, Lark?" Thad grinned at her as he filled two cups with coffee.

"It certainly is, and I can't thank you enough for building a fire for me and having coffee ready," Lark answered, hanging up her jacket and scarf.

"It was Ace's idea for me to start doing that." Thad set the coffee on the table and sat down. "I would have done it on my own if I'd thought about it," he added.

"You make a good brew, Thad." Lark complimented the teenager after she had taken a long, bracing swallow of it.

"Thank you. My mom showed me how. She thinks a man ought to learn how to do things for himself. I'm a fair cook," he boasted with a grin. "Take Ace, now, he can't cook a lick. His mom never taught him how to work around a stove. From what I gather, he's never had to cook for himself. There's always been women around to do for him."

Thad sighed. "I guess that's the way it is when a man is as handsome as Ace is. Women just naturally want to do things for him."

"I guess so," Lark agreed weakly, her heart beating painfully in her chest. She was foolish to think that she was special to Ace. He had known so many women—and would know more once he got his money from Cletus and left the ranch forever.

When Thad had left and she was mixing up flapjack batter, Lark told herself that Ace was an honest man and would keep his word about giving her enough money to get away from Cletus. She should be thankful for that.

Her eyes grew wet. She didn't want Ace's money. She wanted him. She wanted his love.

The men had spent the day hauling hay to the cattle. They spread it in the foothills out of the wind and drove the longhorns to it. The idea was that they would stay there in hopes of getting more feed.

Ace looked up at the black clouds rolling in from the north. It was going to snow anytime now. When he and Thad forked the last of the hay from the wagon, he said, "Let's call it a day and get back to the bunkhouse. My rump is almost frozen."

"Mine already is," Thad complained. And picking up the long reins, he snapped them over the backs of the workhorses.

As the wheels rumbled and creaked through the snow, Ace fell to thinking of nightfall and after supper. He couldn't wait to be with Lark again. There were so many things he wanted to teach her about the art of love-making. If only they could spend a whole night together.

He smiled wryly to himself. They would wear each other out. It occurred to him that Lark could become like a drug to him, if he let it happen. He assured himself that would never happen. He had tied himself to one woman once and it hadn't worked out. He would never try it again. There was something about a marriage certificate that didn't sit well with him. He definitely wasn't a one-woman man.

But Lark was a fine young woman, and he intended to see that she got away from her bastard of a husband. With her beauty and sweetness, it wouldn't take her long to find a man who would love and appreciate her.

Ace frowned as the wagon bounced along. Why didn't that thought appeal to him?

Chapter Twenty

The snow fell silently at first, spreading a new white blanket over the land. Then a roaring wind blew out of the north, daring any human to venture into its path.

"We're in for a blue norther," Newt said nervously when a blast of wind threatened to blow the roof off the cookhouse.

"I don't expect Gibb will make it back from town tonight," Thad said.

"He'll be lucky if he gets back in a week," one of the men said. "That hell out there can last for a week. I remember one time back in the sixties when it snowed for . . ."

As the men sat on, drinking coffee, each had a story to tell.

Lark gave only half her attention to the long-winded tales. Her mind was on the two old people up on the mountain. Was the cabin sturdy enough to withstand the blasts of wind that whistled around the cookhouse? Would their roof stay on?

Ace looked across the table at Lark and saw the worry lines that had gathered between her eyes. "Lark," he said quietly, "your aunt and uncle will be fine. The cabin is protected from the wind by the mountain wall at its back. They're not getting what we are here on the plains."

Her nerves soothed somewhat by Ace's logic, Lark relaxed a bit. When she read the message in Ace's twinkling eyes, it came to her what Cletus's absence would mean to them. They could spend the entire night together. Maybe two nights. Maybe more.

Suddenly she wanted the men gone. She wanted to get into the back room with Ace.

But the boss wasn't there, the kitchen was warm, and the coffee was strong and hot. The men stayed on, spinning their tales. By the time they said good night and stepped out into the blizzard, Ace was impatiently consigning them all to hell.

"Come on, Ace," Thad called. He was the last one to leave.

"I'll be along shortly." Ace frowned. "I'm going to help Lark clean up, then see her to the house."

"That's a good idea. I'll stay and help." Thad started to close the door.

"I don't need your help, Thad." Ace spoke sharply. "Now get on to the bunkhouse. I'll see you later."

"But I don't mind—" Thad broke off at Ace's pointed look. "I'll see you later. Don't you understand English?"

The coldness in Ace's tone made the teenager quickly step outside and close the door behind him.

"I think you've hurt his feelings," Lark said as she began clearing the table.

"He'll get over it tomorrow." Ace started stacking dirty dishes. "I'll make it up to him."

He followed Lark to the sink, and when he saw her pumping water into a basin he said coaxingly, "Can't the dishes wait until tomorrow morning? I can think of better things to do."

"So can I." Lark smiled up at him. "But tomorrow morning I have to make breakfast for the men, and I don't want to have to wash dishes before I can start cooking."

"All right." Ace sighed. "Let's get it done." He reached down and gave her shapely rear a light pinch. "I can't wait much longer to get you in my lovin' arms again."

Lark's pulse picked up. She'd never washed dishes so fast in her life.

The wind was still a demon, roaring around the long building when the dishes were done and the table was set for tomorrow's breakfast. It had found its way under the door and around the window frames, piling snow on the sill.

Lark's feet felt like chunks of ice in her thin, worn shoes, and she kept thinking how cold she and Ace would be on the mattress. They would be practically sleeping on the floor with only a thin blanket to cover them.

"It's growing colder by the minute," Ace said, coming into the kitchen with an armload of logs he had taken from the many cords of wood stacked against the building. "I hope the longhorns have enough sense to stay in the foothills, where they'll get some protection."

When he dumped the split aspen logs into the wood box and then sat down to remove his boots, Lark stopped him.

"Don't take them off," she said.

"You want me to sleep with my boots on?" Ace gave her a quizzical look.

"Silly, of course not. But I have an idea. I've been thinking that we should spend the night in the house, where we can keep warm."

"Well, now, why didn't I think of that?" Ace jumped to his feet and grabbed Lark's jacket off its peg. "Come on, woman, let's get going."

As they battled the wind toward the dim shape of the house, Ace had to hang on to Lark to keep her from falling. As they trudged along they could hear nearby trees cracking in the icy grip of the blast.

Finally they were stumbling up the porch steps. When Ace opened the back door he had to hold it against the force of the wind until Lark stepped inside.

The kitchen still held heat from the day, but the fire in the range had about gone out. Ace felt pity for Lark when he helped her out of the thin jacket. He had seen the sheepskin-lined mackinaw her husband wore. He pulled a chair up close to the stove and set her down on it. He knelt down beside her then and began to briskly rub her bluish hands, which had worn no gloves. When the flesh began to turn pink he rose and stocked the big black stove with more wood.

"Feeling warmer now?" he asked when Lark smiled up at him.

"Much better. Come sit by the stove so you can warm up too."

"I know a much better way to get warm," Ace said huskily as he took off his jacket and hung it up beside hers.

"Oh, you do, do you?" Lark's eyes sparkled up at him.

"Yes, I do," Ace answered and scooped her up into his arms.

As she clung to his shoulders he whispered, "Which way to your bedroom?"

Lark laid her head beneath his chin and pointed him in the right direction.

Ace set her on the floor when they reached her room so he could strike a match and light the lamp on the bedside table. He silently turned to Lark then and began to slowly undress her. There was no need for hurry tonight. They had the whole long night ahead of them.

As each piece of clothing slid down Lark's body, Ace let his lips linger on the bare flesh revealed. When her camisole was pulled down to her waist, baring her breasts, he went down to his knees. He gazed at their jutting beauty a moment; then, cupping them in his palms, he lifted one to his mouth. His tongue laved the pink, hard nipple a moment before he drew it into his mouth.

Lark moaned softly when his lips began to tug at her, and she clutched his shoulders to keep from falling, her desire for him was so great.

She grew weaker as he took turns suckling each nipple. Finally, she could bear no more and moaned. "I hurt so, Ace."

He stood up and led her to the bed. He turned the covers back and gently pushed her down. He sat down beside her and kicked off his boots. He stood up then and began undressing.

When the last piece of clothing, his underwear, lay on the floor, he stood bare before her, his eyes inviting her to look at his hard, pulsating manhood.

Lark gazed hungrily at the long shaft that had given her so much pleasure in the back room of the cookhouse. Did she dare adore it the way she wanted to? she asked herself. Would Ace be shocked if she leaned up and kissed him there?

The decision was taken from her. Ace had read the desire in her eyes. He knelt on the edge of the mattress and said huskily, "Do what you want to Lark. If you desire, put your soft lips on me."

Lark hesitated briefly, then made her wish come true.

When her drawing lips became more than he could bear, he slipped away from her and knelt between her legs. He adored her then in the same way she had loved him until she was sobbing for relief. He rose up and, positioning himself between her legs, slid inside her.

The room was filled with the rocking and creaking of the bed. A short time later that noise was mingled with Lark's cries of delight and Ace's deep groans as he bucked against her.

They didn't sleep that night. They only rested occasionally to gather the strength to come together again.

They had two nights of almost uninterrupted lovemaking. In the daylight hours both resumed their usual day's work. Ace told the men that he was sleeping nights in the cookhouse while Gibb was away.

He told them a hungry animal might come nosing around and would scare Lark.

The men pretended to buy his story, but he could tell from the looks some of the men exchanged that they didn't quite believe him.

On the third morning, when Ace and Lark looked out the window they saw that the snow had stopped, and not a breath of air stirred.

"He'll be coming home today," Ace said, standing behind Lark, his arms wrapped around her waist.

"Yes," she answered on a despondent note. "I'm going to miss our time together dreadfully." After a moment she laughed lightly. "It's probably just as well he is coming home. We've worn each other out. I think I've lost ten pounds."

"You haven't lost anything up here." Ace moved his hands to cup her breasts. "They're just as perky as ever." He turned her around until he could capture a nipple between his teeth. His lips drew on it a moment, then, lifting his head, he murmured into her hair, "Do we have time to go back to bed for a while?"

Lark was tempted. But Cletus could be returning any minute, and she must have breakfast started.

"I'm sorry, love"—she stroked his bearded cheek—"but we'll have to wait until we're in the little back room tonight."

"I guess so." Ace sighed and walked over to the bed to retrieve his clothes from the floor.

When he was ready to leave he cracked the kitchen door open and peered toward the bunkhouse. When he saw that all was quiet there, he hurried toward the cookhouse.

When Lark followed him fifteen minutes later, he had built a fire and had a pot of coffee brewing.

Then, in the habit they'd started during Gibb's absence, Ace helped Lark to make breakfast.

They had bacon and eggs on the table at the usual time. On the dot of seven o'clock, the men came tramping in, their faces red from the short walk from the bunkhouse.

They had just started to eat when the door opened and Gibb stormed into the kitchen. The way he slammed the door behind him, and the black scowl on his face, alerted everyone that he was itching to find fault with something, or someone.

Lark didn't need to be told that she would bear the brunt of his anger. Filled with dread, she watched him hang up his jacket and throw his hat on the floor. She hurried to fix a plate for him and slid it in front of him when he sat down.

She had barely returned to the stove when Gibb dashed his breakfast to the floor. The heavy china shattered, sending shards all over the floor.

"Bitch!" he shouted. "You've grown awfully brave in my absence to serve me a cold breakfast. It looks like I'll have to remind you of a few things." He jumped to his feet, his chair going over backward. When he started toward his terrified wife, a cold voice stopped him.

"How are things in Dogwood, Gibb? Is the town pretty well snowed in?"

There was no threat in Ace's words, but there was a definite warning in his tone.

Gibb turned his big, bushy head around to glare at Ace. Then he remembered the hard punishment he had seen his cowhand's fist deliver, and he looked away.

"Pretty bad," he said, and picked up his chair and sat back down. As he began telling how weather-bound the town was, Lark filled him another plate, which was as steaming hot as the one he had dashed to the floor.

She had escaped his wrath for the time being, but the time would come when she would be alone with him.

When Gibb finished talking about Dogwood, he asked with beetled brows, "Did things go as usual here at the ranch while I was gone?"

Though the question was asked in general, it was Ace he looked at.

Ace returned his gaze with cold eyes. "Everyone knew what was expected of him and has done it. Your wife did the same. There will be no need to remind her of whatever it was you threatened her with."

Gibb made no answer. To save face in front of his men, however, he tried again to glare Ace down. Again he failed. He bent his head over his plate and began shoveling the food into his mouth.

Breakfast was a silent, hasty meal. Within twenty minutes only Lark, Gibb and Ace remained in the kitchen.

"Is there something on your mind, Brandon?" Gibb asked sourly.

"Yes," Ace answered quietly. "I want to remind you that I don't like the sight of bruises."

"All right!" Gibb said savagely. "You won't see any."

"Good." Ace nodded. "I'll go help the men get some hay to the cattle."

He didn't look at Lark as he pulled on his jacket and walked outside.

Gibb finished his coffee and stood up. When he put on his jacket and took hold of the doorknob, he said in a growl, "I'd better find the house in tip-top shape."

Chapter Twenty-one

The terrible blizzard that had visited them had filled the ravines and low spots. Eight feet of snow lay on some places in northern Colorado.

Ace looked up at the cold, white sun moving westward. He wished it would move a little faster. He was cold and tired. He and Thad, working as a team, had been fighting snowdrifts since early morning, helping to bring hay to the hungry, bawling cattle. More times than not he and the teenager had walked ahead to clear a path for the workhorses that pulled the wagon.

When they came to a windblown stretch of range where the team could navigate on their own, Ace began to daydream of Lark and what the coming night would bring. Two hours of making love. Not nearly enough time to spend all his passion on her, but better than nothing.

A troublesome question he'd been asking himself lately slipped into his mind. Was this seemingly never-ending desire to possess her something he should give some serious thought to? Was he about to make the same mistake of thinking he was falling in love with a woman?

He must begin to curb this passion he had for Lark. Come spring he wanted to ride away without any regrets, any feelings of guilt. He would have enough on his mind just trying to get his horse ranch together.

Ace forced himself to dwell on his dream. He knew where to look for the horses. In Utah. Not far from where he had been born and grew up, there were hundreds roaming free and wild. He could even live with his mother while he chased and captured them.

"Hey, Ace," Thad broke into his plans for his future, "isn't that Ben and his old Indian friend helping themselves to some of our cattle?"

"Where?" Ace shaded his eyes against the sun.

"Up there at the edge of the foothills." Thad pointed south.

Ace chuckled his amusement when he spotted the pair. They were indeed rustling some of Gibb's longhorns. The wily old men had devised a perfect way to get the animals to the Indian village. Each man had apparently followed the wagon at a distance and gathered up some of the hay that had been spread for the cattle. They now dropped a handful of the dry grass every few yards, luring the hungry animals to follow them. Six young steers were eagerly trotting along behind them. He figured they had about a couple of miles to go before arriving at their destination.

"What should we do about it, Ace?" Thad asked as he reined the team in.

"We're not going to do anything about it. Let them have the animals. Hungry wolves will kill more than those two old men can steal. The village people have found a way to survive this brutal winter. They will go to bed nights with full bellies."

"Yeah, I expect they'll do that all winter." Thad grinned. "And if old Ben can get out and rustle cattle, I guess he and Aunt Lucy are doing all right."

"I expect so," Ace agreed with a pleased laugh. "Lark will be glad to hear that. She's been worried about them."

Ace looked at the sun again. "Let's spread the rest of the hay and call it a day. It's gonna take hours before I thaw out."

Two more days until Christmas, Lark thought as she made her way over the frozen, rutted path to the cookhouse.

As she stepped into the warmth of the big room, she was remembering how special that day had been when her mother and father were still alive. There would be a big fir tree set up in a corner, its pine fragrance filling the room. It would be decorated with ornaments that she and her mother had cut from colorful materials and felts. There would be strings of popcorn and cranberries draped among the branches. Beneath the tree there would be the Nativity set Pa had carved from hard oak. And at the very top of the tree there would be a beautiful angel smiling down at them.

Lark remembered with a smile how on Christmas Eve she would hang her stocking on the mantel, which had been draped with pine boughs and red berries.

Aunt Lucy and Uncle Ben, bless them, had tried to make the day special for her also. But they were always short of money and Christmas gifts.

She hadn't complained, though. She had known that there was an abundance of love to draw upon from those two dear old people.

There would be none of this in the Gibb household, Lark thought as she hung up her jacket and rolled up her sleeves. December twenty-fifth would be spent like any other day. Work and more work.

She wished that she had something to give to Ace and her aunt and uncle. As she rolled out a piece of pie dough, she prayed that her relatives up in the old cabin were all right. Would they remember that Christmas was almost upon them?

The apple pie was ready to go into the oven. That done, Lark turned her hand to preparing supper.

When she tugged the mattress from under the small cot, Lark's lips twisted in a wry smile. She and Ace still bemoaned the loss of her big, comfortable bed and the warmth of the house. She had brought an extra blanket from the house, but they still felt the chill in the air. Unless, of course, they were making love. The covers were kicked to the floor then.

She straightened up from smoothing the blankets just as Ace rapped on the door and stepped into the kitchen. She gave him a bright smile, then looked at the package he held under his arm. "What have you got there, Ace? Some clothes that need mending?"

"Now when have I ever brought you mending to do for me?" Ace pretended hurt feelings.

"You never have, but I would like doing things like that for you."

"Honey, you do things for me every night." Ace's eyes darkened as he thought of those things.

Lark blushed. "You do things for me too."

Ace held out the paper-wrapped bundle. "Merry Christmas, Lark," he said softly.

Lark stared at him in wonder for a moment, then cried, "Oh, Ace, you remembered that Christmas is almost here. I thought I was the only one to realize that the day was approaching."

"You thought wrong, then. Every man in the bunkhouse, except Newt, sent gifts of money to their families two weeks ago. Newt claims he has no relatives."

Lark wanted to ask Ace if he had sent holiday greetings to anyone, but was afraid of his answer. But then, if he had sent messages to women friends, he wasn't likely to tell her. He never said much about the women who had been involved in his life.

She wondered if he'd have much to say about her when he was around family and acquaintances again. As for that, would he even mention the young woman he had made passionate love to during long, cold Colorado nights? He never hinted at their having a future together.

Lark sighed inwardly. Making love to her was only a job to Ace, a job for which he was going to be paid handsomely. When the time came he would ride away, probably never giving her another thought.

"Aren't you going to open my gift?" Ace teased. "It won't bite you."

Lark put aside her gloomy thoughts and untied the string tied around the brown paper package. When she laid the wrappings open she gasped in surprise and pleasure. It was a bright red sweater.

"Oh, Ace, it's beautiful," she cried, lifting the garment up and holding it against her chest. "How warm it is going to feel."

Lark remembered something that brought the corners of her lips dipping down. She wouldn't dare wear it. "I won't be able to wear it, Ace." Her voice trembled slightly. "I'll have to keep it hidden from Cletus."

"No, you won't. Whenever you go outside, wear it under your jacket. If he notices it, which I doubt he will, tell him that your aunt knitted it for you." Ace motioned at the wrappings. "There's a pair of matching mittens too."

Lark pulled one of the pair over her red, chapped hands and looked up at Ace. "I feel bad that I don't have anything for you."

"Of course you have something for me." Ace took her arm and led her toward the small back room. "You can give it to me now," he added huskily.

In seconds their clothing was discarded and they were lost in their need of each other.

Later, when they were getting back into their clothes, Ace said, "Newt is going to try getting up the mountain to your aunt and uncle tomorrow. You can try out your new sweater when you ride up with him."

"Cletus won't let me go," Lark said dejectedly.

"You just be ready to go," Ace said as he shoved the mattress out of sight. "I'll see to it that you can go. I'll just point out to him that it's only natural that you'd want to see your relatives on Christmas Eve."

"He must like you. You always seem to get your way with him."

"Like me? That's a laugh. That man doesn't like anyone. The truth is, he's afraid of me. He saw me fight in Dogwood's saloon one night. He doesn't want a taste of my fists. Besides, he thinks I'm going to father a child for him."

Ace gave Lark a lingering kiss, then left her as she buttoned up her bodice.

Lark felt sorry for the team as they fought their way through the snow. Newt reined them in every half hour to let them rest awhile. When they came to drifts too high for the horses to get through, he would bring them to a halt and jump from the wagon. He would take from under the seat a shovel and clear away a couple of feet of snow so that the animals could move on.

The usual half hour it took to reach the foothills stretched into an hour today before they were climbing toward the cabin. When they finally approached the log building, Lark saw smoke curling out of the chimney. She couldn't wait to sit before the heat of the fire. Even with the warm sweater Ace had given her, she was cold. And her feet felt as if they were sitting in buckets of ice water.

When she and Newt stumbled into the cabin they were greeted with joyous cries of welcome. "Lark, honey, you look frozen!" Lucy exclaimed, full of concern. "Come by the fire and let me help you out of your jacket, and get your shoes off too."

"Newt is cold too," Lark said, remembering her companion.

"Don't worry about me, Lark. As soon as I unload the wagon and put the team in the shed, I'll be right in."

When Lark had her stockinged feet propped on the hearth of the brightly burning fire, she looked around the room. How different it was from that day when she and Uncle Ben and Aunt Lucy had walked into it. The furniture and carpeting she and Ace had smuggled from the big house had made the room cozy and inviting.

She smiled when she saw the pine boughs attached to the edge of the mantel, and a wreath of the same pine hung at the window. It pleased her that the old folks had remembered the holiday season. She sniffed the air and breathed in the aroma of baked cookies and tangy pine.

"You've got everything looking so nice and homey, Aunt Lucy," she said when the old woman brought her a platter of sugar cookies and a cup of steaming coffee.

"Thank you, dear. I can't remember the last time I kept house. It's been a long time, that I know."

Lucy sat down beside Lark. "Ben and I have been hoping and praying that we would get to see you for Christmas. We thought sure the weather would keep you away."

"It almost did. Newt and the horses are exhausted."

"I suppose you're all set for Christmas," Lucy said with a smile. "I imagine your home is decorated and all."

"Oh, yes." Lark smiled as she lied. "I'm sorry I wasn't able to get to town and get some shopping done for you and Uncle Ben."

"Don't worry about that, child. Just seeing you is gift enough."

Before Lucy could say more, Ben and Newt came

bustling into the cabin. When they made straight for the fire, Lucy jumped up, exclaiming, "You look absolutely frozen, Newt. Take my seat while I go pour you and Ben a cup of coffee."

"Bring the whiskey bottle too, Lucy," Ben called. "Newt has a lot of thawing out to do."

In a short time Newt's stockinged feet were stretched out beside Lark's on the hearth. The weather was discussed, along with the hard times the blizzard had brought to man and beast.

"I expect wolves will get a lot of Gibb's cattle," Ben said, then added, "He's got so many he probably won't even notice the few head that are missing."

Lark looked straight ahead into the fire and bit her tongue not to laugh out loud. Ace had told her about the steers her uncle and the old Indian had rustled from her husband. Her rascally old uncle was worried that he and his friend might be found out. Keeping a straight face, she said, "A few, Uncle Ben? He'll lose at least a couple hundred."

"No foolin'." Ben brightened up. "Imagine that."

Lark knew what he was thinking. It would be safe to take more of the Gibb cattle.

The warmth and murmur of voices soothed Lark into a half sleep. When Ben saw her nodding off he said, "Don't fall asleep, Larkie. You've got some presents to open."

"I do?" Lark's eyes popped open.

"You sure do." Ben's eyes sparkled. "Bring the packages from the bedroom, will you please, Lucy?"

When Lucy returned from the small bedroom, she brought with her three paper-wrapped bundles. One was a large one and the other two somewhat smaller.

"Open the big one first," Ben urged excitedly.

"It's from the Ute chief in the Indian village."

He didn't add that it was a gift in appreciation of the cattle he and Ragged Feather had driven to the chief's starving people. Nor did he tell her how the man had said in scorn, "We have seen the thin jacket her husband provided for her."

When Lark opened the brown paper she couldn't speak for a moment. She was overwhelmed with surprise and joy. She could only stare at the fur-lined doeskin jacket with attached hood. She smoothed her palm over the intricate beadwork decorating the garment. She marveled at the softness of the skin, the silky feel of the beaver lining. No cold air would penetrate this coat.

She lifted her gaze to Ben and, with tears swimming in her eyes, said, "Please tell the chief that I will treasure his gift always."

"He will appreciate that you said that," Ben said, and handed her a long, flat package. "Open this one next."

When Lark tore away the paper she gave a cry of delight as she looked down on a pair of knee-high, fur-lined leather moccasins.

"They're from Ragged Feather," Ben said proudly. "His granddaughter made them. She rubbed bear grease into the leather so that they will shed water."

"Why don't you try them on, Lark?" Newt suggested.

Lark undid the ragged laces of her shoes and slid her feet into the softness of the footwear. She looked up with a wide smile. "They fit perfectly. I will wear them home."

"This one is from me and Ben." Lucy handed her a wide, flat package. "It's not so grand as the others, but it will go very nicely with your new sweater."

Lucy had knitted her a white scarf. "I love it, Aunt Lucy." Lark jumped up and kissed her aunt on the cheek. "This is the best Christmas I've ever had."

"I hate to break up your visit, Lark," Newt said, reaching for his boots, "but it's time we got started down the mountain."

"Yes, it is," Lark said reluctantly and stood up. She bent over and picked up her old shoes. She stood a moment looking down at them, and then with a jerk of her hand, tossed them into the fire. The moccasins would see her through the winter and, after that, she would go barefoot if necessary.

She hesitated a moment, then tossed her old worn jacket onto the flames. The three people watching her nodded their approval when she pulled on the chief's Christmas gift.

When good-byes were said, Lark pulled up the hood over her head. She was toasty warm all the way home.

Chapter Twenty-two

Ace had been walking along the riverbank for over an hour. He had much on his mind. He had a decision to make.

The months of January and February had been bitterly cold, with gray skies and blustery winds.

It was March now, and for two weeks male cardinals and trout swimming in the creeks had been telling him that spring was on the way. The long, cold months were coming to an end. Then yesterday the chinook winds blew in and the snow rapidly began to melt.

It was time for him to move on. It was time to have a talk with Gibb, to tell him his lie.

A devilish light grew in Ace's eyes. He wished he could be here when the rancher discovered that he had been taken advantage of. What a rage the fat man would go into when he also realized that Lark and her relatives had gone away. The bastard wouldn't mind losing his wife and the two old people. The thing that would drive him mad was the baby Lark supposedly carried. And he mustn't forget the added loss of the money Gibb had put out to get an heir.

"I might as well get it over with," Ace muttered, and turned around to retrace his footsteps back to the ranch. He wanted things settled before suppertime.

As he walked past the cookhouse window he saw Lark moving around, preparing the evening meal. *You won't have to be his slave much longer, Lark,* he thought. *This time tomorrow you can start making plans to get away from here.*

Ace had to knock twice on the door before Gibb opened it with a disapproving frown. "Go around to the kitchen door," he ordered. "I don't want you tracking mud on my parlor floor."

Ace condemned his boss to hell as he walked around the house and knocked on the back door. When Gibb admitted him into the kitchen, he purposely didn't wipe his feet.

Gibb frowned at the mud and gravel tracked across his floor and growled, "What do you want to see me about?"

Ace, uninvited, sat down at the table. "I've come to finish our business deal," he said bluntly.

"What do you mean, finish it?" Startled, Gibb sat down also.

"I mean just what I said. Lark is with child."

Elation spread over Gibb's face. A split second later, though, his forehead was creased with his habitual frown. "It took you long enough," he said with a growl. "I was beginning to think that your seed wasn't any good. When will the baby arrive?"

Ace paused a moment. It hadn't occurred to him that he would be asked that question. He thought a moment, then said blandly, "Eight months from now."

Although he had tried to hide it, Gibb's excitement was evident in the way he began to rub his hands together. "Before the year is out I will be a father. I can't wait to see how people around here are going to react to that."

When Gibb stopped gloating, Ace said, "I've come to be paid for my services."

Gibb stared down at his clasped hands a moment; then, giving Ace a sidelong look, he complained, "I don't think I should have to give you the full amount we agreed on. After all, you enjoyed all winter, mating with Lark. Don't try to tell me that you didn't enjoy it. I heard you moanin' and groanin'."

"Whether I did or not, that has nothing to do with our agreement." Ace's eyes stabbed the man he so detested. "The important thing is that I got your wife with child."

"Even so, I still think—"

"Look," Ace said impatiently, "a deal is a deal. I don't think you want me to hang around the area, maybe accidently let slip that I fathered your heir."

"You'd do that, wouldn't you?" The rancher glared at him.

"You damn betcha." Ace gave him a wolfish grin.

Gibb could hardly control his rage. This man he both admired and hated had him over a barrel. To save face he would have to hand over a good sum of money. "I'll go get your damn money," he grated out, and left the room, slamming the door behind him.

Ace's lips tilted contemptuously. He had expected the miser to argue about the deal they had made and had been ready for him.

Gibb was gone several minutes before he returned, a thick stack of bills in his hand. He slapped them down in front of Ace and growled, "I expect you to be off the ranch tomorrow morning. And I want you to get the hell out of Colorado."

"That's my plan." Ace folded the greenbacks and slipped them into his vest pocket. He stood up and gave his ex-boss a grin. "I've enjoyed doing business with you. I hope you enjoy your heir."

Gibb's answer was an angry growl as Ace opened the door and stepped outside.

Lark shoved a loaf of sourdough into the oven and closed the heavy door. When she straightened up and glanced out the window she saw Ace leaving the house. Why had he gone to see Cletus? she wondered, worrying her bottom lip. Had Cletus called a halt to their nightly lovemaking? Did that mean that he wasn't going to keep the agreement he had with Ace? Ace would be so disappointed. All his plans to build a herd of horses would be for nothing.

With a weary sigh she sat down at the table. She had something equally important to think about. She was three months pregnant.

It had been hard to keep it a secret. She still had morning sickness. Retching every day had caused her to lose weight. However, that was a blessing in some ways. She showed no signs of being with child.

One question had nagged her all these months: Should she tell Ace? At first she hadn't told him because she feared he would tell Cletus and then ride away. She wanted to hang on to him as long as possible.

But spring was here now and Ace would be wanting to leave, to get on with starting his ranch. Any day now he could go to Cletus and tell him that his wife was pregnant—which to his way of thinking was a lie.

Lark stood up and paced the floor. She must decide whether she would tell Ace that he was to become a father in the fall. If she had thought he loved her, she would have told him a long time ago. But so far that word hadn't been mentioned between them.

Still undecided on what to do, Lark stood up and began preparing supper.

As Ace sat in the bunkhouse, waiting for supper with the other men, his hand kept stealing over his vest pocket. Excitement rushed through him every time he felt the roll of money. The means of a secure future lay there.

However, the stirring of his blood slowed down a bit when he remembered that tonight he would say good-bye to Lark. It would be one of the hardest things he'd ever done in his life. Would it be hard on her too? She had never said that she loved him, had never even hinted at it. She seemed only to wait for the day she could take her aunt and uncle and get away from Gibb.

By the time the wall clock showed seven, Ace had convinced himself that he wouldn't be leaving a heartbroken Lark behind.

The men ate their meal in their usual manner, with

no words spoken, heads bent over their plates. Except for Ace, Lark noted. His eyes sparked and he could hardly sit still. She wondered if his visit to Cletus had anything to do with his behavior. Evidently her fear that Cletus was going to call a halt to their meeting was unfounded.

The meal was eaten and Gibb had still made no appearance for his supper.

She wondered about that after the men left when she put the kitchen in order. It wasn't like her husband to miss the evening meal. She concluded that Cletus had probably gone into town. She walked into the small back room. She tugged the mattress out from under the cot and smoothed the blankets. It took but a moment to get out of her clothes and then slide under the covers. Ace would be here any minute.

She heaved a heavy sigh. Two hours spent with him every night wasn't nearly enough anymore. She wanted to fall asleep in his arms, awaken there the next morning. It appeared to be the same with Ace. He was always reluctant to leave her when their allotted time was up.

A bit of unrest settled over Lark. Ace still hadn't said that he loved her, though. But what was that old saying? Actions spoke louder than words. His actions, his passion said that he loved her. Maybe Ace was the sort of man who didn't speak his feelings.

For her part, though, she longed to express her love for him. She wanted to tell him that she didn't know if she could bear for him to leave her.

She had faith, though, that Ace would give her enough money to get away from Gibb. She shook her head at that thought. She could move a thousand miles away, but that wouldn't stop her from loving Ace, wanting to be with him.

As Lark gazed through the window at the white moon hovering in the sky, her thoughts continued to be gloomy. Lately, Ace had been talking about the horses he would capture and the ranch he intended to build up. He talked about how at first he would live with his widowed mother while he chased the wild ones. He dreamed aloud how he would tame them to saddle, then sell them.

"Give me five years, Lark," he had said once, "and I'll be one of the largest horse breeders around."

He had never said, though, what would happen when he became a man of means. He never said anything about her being by his side as he made his dream reality.

"Maybe he takes it for granted that I'll be his help-mate," she whispered into the darkness as she waited for Ace to come to her.

But as the time ticked by she became nervous and excited at the same time. She had made up her mind that tonight she was going to tell Ace the truth: to-gether, they had conceived another little human be-ing. She had decided that whether Ace loved her or not, he had a right to know that he was going to become a father.

When Lark heard the outside door open and Ace's footsteps coming toward the little room, she forgot everything but the two hours she would be held in his arms.

In the light from the kitchen she watched Ace get out of his clothes, then felt him slide in beside her. His arms immediately reached out and drew her softness against his hardness. He bent his head, and the kiss he settled on her lips was soft, yet demanding. He smoothed his palms over her body, as though to impress it on his mind for all time. When he drew a pebble-hard nipple into his mouth, Lark cried out, "Now, Ace, now."

She sighed in anticipation as his hardness slid inside her. She clutched his shoulders, murmuring her pleasure as his manhood slowly thrust in and out. She had never known such tenderness from Ace as twice more they made love.

At last, spent and weak, they lay side by side, catching their breath. When Ace's breathing returned to normal he leaned on an elbow and gazed down at Lark. As he stroked the damp curls from around her face he asked with a teasing grin, "Did I please you, Miss Lark?"

"You know you did." Lark lifted a hand to his cheek. "You always do, but tonight was different, so satisfying."

Ace's smile faded and his eyes became serious. "I wanted tonight to be special," he said softly.

"Oh? How come?" Lark asked, knowing that she wouldn't like his answer.

"I talked to Gibb this afternoon. He believed me when I told him that you were expecting."

Lark's body went still and her throat tightened. She had to swallow twice before she could ask unsteadily, "What did he have to say about that?"

"He tried to hide it, but he was as pleased as a bear with a honey pot. For the first time since I've known him, I saw him half smile."

Ace lay back down and, chuckling, said, "The old bastard tried to get out of paying the whole amount we had agreed upon. I had to do a little blackmailing to get the promised amount. When he reluctantly handed the money over, he said that he wanted me off his ranch by tomorrow morning. Also that I should leave Colorado altogether."

With her breath held, Lark waited for Ace to say that she would be leaving with him. When those words were not forthcoming she felt as if there were a big piece of ice in her chest.

She composed herself with an effort before asking weakly, "Will you do as he says?"

"You know I will. I'm leaving at first light in the morning. I put the money I promised you on the table in the kitchen. Have you decided where you'll go when you leave here?"

Where would she go? Lark pushed back the sob that had risen in her throat. She had never given it that much thought. In the back of her mind she had believed that when she left Cletus, it would be to go with Ace.

She finally managed to say, "I have a couple places in mind. I haven't decided yet."

Into the short silence that grew, Ace said softly, "I'll never forget you, Lark."

"Nor will I forget you, Ace," Lark whispered, wanting to put her arms around him and beg him to take her with him.

She lay quietly, however, knowing that if she did that she would only embarrass him. He had a fondness for her, but no love.

"Well." Ace sighed and sat up. "I guess I'd better get going. I don't think I was supposed to come here tonight."

When Lark sat up beside him, Ace wrapped his arms around her and gave her a warm, lingering kiss.

"Take care of yourself, Lark. I wish you all the luck in the world."

"I wish you luck in building your horse ranch, Ace," Lark said huskily.

He was gone then, and Lark let her hot tears fall when she heard the kitchen door open, then close. For a moment she was on the point of running after him, to tell him about the baby she was carrying. She knew that he was an honorable man and would insist that she divorce Cletus and marry him.

Lark shook her head and said to herself, "I couldn't do that to Ace. He doesn't need a wife and child holding him back while he's trying to get his ranch started." Besides, he didn't love her, and in time he would grow to hate her. She couldn't bear for that to happen.

The excitement that had gripped Ace all afternoon and evening continued as he walked along the muddy path to the bunkhouse. He now had the money to start the biggest adventure of his life. It wouldn't be easy, he knew. Each day of the week there would be at least twelve hours of backbreaking work, with the hot sun burning down on him, and sweat pouring down his face and stinging his eyes. All that he didn't mind, though. In the end he would have won something worth having.

As he walked along he visualized the wild horses that ran free in Utah. Many times he had watched and admired the handsome stallions and their harems. Many of the mares showed signs of high breeding. Wild stallions were always stealing mares from ranchers. He would get some real beauties.

He recalled the rolling hills where his mother

lived, and chose the spot where he would build his cabin before another winter set in.

Then suddenly the thought of walking out of Lark's life, never to see her again, put a damper on his high spirits. He would miss her, he knew, but that would pass. There was no place for a wife in his life. He had a roving eye for beautiful women, and he knew that in time he would resume his ways of dallying with them.

He grinned wryly. He would probably never change until he was too old to chase them.

Ace left off thinking of his past and future when he approached the bunkhouse and Thad spoke to him out of the shadows.

"Why aren't you in bed, asleep?" he asked, stepping up on the porch and sitting down beside the teenager. "We had a hard day chasing those wild longhorns all over creation."

"I could ask you the same question." Thad squinted at him from the dim light shining through the grimy windows of the bunkhouse.

"You could," Ace answered, gazing up at the moon that slid in and out from behind the clouds. "I've been saying good-bye to Lark."

"What do you mean, saying good-bye?" Thad brought his chair down from its tilt against the wall. "Are you going somewhere?"

"Yes, I am, Thad. I'm leaving in the morning."

"For good?" There was alarm in the young man's voice.

"I'm afraid so, kid."

"But why? You've seemed pleased enough working here."

"Thad, I told you when I first signed on here it was

only for the winter. Spring is here now and I'm moving on."

"Where to? Another ranch? The work will be the same, whatever ranch you choose."

Ace ignored the first question and answered the second one. "I'm not going to another ranch. I find that I'm not cut out to take orders. Especially from a man like Cletus Gibb. I have plans of building my own ranch. A horse ranch. My mother has land in Utah. That's where I'm heading."

"I'll go with you," Thad said eagerly, sitting forward. "I've saved most of my pay."

"Thanks, kid, but I'd appreciate it if you'd stay here and try to help Lark in any way you can. Gibb eased up on her because he was afraid of me. I'm afraid that when I've gone he'll start abusing her again. You're a big fellow for your age, and if you let him know you're not afraid of him, it might help Lark a lot. You might even help her get away from him someday."

"She sure needs someone to help her," Thad agreed, "but I'm not going to hang around here the rest of my life."

"I've got a feeling she'll be leaving before too long."

"Well," Thad said reluctantly, "I guess I can stay for a while."

"Thanks kid." Ace rose to his feet. "Let's turn in now. It's late, and I want to get an early start in the morning."

"How early?"

Ace hesitated a moment, then said, "Around eight o'clock. We'll say our good-byes then."

Chapter Twenty-three

There came the first faint gleam of light over the horizon. Ace sat on the edge of the bed and donned his pants and shirt, pulled on his boots. When he had strapped on his gun belt he quietly opened the door and stepped outside. He softly closed the door on the snoring men. As he walked to the barn the stars faded and the shadows lifted from the distant river.

When he walked into the barn Sam whinnied a muted greeting. It was as if the horse knew not to make too much noise. "Are you ready to do some riding, fellow?" he asked as he settled the bit into the gelding's mouth. "We've got a ways to go," he added, placing a folded blanket on the broad back, then setting the saddle on top of it.

Ace swung the saddlebags across Sam's strong neck, then walked over to a mound of hay. Bending over, he dragged from it his gear and a rolled-up bundle of clothing. When he had fastened everything behind the cantle, he led the horse outside. He swung into the saddle and sat for a moment, gazing at the dim outline of the cookhouse and the big house. He pictured Lark curled up in sleep and wondered if she was sad that he was leaving.

His gaze moved to the cookhouse, and he recalled the many evenings spent there with Lark. How wonderful those hours had been, her soft body beneath him, her arms wound around his shoulders as he made love to her.

He sighed heavily. As he had told her, he would never forget her. For a long time he would be hard put not to compare other women to her.

"Stop such thinking," he muttered, and gave Sam a nudge of his heels.

As they headed in the direction of Utah, Ace felt bad that he had lied to Thad about the time of his departure. He so hated good-byes. It had been hard enough to take his leave from Lark.

The sun rose higher, bright and warm on Ace's head and thighs as he held Sam to a canter. The big gelding wanted to stretch out his long legs and run, get rid of his excess energy. But Ace held him in. He wanted to cover as many miles as possible today, and he wanted Sam to conserve his strength, not spend most of it in a few miles of hard gallop.

It was around ten o'clock, Ace judged by the sun, when he rode out of a stand of aspen that was just beginning to bud out. After a hundred yards or so he came to a creek. It was wide with water from the snowmelt up in the mountains. There was a clump of willows on one side of it, and he reined Sam in and dismounted. While the gelding drank deep, Ace decided to replenish his canteen. He might not come across another stream the rest of the day.

He had just knelt on the bank and dipped the canvas-covered container into the clear water when a bullet sang past his ear.

"What the hell!" he swore. He jumped to his feet and started running toward Sam. He grabbed his rifle from its sheath behind the saddle and sprinted back toward the willows, thinking that they would give him scant protection because they weren't leafed out yet. When he ducked beneath the ground-hugging branches, another shot kicked up dirt and gravel at his heels.

That bastard, whoever he is, is trying to kill me, he thought. He jacked a round into the rifle's chamber.

Who would want me dead? he asked himself as he hunkered down behind one of the larger tree trunks. He knew there were some men who didn't especially like him, but he didn't think any of them would want to see him dead.

When several minutes passed and no more shots were heard, Ace moved out of cover. He let out a savage oath when he recognized the big stallion racing away—Cletus Gibb's big black. "You miserly bastard!" he shouted, and took aim at the fat body bobbing up and down in the saddle.

Even as he squeezed the trigger, Gibb disappeared behind a small knoll.

"You back-shooting coward, you meant to kill me," he yelled, shaking his fist at the spot where he had seen Gibb. "You meant to steal back the money you gave me."

He swayed between the choice of chasing after

Gibb and putting a slug in his fat rump, or moving on toward his destination. He decided that the back-shooting skunk wouldn't follow him any farther and swung onto Sam's back.

Sunset was a blaze of red and yellow in the west when Ace started looking for a place to make camp. For the past hour he had been following a river that wound its way in the direction he wanted to travel. He soon found a likely spot in another stand of wil-lows. He would be well hidden here from anyone riding by. There were renegade Indians in the area, as well as cattle rustlers. There were plenty of men who would kill just to get their hands on Sam.

He rode the gelding onto the wide gravel bank and dismounted, dropping the reins so that Sam could drink as long as he wanted to. When Sam had had his fill and lifted his head, Ace led him among the trees. There he staked the gelding in a patch of tall, tender grass.

As the handsome animal cropped his supper, Ace began to gather dead limbs from beneath the trees to make a campfire. When he had a fire going, bordered by large rocks he had gotten from the river, Ace picked up his rifle and struck off toward a stand of trees a few hundred yards away. There was at least another hour of daylight left. Maybe he could shoot a young turkey for his supper.

He was back at his cookfire within fifteen minutes. He hadn't found a turkey, but his rifle had brought down two prairie chickens that had gone to roost in a pine tree.

The small hens, dressed and roasted on a spit,

were soon eaten, their bones tossed into the fire. As Ace sat before the fire, having a smoke and watching the river slide by, his thoughts turned to Lark.

She would be serving the cowhands their supper right about now. Her graceful body would move around the table, growing tense when she drew near her husband.

Ace thought next how later, if he were there, he would join Lark on the mattress in the back room of the cookhouse. He felt a rush of hot blood as he recalled the sweet fire of her kisses, her hands stroking over his body.

"Enough of that," he said so loudly that Sam lifted his head and looked at him. "I will not think of her again," he vowed as he added more wood to the fire. He would awaken at intervals during the night to replenish the fire. There was always the chance that a bear or a pack of wolves would scent Sam and come sneaking around camp in the hope of bringing the gelding down.

After a wide yawn Ace unrolled his blankets close to the flames and took off his boots and gun belt. He shoved his Colt beneath the blanket and stretched out between the covers.

It had been a long day, and he soon fell asleep to the whisper of the night wind.

Lark awoke in the early dawn. Ace had left the day before. That was the first thing that popped into her mind. She would never see him again. He would never know that they had created a child together. She had gone through the previous day in a daze, unaware of what happened around her.

What would her life be like now? she wondered

miserably. Cletus no longer had to fear Ace's fists, and he would treat her more cruelly than ever to make up for all the times he had held back because of his hired man. He would no doubt put her to shoveling out the stables again and to doing any menial work he could think of.

Her face lost its color at a sudden thought. She was three months pregnant, a time to be very careful that she not lose the baby growing inside her. Would the hard labor she would have to do from now on cause her to miscarry?

"Dear God," she whispered, "I mustn't lose Ace's baby. His son or daughter will be all that I'll ever have of him."

She gazed at the window, gray in the early morning light. For her unborn child's sake, should she leave Cletus right now? Ace had told her to do that. What he didn't know was that she was expecting, that she was sick most of the time. Sometimes she could barely stand up.

Besides, where would she go? Right now her mind was too clouded by pain and loss to make a logical plan. And there were her aunt and uncle. She would have to explain to them that once again they would be moving on. They would ask so many questions.

Lark heard the rooster crowing in the chicken pen and knew it was time she dragged herself out of bed and over to the cookhouse.

She found the long room warm as usual, and the coffee made. Thad was not there, however. As she prepared breakfast, she kept reminding herself not to let her face show her sadness, her despondency. Cletus had been gone most of the previous day. Now that he was back, it would please him to see her grieving over Ace.

It was close to the time for the men to start arriving when the odor of frying bacon started a roiling in Lark's stomach. She rushed outside and, standing at the corner of the building, had dry heaves.

When later she served the men their breakfast, her pale face and strained features drew looks of pity from them. Those looks turned hard when once again Gibb reverted to his old self and began ordering her around.

"Stand ready to keep the men's cups full of coffee," he growled at her.

The beginning of his revenge, she thought as she carried the big pot from the stove and started filling any cup she found empty. When she came to Thad, her hands shook a little as she looked at the empty space between him and Newt. Ace should be sitting there.

Thad and Newt shook their heads that they didn't want any more brew. She knew that they did; they were both big coffee drinkers. They only refused more to make it easier on her.

When Lark returned to the stove and stood ready for Gibb's next order, Newt said, "I'm taking some grub up to the old folks this morning, Lark. Do you want to ride along with me, visit with your aunt and uncle for a while?"

Eagerness brightened Lark's dull eyes. She longed to see the old couple, especially Aunt Lucy. She needed to tell the old lady that she was going to become a great-aunt, and to tell her about her aches and pains.

Before Lark could open her mouth, Gibb said roughly, "She can't go lolly-gagging today. She has too much work to do."

Lark visibly shrank in her disappointment. The men gave Gibb a hard, dark look and, as one, stood up and left the cookhouse.

"I'll have another cup of coffee," Gibb said in a growl when the door closed behind the men.

When Lark brought the pot to the table, she saw that his cup was still three-quarters full. When she would have added more to it, he grabbed her wrist and squeezed so hard she was afraid he would crush the bones.

"Get me a fresh cup, bitch," he snarled. When another cup was placed before him, he looked at her and sneered, "The party is over. Things will go back to normal now. When you've cleaned up in here, get your lazy self down to the barn and start shoveling out the stables."

The pain in her back, the ache in her wrist and the queasiness in her stomach became too much for Lark. She was going to be sick. She rushed to the door, tore it open, and got outside just as she started heaving.

Gibb had followed her, and his fat face wore a satisfied look as he watched her retch. When she had finished, her body weak and trembling, he said sanctimoniously, "That is your punishment for wallowing around in sin all winter. A woman has to pay for her pleasure, one way or the other."

Lark could only gape after her husband as he waddled off toward the barn. "You hypocrite," she ground out, "blaming me for doing what you ordered me to do."

Chapter Twenty-four

Newt pulled the team up alongside the porch. When Ben opened the cabin door he grinned down at the old man and said, "Brought you some grub."

"I hope you didn't forget my tobacco," Ben said anxiously.

"I remembered." Newt laughed as he jumped to the ground. "It seems to me that you're smoking more than usual."

"I've been sharing it with my friend, Ragged Feather."

"You two are pretty chummy, aren't you?" Newt remarked, hauling a full gunnysack from the wagon.

"Yeah. He's the best friend I ever had."

"Good morning, Newt." Lucy came out onto the porch and smiled at him. She looked past his shoulder then and said, "I was hoping that Lark would be with you."

"She couldn't make it today. She's feeling poorly."

"What's wrong with her?" Ben and Lucy asked in unison, alarm in their voices.

"I don't know, but she looked sickly this morning."

Ben gave Newt a hard, steady look. Then he ordered, "Come on in, Newt. I'm going to ask you some questions, and I want the truth from you."

Uneasy, wishing that he hadn't mentioned that Lark didn't look well, Newt followed the old couple into the cabin. Ben motioned for him to sit down at the table, and he and Lucy joined him when he pulled out a chair.

"Now then, Newt," Ben began, "do you think Lark is happy in her marriage? Does Cletus Gibb treat her right?"

"Hell, Ben, I wish you wouldn't put me on the spot like this," Newt complained.

"Well, I'm doing it, and I expect an honest answer from you."

Newt stared down at the floor. Should he tell the old folks the truth or lie to them? What could they do about it if he did tell them that Gibb treated Lark shamefully?

And yet, he felt they should know that their niece's husband worked her like a slave, and that somehow they should get her out of Gibb's clutches before he worked her to death.

With a sigh, Newt lifted his gaze to the waiting Ben and said, "The truth is, he don't treat her good at all. He makes her work like a slave, and sometimes he strikes her."

Lucy's face blanched and Ben swore furiously.

"We've suspected that things haven't been the way they should be down there." Ben stood up and paced the floor. "Ragged Feather has mentioned a few things that have been spoken around the village campfire."

Her eyes swimming with tears, Lucy choked out, "No telling what that dear girl has been going through so that Ben and I can have a roof over our heads and food in our stomachs."

"Lucy, get your coat on while I go saddle the horse," Ben ordered as he pushed his chair away from the table. "We're riding down there right now, and we'll find out just what's going on."

"I doubt that he'll pay any attention to what you say to him," Newt cautioned. "Ace used to keep him in line a little, but he quit the ranch yesterday."

"Oh, dear, I'm sorry to hear that," Lucy said as she left the table. "He's such a nice young man, and he was a good friend to Lark."

"Come on, wife, let's go." Ben held Lucy's coat for her to slip into. "We'll see you later, Newt," he said, hurrying Lucy out the door.

The old nag was carrying them down the mountain before Newt finished carrying in the supplies.

Lark had finished washing the dishes and sweeping the floor when she saw Gibb ride past the window, headed toward town. She leaned against the table, her hands supporting her back. If only she could lie down for a while. She could forget that, she thought. She had a full, hard day ahead of her.

She pulled together her small reserve of strength and readied herself to start cleaning the stables.

When Lark walked up to the barn she found that Thad had led the horses out of the stalls and turned them loose in the corral a few yards away. At least I don't have to do that, she thought, and started to enter the big building. She met Thad coming out.

As soon as he saw her, he took one look at her pale, drawn face and demanded, "What are you doing down here, Lark?"

She gave him a wan smile. "I'm to take up my old chores again."

"Like hell you are. You look ready to fall on your face." He took her by the arm and led her to the oat bin placed against a wall. "You sit down here. I'll have the stalls cleaned out in no time."

"But, Thad, what if Cletus comes back and finds you doing my work? He won't like it at all."

"He's going to be gone for at least an hour, and I'll be finished by then. You sit there and relax."

Lark tried to relax, but the pain in her back had become so severe she felt ill from it. As if from a distance she heard Thad talking to her and she tried to focus on his face and words. Then everything began to grow dim around her and she knew she was going to faint. With her last conscious effort she called out, "Thad, help me!"

Thad threw down the pitchfork and reached Lark in time to keep her from falling to the floor. He put one arm across her back and the other under her knees and straightened up with her in his arms. He hurried toward the house then, at a half run.

He was about to climb the steps to the porch when an anxious voice called out, "Thad, what's wrong with Lark?"

"She's fainted, I think." Thad's voice was husky with anxiety and concern.

Lucy hurried forward and took over. "Get her to bed," she ordered, "then ride to town and bring back the doctor. She doesn't look at all well."

None of the three knew which room to put Lark in. Lucy ran ahead, opening doors that led off the long hallway. When she opened a door and recognized Lark's old robe lying across the foot of the bed, she directed Thad to lay her there. When Lark was lying in a comfortable position, Lucy shooed the men out and began undressing her niece.

Lucy shook her head and clucked her tongue when she removed her niece's clothes and saw the emaciation of her body. Lark was a shell of her old self. Her shoulder bones and hipbones jutted out sharply, and she could have counted her ribs.

Her last discovery made her cry out in dismay as her gaze fell on Lark's small but protruding stomach. "Dear Lord." Lucy's eyes filled with tears. "She's with child." As she rushed to the dresser to find a gown for Lark, she breathed a prayer over and over. "Please don't let her lose the baby."

Lucy had put Lark into a worn gown and was chafing her hands when Newt rushed into the room. "Ben just told me that Lark is sick. He said she fainted. Is she all right?"

"I don't know, Newt. She's so thin and run-down. I looked in the kitchen to find something to feed her." Lucy paused and shook her head. "That room is as bare as a rock. I don't think the stove has ever been used."

"Lark has been preparing our food in the cookhouse. I'll go see if I can find something there. We had some chicken soup with our supper last night. Maybe there's some left over."

Newt had barely left the room when Lark stirred and opened her eyes. "Aunt Lucy," she exclaimed when her eyes focused on her aunt. "What are you doing here?"

"Don't excite yourself now," Lucy soothed. "Your uncle and I decided to come visit you. We arrived in time to see Thad about to carry you into the house. You had fainted in the barn."

Confusion furrowing her brow, Lark stared at Lucy. Then slowly the events in the barn came back to her. "I remember now," she said. "It's my back. It ached so I could hardly bear it."

"Does it still hurt?"

"It's not so bad when I'm lying down."

Lucy picked up Lark's thin hand and, stroking it, chastised gently, "Why didn't you tell me that you are expecting?"

"You know, then?" When Lucy nodded gravely, she said, "I didn't want you worrying about me." She gave a small laugh. "Of course, I couldn't have kept it from you much longer."

Lucy waited a moment; then, still holding her hands, she said softly, "You're in danger of losing your baby, honey. I sent Thad after the doctor."

Alarm leaped into Lark's eyes. She mustn't lose Ace's baby. It was all she had left of him. And Cletus, what would he say about having a doctor come to the house?

She looked up at her aunt. "I'm afraid that Cletus won't like it that a doctor has been sent for."

"Doesn't he want the baby?" Lucy looked surprised.

"Oh, yes, he wants it very much."

"Well, then, if he's got an ounce of sense, he'll realize that if you don't get well, you will lose his heir."

"Maybe you're right." Lark nodded, feeling a little

relieved at her aunt's logic. "I guess if the doctor says that I need to rest a few days, he'll probably believe him."

They both looked at the door when Newt came through it. He carried a tray holding a bowl with delicious-smelling steam rising from it. "Good, you're awake, Lark." He beamed at her as he placed the tray on the bedside table. "I found some of your chicken soup and heated it up. You'll feel better when you get some of it down you."

"I am a little hungry," Lark said, smiling her thanks.

"Pull her up and prop the pillow behind her, Newt," Lucy ordered. When Lark was made comfortable, Lucy set the tray on Lark's lap and handed her the spoon that lay beside the bowl.

Lark had finished eating half the soup when Thad arrived with the doctor. Ben followed close behind them.

"You remember Dr. Randal, Lark," Thad said. "He'll find out what's wrong with you."

The doctor took one look at Lark, then said briskly, "Take away the tray for now. Then all of you leave the room. And close the door behind you."

Lucy gave him a sharp look. She did not like his manner. Nevertheless, she took the tray and placed it back on the table, then reluctantly left, giving the door a good slam when she closed it behind her.

"Well, young lady," the doctor said, smiling down at Lark, "what seems to be the trouble with you? Young Thad said that you fainted."

"Yes, I did," Lark answered, looking a little embarrassed. "I've never done that before."

"Why do you think you did it this time?" Randal

asked, picking up her wrist and putting his fingers on her pulse.

After a slight hesitation Lark decided that she might as well tell him about her condition. He would probably discover it anyway. She looked up at the doctor and gave him a half smile. "Maybe because I'm expecting?"

Randal chuckled at her half statement, half question. "That's not an unusual occurrence," he said. "Is anything else bothering you?"

"I do have this pain in my lower back. Sometimes it is so severe I can hardly bear it."

Dr. Randall studied her a moment, then asked, "Does it burn when you relieve yourself?"

"Why, yes, it does. I feel like I'm on fire."

"Turn over on your stomach," he ordered.

When she had rolled over, Lark blushed when he lifted her gown to her shoulders and started pressing his palms on her lower back. Only Ace had ever seen her bare behind.

A few minutes later her gown was pulled down and she was told she could roll over on her back. When she had pulled her gown down around her feet and pulled the covers up to her waist, she looked at the doctor and waited for him to speak.

Dr. Randal sat down on the chair Lucy had pulled up to the bed. His voice was grave when he said, "You are a very sick young woman, Mrs. Gibb."

Before the doctor could say anything further the door banged open and Cletus came stomping into the room. His fat face was red with fury. "I never gave orders for you to come to my house," he shouted at the doctor. "What's she trying to pull to keep from doing her work?" He shot Lark a menacing look.

The man of medicine rose to his feet and glared back at Gibb, his sharp blue eyes gradually staring the raging man down. When Gibb stopped ranting, he said quietly but clearly, "Your wife is seriously ill. She has albumin poisoning. If I don't get her kidneys cleared up, you stand a chance of losing her. For sure she will lose the child she is carrying."

Lark let loose a despairing cry and Gibb grew pale. He stepped closer to the doctor. "What can you do to save the baby?" His voice was raspy.

Randal gave him a cold look. "I have to save the mother first. I think that can be done with medication and plenty of bedrest. She is going to need both."

"What do you mean, plenty of bedrest?" Gibb sent Lark another threatening look.

"I mean just what I said. I want her to stay in bed for the next two weeks so that the medicine can work. If she's to carry this child the whole nine months, she has to take it easy. That means no hard work, no cooking for your hired help, no bending over a washboard cleaning clothes, and no scrubbing floors. I want her to sit in the sun a lot and eat good, healthy food. She must eat a lot of red meat to build up her strength so she can birth your child. She is very run-down."

Gibb was practically hopping up and down in his rage at the end of the doctor's harangue about Lark's illness and the care she was going to need. "Are you saying that I'll have to hire a cook, have some woman come in here and do my wife's work?" he shouted, his face beet red.

"That's exactly what I'm saying. And she'll need someone to wait on her for the next couple of weeks. Will you be able to do that, Mr. Gibb?"

Lucy had been watching Gibb all the while Randal spoke. She saw a flickering gleam in his small eyes and knew what it meant. He would agree to take care of Lark, but she knew that the only thing he would do was give her the medicine. Then as soon as she showed signs of recovery, he would have her up and working like a slave again.

Before Gibb could speak up, Lucy said clearly and firmly, "I'll take care of my niece." Her eyes dared Gibb to say no.

"She'll be in good hands then," Randal said, and closed the little bag that accompanied him everywhere he went. As he rose and walked to the door, he said, "I'll stop by tomorrow and see how she's coming along."

Gibb stared after the doctor until he went through the door; then he whipped his head around, his beady eyes glaring at Lucy. Before he could start in on her, the small, quiet-mannered woman became like a mother bear defending her cub.

"Don't try to put the evil eye on me, Cletus Gibb." Her soft blue eyes had become like pieces of ice. "I know now that your words and actions up on the mountain were only a pretense to convince Lark to marry you. You are an evil, amoral man. For all you care, my niece can die. Well, I'm not taking a chance of that happening. I'm staying here until she delivers her baby."

"The hell you are!" Gibb spluttered, his face twisted in rage. "I'll not have you in my house mollycoddling your niece, making her lazier than she already is."

Ben caught his wife around the waist as she sprang at the rancher. And although she was held fast, the little woman continued to berate the man she so detested. "The only way you'll get me out of your house, mister, is if you bodily force me out. If you do that I'll have you arrested for laying hands on me so fast your fat head will spin."

Defeat was apparent in the way Gibb's fists uncurled. He knew by the wild look in the small woman's eyes that she would do exactly what she threatened. He knew also the scandal he would create if he put his ailing wife's relative out of his home.

Ruing the day he ever met the Elliot family, Gibb gave Lucy one last hate-filled look before stomping off toward the door.

"You'd better hire a cook as soon as possible," Lucy called after him. "Your men are going to expect their meals."

Her answer was a slam of the bedroom door.

Lucy's body suddenly went limp, all the fight gone out of her. Ben helped her to the chair. "Boy, Lucy," he said, easing her down, "I never saw you so worked up before."

"I never saw one of my loved ones so abused before." Lucy rested her head on Ben's waist. "God forgive me, but I wanted to kill him."

"You're not the only one." Ben stroked her graying hair.

Lucy turned her attention to the wide-eyed Lark. "I guess I shocked you too, didn't I, honey?"

"You sure did, but you pleased me too." Lark grinned at the little woman. "You reminded me of a bantam rooster fighting a wild turkey. I didn't think for a minute that you would win, but you sure did."

"Yes, I did"—Lucy nodded—"but I guess we'd better not press our luck. Maybe it's best that you return to the cabin, Ben."

"I was thinking that too," Ben agreed. "But I'll stop by every couple of days to see how Larkie is doing and to make sure that no-good Gibb is behaving himself."

He reached down and squeezed Lark's hand, then kissed the top of Lucy's head. With a smile, he left them.

"Now, Lark, dear"—Lucy stood up—"let's get some of Doc's medicine in you."

Chapter Twenty-five

Twilight had set in when Ace sat down in front of the cookfire. The sun had disappeared behind the peaks of the mountains to the west, but there was still a little daylight left.

He placed his tin cup of coffee on the ground and reached into his vest pocket for the small white bag of tobacco and the packet of thin rolling papers. As he drew on his smoke and sipped his coffee, he gazed at the half-finished cabin he had been working on every chance he got for the past three months. His own building on his own land, he thought proudly. It was his mother's land, actually, but it would be his one day.

He had given a lot of thought to where he would erect the place. He was building his new home facing east at the bottom of a tall knoll. It would protect the house from the cold winds that swept off the mountains in the winter.

If he turned his head and looked behind him, he would see the river a quarter mile away, sliding smoothly along. He would also see three large holding corrals. One held the stallions he had captured, big handsome fellows, and one held the special mares he had been putting to the best stallions. They would drop some fine foals. The third pen, made of aspen poles, was for breaking and branding the wild ones.

Ace gazed out over the valley where his horses—piebalds, pintos, mustangs and other mixed breeds—grazed. These horses had been tamed and were left to shift for themselves. However, a young lad of ten watched that they didn't return to the wild.

Benny, the youngster was called. Benny Richards. He was a laughing, carefree boy, always ready to do what he was told. And so were his two older brothers. There was fifteen-year-old Drew, a quiet young man who still grieved over the loss of his parents. Then there was seventeen-year-old Matt. He was a hard worker and had a way with the wild horses they captured. He tamed them with gentleness, not brutal force. He was going to make a handsome young man, and was now at an age when he was very interested in the opposite sex.

Ace stared into the fire, remembering the day he'd met them. He had been on the trail three days and was only a day's ride from his mother's place the morning he came upon the brothers. They had been standing shoulder to shoulder, staring down at two fresh graves. When he dismounted and walked up to them, he noted that the youngest one had tears in his eyes and that the two older ones were choking back their own tears. When they became aware of his presence he asked quietly, "Indians?"

The oldest boy, a teenager, nodded. "Renegades. Me and my brothers were out hunting game when they struck. That's why we're still alive.

"When we got back, the cabin and barn were burned down and our cow and draft horse had been taken. And"—the boy had choked on the words—"Ma and Pa were dead. Scalped."

The youngest rubbed his knuckles across his wet eyes and, jerking a thumb toward a stand of aspen, said, "They missed our two horses, though."

Ace looked where the boy pointed and thought to himself that the renegades probably hadn't wanted the two old nags.

"What will you fellows do now?" he asked. "Do you have relatives to go to?"

The older boy shook his head. "We have an uncle in Missouri, but he has all the mouths he can feed now. Maybe we'll try some ranches. See if we can get hired on."

You two older ones might find jobs of some kind, Ace thought, *but no one would hire the button. He's too young to be of any help on a ranch.* He felt sure that the older brothers would not abandon their young sibling.

"While you think on it," he said, "let's ride on a piece and make some breakfast. I'm hungry; what about you fellows?" Actually, he'd had his morning meal at dawn, but the boys didn't have to know that.

"That sure sounds good to me," the youngest boy

had agreed readily, and received a cuff from the third brother.

He mounted and sat quietly while the three brothers gazed down at their parents' graves again, saying a last good-bye. They set off then, the youngest sharing Sam with him, and the other boys each riding one of the old horses.

Half an hour later they drew rein beside a wide creek of clear running water. While the oldest boy led the horses to drink, the middle brother built a fire from pieces of dead branches lying about. Ace put on a pot of coffee to brew, and the brothers sat down and watched him fry the last of his salt pork and some pan bread.

When he called them to eat, the oldest stuck out his hand and said, "We're much obliged for the grub, mister. Our name is Richards. The tadpole is Benny; he's ten years old. And that's Drew." He pointed at the other brother. "He's fifteen. And I'm Matt. I'm seventeen."

He had shaken hands with the three, then said, "I'm Ace Brandon." Then he added with a grin, "I'm thirty-five."

The growing boys had made short work of their breakfast. When they sat around the fire later, drinking coffee, Benny asked, "Are you a cowboy, Ace?"

"Naw." Ace shook his head. "I tried it once and didn't like it. I don't care for cows. They're dumb critters. I lean toward horses. A day's ride from here I intend to start a horse ranch."

Matt's head snapped up, an avid look in his eyes. "A horse ranch," he said softly. "Working with horses all day wouldn't even be work."

"You think not?" Ace laughed. "I'm talking about

chasing wild ones, taming them and breaking them to saddle so that I can sell them. It's backbreaking work chasing them down. You ride ten to twelve hours a day in heat and dust, and sometimes you get caught in storms. That doesn't sound very exciting to me."

"It does to me," Matt said. "I think it would be a grand feeling, running your horse at a flat-out gallop, chasing the beauties."

"Me too," Drew agreed eagerly. "It sounds like a lot of fun."

He had smiled to himself at their adventurous spirit. He had been the same way until life knocked some sense into him. How hard was life going to be on them? he wondered. If they were able to stay together, they could make it to manhood. At least Matt and Drew could, but what about freckle-faced Benny? Would his brothers be able to hold down jobs and take care of him as well?

Before he completely realized it, he'd made a decision. Matt and Drew were young and tough, and chasing wild horses would be a frolic for them. As for Benny, he could do odd chores around camp, and maybe learn how to cook for them.

When they were about ready to mount up and ride on, Ace casually asked, "Would you fellows be interested in helping me get my ranch started?"

All three swung around to stare pop-eyed at him. Finally Matt, his eyes glittering at the thought, exclaimed, "You mean chase the wild ones?"

"That's what I mean. Keep in mind, though, it's hard work. You'd probably have saddle sores on your rumps the first week."

"What's a few sores on your behind," Drew said,

laughing, "when all you have to do is ride all day?"

"Don't forget there's the taming and branding of them. That's no picnic, I assure you."

"That wouldn't bother us, would it?" Benny looked at his brothers.

There was silence for a moment, and then Matt said kindly, "You're not ready to chase horses yet, Benny."

When the youngster's lips drooped and it looked as if he might cry, Ace explained, "I have another job in mind for you. One that is equally important. I would like for you to look after the horses we drive in, see to it that no wolves or bears get to them."

Benny's face brightened. "I could do that. I'm a pretty good shot with a rifle, ain't I, Matt?"

Matt shrugged, then teased, "I guess you could hit a bear if he stood still for you."

"You know I'm better than that." Benny threw himself at Matt. Both were laughing as they rolled around on the ground.

As they mounted up and rode away from camp, it was evident from Matt's and Drew's relaxed bodies that the weight of deciding what was to become of them had been lifted from their shoulders. They still grieved for their dead parents, but they also talked about the great adventure that lay ahead of them.

They had ridden all day, stopping twice at a stream to let the horses drink. At the last stop, Ace had passed out strips of beef jerky for their lunch. It was the only food he had left.

It was close to sunset when they entered Utah, and an hour later when they arrived at his mother's place. His mother, Betty, had been sitting on the front porch, and when they dismounted and she recognized him, she hurried down the steps, greeting him with loud cries of pleasure.

"It's about time you showed your face," she chastised as Ace grabbed her around the waist and lifted her up to spin her around.

"I was getting quite concerned about you," she said when she was set back on her feet. "I didn't know if you were alive or dead."

"As you see, I'm very much alive." He hugged her shoulders. He turned to the boys then, who stood watching the reunion with smiling faces. "Ma, I want you to meet three friends of mine."

Betty shook hands with each boy as she was introduced. When Ace came to Benny, her eyes softened and she smoothed the tangled hair off his brow. "I bet you're hungry, Benny." She put an arm around his narrow shoulders. "Come along inside," she said, leading the way up the porch steps. "I have a big pot of ham hocks and pinto beans I'll heat up."

"Do you have corn bread to go with it?" Benny asked hopefully.

"I sure do." Betty opened the kitchen's screen door. "I've also got a pitcher of cold milk to go with it."

All four males ate with hearty appetites. After Ace had rolled a cigarette, he told his mother of his plans for a horse ranch, and how the boys had lost their parents.

"I'm sorry about your parents, boys," Betty said gently, smoothing Benny's hair again. "Do you have relatives to go to?"

"They're going to be working for me," Ace answered before Matt could explain that they had no one. "They're going to help me chase down the wild ones. I hope that by this fall I'll have a herd to drive to Denver and sell."

"I can't tell you how happy I am that you are finally settling down," Betty said, her pleasure evident in her shining eyes.

Matt and Drew were eager to talk more of the horses they would capture, but Ace saw that young Benny was about to nod off. "I think we're about ready to turn in, Ma," he said. "We had a long ride today."

"Well, let's see now. Where can I bed you all down?" Betty said. "There are only two bedrooms, you know."

"Don't worry about it, Ma. If you'll give us some blankets, me and the boys will be real comfortable sleeping on the hay in the barn loft."

"I expect you would, but maybe Benny can sleep in your old room, Ace."

When Matt pulled the half-asleep Benny from his chair and followed Betty out of the kitchen, Ace realized how lonesome his mother must have been, living alone at the old homestead. Benny would be the recipient of much affection and tender care.

"Help yourself from the linen closet, Ace," Betty called back as she opened the door to his old room. "You'll find plenty of blankets and quilts."

A few minutes later he and the two brothers were comfortably stretched out on a pile of fragrant hay. They fell asleep almost immediately.

They were up at the first flush of dawn. Betty had breakfast waiting for them. "Where's the sprout?" he asked as they sat down at the table.

"He's still sleeping. The poor child was worn out. I thought it best to let him rest."

If he let her, Ma would spoil Benny rotten, Ace thought as he dug into bacon and eggs. When each of them had drunk two cups of coffee and he had smoked a cigarette, he and the boys rode off on their first hunt for wild horses. This had been the beginning of the routine they would follow seven days a week.

Ace tossed his cigarette butt into the campfire. The boys had long since rolled up in their blankets; it was time he did the same. Tomorrow they would start breaking the horses they had gathered all week.

As tired as he was, though, he dreaded going to bed. He could keep his thoughts off Lark during the day, but once he lay down and all was quiet, she came to him. Her soft body would press against his, and her smooth arms would wrap around his shoulders.

Every night he asked himself the same questions: Where was she? Was she all right? Why hadn't he insisted that she tell him where she was going?

Chapter Twenty-six

The last day of July was stormy. The wind lifted Lark's long hair, ruffling and tangling her curls. She was big with child now, and she stepped carefully as she walked away from the cookhouse.

It was her habit to spend some time with the cook, who had been rehired two months ago.

She had liked Randy right off; no one knew his last name. He was somewhere in his mid-fifties, tall and lanky, with thinning hair. He had a droll sense of humor, and during the time she spent with him she was able not to think of Ace. As she sat with the cook, drinking coffee and chatting, she didn't wonder where Ace was, what he was doing.

Did he ever give her a thought? she wondered as she approached the house and climbed the steps to the porch. Did he ever recall the hours they had spent together in the cookhouse all winter?

She doubted it. Making love to her had been a job to him; probably he was so busy chasing wild horses, she never entered his mind.

Lark paused on the edge of the porch and shook her head at the cursing and yelling going on inside the house. It was a three-way screaming match. The combatants were her aunt and husband and the Mexican woman Cletus had hired to keep the house clean.

It hadn't taken Cletus long to discover that Rosa Santiago wasn't the housekeeper that his wife was. Lark remembered how he had ordered her to oversee the woman's work. But Aunt Lucy had refused to let Lark guide the woman about the way Cletus wanted his house kept.

"He'll only wind up accusing you if everything isn't done to his satisfaction," she explained. "You'd get all nervous again and maybe have a set-back." He had demanded then that Aunt Lucy keep an eye on Rosa, see that she cleaned his house properly. She had refused, and it had been a bone of contention between them ever since.

The argument today was because Rosa hadn't swept underneath Cletus's bed, and he was tossing insults at both women. And they, as usual, were hurling them back.

Lark sighed and took a step forward just as Gibb came bursting through the door. His heavy body rammed into her, and suddenly she was falling backward, down the stairs.

As her head hit the gravel path, she heard Aunt Lucy screaming; then everything went black.

*　　*　　*

She came to in her bed with three people looking down at her. Aunt Lucy's eyes were swimming with tears, Dr. Randal looked concerned, and Cletus looked angry.

She started to speak, to ask what had happened, but her words were cut off. Her stomach had contorted with a cramp that made her cry out. *Dear Lord*, she thought, *am I having my baby or am I losing it? The little one shouldn't arrive for another two months.*

"You can leave, Mr. Gibb," Dr. Randal said, rolling up his sleeves. "I'm going to examine your wife now. And you, Mrs. Santiago," he said to the housekeeper, "heat me a lot of hot water and tear some sheets into strips."

When Rosa started toward the door, Gibb pushed her aside and stomped out ahead of her. The Mexican woman started to lay into him but stopped. Her face said that she had realized that this was no time for them to have a screaming match.

Dr. Randal made his examination and reported to Lucy and Lark that everything looked fine, that it didn't look as though there would be any problem bringing the little one into the world. "It should arrive in three or four hours."

"Three or four hours," Lark exclaimed, reaching for Lucy's hand.

"I know it's not easy giving birth, Lark," Dr. Randal said gently, "but that's how it's been since Adam and Eve. You're a strong young woman now, and when you hold your baby in your arms, every pain will be worth it."

An hour later as yet another pain gripped Lark, she wondered about Randal's words. She wanted to cry out to Ace, but knew she didn't dare. Aunt Lucy and the doctor would think it very strange that she wanted Ace and not her husband at her side.

The afternoon wore on and three hours passed. Lark was exhausted and was sure she couldn't go on. The pains were coming close together now, with no rest between them. She looked at her aunt with beseeching eyes.

"I think it will be over soon, honey," Lucy said gently, and looked at the doctor for confirmation.

He nodded. "The next pain you have, Lark, bear down hard. I think one more contraction should do it. I can see the baby's head."

"Is it alive? Is it all right?" Lark panted.

"It appears to be. But keep in mind that it's a seven-month baby and will be small."

"We don't care how small it is. Just so it's all right." Lucy looked hopefully at the doctor. "We can make it grow big."

Lark labored another half hour before giving birth to a little boy. He was small, only about four and a half pounds. However, the lusty cry he let loose when slapped lightly on his little bottom said he was very healthy.

With a wide smile Dr. Randal handed the infant to Lucy to wash and dress, then turned to attend the spent Lark. When he had finished making her as comfortable as possible, he went in search of Rosa. Lark's bed linens had to be changed.

He found Gibb in the kitchen also. "Well, what is it?" he demanded gruffly.

"You have a son, Mr. Gibbs. He arrived early, as you know, and is on the small side right now. But he is healthy."

"A son, by God." Gibb slapped his hand on the table, a look of satisfaction on his face. "I'll go see him now."

"You can see him after Rosa has changed Lark's bedding and the baby is cleaned up," Randal said firmly.

Gibb made no reply, only glared at the doctor. He had learned that he always lost his arguments with the sharp-tongued man.

Twenty minutes later Lark was lying between clean linens and wore a fresh gown Rosa had helped her into. She looked eagerly at her aunt as Lucy approached the bed, the blanket-wrapped baby in her arms.

"What's wrong, Auntie?" she asked anxiously when she noticed the bewildered look on Lucy's face. "Is my son all right?"

"He's fine, honey," Lucy said, laying the infant in Lark's waiting arms. She looked over her shoulder to where the doctor and Rosa were engaged in conversation. She leaned down then and whispered, "Lark, the little one is the spitting image of Ace Brandon. How can that be?"

"It's a long, unbelievable story, Aunt Lucy. I'll explain everything to you when we're alone and have more time," Lark answered as she gently stroked the fine, black curls on her son's head. "All I can say now is—" Lark was interrupted as Gibb came bursting into the room.

"I've come to see my son," he said loudly, making the baby jerk and whimper.

"You're going to give your son a heart attack if you don't lower your voice," Dr. Randal said coldly.

"He'll have to get used to my voice," Gibb remarked more softly. He leaned over the bed and pulled the blanket away from the baby's face. "He's awful little." He frowned. "It don't look like he'll be the size of his father."

"He'll be fine. A couple months from now he'll be double the size he is now."

Gibb straightened up and asked, "When can she get up, Doc?"

"If you mean your wife, it will depend on how long it takes her to regain her strength. She had a hard labor. I imagine ten days to two weeks should see her on her feet."

"That long?" Gibb said grumpily, then gave Lucy a malicious look. "That's the day you get out of my house, old woman. And that useless Mexican can get too." He started waddling toward the door, still talking. "And the cook goes too. I'm gonna get things back to normal around here." He slammed the door behind him, making the infant whimper again.

Dr. Randal closed his bag. As he shrugged into his coat, he looked at Lark and warned, "You'd better take your baby and get away from that man as soon as possible. He'll be the death of you if you stay here."

"She'll not stay here, Doctor," Lucy said, fire in her eyes. "We'll be gone just as soon as Lark is able to travel."

"Good. I'll look in on you tomorrow, Lark."

He was gone then, and Lucy and Lark were alone. Lucy sat down on the edge of the bed and helped Lark put her fussing son to her breast. "What will you name him, Lark?" she asked when she saw the baby greedily having his first feeding of his mother's milk.

"I've always liked the name Aaron."

"That's a good, strong name." Lucy nodded, then took Lark's hand. "Now tell me why Ace Brandon is the father of your child," she said quietly.

Lark sighed, then began the lengthy story.

When she finished, Lucy said, "So you fell in love with each other."

A sad smile stirred Lark's lips. "Let's just say that I fell in love. When Ace told Cletus what he thought was a lie, that I was with child, he took the promised money and rode away." A tear slipped down her cheek. "He has no idea he has a son."

"I'm so sorry, Lark." Lucy stroked her sweat-damp hair. "Ace didn't strike me as a man who could just ride off without a word of where he was going."

"It's simple enough, Auntie," Lark said wearily. "Making love to me was only a job to Ace. I think he grew fond of me, but that was all."

"All right, honey, that's all behind you." Lucy became all business. "We've got to make plans about how to get you away from here before that monster starts putting you to a workload that will kill you."

"That's been my problem all along. I didn't know where to go. Then there was my poor health."

"Well, we've got to get away from here. We've got to think of something. We've got to go somewhere that he will never think of looking for you."

"Maybe Thad could come up with an idea," Lark said. "I'm sure we can trust him."

"That's an idea. Your uncle will be coming down tomorrow to see how we are. I'll have him find Thad and bring him to the house."

Lark was suddenly animated. Her eyes now alive with hope, she said, "If Thad can come up with a plan, Ace left me enough money to get us settled someplace. I think there's enough to buy a small house in some town. I'll find a job as housekeeper there, and you and Uncle Ben can take care of Aaron."

Lucy became caught up in Lark's excitement. "I'll tell Ben to get our clothes and our few belongings together. You and I will do the same thing here."

Lark laughed bitterly. "It won't take long to gather up my things. Except for my Indian jacket and moccasins and the sweater Ace gave me for Christmas, the rest of my clothing should have been thrown away years ago."

"Don't forget the baby's clothing." Lucy smiled. "That will make quite a bundle. We did nothing but make clothes for him while we were waiting for his arrival."

She stood up and, taking the sleeping Aaron away from Lark's breast, said, "You rest now, Lark. Get some sleep. I'm going to my room to do some thinking."

Chapter Twenty-seven

Ace watched his mother fuss over Benny as they sat at her table finishing off supper with berry pie and coffee.

They looked forward to Sunday evenings. That was the one day in the week when they had a good meal. The rest of the week they made do with what young Benny put together.

For the first three weeks, his cooking was hardly edible. The meat was burned on the outside and raw in the middle. His biscuits were so hard there was a danger of breaking a tooth when you bit into one.

However, with Ma's guidance and written instructions for Benny, they were now able to digest most of what he served them. At any rate, they were all so beat at the end of the day, they hardly knew what they were putting into their mouths anyway.

Their hard work was paying off, though. They now

had over two hundred horses. Half, however, were penned up in a dead-end canyon, waiting to be broken to the saddle before they could go to market.

Ace rolled a cigarette and struck a match to it. As the smoke curled from his nose, he looked through it at Matt. "How many three-year-olds do you think we have ready for sale?"

Matt was thoughtful for a minute, then answered, "I think about fifty tamed ones, and about the same number of wild ones from the canyon. Why do you want to know?"

"I've been thinking about driving a herd into Denver. See what we can get for them."

All three Richards leaned forward, their eyes sparking with excitement. "When, Ace?" Matt asked.

"I think in a couple of days. That should give us enough time to cut the three-year-olds away from the others, get them ready to travel."

"Boy, oh, boy, I can't wait to see a real city." Matt's eyes gleamed at the thought. "The only town we've ever been to is the little place a few miles from our homestead. Beside the livery at the end of the street, there were only three places of business. There was a saloon, a mercantile and a—" He gave Betty an uncomfortable look and mumbled, "One of those places."

Betty turned her head to hide her tickled smile when Benny asked, "What do you mean, one of those places, Matt?"

When Ace saw that the embarrassed Matt wasn't going to answer his brother, he said, "I think he means a schoolhouse, Benny."

"Oh, that. It's not in town, Matt." He looked at his brother. "The schoolhouse is a mile out of town."

"I guess I forgot," Matt mumbled, wishing he could give Benny's hair a good yank.

"Will we stay awhile in Denver, Ace?" Drew asked.

"I don't know. Long enough for you boys to get your hair cut. All three of you look pretty woolly. You need some new duds too. The seats of your pants are so thin you're in danger of showing your bare rumps."

"I can't wait to buy some candy." Benny's freckled face glowed with anticipated pleasure.

A small frown creased Ace's forehead. He hadn't planned on the youngster going with them. He intended to spend most of his time in the Lady Chance. He wanted to renew his acquaintance with the dancers there. After a couple of nights of romping with them, he'd forget all about Lark. He'd be able to sleep peacefully at night again.

He didn't want to let the boy down, though, to see the disappointment that would kill the light in his eyes. Benny had worked hard at the job given him. He had managed to turn into a fair cook, and he was diligent at keeping an eye on the horses that were allowed out of the pens.

The youngster was part of the crew. His brothers would have to look after him.

"What about the rest of the herd?" Drew asked; he was the thoughtful one of the brothers. "Someone has to keep an eye on them. And hay has to be brought to the ones penned up in the canyon."

"I've been thinking about that," Ace said, then looked at Betty. "Ma, could you spare your handyman, old Elisha, to look after the horses while we're gone?"

"He'd jump at the chance." Betty chuckled as she refilled Benny's glass with more milk. "He has so little to do around here, he's bored half the time." She gave Ace a sober look. "You make sure you watch out for Benny. I don't want you taking him into the Lady Chance."

"What's the Lady Chance, Ace?" Benny wanted to know.

"It's a saloon, huh, Ace?" Matt said, his eyes shimmering in the hope of finally being able to enter such an establishment.

Betty read what was going through the teenager's mind and spoke up before her son could. "That's right, Matt, and no place for you and Drew to visit."

She looked at Ace for confirmation. He nodded. "Ma's right. Next year when you're eighteen, Matt, you can go with me and have a drink. Drew, I'm sorry, but you've got to wait another three years." Drew only shrugged indifferently. A saloon held no appeal for him.

"What about me, Ace?" Benny piped up. "When can I go have a drink?"

"Well, tadpole"—Ace ruffled his hair—"you've got eight long years before you can visit a saloon."

When Benny complained that that was a long time to wait, Betty soothed, "Don't fret, Benny, you can still have a good time in Denver. There are a lot of stores you can walk around in."

"I guess so," Benny said, his tone saying he wasn't fully convinced.

"You fellows had better turn in." Ace stubbed out his smoke. "I want to get back to the horses before daylight."

Matt and Drew stood up and said good night to Betty. When they left for the barn, Benny said a sleepy good night and went to his room.

"They're nice boys," Betty said. "So well mannered."

"Yes, they are. I've grown fond of them. They're beginning to feel like family."

"Speaking of family"—Betty stood up—"a letter came for you last week. I think it's from Roxy."

"I hope my little cousin is all right," Ace said, taking the envelope and tearing it open. He scanned the contents rapidly:

Dear Ace,

I hope it doesn't take this letter too long to get to you. The reason I'm writing is that Belle is getting married. She wants me and you to stand up with her. She says we're the only family she has.

She met Harry Grayson six months ago when he came to the Lady Chance seeking a job as a dealer. He is almost as good as you with a deck of cards. Anyway, they fell in love and want to get married as soon as possible. Belle says that she will wait a month for you to show up. I hope you do, real soon. I've missed my rascal cousin.

The family is fine. Jory has grown so much you won't recognize him. Tanner says hello. Your old room is waiting for you. Love, Roxy.

"It must be good news, the way you're smiling," Betty said as Ace folded the letter.

"It is. An old friend of mine is getting married. She wants me and Roxy to stand up with her."

"That's nice. Is everything all right with Roxy and her family?"

"She's fine. Read her letter." Ace slid the two sheets to her as he stood up. "I'm going to bed now, Ma. I'll see you in the morning."

As he stretched out on his bed of hay Ace chuckled at the idea of Belle Lange, madam of Denver's busiest brothel, getting married. But in his heart he knew she would make a fine wife.

"Keep them from balling up at the river crossing," Ace called out as he reined around and chased after a pinto that had broken away from the herd.

He and the boys had been on the trail for two days, driving the horses ahead of them. Once they crossed the river, they would be only a couple of miles from Denver.

The horses were tired and gave Ace and the boys no trouble as they swam to the opposite shore. When the last one lunged out of the river, water sluicing down its hide, Ace stood up in the saddle and yelled, "Haze them out."

It was high noon when they entered Denver's main street, sun-baked in the summer, muddy in the winter. The town lay asleep under the glaring noonday heat as the horses trotted through on their way to the outskirts of town. There were large holding pens there, used mostly by ranchers when they drove cattle in for loading onto trains.

There were few people on the street, none that Ace recognized. When they rode past the Lady Chance, it looked pretty dead in there also, from what he could see through the window from the street. He wasn't surprised to see nothing going on at the pleasure house. The girls would be sleeping after a busy night.

Old Cal, who ran the livery, must have heard them coming, for he had removed the poles from a portion of the corral and waited for the horses to come pushing inside.

"Them horses yourn?" The old man gave Ace a wide, toothless smile when he recognized him through the roiling clouds of dust.

"They sure are, Cal. Every last one of them. Me and my crew chased them down and tamed them. I'm hoping to sell these beauties."

"By cracky, I never thought to see the day handsome Ace Brandon would do hard work." The old man cackled. "How come you ain't dealin' cards in some saloon?"

"Well, Cal, I realized one day that there was no future in playing poker, and I decided to do something about it. I'm building myself a horse ranch. This is my first herd to sell. Do you know of anyone looking for some fine horseflesh?"

"Ranchers are always lookin' for good stock, and the army back East is on the lookout for horses too. In fact, one of their buyers came to town yesterday. He checked in at the boardinghouse, but he spends most of his time at the Lady Chance. He's most likely there now."

"Thanks, Cal," Ace said as he dismounted and ran to help Matt and Drew replace the poles in the corral. After he checked the long tin trough to see that it was full of water, he said to the brothers, "Let's put up our horses here at the livery and walk back into town. I've got to stop at the Lady Chance a minute. Then we'll grab something to eat and find a place for you fellows to stay while we're here."

When they had walked the three blocks to the saloon, Ace led the way up the wide steps to its porch. "You boys wait for me out here." He motioned to a line of chairs set against the wall. "I won't be long."

He stepped into the saloon, resplendent with a long mirror behind a carved mahogany bar, chandeliers and paintings of nude women. Just as I left it, he thought, his gaze going over the many games of chance in progress at the poker tables. Four men sat at one table, their eyes on the cards they held in their hands.

He was walking toward the bar when his name was squealed. With a happy laugh he caught Belle's plump body in his arms as she came hurtling toward him.

"I told Roxy that you'd make it in time for my wedding." Belle gave him a smacking kiss on his whiskered cheek. "Let me take a good look at you. Devilishly handsome, as ever," she said, smiling up at Ace, "but you smell pretty rank."

"Hey, I've been on the trail for two days."

"So what have you been up to all this time?" Belle asked, linking her arm in his and leading him toward the bar.

Over the glass of whiskey she poured him, Ace brought Belle up to date, ending with his venture into capturing and gentling wild horses. "Me and my crew just drove fifty head into town to sell."

"How many men do you have helping you?"

Ace grinned. "Would you believe two teenagers and a ten-year-old?"

Belle shook her head. "Just you and two teenagers? It is hard to believe."

"Well, it's true, and speaking of them, I've got to

find them a place to stay while we're here, and take them to the diner and feed them."

"Why don't you do both right here in the saloon? If you remember, we have a kitchen, and Roxy's old quarters upstairs are empty."

"I don't know about that." Ace pushed his hat forward and scratched the back of his head. "I promised Ma that I wouldn't take them into the saloon."

"You wouldn't have to. The kitchen has a back door, and there are back stairs to Roxy's old rooms."

"That's right. I'd forgotten." Ace's eyes crinkled with affection as he squeezed Belle's shoulders. "You've solved both my problems. And as I remember, Pee Wee is a fine cook."

"That he is. I'll go tell him now to start four steaks to frying."

"And I'll take the boys upstairs to get cleaned up."

"After you've cleaned up and shaved, check out your suits. Decide which one you're going to wear when you stand up with me." Giving him a bright, excited smile, she added, "I'm getting married tomorrow."

Ace could only stare after Belle as she went through the kitchen door. Tomorrow? That hardly gave him time to catch his breath.

Chapter Twenty-eight

It was near dark when Lark walked out on the porch and sat down in a chair that was half-hidden by heavy vines.

This wasn't the first time she had been out of bed since Aaron's birth. She had been up and walking around in her room for the past two days. Ragged Feather had told Uncle Ben that she would regain her strength faster that way than lying in bed.

And the old Indian was right. Each day she felt a little stronger. It was important that she regain as much strength as possible in the ten days to two weeks Dr. Randal had given her. She knew that Cletus would demand that she start working again on the tenth day. However, with Aunt Lucy butting heads with him, she felt sure her relative would get her the additional four-day reprieve.

Lark breathed deep of the pure night air. This was

her first time out of the house since baby Aaron was born. Cletus had ridden off right after supper, and if he kept to his usual routine, he would be gone for an hour or two.

She leaned her head back and gazed at the stars that were beginning to show against the dark sky. Thad had been gone for five days, and no one knew where he had gone or when he'd return, if ever. When Uncle Ben was making inquiries of the ranch hands, Newt had said that he thought maybe Thad had gone to visit his folks. None of the men, however, knew where his family lived.

Lark breathed a deep sigh. She was depending on the young man to help her get away, to find a place for her and her family to settle. She couldn't just strike out with a newborn with no destination in mind. She couldn't rely on Uncle Ben. He depended on *her*.

If only I knew where Ace was, Lark thought at the end of a long sigh. *He may not love me, but he would help me. But no,* she thought, *he mustn't know about baby Aaron.*

Lark was about to set the rocker in motion when she caught sight of a figure slipping from behind the cookhouse. It paused a minute, then began edging toward the house. From the stealthy movement, it was plain whoever it was didn't want to be seen lurking around.

What did he want? What was he after? The house was in darkness. Did he plan to sneak inside and steal anything he found of value?

Panic gripped her when the figure moved from behind a tree and darted to the side of the house. She was about to rise and go inside and bar all the doors when she heard the sound of galloping hooves coming toward the ranch. It had to be Cletus. No one else would be galloping that way in the dark.

Lark started to stand up again, her fear of Cletus finding her outside greater than her uneasiness about the man standing only a few feet from where she sat. Again she sat down, however. Cletus had ridden the lathered stallion into the yard and brought him to a rearing halt close to the porch steps. She held her breath and shrank back in the shadows when he dismounted and sat down on the bottom step.

While she wondered about his strange behavior, the man at the corner of the house appeared suddenly. He walked to Cletus and sat down beside him. Lark leaned forward when the man began to speak.

"I got the message that you wanted to see Half Moon. I am here. What do you want?"

Lark unconsciously moved to the edge of her seat. She, too, wanted to know what business her husband had with the Indian.

Without hesitation Gibb answered. "I need a woman who can suckle my baby son. His mother is going away, and I hoped that you might know of a woman who could take her place."

Lark almost gasped aloud her outrage. What did this cruel, manipulative man have in mind? Did he think that she would willingly hand over her son to some unknown Indian woman and ride away without protest? She knew he wasn't very bright, but she didn't think he was that stupid.

A thought came to her that left her weak. Could Cletus possibly be planning to do away with her and Aunt Lucy and Uncle Ben?

She listened closely when the Indian began to speak again. "I know of no such woman at this time. Me and several braves have broken away from the village. As you probably know, we are renegades. There is one woman among us who will be dropping her baby in a couple weeks or so. She will be able to give your son nourishment. You can have her . . . at a price."

Overwhelmed at all she had heard, her head buzzing with the possible danger to her and her relatives, Lark paid no attention to the dickering going on between her husband and the Indian. She had heard all that was important to her. She must take her son and get away from this madman.

The sun was high and hot as Ace lounged against a supporting post of the saloon. He had been waiting close to twenty minutes for his cousin Roxy and her husband to come riding down the street. His mood was growing darker by the minute. Why did Belle want to get married anyway? She had gone all these years without a wedding band on her finger.

He ran a finger around the inside collar of his pristine white shirt and shrugged his shoulders uncomfortably inside the pearl gray suit jacket. It had been a long time since he had been all decked out in tight-fitting trousers, string tie and polished boots. He longed for his comfortable denims and loose shirts and his old, worn, scuffed boots that didn't pinch his feet.

Ace spit out onto the street. He guessed he could survive one day of being uncomfortable. The only things worse than his clothing were his raging headache and roiling stomach. How much had he drunk last night, anyway? Too much, that was for sure.

His mind went over the events that had taken place since his arrival in Denver.

He settled the boys in Roxy's old quarters over the saloon and waited while they washed up and brushed some trail dirt off their clothes. He led them then down the alley to the back door of the kitchen. There they devoured the steaks Pee Wee placed before them. When all three were rubbing full bellies, Ace handed Matt some bills and told them to go look over the town. "Behave yourselves," he cautioned, "and keep an eye on Benny."

When they had left, full of excitement, eager to check out the first big city they had ever been in, he carried water to his old room and took a long bath.

He had just toweled off and slid his legs into a pair of trousers he had taken from his crowded wardrobe when a rapping sounded on his door. He pulled on a white shirt before opening the door.

"Cousin Roxy." He laughed as the beautiful, black-haired woman threw herself at him.

"I've missed you," she cried as Ace gave her a loud kiss on the cheek. She let out a screech then and hit him on the shoulder as he deliberately rubbed his whiskered jaw on her tender cheek.

"You're as ornery as ever." She hit him again before twisting out of his arms. Her eyes twinkled with affection as she said, "You'd better shave that brush off before the girls see you. Otherwise they'll run away."

"I doubt that." Ace grinned confidently. "Have you hired any new dancers while I've been away?"

"A couple. One won't interest you, though. The other one is just the kind you like. She's a tall blonde. Her name is Dolly."

"Can't wait to meet her," Ace said as he lathered his shaving brush, then spread soap across his jaw and cheeks. As he shaved they brought each other up to date on what had been happening in their lives since the last time they had seen each other.

When Ace told Roxy about the horse ranch he was building, she said after a pause, "I think a horse ranch is a wonderful idea, Ace, but that kind of life will be so different from what you're used to. Aren't you afraid you'll tire of it and want to get back to the excitement you've enjoyed for so many years?"

"I won't," Ace answered promptly. "My old life was leading me nowhere. I realized one day that it was time I settled down to something that would give me a worthwhile future. A well-run ranch would support me in my old age."

Roxy studied her cousin a minute, then said with a half-teasing note, "I wonder who the woman is that started you thinking so seriously."

"A woman had nothing to do with it," Ace snapped.

Roxy thought his denial came too quickly, and she pressed him further. "Are you sure? Your face has taken on a bright shade of red."

"You're loco. Have you ever known me to let a woman influence me in anything?" Ace demanded, toweling off his face and glaring at her in the shaving mirror attached to the wall.

"I think it's possible the right woman, a good woman, could change your bullheaded thinking." Her eyes full of mischief, Roxy asked, "Did you meet a good woman on your travels, cousin?"

Lark's lovely face swam before Ace. He had met a good woman, a special kind of woman. And she had encouraged him to build up a horse ranch instead of *running cattle. He had never paid any attention to what his now-dead wife had suggested they do.*

He rinsed off his straight razor, did the same to his shaving mug. As he buttoned up his shirt he said, "Stop your foolish talk and take me to meet the new dancer."

Ace thought of the new dancer, Dolly, as time dragged on and Roxy still hadn't made an appearance.

Dolly was tall, with long legs and blond hair. She would have been very lovely except for the sharpness of her blue eyes. They signaled to him that she knew her way around men, knew just how to satisfy them.

Ace remembered with a wry smile the frustration that followed their meeting. They had a couple of drinks at the bar, played roulette for an hour or so, then went to his room.

As soon as the door closed behind them, Dolly was all over him, unbuttoning his shirt, undoing his trousers. In a flash she was out of her skimpy dress and they were falling onto the bed.

Her body was soft and her lips hot as they moved from his chest down past his waist. There she paused, giving him a look of surprise. His manhood hadn't stirred, was as flat as one of Benny's pancakes.

"What's wrong?" she asked.

Frustrated and embarrassed, he answered apologetically, "I guess I'm tired from herding horses all day."

"Well, then," Dolly purred, "I can fix that."

As her lips came down over him, Ace thought of Lark and wanted to push Dolly's head away. From the time they'd stepped into his room, Lark had been with them. Her tear-wet eyes had gazed at him accusingly.

He endured Dolly's ministrations until she gave up

*in defeat. "You're more than tired, mister," she said
sarcastically. "You're dead."*

You're wrong, lady, *he thought as Dolly pulled her
red dress over her head.* Lark makes me come alive
with only one stroke of her hand.

*When the new dancer flounced out of the room and
he still couldn't shake Lark from his mind, he went to
the bar. There, he drank until the bartender had to help
him to his bed.*

As he continued to wait for Roxy, he came to a
conclusion. He must find Lark, determine why she
had such a hold on his mind.

A moment later Ace straightened away from the
porch post. He recognized Roxy's surrey coming
down the street. Jory sat beside her, grinning and
waving to him.

"Hi, button." He smiled at the boy and ruffled his
hair. He scowled at Roxy then and half snarled, "It's
about time you got here."

"Boy, you're in a mood," she griped and, clucking
at the horse, sent the delicate vehicle down the street
toward the church.

As the surrey rolled down the street, stirring up
clouds of dirt, Thad watched Ace climb into the
fancy rig with narrowed, suspicious eyes. He had
been about to cross the street to greet his idol when
the pretty woman and young boy drew up. From the
way the youngster greeted Ace and the cross looks
exchanged between Ace and the woman, it looked to
him as though they had known each other for a long
time. In fact, they acted like a married couple, a pair
that had been wed for some time.

"Who are you gawking at?" asked his companion,

a man in his mid-twenties who looked much like Thad.

"Do you know that man who just rode away with that woman and young boy?"

"Nope. Do you?"

"I thought I did," Thad answered, a bitter note in his voice. "I guess I was mistaken."

"If we're gonna drop in on Aunt Bertha, we'd better get going."

"Yeah, Coy," Thad answered, and followed his brother to where their horses were hitched in front of the mercantile.

As they rode out of town, going in the direction of the Sheldon farm, Thad continued to think about Ace and his two companions. It appeared to him that all this time Ace had had a family of which he never spoke. But why would he keep it a secret? Why would he stay away from a wife and son for such a long time? Had he and his wife quarreled? Had Ace been lying about building up a horse ranch?

"Damn it," he muttered under his breath, "couldn't he have told me? And did he have to just ride away without saying good-bye?"

The more Thad pondered, the more his liking and respect for Ace dropped down. The fancily dressed man he'd seen today was a far cry from the man Ace had pretended to be at the ranch.

When he and Coy reached the farm, Thad's thoughts were interrupted by a loud whoop and the sound of his name being called out. He turned around to see his cousin, fifteen-year-old Paul Sheldon, loping toward him. His mother and Paul's mother had been Franklins before they married.

They had homesteads about thirty miles apart.

The two families were close-knit, and it showed in the rowdy, though affectionate, way the cousins greeted each other. "What are you fellows doing in Denver?" Paul asked. "Don't you work for that rancher anymore, Thad?"

"Yeah, I still do. I came home to spend a week with the family, and thought that on the way back to the ranch I'd stop in and spend a while with your ma and pa."

"They'll be happy to see you. Let's go on inside."

Bertha's greeting of her nephews was a little more subdued than her son's had been, but hearty nevertheless. When she had made inquires about her sister's health, she seated Thad and Coy at the table and served them vegetable soup and thick slices of fresh-baked bread while Paul went to find the rest of the family.

The others came bursting into the kitchen just as Thad and Coy finished eating. They were a healthy, hearty-looking group, from their uncle Ben right down to six-year-old Sissy.

As they all sat on the porch, catching up on family news, Ace wasn't far from Thad's mind. What puzzled him greatly was that though Ace appeared to be married and had a son, he had seemed sincere in his desire that Thad stick around the ranch to look after Lark.

Lark did need to be looked after; Thad felt sure of that. Suddenly he wanted to get back to the ranch. Something told him that all was not well there.

Against his relatives' protests, he explained that he had been away from the ranch for a week and had to get back. They understood that—a man's job was important—and after shaking hands with everyone, he rode away with several hours of daylight left to guide him along the way.

Chapter Twenty-nine

"Thad's back." Ben burst into the ranch house's kitchen. "I just saw him ride up."

"Thank God," Lark and Lucy cried in unison.

"Go fetch him, Ben," Lucy ordered.

Ben turned to leave the kitchen just as Thad stepped up on the porch. "Come in, come in," Ben welcomed the teenager. "Are we glad to see you!" He pulled a chair away from the table. "Take a seat." When Thad sat down, Ben asked, "Where have you been, anyway?"

"I went to visit my folks. I hadn't seen them for a while. What's been going on while I was away?"

"A lot, son, a lot. First off, does Lark look any different to you?"

Thad looked at Lark, who sat smiling at him. After he studied her a minute he said, "She looks the same to me, only a little thinner maybe."

"She is thinner, boy. She had her baby while you were away. It came two months early."

"Congratulations, Lark." Thad gave her a wide smile. "What did you have, a boy or a girl?"

"A little boy. I named him Aaron."

"He's a handsome little fellow," Ben added proudly.

"I expect Gibb is happy," Thad muttered.

"That no-good polecat," Ben grated out. "Wait until I tell you what he's up to."

"Anything that man would do wouldn't surprise me."

"This might. At least it will make you madder than hell. Lark overheard him making plans with a renegade Indian to bring him an Indian woman to nurse and take care of little Aaron. He said that Lark was leaving him."

Thad sat in stunned silence. The man was more evil than he'd thought any man could be.

He looked at Lark and said, "You must take your aunt and uncle and baby and get away from here as soon as possible. I think that man is planning to kill you and your aunt and uncle."

"We know that, Thad," Lark said, "but we have no idea where to go. This country is strange to us. We've been waiting for you to return to suggest someplace we could go that Cletus wouldn't think of looking."

"I've just come from Denver, but that would be the first place he would look. Any other large city would be too long a trek with an infant."

Tears stung Lark's eyes. "I can't let him have my baby," she said between sobs.

"Hold on now, Lark," Thad said soothingly. "He's not going to get your little one. There's got to be a solution. I have to think on it a minute."

"Think, Thad, think," Ben urged. As though to help Thad along, everyone grew quiet.

A full minute ticked by with Thad staring down at his clasped hands. He looked up then, an excited gleam in his eyes. "I know the perfect place, if you all wouldn't mind living in the country."

"Me and Lucy wouldn't mind." Ben moved to the edge of his seat. "We were raised in the country."

"And I lived on a farm until I was ten," Lark added eagerly. "What have you come up with, Thad?"

"I'm gonna take you to where I just came from. My parents' farm. It's way out in the country. Ain't nobody around for miles. Gibb would never think to look there."

"But couldn't he track us?" Ben asked with a frown.

"That's the beauty of my plan. He can track us to the North Platte, but there he will lose us. He won't know whether to go upriver or down. We can travel by boat practically all the way to the farm. After we come to our landing spot we'll only have to walk about a mile."

"It's a great idea, Thad, but won't your parents mind having strangers with a baby piling in on them?" Lark asked anxiously.

"Ma will love it. She gets lonesome, hardly ever having any womenfolk to talk to. And there's plenty of room. When Pa built the house, he and Ma planned to have a big family." Thad grinned. "They only had me and my brother Coy. Ma will love having a baby in the house again."

"If you're sure, we'll really appreciate it, Thad." This time tears of thanksgiving swam in Lark's eyes.

"When will we leave?" Ben asked. "Gibb expects Lark to be slaving again for him by the end of the week. If we're all still alive," he tacked on.

"No one saw me ride in, so I'm going to leave again while everyone is away. Gibb will probably think that I've drifted for good and won't connect me with your disappearance. I'll need time to scout out a good, sound boat. In the meantime, Ben, get together a two-days' supply of grub, and bedrolls for you and the women. We'll be leaving the river and sleeping on the ground at night."

Ben nodded, then asked hesitantly, "Can my friend Ragged Feather come with us?"

"I don't know how my Ma would feel about an Indian living in her house." Thad grinned. "But I'm sure she'll warm to the idea once she meets him. Let's ride down to the river and pick a place where we'll meet when the time comes."

"Do you have any idea when that will be?" Lark asked.

"I figure around three days."

A fog had risen from the river and now crawled low on the ground as Ace and his young companions kept their horses at a lope this early morning. Ace would have preferred that their pace be a hard gallop. He wished that he could snap his fingers and be back in Utah with his wild horses.

There were two things he was in a hurry to do. Number one was to get another herd of horses to Denver as soon as possible. The army man he had met with the day after Belle's wedding had bought his whole herd at top price. He wanted an additional hundred head as soon as possible.

But even more important than bringing more horses to Denver was his determination to find Lark. He knew now that he loved her, truly loved her, and not for her body alone. Ever since he'd told her good-bye that night before leaving her, he hadn't felt whole. Nor would he until he was with her again.

Would she have him, though? he asked himself. He felt certain that she enjoyed their lovemaking as much as he did, but what had she felt for him as a person, as a man? She had never by word or action shown anything except affection. He was on fire to find out.

Behind him he could hear Matt and Drew talking about their two days in Denver and the plans they had for when they helped him drive in another herd. Benny tried, unsuccessfully, to tell about the fun he'd had with Jory. Roxy had taken him to the Graylord ranch to spend the day. The boy was all fired up to work on a cattle ranch when he grew up.

But his two brothers loved horses. They talked, ate and slept horses. Their plans for his horse ranch were as big as his: one day it would be the biggest and best in all of Colorado.

Each day his fondness for the boys grew. He couldn't visualize a life without them in it.

What was he to do with them when he went in search of Lark? he wondered. He couldn't take them with him. He had no idea how far away she was or how long it might take to find her. That problem was solved when he hit upon the idea of leaving them with Roxy. Matt and Drew would be a big help to Tanner, and the button would pal around with Jory.

The sun rose, and the air grew hot and close. By noon everyone was sweaty and uncomfortable, and the brothers no longer talked to each other. It was around two o'clock, after they'd stopped to eat the beef sandwiches Pee Wee had made for them, that Ace noticed a dull pall hanging over the mountains. Damn, he thought, we're going to be caught in a storm. "Come on, boys," he urged. "Let's mount up and ride. It's going to storm any minute and we've got to find some kind of shelter. It's dangerous as hell to be caught out on the bare plains in an electric storm. Head for the foothills. Maybe we can reach them before the storm breaks."

As they raced their horses along at breakneck speed, the air grew so humid it felt like breathing steam into their lungs. They were about a quarter of a mile from the edge of the timberline when a jagged streak of lightning split the sky. The roll of thunder that followed shook the ground beneath them. Ace felt Sam quiver and knew that the gelding was terrified.

They were almost in the woods when Ace saw a white wall of rain rapidly coming toward them. At the same time he heard the thunder of galloping hooves coming up behind them. He shot a look over his shoulder and saw at least twenty wild horses following a big white stallion.

Their tails streaming behind them and their eyes rolling in terror, they swept past him and the boys as though they weren't there. They all entered the fringe of aspen and pine at the same time. The wild ones kept running at full speed, but Ace slowed the gelding down so he could keep an eye out for a cave or some kind of cover for protection. It was almost as dangerous among tall trees as it was to be caught on the open range.

Ace muttered his thanks when he spotted a black opening in the grayness of the forest. The next streak of lightning showed him a cave. "This way, boys," he shouted, and turned Sam's head in the direction of shelter.

The cave was shallow but long. The rain hit just as they dismounted and led the horses into the dark opening. Since they could no longer see the lightning and the sound of the thunder was muted, the nervous horses settled right down.

The next few minutes were spent unsaddling the horses. Then, as Matt gathered dry wood from the cave floor and started a fire, the others stood at its mouth watching the rain slash at the trees as the storm raged on. Darkness came quickly to the sodden forest, but the flames from the fire pushed the damp gloom away.

Ace knew that Benny was too shaken up to prepare the salt pork and beans that would be their supper, so he took on the chore.

As he set a pot of coffee to brewing and laid strips of meat in a battered skillet, Matt came and hunkered down beside him. "Did you see that band of wild horses that flew past us back there?" he asked, his eyes glittering in the firelight.

Ace grinned at the teenager's excitement. "You damn betcha. Do you have any ideas about them?"

"You know I do. If we can get them home, they will make up the hundred head that army man wants."

"They sure would," Ace agreed, then asked, "Do you have any idea how we're going to get them home? If it was just you and I and Matt we'd drive them the way we have all the others. But there's the button to think about. He's too young, and it's too dangerous for him to be chasing wild horses."

"I've been thinking on that too." Matt picked up a twig, snapped it in two and tossed it into the fire. "I ain't come up with any ideas yet."

"I've got one idea," Ace said, giving the heating beans a stir with a long-handled spoon. "That little mare of Benny's is horsin'. If that big wild stallion gets a whiff of her, he and his herd might try to follow us."

"I think that's a great idea, Ace," Matt said, admiration in his tone.

"Well, maybe. The trick would be to keep him far enough behind us so that he couldn't steal her."

"I believe we could do that. Of course I would ride the mare, in case he got too close. How do we get close enough to the stallion so that he can smell her?"

Ace stared thoughtfully into the fire. Then he raised his head and looked at Matt. "Tomorrow morning, early, you mount the mare and track the herd to where they spent the night. Get close enough for the stallion to smell the mare, then turn around and ride back down here. We'll be saddled and waiting for you."

The meat was fried and the beans hot. Ace pulled the brewed pot of coffee off the fire and called out, "Time to eat, you fellows."

When the meal was eaten and each had a tin cup of coffee in his hands, Ace told the younger brothers about his plan to lure the wild herd home.

"Boy, oh, boy," Benny exclaimed, "I'm finally going to be in on a wild-horse chase."

"We're hoping there won't be a chase, Benny,"

Matt said, "and I'll be riding your little mare."

"That's not fair," Benny said, bristling. "She belongs to me. Ace gave her to me."

"Do you want to lose her to the stallion?"

"Of course not."

"Then shut your yap."

Benny knew by his brother's tone that Matt was aggravated and that if he continued to argue, he might get a cuff to his head. He said no more, only stared sullenly into the fire.

The deepening twilight turned to darkness. Ace stood up, stretched, then said, "Unroll your bedding, fellows. We want to be up in the morning before the wild ones start moving out."

He watched with amusement as Benny spread out his blankets only a foot away from his own. The button wasn't as brave as he would have them believe.

The thunder was a distant rumble now and it had stopped raining, Ace noticed as he stretched out on his hard bed. He stared into the fire for some time, his mind on Lark. Where was she tonight?

Chapter Thirty

Lark tied a string around the rolled-up bundle of baby clothes. When she had slipped it into a fustian bag, she shoved it out of sight under the bed. She had kept out what she thought she would need for the baby until it was time to leave tomorrow. She did the same thing with her own meager wardrobe and shoved it under the bed also.

Her emotions had been up and down all day. Thad had told Uncle Ben this morning that tomorrow they would leave. One moment she was filled with the excitement of finally getting away from a husband who had been unbelievably brutal; then the next minute she was filled with nervous tension. She was sure that Cletus would learn of her planned flight and wouldn't let her take the baby with her.

When Lark heard her uncle arrive she checked on

304

her son, then joined her aunt and uncle in the kitchen.

Ben gave her a wide smile from his seat at the table. "Do you have everything ready?" he asked.

"Yes, I do, Uncle Ben, but you don't look all that happy about leaving. How come?"

A long sigh escaped the old man before he said, "I'm gonna miss my friend Ragged Feather."

"Didn't you tell him that he is welcome to come with us?"

"I told him, but the old fool doesn't want to go. He said that he was heading for the sunset of his life, and that when it was time, he would go to the mountains where he was born and die there."

"I'm so sorry, Uncle Ben." Lark reached across the table and squeezed his knobby hand. "I know you'll miss him. Maybe you can make another friend where we're going."

"No, I won't. I won't even try to."

"We'll see." Lucy patted his other hand. "Maybe Thad has a grandfather."

"He doesn't. There's just him and his mother and an older brother named Coy." He paused a moment, then added, "He's got an aunt and uncle and a bunch of cousins, but they live about thirty miles from his parents' farm. Probably won't see anybody very often," he complained.

To put his mind on something else, Lucy asked, "Did Thad say anything about Denver? How big is it? Does it have a lot of stores?"

"He didn't say, but I've heard tell it's a good-size city. I expect it has a lot of stores."

Ben's face brightened after a while. "Thad did say that he saw Ace in Denver one day."

"You don't say!" Lucy exclaimed. "What did Ace have to say? Is he living in Denver now?"

"Thad didn't talk to him. Ace was with a fancily dressed woman and a young boy. He said that they acted like a family, and he figured that Ace might be embarrassed if he walked up to them and spoke. The boy feels bad that Ace had a wife and family all this time and never mentioned it."

Ben shook his head. "It just goes to show you a person never knows who to trust these days. I thought sure Ragged Feather would jump at the chance to go with us. He's only got one daughter, and his son-in-law begrudges him every mouthful of food he swallows."

Lark felt sick to her soul. Although she hadn't faulted Ace for not loving her, not taking her away with him, she had never dreamed he had a son. He had told her of the wife that had died, but hadn't spoken a word about any other woman he was involved with. Hadn't it bothered him, made him feel guilty when he made passionate love to her all those months ago?

Later that night, when Lark went to bed, her baby sleeping in the curve of her arm, she promised herself that she would never love another man again. She would never let one get that close.

The baby's fussing awakened Lark. She snuggled his small head against her body and untied the ribbons of her gown. She cooed soft, loving words as she bared her breast to him. As the little one nursed, she stroked a gentle finger between his closed eyes, wishing he didn't look so much like his father. It would be very hard to forget Ace with a constant reminder of him in his son.

"But I will do it," she whispered, then looked up when Lucy entered the bedroom.

"I thought I heard little Aaron," Lucy said cheerily, gazing fondly at the mother and baby.

"What time is it, Auntie?" Lark asked as she removed the sleeping baby's slack mouth from her breast.

"The clock just struck eight. It's a beautiful day for us to make our escape."

"Has Cletus left the house yet?" Lark swung her feet to the floor and stood up. She wanted to move around, but she didn't want to chance Gibb's coming into the room and catching her.

"No, he hasn't." Lucy frowned slightly. "He's usually out of here by seven. I can't imagine what's keeping him. He's up. I heard him moving around in his room."

Alarm jumped into Lark's eyes and her fingers trembled as she retied the gown's ribbons. "Do you think he's found out that we're leaving today?"

"Now, don't go getting yourself all worked up," Lucy soothed gently. "There's no way he could. There's only the four of us who know we're leaving." Lucy turned back to the door. "I'll go fix you some breakfast, and in the meantime you pray that he leaves the ranch today."

"What if he doesn't? How will we get away?" Panic rose in Lark's voice. "What if we're still here when that Indian woman comes to take care of Aaron?"

"You're borrowing trouble, Lark. He's bound to leave the house sometime today. We'll need only a few minutes to get out of here. I'm sure Ben is nearby, waiting and watching."

"That's true." Lark perked up a bit. "I'll get dressed and change the baby, so we're ready to leave the moment we get the chance."

Lark had eaten her breakfast and was on tenterhooks by the time Gibb went stomping out of the house around nine o'clock. As soon as the door slammed behind him Lucy and Lark ran to the window. "I wonder who they are?" Lucy asked, referring to the four mounted men who sat in the barnyard.

"I don't know," Lark answered, "but I'll bet they're the ones that made Cletus leave the house."

"One of the men is wearing a star, Lark," Lucy exclaimed. "I bet he's heard that Gibb has those expensive bulls."

Before Lark could make a response, Ben appeared at the window. "Come on," he said hurriedly, "let's get out of here while he's occupied with those strangers."

While Lark wrapped the baby in a blanket, Lucy dragged the two bundles of clothes from under the bed and tossed them to Ben. Lucy climbed out of the window then, and Lark handed her the baby. A second later she was through the window and taking the infant from her aunt. They struck out running toward a small knoll that hid the river a quarter mile away.

As they topped the hill and saw the gleam of the river below, they heard Gibb yelling and swearing. Ben paused and said, almost out of breath, "You two go on to the river. Thad is waiting beside that big cottonwood. I'll just be a minute. I want to say goodbye to Ragged Feather. He's waiting for me in that patch of aspens beyond the barn."

"You be careful that Gibb don't see you," Lucy warned, and she and Lark hurried on to the river.

They were almost at the cottonwood and could see Thad hunkered down beside the trunk, when they heard the deadly staccato of gunfire.

"What was that all about?" Thad asked, coming to meet them.

"I don't know," Lucy said, looking nervously over her shoulder. "I hope Ben isn't in the middle of it."

"Where is he?" Thad asked. "We've got to get going."

"He went to say good-bye to that old Indian." Lucy snorted; then her face lit up with relief. "Here he comes now," she said as Ben came loping toward them.

"What was all that shooting about?" Thad asked as he dragged a boat from under a patch of tall reeds and cattails.

"I couldn't see very clearly, but I think Gibb was shooting it out with the four strangers who showed up a short time ago. I hurried up and got away from there," he added with a note of wry humor as he helped Thad push the boat into the water.

He held the big vessel steady then as Thad helped Lark and Lucy climb into it. When they were seated, he jumped in. Thad gave the boat a shove and took a seat in its middle.

The boat floated, half circling until it edged into the current. Thad picked up the oars then and dipped them into the water. With long, powerful sweeps they glided down the river.

Lark, facing Thad, clutched her son to her breast and returned his wide smile. At last. At last she was leaving her life of hell behind.

Chapter Thirty-one

The eastern horizon had been pink and light yellow when Ace shook Matt awake. "Roll out, kid," he'd said. "Light's coming fast. The horses will start moving out anytime now. They'll want to graze."

Matt had pulled on his boots and poked Drew. "Time to get up."

Drew opened his eyes, rubbed them, then gave Benny's shoulder a shake.

"I don't know when we'll eat today," Ace said as he handed out strips of pemmican. "If we succeed in getting that stallion to follow the mare, we may not eat again until nightfall."

Altogether it took about five minutes for their blankets to be rolled up and their horses saddled. They mounted up and Matt, astride the mare, started up the mountain looking for the wild horses' tracks. Ace, Drew and Benny stayed behind, waiting with bated breath for him to lead the herd past them.

Ace had watched as Matt found the trampled trail made by the horses in their mad rush up the mountain. Suddenly a clarion call erupted, followed by the sound of flying stones and gravel. In the blink of an eye Matt was racing back toward them with the big white thundering behind him. He flew past them, followed by the wild herd.

In what had seemed only seconds they were all out of the foothills and racing across the range. Matt was keeping his head start, but Ace wondered how long the little mare could keep up this pace.

The big white seemed oblivious to everything around it as it thundered along. There was only one thing on its mind: it wanted to add the mare to its harem.

Now Ace looked up at the sun. It was nearing noon, and they had been at a full run since early morning. Sam was tiring, and he knew that the other horses were also. It wasn't long before the pace changed from a hard gallop to a slow lope. But not once did the stallion lose sight of the mare.

It was near sunset when both men and horses had reached exhaustion. Ace rode up to Matt and the tired mare. "We'll make camp here," he said, "and let the horses rest and graze. Keep the stallion away from the mare while I cook us some grub."

"How in the hell do I do that? He wants her bad, Ace."

"He's pretty worn out now. If he gets too close, whack him across the face with your rope."

"I'll try, but you be ready to help me if I need it."

"Don't worry about it. I'll be keeping an eye on you."

311

Drew had a fire going and Benny had fallen asleep, his back propped against a tree trunk. Ace smiled his amusement as he started a pot of coffee to brewing. The button was worn out.

When the aromatic smell of strong coffee rose from the fire, Ace started a skillet of salt pork frying, then opened two cans of beans and dumped them into a pan to warm up on a bed of red coals.

Still hunkered beside the fire, he twisted his body to see if Matt was having any trouble keeping an eye on the herd. He was in time to hear the teenager swear a string of oaths and slap his rope across the white stallion's face. The stallion shook its head, stamped its great hooves; then, its tail raised high, it trotted a short distance away. That's a mean bastard, he thought, and Matt was having a hard time controlling the mare. The horse wanted to answer the stallion's shrill whistle.

"I'd better keep watch tonight," he said to himself. "That white brute seems determined to add the filly to his herd."

The rough meal was ready and Ace called, "Drew, wake up Benny. It's time to eat." He walked the short distance to where the horses were still grazing and, cupping his hands to his mouth, yelled, "Grub's on, Matt."

"You gonna leave the herd unattended, Ace?" Drew asked as he and Benny filled their tin plates. "Won't they take off?"

"Nah." Ace shook his head. "They're tired and will graze half the night. As for the stallion, he won't go far as long as he can smell the mare."

As the boys ate like young wolf cubs, the white stood on a small knoll whistling and screaming,

sending a bold challenge to those who were keeping
him away from the mare.

Ace was debating opening another can of beans
when the boys poured themselves coffee and sat
back, full and contented. He didn't know which boy
started it, but suddenly Matt and Drew were grap-
pling on the ground, each struggling to pin the other
one down. He started to stand up, to break them
apart, then saw the laughter on their faces. They
were only horsing around.

He shook his head. After the day they had put in,
how did they have enough energy to wrestle each
other? He glanced at Benny. The boy's pouting lips
told him that the youngster was put out that he
wasn't included in the good-natured melee his brothers were enjoying.

It's a good thing you aren't, Ace thought with a grin.
They'd have mashed you into the ground by now.

As suddenly as it had started, the roughhousing
was over. Their faces red and sweating from their
exertion, Matt and Drew sat back down and had another cup of coffee.

The campfire crackled and twilight deepened. Ace
was thinking of Lark when Benny broke the companionable silence.

"Ace," he said, spiteful mischief in his eyes, "Matt
was bragging to everyone in Denver that he's a mus-
tanger."

"Shut your yap, Benny!" Matt glared threateningly
at his troublemaking brother, his face an embarrassed red.

Ace shook his head. He knew what the tadpole was
up to. He wanted to get at Matt because he had been
ignored in the rough-and-tumble horseplay. He

knew also that Drew would be the next to receive the same treatment. Benny had to be taught not to be a tattletale. He lifted a flaming twig from the fire and brought it to his cigarette. He leaned back against his saddle then, drew on the smoke and said, "Matt and Drew have been chasing the wild ones for some time now. Both your brothers can honestly say that they are mustangers."

With a flash of pride in his eyes, Matt said gleefully, "There, you little runt. Why don't you go to bed now."

Before the red-faced Benny could make a retort, Ace said, "I think we'd all better turn in. We've got the same hard day tomorrow as we had today. I'll take the first watch, Drew, and wake you up at midnight to take over. Benny, before you hit your bedroll, wash up everything, and ready camp for tomorrow morning."

Before Ace mounted the mare, he gave Sam an affectionate pat on the rump. The horse was gelded, as were the horses that Matt and Drew rode. Wild stallions felt no animosity toward neutered ones. Matt had put him wise to that. The kid really knew horses, he thought as he mounted the mare and rode to within a few yards of the herd.

Ace had barely taken up a position that allowed him a complete view of the horses when, with flaring nostrils and flying mane and tail, the stallion came racing toward him, trumpeting its fury at the man who was keeping him from the mare. Ace hurriedly checked the Colt at his right side and snatched the coiled rope from the saddle horn. He was just in time to whack it against the furious face and bared teeth. With a vindictive scream the stallion wheeled and galloped away, but only a short distance.

Twice more the white charged Ace. Ace was growing impatient at the animal's determination to get at the mare. "You rogue bastard," he gritted out. "You have a meanness in you that tells me you will never be tamed."

I don't think I want you around the boys, he thought. *Matt doesn't have the strength to handle you, and I don't have the patience. Furthermore, I'd feel guilty selling you to the army man. I wouldn't want to have it on my conscience that you might stomp a soldier to death. I don't know what to do with you.*

Ace lost sight of the stallion and relaxed. He knew the animal wouldn't go far from the mare.

He was totally unprepared when suddenly the big rogue was behind him, rearing up, its deadly front hooves descending toward him.

Ace's reaction was swift. As he threw himself out of the saddle, he pulled his Colt and rolled as he hit the ground. He leaped to his feet, gun ready as the stallion circled around the mare, its nostrils flaring, blood in its eyes. As the horse reared up, ready to strike out with its powerful legs, Ace squeezed the trigger.

With only a stunned grunt, the handsome horse went down, shot through the heart.

Ace stood, trembling, the Colt dangling from his limp hand. He had never before looked death in the face. The boys were running toward him then, their faces pale in the light of the full moon.

"Are you all right, Ace?" they asked in unison. They grew quiet when they saw the motionless body of the big white on the ground. Matt walked over to the fallen animal and knelt at its head. As he stroked a hand over the proud neck, he whispered, "Why couldn't you behave yourself?" With tears shimmering in his eyes, he looked up at Ace. "He was a rogue, wasn't he?" When Ace only nodded, he added, "We could never have tamed his wild heart."

Ace laid a hand on Matt's shoulder and squeezed gently. "That's right, son. I never would have felt easy when he was around you boys."

The herd had spooked at the blast of gunfire and run a short distance away. When they returned shortly and resumed grazing in the night, Ace said, "Drew, would you take over for me for a while? I'm beat, physically and mentally."

The pink freshness of the sunrise shone on the dew-wet grass when Ace and the boys awakened the next morning. They had overslept a little due to the interruption of their sleep earlier in the night.

Their first action was to check whether they still had a herd. Ace grinned at Matt and Drew. The horses were still there, grazing in the cool morning breeze.

"Let's grab a bite to eat, then see if the horses will still follow us," Ace said.

Benny prepared the morning meal, and when the salt pork and skillet bread was eaten, washed down with strong coffee, they saddled up and prepared to head out. Ace looked over his shoulder as they rode away to see if they were being followed.

They were. Matt looked at Ace with a wide grin. "There are a few horses in that bunch that will try to get to the mare now that their leader is gone. There will probably be a fight to see who will replace him."

Ace glanced back again and saw that Matt was right. There were three young, fully grown horses in the lead of the herd. Could they handle three? Ace worried.

He found, however, that the young horses were easily repelled when they came too close to Benny's pet. Being able to relax and just ride along was a lark for the brothers. The steady, uninterrupted pace allowed Ace to think of Lark, to plan how he could track her down.

It was near sunset when they crossed over into Utah, and half an hour later they gazed down from the top of a rocky knoll at the half-finished house and the corrals basking in the westerly sun.

With a whoop the boys touched spurs to their horses and raced down the hill. The herd followed them, all the way into one of the corrals.

When Ace rode up, Elisha was coming up from the river, a fishing pole and two fish on a string in his hand. He and Ace spoke together a minute. Satisfied that everything had gone well in his absence, Ace called to the brothers, "Let's get on to the farm and have a good home-cooked meal for a change."

Mrs. Brandon saw them coming, racing toward the house at a full gallop. A tender smile curved her lips when she saw young Benny riding several horse lengths behind his brothers and her son. Poor little fellow, she thought, he is always trying to catch up with the older boys.

They will be hungry, she thought. Betty chewed on her thumbnail, wondering what she could prepare in a hurry. Big juicy steaks came to mind, and she was in luck. She had just bought a quarter leg of beef, and the farmer had been good enough to slice most of it into steaks. The rest he had cut into stew meat.

She was on the porch to greet them when they came thundering into the yard. Benny slid off his horse and ran to hug her around the waist. Ace and his brothers looked at each other and grinned. Ace made up his mind on the spot that Benny was staying with his mother when they drove the next herd to Denver.

Matt and Drew removed their dusty, disreputable-looking hats and smiled a shy greeting at Betty. Her son, however, caught her up and swung the little woman around until she beat him on the shoulders, demanding to be put down.

As they followed Betty inside, Ace asked, "What have you got for three hungry men to eat?" At Benny's injured look he added, "And one skinny little tadpole."

Betty scolded him before saying, "By the time you wash up and change into clean clothes, I'll have supper on the table. You'll just have to wait and see what it is."

A lot of splashing took place on the back porch as Ace and the boys scrubbed the dust and grime off all exposed flesh. By the time they had changed into the clean clothes Betty had waiting for them, the steaks were on the table.

Cries of appreciation sounded as they took seats and dived into the tender meat. Betty let them eat in silence until they sat back with contented sighs. As she poured coffee she asked, "So how did the drive go? Did you find a buyer for the horses?"

"Yes, we did," Ace answered. "An army man

bought them all. And what's more, he wants another hundred head within a couple weeks."

"Two weeks? Will you and the boys be able to tame that many in so short a time?"

"We'll be putting in ten and twelve hours a day, but we can do it." Ace looked at Matt and Drew to verify his statement.

Matt used his favorite expression. "It will be a lark."

"I'll be glad when we've delivered the herd to that army man in Denver, though," Ace said. "Driving a hundred head isn't going to be an easy task."

"I almost forgot." Betty stood up and left the table. "A letter came for you a couple days ago. It has an army post return address on the envelope."

Ace's high spirits dropped to his dusty boots. Perhaps the army scout had changed his mind, and he didn't want any more horses. He tore the envelope open, extracted a sheet of paper and read the message on it:

Dear Ace Brandon,

I have just received word from my superior that he needs the additional horses as soon as possible. To hasten your progress I am sending four men to your place. They will drive the horses to Kansas, where they will be put into boxcars to finish the trip to our headquarters. The soldiers will arrive within two weeks. The sergeant will give you a check for the number of tamed horses you have for him.

Ace dropped the letter and looked up at the expectant faces gazing at him.

"Is it good news?" Matt asked.

"It couldn't be better." Ace's white teeth flashed in a wide smile. "Instead of passing the letter around, I'll read it out loud."

Chapter Thirty-two

The flowing river gleamed under the hot sun as Thad steadily pulled the oars through the water with strong, sure strokes. He would have liked to stay close to the shore, where the great willow trees spread their thick branches out over the water, providing cover. The water was shallow there, though, and he would be too easily grounded.

Lucy and Lark had pulled on bonnets, and Lark had arranged a small blanket like a tent over the baby. They would not suffer too greatly from the sun. At least the air was cool on the river.

Thad looked at Ben, who sat with his back to them. The old fellow had hardly said two words since they'd started out. Usually he was a garrulous fellow, always having something to say about anything and everything. It must have been hard on him to say good-bye to old Ragged Feather, Thad thought.

His gaze fell on Lucy. She sat quietly, enjoying the scenery as it passed by. It was evident by the serenity on her face that she was happy Lark was escaping her life of hell.

He looked at Lark and tried to read her face. There was a look of relief on her features; still, there was a sadness in her gray eyes. What was she thinking?

Lark was glad that they had successfully fled Cletus, but she knew that her problem had not really been solved. She and her family couldn't pile in on strangers and live with them for the rest of their lives. It could only be a temporary arrangement. She was grateful to Thad for rescuing them; his plan would give her time to figure out where they could go and still be safe from Cletus. After all, she was still his wife; he could legally take baby Aaron away from her.

She hugged the infant close to her chest. She would go anywhere, do anything, before she let Cletus Gibb get his hands on her son. When Ace slipped into her mind, she firmly pushed him away. He would never be a part of his son's life. He already had a family and another son.

Around noon Thad passed around a leather bag containing strips of dried beef. To everyone's surprise, the meat was delicious. The baby fussed for his lunch, and Thad looked away when Lark brought the little one to her breast.

The afternoon wore on, and when the red ball of the sun was partway behind the horizon, Thad turned the boat toward the shore.

"This is where I always camp when coming from or to the farm," he explained as he nosed the boat onto the edge of the gravelly bank. "It's one of the few places along the river where the water is deep enough for a vessel to land. You'll find my campsite over there in that patch of willows."

The boat rocked slightly as Thad helped first Lark, then Lucy to step onto solid ground. Ben hopped ashore then, carrying the bedrolls. Thad followed with the camping gear and grub sack in his hand.

While Lark and Lucy waited out of the men's way, Thad and Ben pulled the boat up on the bank. When they had anchored it to a tree, Thad smiled and said, "This way, ladies." They followed him up a beaten path to the willow growth.

Thad's campsite had a look of permanence. He had dug a hole about three feet wide and a foot and a half deep and lined it with good-size rocks. He had placed four short logs around the fire pit, places where a man could sit as he ate or simply gaze into the fire and maybe dream. Off to one side, stacked neatly, were a water pail and dipper, a coffeepot and a skillet. A large piece of canvas covered everything.

While Thad and Ben went about setting up camp, Lark sat down on one of the logs to nurse her fussing baby. There was a break in the willow foliage where she had a good view of the river flowing by. *There is a loneliness about it,* she thought. *It's as if no human being has ever traveled this river before us.*

She shook off her morbid thoughts and began to wonder what kind of reception they would receive from Thad's parents when they arrived uninvited. Would they be welcomed with smiles or with suspicion? Maybe Thad's family was of the belief that a wife should stay with her husband no matter how cruelly he might treat her?

Lark was hoping that Thad had inherited his kind and thoughtful ways from his parents when that young man approached her with a tin plate heaped high with fried bacon and warmed beans. Lucy, walking behind him, carried cutlery and a cup of coffee. She took the baby from Lark and laid him on a bedroll that had been unfolded.

Lark hadn't realized how hungry she was until she started eating. It was evident that her companions were equally hungry, the food disappeared rapidly from their plates.

Later, as they sat around the fire, drinking coffee, Ben asked, "What time do you think we'll be arriving at your parents' farm tomorrow, Thad?"

"In the late afternoon," Thad answered as he opened up the other bedrolls and placed them around the fire. He added with a grin, "Just in time for supper."

A few minutes later Lark and Lucy walked farther into the willows to answer nature's call. When they returned to the fire they said good night and lay down on the blankets. The men were left to clean and tidy the camp.

As Thad had promised, the next day near sunset, the boat drifted around a bend in the river and a column of smoke was spotted. "The farm is just a short distance away," Thad said with excitement in his voice. "That smoke is coming from the kitchen chimney. Ma is making supper."

Another curve of the river showed the farm sitting on top of a small knoll. Thad guided the boat toward a sloping bank. When it nosed into the mud and gravel, he and Ben jumped out and held the boat steady for Lark and Lucy to disembark. Then Thad, carrying the baby, led them up a path that went to the big farmhouse.

Two men were washing up on the back porch, and Thad called out, "I hope we're in time for supper."

As the men turned around to look at them, a tall, rawboned woman stepped outside. A warm smile of welcome appeared on her pleasant face. "You must be Lark and Lucy and Ben," she said, holding out a work-roughened hand to Lark.

Lark's tense shoulders relaxed. They were welcome. She smiled, and as she shook the proffered hand, she said, "I guess Thad has spoken of us."

"Yes, he has, dear, and my heart goes out to you. You are safe here with us." When she had shaken hands with Lucy and Ben, she introduced the two tall men who stepped up beside her. "This is my husband, Richard, and my son, Coy, and I'm Elizabeth."

Richard was a sober-faced man, but when he smiled his whole face lit up. Lark thought she had never seen a man more handsome than Coy, and wondered why he was still single.

"Give me the baby, Thad," Elizabeth ordered, reaching for Aaron, "and we'll go inside so you folks can freshen up a bit before supper. We'll eat in about half an hour."

The room Lark was shown to was a back room on the first floor. It was furnished with simple, sturdy furniture. The big bed with a bright quilt on it looked very inviting, and she wondered if she would have time to stretch out on it for a few minutes before supper.

Lark changed the baby into fresh clothing; then, finding water in the pitcher beside a china basin, she washed her face and hands and changed into a clean, faded dress. She lay down beside her son and fell asleep immediately.

Clouds of dust rolled around the feet of the horse as it tried to buck Ace off its back. Ace hung on grimly as Matt and Drew cheered him on from their perch on the top rail of the breaking pen. This was the last wild one to be tamed. After two weeks of backbreaking work he would have the hundred head that the soldiers wanted.

The horse gave one last stiff-legged jump, then stood in defeat, its sides heaving and its head hanging. Ace slid off its back and wiped a sleeve across his dusty, sweating face. He gave the animal an affectionate pat on the rump, then limped over to where the boys waited with huge grins on their faces.

"That devil sure gave you a good workout, didn't he, Ace?" Matt said, amusement in his eyes. "I bet you won't be able to sit down for a week."

With a laugh Ace grabbed the teenager's head in a hammerlock and rubbed his head with his knuckles. "Are you trying to say that I'm getting too old to break the horses?"

"Of course not," Matt denied, but when Ace released him and Matt stepped out of his reach, he said, "I could have broken him in half the time."

"Oh, you could, could you?" Ace lunged at the grinning teenager, who, with a taunting laugh, adroitly sidestepped him. "I'll get you later," Ace promised good-humoredly, and limped off toward the river.

On its sandy banks he took off his hat and boots and waded out into the water. Matt and Drew were right behind him, yelling and splashing water, seemingly trying to drown each other.

Ace didn't join in the horseplay. Every bone in his body ached. Maybe he was getting too old to break the wild ones. Matt and Drew had broken as many horses as he had, maybe more, and were still able to tumble and play like a pair of young pups.

Later, as they sat on rocks in the sun letting their clothes dry on their bodies, Matt looked at Ace and asked, "Are you sure me and Drew can't come with you to Denver?"

"Yes, I'm sure. I've told you that a dozen times. I want you and Drew to stay behind and keep an eye on things until I get back."

"Old Elisha could do that," Drew said. "He'd do anything to keep from going back to the farm."

"Look," Ace said, exasperated, "you can't come with me because I have some personal business to take care of."

Matt slid him a sly look. "Could that personal business have anything to do with a female?"

"It might," Ace snapped. "Do you think it's impossible for a woman to be interested in me?"

"Well"—Matt pretended to be thoughtful for a moment—"I expect some dried-up old maid might agree to let you come courting." He barely dodged the rock Ace tossed at his legs.

Although Ace knew that Matt's teasing was all in fun, it nevertheless started him thinking. What if Lark thought he wasn't good husband material because of his age? Just because she enjoyed making love with him didn't necessarily mean that she would want to spend the rest of her life with him. She was young and beautiful, and could have most any man she wanted.

Before he went to sleep that night, Ace knew one

thing for certain. He was going to find Lark and ask her a certain question. Her answer would give him either great happiness or deep despair.

The sun was barely up the next morning when Betty went to the barn and shook Ace awake. "Get up, son. Those soldiers are here for the horses."

"Ask them in, Ma." Ace sat up and reached for his boots. "Maybe they'd like a cup of coffee."

Matt and Drew had also awakened, and they walked to the house with Ace. The army men stood up from the table when Ace and the boys walked into the kitchen. Within fifteen minutes their business had been taken care of and Ace had a good-size check in his hand. Matt and Drew led the soldiers to the holding pens.

"Ma," Ace said a little while later as he stood in front of a small mirror in the kitchen lathering his face, "if you don't mind, I'd like to leave the tadpole with you while I go to Denver."

"That will be fine. Benny is good company for me. What about Matt and Drew? Are they going to Denver with you?"

"No, they'll be staying on to look after the few horses we've got left."

"How long will you be gone?"

"I don't know. It depends on how things go. Maybe a week, maybe a month."

Half an hour later Ace kissed his mother and mounted Sam. He had decided that he would go to the Gibb ranch first. Lark might still be there, although he doubted it. At any rate, he might discover where she had gone. Young Thad would probably know.

LARK

* * *

When Ace topped the small knoll behind the ranch, he reined in and looked down at the buildings below. He frowned as he studied the place where he had once worked.

Damned if the place doesn't look deserted, he thought, looking over the weed-filled yard, the closed-up house and cookhouse. The corrals next to the barn that had held Gibb's prize bulls were empty, and no one was moving about.

The barn door stood open, however, and Ace nudged Sam into a lope down the hill.

A few scraggly-looking chickens ran squawking out of the way as Sam went clattering into the barnyard. His gaze roaming over the dilapidated-looking area, Ace slid out of the saddle and lopped the reins over a post. As he stood at Sam's head, wondering what to do next, a tall form darkened the open barn door. He recognized the drawling voice that called out to him.

"Hey, Ace, you ol' son of a gun, what brings you back here? Tired of chasing mustangs already?" Newt walked toward him.

"No, I'm still tracking them down." Ace grinned at the middle-aged man as he shook his hand. "I've tamed and sold a hundred and fifty head and now I'm taking a little rest."

He looked over at the empty corrals. "What's been going on around here?" he asked, looking back at Newt. "The place looks dead."

"It practically is." Newt leaned against the corral. "A few weeks ago a sheriff came riding in here with three men. One of them was a big important-looking rancher. As soon as he spotted the bulls in the pens,

329

he started yelling that the animals were his, and that the sheriff should arrest Gibb for stealing them. Gibb, he starts yelling back that the bulls were his, that he paid good money for them. You never heard such a ruckus, yelling and cussing and threatening. And when the rancher started to charge at Gibb, the sheriff pulled his gun and stepped between them. When he told Gibb that he was arresting him for the theft of the bulls, Gibb's face got all puffed up and he pulled his gun.

"Well, by this time the posse had their guns out, and they started spraying bullets around, in case any of us ranch hands were going to help Gibb. Which we weren't about to do.

"When Gibb came charging at the sheriff, I saw the man crouch and fire. The shot went wild, but Gibb fell to the ground, dead from a bullet between his eyes.

"Now here's the strange part of the whole thing. Just as the lawman squeezed the trigger, I heard the sharp report of a rifle. I looked up at the knoll in back of the house and saw gunsmoke lifting up from among the pines there. And, Ace, I swear to you, I saw old Ben hightailing it away from there, a rifle in his hand. It was him that got Gibb. He wanted revenge for the way Gibb was treating his niece. But he wasn't the only one who hated the bastard. I was the one who wounded him in the shoulder that time."

"I'll be damned." Ace shook his head in disbelief. "Have you told anyone about Ben?"

"Naw. Why get the old fellow in trouble? I felt like shaking his hand for doing it."

"I'm surprised that Lark and her aunt and uncle

were still here. I figured that they would have run away from Gibb."

"They didn't take off until the day the sheriff and his men turned up. I spotted them running down the valley."

"Do you know where they were going?"

"No. They were very secretive about it."

"I suppose Thad was with them," Ace said hopefully.

"No, he disappeared a week or so before Lark did."

"Then Lark probably doesn't know that Gibb is dead," Ace said, "unless she knew that Ben shot him."

"I doubt that. She would have been against the old man's taking a life."

Ace nodded. Lark would never countenance such an action. Old Ben must have done it on his own.

But where were they? There were two reasons for him to find Lark now. She didn't know it, but she was a very wealthy widow. All the more reason she wouldn't want him. Gloom settled over him.

"Everybody left after Gibb was planted," Newt said, bringing Ace back to the present. "Couldn't blame them for not sticking around when there was nobody here to pay them. I've been hanging around in case Lark hears about Gibb and comes back. I've about given up, though. I can't keep herd on the cattle by myself, and I'm getting pretty low on money for grub."

Ace reached into his vest pocket and pulled out several bills. "Here's a month's wages. I'd appreciate it if you'd stay on while I look for Lark."

"Much obliged, Ace," Newt said, then asked, "Where are you going to look for her?"

"Damned if I know. I'm going to look up Thad first. He might know where she went. He told me once that his family lived outside Denver. I'll look for him there."

Chapter Thirty-three

Lark stared down at the bed, studying the three new dresses spread out there. She smiled wryly. They were just the sort Elizabeth would have chosen for herself, dark and plain and serviceable. There wasn't a piece of lace on any of them.

But she'd had to depend on the well-meaning woman to decide what to buy for her. Her old dresses were so threadbare, she'd been ashamed to be seen in town in them.

As Lark pulled one of the unattractive dresses over her head and buttoned up the bodice, she knew she owed Elizabeth a debt of gratitude. Thad's mother had offered a safe haven when she needed it most. But it would soon be time to move on. She wouldn't feel truly safe from Cletus until she put many miles between them.

There was a second reason she must move on. Coy.

He was becoming too interested in her. As handsome and as nice as he was, she had no intention of chancing her heart on another man. She had done so with Ace and had been badly hurt. She was still battling to get over him. Every time she looked at baby Aaron, she saw his father in his tiny features.

As Lark brushed her hair she heard Uncle Ben talking with someone outside her window. He was coming out of that gloomy spell that had come over him after leaving his old friend Ragged Feather behind. He was almost as talkative as ever.

She heard Lucy's laughter ring out from the kitchen. She and Elizabeth got along fine together, working in the kitchen or out in the garden patch. She sighed as she laid the brush down. She hated to disrupt the old folks' lives again, but she must if she was ever to have peace of mind.

"You about ready to go, Lark?" Thad rapped lightly on the open door, then stuck his head into the room.

Lark smiled at him and picked up her small drawstring purse. "I'll just have a few words with Aunt Lucy and then we'll go."

In the kitchen she explained to Lucy that she had nursed Aaron about ten minutes ago. "He should sleep for the next three hours or so. We'll be back before then. I only need to purchase some underclothing and a pair of shoes, and maybe a hat. Do either of you ladies want anything from town?"

Both women shook their heads, but when she and Thad stepped out onto the porch Ben reminded her to buy him some tobacco.

Coy stood ready to help her into the wagon. She settled her skirts around her ankles, and the three of them started off to Denver.

The whole valley was in fog as the wagon rolled along, and not much was said until the sun began to burn it away. Conversation picked up then, and easy chatter and light laughter took over.

Coy kept the team at a fast clip, and they were soon riding down Denver's main street. When they drew abreast of the biggest mercantile in town, Coy pulled the horses in. Excitement grew inside Lark. For the first time in her life she would be able to walk into a store and buy almost anything she liked.

Coy had jumped from the wagon and now raised his hands to help her down from the high seat. As she went into his arms the smile on her face died.

Across the street, in front of a saloon, Ace stood talking to a beautiful young woman. "That's the woman I saw him with before," Thad said as he climbed down beside her.

Lark told her legs to move, but they seemed to be paralyzed. As she stood, glued to the ground, the woman turned and walked into the saloon. She saw Ace start to step off the wide porch, then pause abruptly.

Their gazes locked across the street.

Ace froze as if he had been poleaxed. Surely he wasn't seeing what he thought he was. It couldn't be Lark staring at him from across the street. He felt the leap of his pulse, the rapid beat of his heart, and started across the street.

As he drew near Lark, everyone around her melted away as if in a misty fog. His eyes devoured her. He wanted to fold her into his arms and just hold her close. He wanted to feel her softness once again, to breathe in the essence of her. It had been so long.

His arms were about to reach out to her when he saw the coolness in her gray eyes. They did not reflect the joy, the love, that burned inside him. He fought back his bitter disappointment and said softly, "It's good to see you, Lark. I've been wondering where you and your family had gone to. Are you living in the area now?"

"It's good to see you, too, Ace," Lark said. Then after a slight hesitation she added, "We're living in the area for the time being. We're staying with Thad's parents."

The two men with Lark began to take shape, and Ace recognized the teenager. "Thad!" he exclaimed, surprised and delighted to see the young man. He held his hand out to him. "How are you, fellow? I'm pleased that you've been taking care of Lark like I asked you to."

"I'd have done it on my own," Thad muttered and barely shook Ace's hand.

Ace gave him a curious look. The kid seemed put out. Why? He looked at the tall young man standing next to Lark.

"This is Coy, Thad's brother," Lark said when Thad failed to make the introduction.

Again Ace held out his hand, and again it was only halfheartedly taken. What the hell is going on? he thought, becoming a little impatient. What had he done to make Lark and Thad treat him almost like a stranger? And what was in the brother's craw? He knew damned well he had never done anything to him.

"Are you going to be in town long?" he asked, turning back to Lark.

"Only long enough to pick up a few things in the mercantile."

"Couldn't you take the time to step into the café with me and have a cup of coffee while we catch up on what we've been doing the past months?"

"I'm sorry, but Aunt Lucy and Thad's mother are waiting for me to get back. It's washday and there's a lot of clothing to be scrubbed."

Ace's eyes hardened at the proprietary way Coy took hold of Lark's arm and turned her toward the store. Is that the way the wind blows? he wondered. Was the good-looking farmer courting Lark?

Desperate to keep Lark there, to keep her talking to him, he blurted out, "I guess you weren't too broken up when Gibb met his?"

Lark stopped and whirled around. "What do you mean?"

"I'm sorry, Lark, but I thought you probably knew he was dead. A couple weeks ago a sheriff showed up at the ranch. According to Newt, there was a gun battle. When the smoke cleared Gibb lay dead."

Lark's face had gone white, but her eyes burned like a banked fire. She wouldn't have to fear Cletus Gibb ever again. She wouldn't have to run from him, to hide from him. She could go where she pleased, do what she pleased.

The blood drummed in her head, rang in her ears. When it looked to Ace as if she was about to faint, he pulled her away from Coy and said in a no-nonsense tone, "You're coming with me, Lark, before you fall flat on your face."

Chapter Thirty-four

Lark only half heard Ace say, "Thad, I'd like to have a private word with Lark, if you don't mind waiting out here for her."

She heard Thad grumble an answer. Then they were inside the diner and Ace was helping her to sit down. The escape from the hot sun into the coolness of the eatery began to clear her head. When Ace sat down across from her in the booth she had control of her racing thoughts. She welcomed the cup of coffee the waitress brought to her. She needed something to hold in her hands to keep them from reaching out to Ace. He looked so good, so dear. Memories of their nights together came flooding over her. They were so strong, so clear, she almost cried out.

She jerked her gaze away from him and directed it to the big window opposite where they sat. That act was her salvation. The other woman in Ace's life stepped out of the saloon across the street. The beautiful woman stood a moment in her fancy silk dress, a hatbox hanging from her arm. She held a black lacy parasol over a head piled high with black, glossy curls. She stepped off the porch, looked up and down the street, then walked down the wooden sidewalk, her dress swirling smartly around her ankles.

Black jealousy gripped Lark. She looked back at Ace and wanted to slap his handsome face. How could he look at her with that softness in his eyes, as if he were joyful to be with her again?

"I'm surprised you didn't know about Gibb," he was saying. "Newt said he saw you and your folks running away from the house just as the gunfire started."

She was tempted to jump to her feet and leave the café without answering him. What did he care if she knew about Cletus's death or not?

To her own disgust, she found herself telling him what had happened that day. "I could hear the gunfire when we ran from the ranch, but I didn't look back. We were running as fast as we could to where Thad waited for us at the river. We climbed into a boat that he had hidden there. It took days for Thad to row us upriver to where his parents' farm is located."

"Well," Ace said when she had finished, "you're the owner of Cletus's ranch now, Lark. When are you going to take it over?"

"Oh, dear," Lark half whispered. The startled look that came into her gray eyes told him that she hadn't thought of that. "Are you sure it belongs to me now?"

"Sure it does. You're Gibb's widow."

Lark stared down into her coffee for a long time.

Finally she looked up at Ace and said, "I don't know if I could bear living in that house again. I was so miserable and unhappy there."

"You can do it. You must. What you just said proves that you deserve it. It would be altogether different now."

"But to operate such a big holding. I wouldn't begin to know how to go about it."

"You don't have to know how. You've got Newt, who has stayed on, as well as Thad to depend on. The other help will come back as soon as they hear you have taken over. Even the cook would return."

"I don't know. It seems like a big undertaking for a woman," Lark said, very doubtful.

"Look, Lark, if something isn't done about the place pretty soon, rustlers are going to drive away all the cattle. I don't think you want that to happen."

"I don't know what to do," Lark cried, resting her forehead on her knotted fists. She was torn between her desire to keep the ranch, which she felt she deserved, and her fear that it was not wise to settle into a place so close to Ace. Sooner or later he was bound to find out about Aaron. And what would be the outcome of that? What would Ace do?

The thought came to her that he probably wouldn't do anything. If and when he realized he had sired the little one he would probably ignore the fact. He was obviously living with the mother of his other son. Perhaps he'd finally married her. In any case, he'd already made his choice.

"I'll have to think it over," she said finally. "Thanks for the coffee."

"When will I see you again?" Ace followed her out onto the street.

Lark gave him a puzzled look. Did he think that they would be picking up where they had left off? He couldn't be that stupid.

"I have no idea," she answered coolly. "We'll probably bump into each other from time to time."

"I'd like to see you more often than that," Ace protested. "I'd like to help you get started operating the place."

"I don't think that's a good idea. You have your life and I have mine. They're very different."

"But they don't need to be. We could work something out."

Ace said no more. They had joined the brothers now, and the two of them flanked Lark as though to protect her from him as they hurried her into the store.

Something strange is going on here, Ace thought as he crossed the street to the Lady Chance. He could understand Lark's coolness. After all, their liaisons had not been prompted by love, at least not at first. But Thad? The teenager used to dog his heels, hang on his every word.

He was going to get to the bottom of it, he promised himself as he entered the saloon. And he was going to find out where the brother Coy fit into the picture. He would wait a couple of days, then ride out to the Gibb ranch. Lark should have made up her mind about the place by then.

It had taken Lark about half an hour to make her purchases. The only added thing on her list was a riding skirt that caught her attention. She would need one in case she decided to move back to the ranch, for if she did take over the running of the place, she intended to be a major part of its operation. She would not play the grand lady, sitting idle indoors. She would be out with the men, learning from Newt.

However, when she and the brothers rode out of town, she still hadn't made up her mind. She feared she would be taking a big chance, living where Ace could find her at any time. If he pursued her, would she be strong enough not to give in to him?

One minute she told herself that she would, that it was different now that she knew he had another woman. The next minute, though, she remembered how wonderful their lovemaking had been, how she still longed for those sweet nights, lost in each other's arms. Could she trust herself to remember that Ace had a family? Could she remember that she would only be inviting more heartache?

"That was quite a shock Ace gave us, wasn't it?" Thad asked.

"It certainly was," Lark agreed. "I'm still reeling from it. I can't believe that I am finally free from Cletus, that I don't have to worry about him finding me and taking Aaron away."

"When will you take over the ranch?" Thad asked so matter-of-factly it was as if there were no question of her taking ownership of the place.

Lark gave a small laugh. "You too, Thad? Ace was pressing me to claim it as well."

"Hah! That one. It's none of his business what you do."

"Anyway, I'm of two minds what to do about the ranch."

"You've got to be joshing me. Of course you'll take over. Are you gonna let the other ranchers take over that prime range, let rustlers steal your cattle? So what if you hated Gibb's guts? You had every right to, and you have every right to be compensated for his meanness."

The farm came into sight, and when they rode into the barnyard Lark said, "I want to discuss it with you and Auntie and Uncle Ben after supper."

The pleased flush that spread over Thad's face said that he felt honored to be included in a family discussion. "We can talk out on the back porch," he said.

There was that special hush that falls over the land between dusk and dark when Lark and Lucy walked out onto the small porch, followed by Ben and Thad. "What is it you want to talk to us about, Lark?" Lucy asked when she and Lark sat down on the bench flanking the wall and Ben and Thad had taken seats on the edge of the porch floor. "You sounded awfully serious. Is everything all right?"

"Well," Lark began slowly, "it is serious, and everything is better than all right."

Thad couldn't contain the news any longer and blurted out, "Gibb is dead. Shot dead by a sheriff."

There was a silence that seemed to go on forever. Finally Lucy half whispered, "He's dead? I can't believe it."

"It's true, though," Thad began; then, seeing the displeased look on Lark's face, he closed his mouth.

"I'm told the ranch now belongs to me and that I should move back there. I want your and Uncle Ben's opinion on that. Would you two mind moving again?"

"Land sakes no, child. I wouldn't mind." Lucy's

face was beaming at the thought of living in the big house again. "What about you, Ben?" She turned to her husband. "It wouldn't bother you, would it?"

Lark noticed for the first time that her uncle hadn't said a word since the news about her husband was broken. That's strange, she thought. Uncle Ben always voiced an opinion on everything. "Well, Uncle Ben," she pressed, "what do you think?"

Ben cleared his throat a couple of times, then muttered, "It sounds like a good idea."

"That's settled," Thad said, then asked eagerly, "When do we start? We can go by boat. It's still tied up where I left it on the shore."

Lark smiled at his and Lucy's excited faces. She shrugged and said, "I guess we can head out tomorrow."

When the boat bumped onto the muddy bank, the same spot where Lark had boarded it the day she fled the ranch, she was swamped with dark memories. It took her a moment to remember that Cletus was gone, that he would never hurt her again.

She looked over her shoulder at her relatives, and the happiness on Lucy's face made her give thanks that at least her beloved aunt could settle in a permanent home in her old age. Her uncle's stoic expression told her nothing.

Lark hid an amused smile as Thad helped her out of the boat. On a distant knoll, the noonday sun beaming on his white, straggly hair, stood Ragged Feather. How did the old fellow know that we'd be arriving today? she wondered. But maybe this wasn't the first time he had stood there, his gaze on the river, she thought as Thad took the baby from her and led the way up the bank. He could have been waiting for them every day since Cletus was shot.

"Look who's waiting for you," she said to Ben, who was walking beside her.

Ben looked to where she was pointing, slowed his pace, then broke away without a word, walking toward his old friend. "We won't see him again until suppertime, when he gets hungry." Lucy laughed.

Lark was hoping that he would be in a better frame of mind when he showed up. She opened the gate to the white picket fence and walked through it, shocked that the house and yard had taken on such an unkempt appearance in such a short time. The unmowed grass reached past her ankles, and the flower beds that Cletus made her work so hard on now had weeds popping up among his prize rosebushes. Tending to them had been her one pleasant chore. She would get to them tomorrow.

Dust lay thick on the porch and the three chairs there. It was plain a broom hadn't been wielded on the floor for some time. With a sigh she pushed open the unlocked door and stepped inside.

As she walked through the rooms, it was evident that Cletus hadn't been in the house since she had left. The bedrooms she and Aunt Lucy had occupied had clothes strewn about, and the beds were unmade, just as they had left them. Cletus would never have tolerated that.

Baby Aaron stirred and whimpered. After she had changed him into dry clothes, she sat down in a rocker in the parlor and put the little one to her breast. With a shove of her foot, she put the rocker into motion.

"The first thing I'm going to do is change the bedding in our rooms," Lucy said, bustling into the room with a stack of linen in her arms. "Then I'll see what I can rustle up for supper."

"Will you cook in the kitchen, or use the cookhouse?"

"The cookhouse, I think. That's where all the food is stored."

"I'll give you a hand later. I haven't said hello to Newt yet. We have to talk, to make plans."

"Take your time," Lucy said, whipping the sheets and blankets off the bed. "He and Thad are down at the barn talking to each other." She laughed lightly. "Thad is probably telling Newt how the ranch should be run."

Ten minutes later little Aaron was asleep in his cradle and Lark was walking toward one of the empty corrals where Thad and Newt stood in what seemed like serious conversation.

"Hello, Newt." She smiled at the man who had been her friend since the first day she had come to the ranch as Cletus Gibb's frightened bride. "It's good to see you again."

"The same sentiment to you, Lark." Newt held out his hand to her. "It's almost like old times, the three of us putting something over on Gibb."

"We don't have to worry about him anymore, do we?" Lark smiled slightly.

"Thank God for that mercy." Newt smiled openly.

Lark folded her arms on the top corral rail. "What do you think, can we whip this place into shape again? Cletus was a devil straight out of hell, but he did know how to run the ranch."

"It wasn't that he had that much know-how," Newt replied. "He had the best cowhands around to keep everything running smoothly. He was shrewd enough to pay above top wages and to provide the hands with good grub and quarters so that they would put up with him."

"Do you think the men will return to their old jobs?"

"No question about it. Me and Thad are going into town after supper. I guarantee they'll be riding back with us."

"The cook too?"

"The cook too." Newt grinned, then added, "If we can find him."

"And when they get here, what do we do first?"

"That would be up to Jake Henry, the foreman," Newt answered, "but I imagine he would want to get started right away getting the cattle ready for a trail drive to Topeka, Kansas. We'd be getting a late start, but there will be plenty of grass and water along the way."

As the three discussed the many things to be done, the western sky turned pink and yellow from the setting sun. "Is it suppertime?" Thad sent a surprised look at the cookhouse, where Lucy stood outside running a striker around the inside of an angle iron, announcing that the evening meal was on the table.

"I don't know about you men, but I'm starved," Lark said, and pushing away from the corral, she headed for the cookhouse.

"Me too." Thad fell in beside her. "I sure am tired of beans and salt pork."

They found Ben at the long bench flanking the cookhouse wall. Soapy water was splashing all over, and he gave them a wide smile. Lark was relieved when he began complaining about how run-down the place looked. Uncle Ben was back to his usual garrulous self. His visit with Ragged Feather had worked wonders on him.

Mouthwatering aromas hit Lark and the men when they stepped inside the cookhouse. Lucy had prepared big, thick steaks, mashed potatoes and red gravy, string beans and hot biscuits.

When the men sat down at the table and dug in, Lark walked into the small back room. Memories, sweet and bitter, swept over her. Here she had experienced falling in love, had been introduced to the art of lovemaking. Here, also, she had become pregnant with her son.

She had been so happy, convinced that Ace would demand she divorce Cletus and marry him. Then came the bitterness. Before she could tell him he was to become a father, he was telling her good-bye.

And now Ace was back. But not in her life, she vowed.

It was just turning gray outside when Lark jerked awake. She turned over on her back and peered in the semigloom at the man who had been shaking her shoulder.

"What's wrong, Uncle Ben?" she whispered so as not to wake her son.

"Nothing is wrong," Ben whispered back. "The cowhands are back and they'll be wanting their breakfast pretty soon. Newt and Thad didn't bring back the cook, and Lucy can't cook for that many men. I'm afraid it's up to you, honey."

"I'll be right there." Lark sat up, knuckled the sleep out of her eyes and swung her feet to the floor.

Within ten minutes she had splashed water on her

face, gotten dressed, pulled a brush through her hair and was on her way to the cookhouse.

She fell into her old routine as though she had never left it. This time it was very different, though. She was not gripped by nervous tension as she fried bacon and made biscuits and scrambled a dozen eggs. There was no Cletus staring at her, waiting to find fault so that he had an excuse to strike her. This morning she was the boss lady of the ranch, making biscuits for her hired help.

When the men filed into the big room later, they hardly recognized the self-confident young woman who looked them full in the face and smiled warmly at them. Gone was the browbeaten creature who never lifted her gaze from the floor.

They were a little in awe of this new Lark at first, but her easy manner and warm smile soon put them at ease. Before long they were talking almost as much as Ben.

"So you couldn't find the cook," Lark said as she walked around the table filling the coffee cups.

"We found Randy," Newt answered, "but he'd already signed on at another ranch. He's been there a couple weeks, and he feels that the honorable thing to do is to give the rancher a couple weeks' notice. He'll be here then."

As the men relaxed over their coffee, Jake Henry began telling the men what they would be doing for the next three days. "We've got to get ready for the cattle drive. That means a lot of riding to get the cattle together. You'll find them in brush, thickets, ravines and anywhere else the devils can hide. I want to start the drive next Monday."

"We can do it," some of the men said, while others nodded their agreement.

"What about a cook?" Newt remembered they had none. "Randy won't be showing up for a while, you know."

It grew silent in the room, and it was a moment before Lark sensed that everyone was looking at her.

"Hey," she protested, "don't expect me to go on a drive *and* do the cooking. I have a young baby, remember. How could I take care of Aaron and cook for you men?"

"It would only be for a week and a half. Then Randy will have caught up with us. You could go home then," Thad pointed out.

"I could go on the drive and take care of the little one," Lucy offered.

"There you are, Larkie. It's all settled," Ben said with approval.

As Lark gazed at the expectant faces, she realized that she was going to lose the battle. "All right," she agreed, her voice full of doubt. "But the baby is awfully young to ride around in a bouncing chuck wagon."

"It won't hurt him, Larkie," Thad said, using Ben's pet name for her. "Think of all the babies who rode across country in wagon trains. It didn't hurt them."

"How do you know, Mr. Smarty?" Lark snapped. "Were you there?"

"Well, no. But I never heard of one being hurt by it."

"Hah!" Lark snorted. "As if you would."

As if knowing he was being discussed, Aaron put up a loud wail from the back room. Lark joined in the men's laughter and walked into the back room to nurse her son.

Chapter Thirty-five

Ace was saddle weary as he galloped Sam across the range. He had been riding for days, making a trip to Utah to check on Matt and Drew.

When he had realized that Lark wasn't going to fall into his arms, that he would have to do some serious courting, he'd decided he'd better see how the brothers were doing. They were capable young people, but teenagers nevertheless, and he never knew what they might get up to.

He had found everything going along fine. Not only had the brothers been working on the house—the roof was completely finished—but they had captured a dozen fine-looking mustangs.

He hadn't liked the idea, though, that Matt had found himself a pretty little Mexican sweetheart who was now living with him and Drew in the yet unfinished house. He hadn't voiced his disapproval too strongly. Matt was of an age when his hormones were working overtime. He had told himself that it was better that the boy's first experience at lovemaking was with a young woman like that than with a jaded whore. He wouldn't even be allowed to kiss one of the soiled doves, let alone receive any tenderness or affection in the act. He was going to have a serious talk with Matt, though, when he got things on his own plate taken care of.

Sam topped a knoll and the ranch lay below. A satisfied smile stirred Ace's lips. All the cowhands had returned. That meant Lark had taken over. He saw her then. The early morning sun glinted off her head, and her hair had been pulled back and tied with a ribbon.

She was walking from the house toward the barn, wearing a split riding skirt. Did she intend to ride out with the men? Ace asked himself.

His blood pumping a little faster at seeing her again, he sent Sam down the hill.

The early morning air was cool and breezy when Lark left the house and walked to the barn. She wore her new riding skirt and enjoyed the freedom it gave her legs. She could lengthen her stride without having a full skirt and petticoat swirling around her ankles. Her white, flat-crowned hat hung down her back, secured to her neck by a thin strip of rawhide. Later she would welcome its protection against the hot sun beating down on her head.

Thad had a sturdy little quarter horse saddled and waiting for her. She mounted it and waited with the others as Jake Henry gave orders about what was to be done today. He divided the men into groups to flush out the wild longhorns.

"Now, I don't have to tell you to be careful of them devils," he warned. "You know not to dismount for any reason. A man afoot is flirting with death."

He looked at Thad and Newt and started to caution them to look after Lark. She saw the intent in his eyes and her own dared him to speak what was on his mind. He grinned sheepishly and said, "I guess that's it. Start bringing the ornery critters in."

Reins were lifted and the men were ready to ride out when Newt exclaimed, "Isn't that Ace riding up?"

"It sure is," someone agreed.

When Sam thundered into the barnyard, Lark and Thad were the only ones who didn't rein their horses around the gelding.

"Are you gonna hire on again, too, Ace?" Jake Henry asked.

"I'd like to." Ace looked at Lark. "What about it, Lark? Do you need another hand?"

Damn the wily devil. Lark simmered inside. *He knows I have no legitimate reason to say no, especially at roundup time.* A rancher needed every good hand he could hire then. Well, she could put up with him for a few weeks, she told herself. After roundup, she'd ask him to leave. She rolled her shoulders indifferently and made herself say calmly, "Why not?"

She doesn't want me here, Ace thought. *But why?* Why had her attitude toward him changed so? They'd had a firm friendship when he'd said good-bye to her all those months ago. What had happened to change that? *And what about Thad? He acts like I've done him some kind of dirt.*

"Let's get going then," Jake Henry said, and the

men rode off in their designated directions.

Lark noted that the area she and Newt and Thad had been given wasn't too far away from the ranch house. She would be close enough to ride in and nurse her son every three hours or so. She felt that the foreman had had that in mind when he issued his orders.

Nevertheless, she found it wasn't easy racing the horse after stubborn, half-wild cattle, trying to herd them in the right direction.

The sun grew hot; dirt and sweat rolled down her face. She was thankful when three hours passed and it was time to tend to her son's wants.

Newt and Thad paid no attention to her breaking away from them and riding off in the direction of the ranch. They knew why she was going.

When Lark rode up to the barn, Ben was waiting to take her horse. "Aaron is fussing," he told her as she dismounted. "Better go feed him."

As she stepped up on the porch, she could hear her son's angry cries. "What a temper my little man has," she said softly when she entered her bedroom and looked down at the small, red face and tiny waving fists. "Let Mama wash her face and hands, and then I'll take care of your hunger."

"I'm afraid your milk will dry up with all that hard riding," Lucy said, coming into the room and sitting down on the edge of the bed.

"Do you really think so?" Lark frowned as she brought the baby to her breast. "I wouldn't want that to happen."

"Don't fret about it if it happens. We can always get a milch cow. He's old enough to be weaned to a bottle if necessary."

A smile lifted the corners of Lark's lips when a merry Mexican song drifted from one of the back bedrooms. "When did Rosa arrive?" she asked.

"Shortly after you left this morning. She's cleaning Gibb's room now." Her hands on her knees, Lucy pushed herself up. "I'm going to make you a sandwich and a cup of coffee before you go back to work," she said.

"Thank you, Aunt Lucy."

Lucy was about to walk through the door when Ben blocked her way. "Ace is riding up to the barn," he said anxiously. "He may come to the house."

"Oh, dear," Lucy cried. "Is Aaron finished nursing, Lark?"

"Yes," Lark answered, her fingers busy buttoning up her shirt. "I'm going to put him in Cletus's room. If he cries, we'll say he's Rosa's baby. Now don't look so nervous, you two."

When Ace walked into the kitchen a few minutes later, Lucy was calmly making Lark a beef sandwich, and Ben was sitting at the table sipping a cup of coffee. The greeting they extended him was genial enough, but a little reserved.

"Will you have some coffee, Ace?" Lucy invited. "And a sandwich? I'm just now making one for Lark."

"That will hit the spot. I didn't have breakfast this morning." Ace pulled a chair away from the table and sat down. "Is Lark all right? I saw her ride toward the house. Is the heat getting to her?"

"Oh, no," Lucy quickly answered. "She had to . . . er . . . use the privy. A woman can't go behind a bush like you men can."

"That's true," Ace agreed, amusement dancing in his eyes.

"There you are." Lucy looked up and smiled when Lark entered the kitchen. "Ace is going to have a sandwich with you."

Giving Ace a thin smile Lark said, "That's nice," and sat down across from him. While they silently watched Lucy prepare the sandwiches, Ben finished his coffee and walked outside.

"It's hard, chasing them dumb cattle, isn't it?" Ace tried for some conversation.

"Yes, it is," Lark agreed. "You think you have them all going in one direction. Then they suddenly turn and scatter all over the range."

"I think their brains are very small, and mean at that," Ace said with a half smile.

"You still don't like cattle, do you?" Lark asked, amusement in her voice.

"No, I've got no use for the dumb critters."

After a moment's silence Lark said, "By the way, how is your horse ranch coming along? You are working at it, aren't you?"

"Oh, yes. It's coming along fine. I've settled on my mother's land in Utah. The prettiest country you'd ever want to see. Lots of grass and plenty of water. I've got me a house that's almost finished." He paused a second, then bragged, "I've sold two hundred head already."

"Sounds like you've been very busy. Do you get into Denver often?"

"No. Only when I drive my horses in to sell. I furnish the army."

Lark watched Ace's face through her lowered lashes as she asked, "Doesn't your family miss you in your long absences?"

"My family?" Ace thought of the three young boys

he had practically adopted. He smiled then and said, "My family is with me ninety-five percent of the time."

Lark's eyes widened a little at this unexpected answer. He had to be lying. She couldn't imagine that his beautiful, fancy wife would chase wild horses and live in an unfinished house.

"Let me tell you about my family," Ace began, but Lark was on her feet and headed toward the door. "I'll see you later, Aunt Lucy," she said as the screen door slammed behind her.

Anger began to simmer inside Ace. He was getting tired of her coolness, her rudeness. There was no call for it. He snatched his hat up and slapped it on his head. "Thank you for the sandwich, Aunt Lucy," he said, and almost tore the door off its hinges as he snatched it open.

Lark was about to mount the fresh quarter horse Ben had saddled for her when Ace came striding into the barn. She squeaked a strangled cry when he grabbed her arm and swung her around to come up solidly against his hard body.

"What do you think you're doing?" she cried, trying to get her hands between them so that she could push him away.

"What am I doing?" Ace ground out, jerking her up closer to his chest. "I'm going to learn what has put your nose out of joint toward me."

"I don't know what you're talking about." Lark glared up at him.

"The hell you don't. You and Thad and your aunt and uncle act like I'm a stranger that you don't like."

"That's not true." Unconsciously, Lark began to

push her hips at him at the same time she was pummeling his shoulders with her fists.

"It's true. You know damn well it's true. Everything was fine between us when I left you that night. Now, only months later when I see you again, you act like there has never been anything between us. What happened since then, Lark?"

"Nothing happened." The fight was beginning to go out of Lark as a soft warmth began to flow through her body. She stopped pushing against his shoulders. It only brought her tighter against the bulge of maleness she remembered so well.

"Something happened." Ace grabbed a handful of her hair and pulled her head back so he could look into her face. "I'm not letting you go until you tell me what's going on."

Lark could only shake her head and gaze at him helplessly. Pride would not let her tell him how heartbroken she'd been that night when he'd casually ridden away from her.

As Ace gazed into Lark's upturned face, the anger began to ooze out of him as he remembered the many times he had seen her look the exact same way while she lay beneath his thrusting body. A rush of love and desire for her swept through him.

He released her hair and, stroking his hand over her face, whispered, "You are even lovelier than ever. I have dreamed of you so often. I have awakened in the middle of the night aching for you." He stroked a finger across her trembling lips. "Haven't you thought of me a few times, longed for the nights we spent together?"

Lark could only nod her head. A sigh of surrender

feathered through her lips when he picked her up in his arms and strode to a dark corner.

The hay was soft and fragrant where he laid her down. His hands were slow and gentle as he unbuttoned her shirt and spread it apart. She held her breath as he slid her riding skirt down her hips, taking her underwear with it.

He was standing up then, jerking his shirttail from his denims and kicking off his boots. Lark watched eagerly as he shucked off his pants. Her pulse raced when he stood over her, his masculinity thick and hard as she remembered it. She lifted her arms and he came down to her.

There was no foreplay. Both had waited too long for this moment. When Ace positioned himself between her welcoming legs and hung over her, Lark took his largeness and guided it inside her. As he filled her she moaned her pleasure, and Ace groaned his as she wrapped her legs around his waist. He put his hands beneath her small rear and brought her up into the well of his hips. And like old times he began to slowly thrust in and out of her warm moistness.

Both wanting it to last forever, they rocked together until sweat sheened their bodies as they strained against each other. Then suddenly Ace was moving faster, plunging deeper. The explosion came then, their bodies shuddering in a release that left them drained.

They lay inert, breathing hard, too weak to move. After a few minutes' rest, however, Ace was growing hard again. He had just dropped his head to Lark's breast and settled his mouth over a pouting nipple when they heard hoofbeats coming toward the barn. Ace rolled off Lark, and she sat up when they recognized the voices of Thad and Newt as the two dismounted in the barnyard.

"I hope Aunt Lucy will give us something to eat with a cup of coffee," Thad was saying.

"I hope she has some pie," Newt said. Then their voices faded as they walked toward the house.

As Ace and Lark scrambled into their clothes, Ace called himself a damn fool. He had chanced ruining Lark's reputation. His boots tugged on, the top button of his denims unbuttoned and his shirt hanging open, he pulled Lark into his arms and kissed her hard. "We'll talk later," he said. After peering through the barn door to see if anyone was around, he slipped outside. A moment later Lark heard him riding away.

Tears of shame stung Lark's eyes. She had allowed herself to lose control of her body, had let it do as it wished. She had allowed it to answer Ace's hunger.

She buttoned up her shirt and stuffed the tail into her waistband. She spent a couple of minutes smoothing wrinkles and making sure all the hay was out of her hair. Striding over to the fresh horse, she mounted and left the barn.

Her lips were drawn in a tight line and her back was stiff. Never again would that randy wolf work his spell on her.

Chapter Thirty-six

Lark stopped the rocking of the chair with a drag of her foot and removed the bottle's nipple from her son's slack mouth. He had taken to cow's milk without any trouble. Yesterday she'd had to admit that she could no longer nourish the little one. Her eight-hour day of chasing cattle had made it impossible.

Lark dropped a kiss on the soft black hair crowning Aaron's head and, rising, gently laid him down in his own small cradle. She stood a moment, gazing down at the little sleeping face, and sighed. Each day the baby looked more like Ace. If a stranger saw the two of them together, he would know immediately that they were father and son.

I've got to get rid of Ace somehow, before everyone at the ranch sees how much they resemble each other, she thought as she lowered the lamp's wick.

She did not want her innocent little baby being gossiped about.

As Lark prepared for bed herself, she remembered that the trail drive would stop tomorrow. After that she would make it clear to Ace that she wanted him out of her life.

But could she really say the words? she asked herself as she lay in bed, listening to the distant bawling of cattle. They were uneasy and fighting mad at being driven from their hiding places. She knew what they were experiencing. She had felt the same way many times as she and her relatives were forced to move from place to place.

I'll not do that to my son, she vowed. *He will always know security. I'm going to miss my little fellow,* she thought as she drifted off to sleep. Now that he didn't need her to nurse him, it wasn't necessary to bring him along on the cattle drive. He would stay home with Aunt Lucy and Uncle Ben.

Ace leaned against the trunk of a big cottonwood several yards from the ranch house. He was in the grip of a frustration that was fast becoming unmanageable anger. He had been here since dark, determined that he would talk to Lark. He wanted to know why she was avoiding him. He wanted to ask why the sudden change in her demeanor where he was concerned. He wanted to know how she could cling to him in passion one day, then refuse to make eye contact with him the next.

Ace was also doing a slow burn that her aunt and uncle always managed to keep him from her. And that damn Thad was worse than the old folks. He had been sitting on the porch, whittling on a stick ever since Ace took up his watch in the shadow of the cottonwood. He knew that if he approached the house, the kid would gruffly tell him that Lark had gone to bed.

Ace saw the light go out in Lark's bedroom. With a disappointed sigh, he decided that he might as well turn in too. There was no telling how long the kid might sit there, keeping watch.

He was ready to start walking toward the bunkhouse when he saw a horse ride up to the barn. Who was it? he wondered. All the cowhands, spent from a day of hard riding, had gone to bed a couple of hours ago.

His curiosity was piqued further when the rider dismounted and led the horse into the barn. Had Jake Henry hired another hand?

It wasn't until the stranger walked out into the light of the rising moon that Ace recognized him: Thad's brother, Coy. His suspicions that there might be something going on between Lark and the handsome farmer rose up again. Why else would the man be here? He couldn't know much about ranching. He'd be more at home pushing a plow, Ace thought with a sneer.

When Thad's brother sat down beside Thad and they talked together in low tones, Ace decided he couldn't do anything about the newcomer tonight. He had to get some sleep. The ranch would be awake in a few hours, ready to start one thousand head of longhorns on their way to the holding pens in Kansas. He'd settle things between him and Lark tomorrow, that was for damn sure.

* * *

Lark was up an hour before the men. When she walked into the cookhouse she found that her uncle had risen from bed even earlier than she. He had a fire going in the range and a pot of coffee brewing. He had also sliced up a slab of bacon, ready for the frying pan heating on top of the stove. Also, he had set out on the work bench a small basket of eggs and the ingredients for biscuits.

"Thank you, Uncle Ben." Lark kissed his leathery cheek before washing her face and hands in the basin of warm water he had waiting for her.

"I figured you'd be wanting to make the men a hearty breakfast this morning, seeing what a hard day they have ahead of them. I thought to give you a hand."

"It's much appreciated, Uncle." Lark smiled at him as she placed bacon strips in the skillet.

While Lark prepared breakfast Ben set the table. There was a pink flush in the sky when she told the old man to go strike the angle iron.

The men were in high, good spirits when they came trooping into the large room. For the time being they had forgotten the hard work, the danger that lay ahead of them, even the chance of being trampled to death in a wild stampede. All they thought of now was that at the end of the drive they would have money in their pockets and that there would be saloons and whorehouses where they could spend it. They didn't think that in all probability they would arrive back at the ranch with their pockets empty, or close to it.

All the time that Lark kept the bacon and eggs coming to the table, Ace tried to get her attention. Nothing worked. Coy had no trouble doing that, though, he noticed. Lark laughed and joked with him until he was acting like a blushing, blithering idiot. By the end of the meal Ace was ready to punch his handsome face and tell him to get back to the farm where he belonged.

At the same time Lark was ready to punch Ace's pouting face and to tell him to get back to Utah and his horse ranch. He had her nerves frayed, constantly watching her every move. In retaliation she had paid more attention to Coy than she had wanted to. Thad's brother was a nice man and didn't deserve to be led on. She had to gently make him understand that there could be nothing but friendship between them.

Lark gave heartfelt thanks when the men began filing outside, Ace along with them. When she began to clear the table Ben stopped her. "Go on up to the house and say good-bye to your son and aunt," he said. "I'll take care of cleaning up."

"Thanks, Uncle." Lark hugged his bony shoulders. "You and Ragged Feather behave yourselves while I'm gone," she teased with a grin. "And don't take Aaron fishing."

"We won't," Ben answered, his eyes twinkling. "Maybe we'll take him on an overnight hunting trip, though. He'd like sleeping in a bedroll, staring up at the stars while he chewed on a strip of dried beef." They laughed at the nonsense of their conversation, and Lark left the cookhouse.

Dawn had arrived, pure and clear, by the time the men were mounted. Lark and Newt were sitting in the chuck wagon fifty yards or so ahead of them. They would lead the way, choosing the best places to make camp, the best streams where the cattle and the remuda could quench their thirst. When Jake Henry fired his gun in the air, signaling that the drive was to begin, Newt snapped the reins over the team. As the dust rolled from beneath the creaking wheels, Newt said with a wide smile, "We're off, Lark."

Behind them came the men, popping whips and yelling and whistling as they prodded the cattle into motion. They were indeed off, as Newt had said.

The longhorns moved along at a fast clip as they left the home range. They were well rested after having slept all night. But in the early afternoon, as the sun grew hotter, their pace slowed and they became sullen and edgy. The smallest thing could start them stampeding.

Lark was feeling the heat also as she bounced along in the chuck wagon. The sweat gathered between her breasts and at her waistband. She felt sticky with perspiration. When they topped a grassy hill and gazed down into a shallow valley, both she and Newt expressed their relief. A long line of willows met their view. Where those graceful trees grew there was always a river.

The team smelled the water and stepped up their pace. When the animals came to the silent flowing water and dropped their muzzles into it, Lark started to jump from the wagon. She couldn't wait to bathe her face in the coolness of the river.

"Hold on, Lark," Newt cautioned. "We've got to get on. We must be well away from here before the herd arrives. They're gonna hit the water like a thundering herd of buffalo. If we're still here the chuck wagon will be smashed to smithereens, us with it."

When Lark reluctantly sat back down he whipped

up the team. They reached the opposite shore only moments before the longhorns came into sight at a dead run. As they surged forward, bawling and red-eyed mean, Newt brought the team to a halt half a mile away in a thick stand of aspen and cottonwood.

"We'll make camp here," he said, jumping to the ground.

"Isn't it a little early to make camp?" Lark asked, jumping down beside him.

"No." Newt shook his head. "It will be near dark before the men drive all the cattle across the river."

Lark agreed as she looked down at the herd lining the bank for a half a mile. The men were having a hard time keeping any kind of control over the thirsty animals.

Her gaze went straight to Ace, who was riding back and forth among the cattle, popping a whip over the backs of the unruly beasts. Her heart jumped in alarm. What if he should be unseated and go down beneath those sharp hooves? He would not survive.

She remembered that he hadn't tried to talk to her this morning, and she'd felt sure that he would. All day she had wavered between being glad that he hadn't and being disappointed.

"Make up your mind," she whispered as she turned her back to the milling cowboys and the dangerous work they were doing. She couldn't bear to watch them any longer. If Ace went down she didn't want to see it. She set about helping Newt set up camp.

While Newt prepared a fire pit, Lark went through the air-tights she had packed in the chuck wagon. When she had tossed to the ground four cans each of tomatoes, peaches and beans, she took a sugar-cured ham from a box beneath the wagon seat and set it aside. When it came time to start supper, she would slice a portion of it and fry the meat over the open fire.

When she had gathered the ingredients for Indian fry bread, she helped Newt unhitch the team and stake them out in a patch of tall grass. As Newt walked off through the trees she stretched her back, relaxing the muscles that had tightened from sitting in the bouncing chuck wagon. She took another look at the river and the cattle below. Only half of the cattle had been driven across. There was time for a nap.

Lark spread a blanket on the ground and stretched out on it. Two hours went by before she was awakened by Newt shaking her shoulder. In the west gold light shone through the trees.

"The men will have all the cattle on this side of the river in another half an hour," Newt said. "I expect we ought to start supper."

Lark stood up, folded the blanket and tossed it inside the wagon, where she would sleep while on the trail.

While Newt built a fire and put a large pot of coffee to brewing, she let down the wagon's tailgate. After propping it up she placed a stack of tin plates, cups and flatware on the makeshift table. She pulled a gunnysack from the wagon and dumped its contents on the ground. From the jumble she chose a pot and two skillets.

Next, Lark took a butcher knife to the ham, severing from the bone thick slices of pink, tender meat. That done, she opened the air-tights, emptied the beans into a pot and set them close to the flames to heat.

Twenty minutes later when three of the weary men rode into camp, the evening meal was ready. Lark noticed that Ace wasn't with them. She assumed that he had stayed with the group to help keep an eye on the herd. The cattle had settled down to graze on the plentiful supply of grass.

Coy was there, however, in her way every time she turned around. Finally, exasperated, she handed him a plate of beans and meat and told him to go sit down. She was sorry for having spoken so sharply to him when the cowhands let loose loud guffaws and his face turned a vivid red. He stalked off and sat down beside his brother, Thad. She didn't see him again until the next morning.

When the first shift went to relieve the other men, Lark began frying a second batch of Indian bread. She heard the new group ride in, heard Ace's rich laughter ring out at something Newt had said. She didn't turn her head to look at him but kept her attention on the dough sizzling in the skillet.

Then suddenly, as the men were sitting around the fire wolfing down beans and meat, she was all interest. Ace had just said to Newt that he was thinking seriously of leaving them and returning to his ranch. As she listened intently he went on to say, "I don't know why I signed up in the first place, knowing how I hate these mean, dumb longhorns. Besides, I shouldn't be leaving my boys alone for such a long spell."

After a long moment Newt asked with some surprise in his tone, "How many boys do you have?"

"Three," Ace answered proudly. "Fine youngsters.

Matt just turned seventeen, Drew is fifteen and Benny is ten. He's with my mother. He's too young to be left in the care of his brothers."

Ace realized then that his casual remark about the boys had everyone thinking that he was talking about his sons. He started to explain that his "boys" were orphans that he had more or less adopted; then he saw the stunned look on Lark's face and shut his mouth. Let her chew on that for a while, he thought.

He almost gave a sardonic laugh. As if his having three sons would matter to her. She wouldn't care if he had a half dozen sons. He had spoken the truth to Newt when he said that he was thinking of leaving the drive. He had finally been forced to accept the truth that Lark didn't care for him. She enjoyed their lovemaking. There was no doubt about that. She was like a flame in his arms, wanting more and more of him. But a married couple couldn't stay in bed all the time. There had to be love, friendship and respect in the mixture of wedded contentment.

Ace felt that at one time, he and Lark had had all that when they met in the back room of the cookhouse. But it was plain that Lark felt no love or friendship for him these days.

He had come to the conclusion that if he was to get over her, he must put as much distance as possible between them. He would finish out the week and ride away from her for all time.

By the time Lark had finished washing and drying the dishes, twilight was nearly spent and darkness was closing in. The last group to eat would sleep until midnight, then would relieve the first group.

Ace and the two other men spread their blankets back among the trees. Before Lark climbed into the wagon where she would sleep, she mounded ashes over the fire to keep the coals alive until morning.

Lark was wide awake as she lay on top of her bedroll. Over and over she heard Ace's voice talking of his three boys. He must have been only a boy himself when the first one was born. He couldn't have been more than eighteen. Even at such an early age he had already been a randy wolf.

What kind of father was he? she wondered. There had been pride in his voice when he spoke of his boys. He was thoughtful enough of the ten-year-old not to leave him in the care of his brothers.

Lark knew a moment of envy for the three sons who would grow up with their father, never knowing that they had another brother. At best her poor little Aaron might have a stepfather someday. But that time wouldn't be soon. She didn't know if she could ever trust a man again.

Lark was about to drift off to sleep when suddenly there came the mournful yowl of a wolf. Would it startle the cattle into a stampede? She rose up on an elbow and listened intently. Everything seemed quiet at the bottom of the hill, so she lowered herself back down to the bedroll. While she waited for the lonesome cry to sound again, she fell asleep.

Chapter Thirty-seven

As the chuck wagon bounced along, Lark mopped a handkerchief over her perspiring face. She looked up at the turbulent clouds churning overhead. There was going to be a storm. She prayed it would arrive during the daylight hours and not wait for darkness. The cattle were less apt to spook and run when they could see the area around them.

She was driving the chuck wagon today. Newt had expressed the desire to ride. He claimed he was tired of the monotony of poking along, looking at the rear end of the team's rumps. Having no one to talk to and nothing to look at but the rolling plains, Lark found her thoughts turning to Ace.

Tomorrow would end the week's notice he had given before leaving the trail drive. She told herself that she couldn't wait for him to be gone. Her nerves were frazzled. Although she had every reason to feel nothing but scorn for him, his polite coolness toward her was wearing her down. Faced with harsh reality, she knew that in spite of everything she had learned about him, she still loved him.

"But I'll overcome that foolishness," Lark vowed aloud as she flicked the tip of the whip at a fly on one of the horse's rump. She would put all her thoughts and energies on her son and the ranch he would inherit someday. In another week or less the cook would be catching up with them, and she would be free to return home. And not a moment too soon, she thought. She missed her little son something fierce.

It was around two in the afternoon when Lark became aware of storm clouds rumbling behind her and lightning zigzagging across the sky. She was going to get her wish. A storm was going to erupt any minute, and it was going to be a bad one. She could smell sulfur in the air.

She wondered where she could find shelter for herself and the team. They were becoming nervous, flinching at every crack of thunder. If they decided to bolt, she would never be able to control them.

As Lark scanned the area, the storm grew louder and nearer. Every strike of lightning seemed aimed at the chuck wagon. Tears of fear were running down her cheeks when she spotted, in a short, narrow valley, a run-down, deserted homestead. She sent a look of thanks skyward and guided the team toward the forlorn-looking buildings.

The double doors of the barn stood open, and without pausing she drove the team inside the calming gloom of the building. She jumped to the dirt floor and began speaking soothingly to the horses.

She was stroking their quivering shoulders when suddenly a horse and rider loomed in the opening of the barn. Her mouth went dry with fear as a male figure walked toward her, leading the horse. She darted a look at the chuck wagon. Could she get inside it, grab the gun under the seat before the man could grab her?

I can at least try, she thought, and was ready to make a dash for the wagon when a flash of lightning lit up the gloom of the building. She gasped her relief when she recognized Ace.

Ace recovered speech first. "It looks like we're both fleeing the storm," he said with a tentative smile. "My horse picked up a stone," he explained.

Lark gave him a weak smile and said, "I think it will be a bad one."

"I think so too," Ace agreed, looking up at the rotting roof. "I hope this place doesn't leak."

"I'm sure there will be a few places that will stay dry." After an awkward pause Lark said, "I hope the cattle don't decide to run."

"I've been thinking the same thing." Ace walked over to the barn doors and peered into a world that now resembled twilight. "Judging by the dust they're raising, they are still at a walk."

Lark sat down on a bale of moldering straw and let her gaze drink in Ace's broad back, his lean waist, his narrow hips and long legs. A warmth like melted butter spread through her body as she was carried back to the nights spent with him on the cook's narrow bed, then later on a mattress spread out on the floor. She relived the many times those broad shoulders had hung over her, the way the long, muscled legs had slipped between hers. She closed her eyes when she remembered how eagerly, yet gently, he slid his long, throbbing manhood inside her. She caught herself just in time to stop the moan of pleasure that rose to her lips as she recalled the rise and fall of his hips as he thrust in and out of her.

She gave a startled jerk and blushed when Ace came hurrying away from the door, calling out, "It's here!"

The rain was coming down at a slant, and already Ace's shirt was water spotted. In minutes the downpour had found every crack and hole in the roof. Raindrops were peppering the floor in a dozen places.

Lark felt a splash on her face. She jumped to her feet, looking for a dry spot. She spotted a dry corner piled with hay. She made a dash for it at the same time Ace did. As she bumped into him and started to fall, Ace said, "Sorry," and grabbed her arms, keeping her upright.

"I guess we'll have to share," he joked, and they settled down in the small area, their shoulders touching. Ace gave a small laugh and said, "Look, wouldn't you know that the horses are in the driest part of this old barn."

Lark started to laughingly agree, then grabbed Ace's arm and let out a frightened squeal instead. The storm had reached a crescendo of howling wind, streaks of lightning and rumbling thunder. It seemed to be right over their heads, and it was impossible to talk or be heard over Mother Nature's anger.

Ace gathered Lark's trembling body in his arms and held her close. He had his own fear. Were they going to have a tornado, and if so, were they in a deep enough depression to escape it? And he worried also about the longhorns. He could see them running their fool heads off right now. He said a silent prayer that none of the men would go down beneath the thundering hooves.

Ace suddenly became aware of Lark's warm body pushing into his as close as she could. The feel of her firm breasts pressed against his side made him forget the storm going on outside as a different kind of turbulence built inside him. He asked himself if he could keep from unbuttoning her shirt. God knew how he wanted to free one of her breasts, to fasten his mouth on it and twist his tongue around its pink nipple and draw on it until she begged for mercy.

A heartbeat later Ace found that he had no power over his own hand. It had moved to Lark's shirt, his fingers had undone the buttons, and the weight of her beautiful breast lay in his palm.

Lark hadn't stirred a muscle all this time, and Ace wondered if she was aware of what he had done. He argued with himself that of course she knew. She always caught fire when he touched her. He slowly bent his head and lifted the fullness to his open mouth.

Everything was fine until he pulled the nipple between his teeth and started drawing on it. He learned in an instant that she hadn't known what he was doing. She shoved at his head and pummeled his shoulders with her fists.

With a long, defeated sigh Ace raised his head and grabbed her hands. His voice was husky with hopelessness when he said, "I love you, Lark. I don't understand why you can't love me back."

All the anger, the hurt, the unhappiness drained out of her at the sound of the words she'd thought never to hear. When Ace released her hands, they slid up his arms to his shoulders and wound around his neck.

Bewildered by the sudden change in her, Ace stared down at the red lips asking to be kissed. When she slid her hands to the back of his head and gently urged it downward, he gently lowered her onto her back in the straw and covered her lips with a passion equal to the wildness of the storm raging outside.

In their urgency to get out of their clothes, no words were exchanged between them. There was only one thing on their minds: to fuse their bodies, to become one as they had been in the little back room. It took just moments for them to be locked together.

In the hour that passed as they rocked together, noticed neither that the storm was fading away. They only knew that the storm of desire still raged on.

When finally they were sated, the storm was gone and the sun was out again. There was a contented smile on their lips as they climbed back into their clothes and brushed the hay out of their hair.

"Ace, did you love me when we first made love in the cookhouse?" Lark asked as she walked up to him and wrapped her arms around his waist.

Ace dropped a kiss on her forehead. "I'm sure I did, Lark, but I didn't realize it. I thought my feeling for you was only a deep friendship. Then, after I left you I couldn't get you out of my mind. I made love to you every night in my dreams. I finally realized that it was love I had felt for you all the time."

"I think that I loved you even before we made love."

Stroking Lark's back, Ace smiled down at her and said, "We've got to talk, make plans."

"Yes," Lark agreed, her cheek pressed against the steady beat of Ace's heart.

We've got a lot to discuss, she thought. *Not only the son you know nothing about, but also the woman I saw you with in Denver. There's also your three boys. I want to know what you're going to do about them.*

"We'll meet tonight after supper and make our plans," Ace began, then turned his head to look out the barn door when there came the sound of galloping hooves.

"Somebody is in a hurry," he said, and together he and Lark walked outside.

Ace recognized the teenager who jumped off his horse before it had come to a full stop. "What's your hurry, kid?" he asked the sixteen-year-old who worked in the Denver livery.

"Thad told me he thought you was here, but I was beginnin' to think I'd never find you." The words came out in a rush. "Miss Roxy said to tell you to come home right away, that it's very important."

"Did she say why she wants me back in such a hurry?" Ace stepped forward, shaken.

"No, she didn't. She just said to find you as soon as possible."

"Did she look sick?"

"Naw. She just looked mad . . . like a broody hen that's been rained on." After a thoughtful pause he added, "Come to think of it, I saw one thing that might have to do with her wantin' you to get back in a hurry. Your boy Drew came in a few days back, his face like a storm cloud. He and Miss Roxy talked; then an hour later he forked his mount and rode out

378

of town. It was shortly after that when Miss Roxy sent me lookin' for you."

"Oh, Lord," Ace muttered, worry and concern on his face. "What have they been up to now?

"I've got to go, honey." Ace turned to Lark. "I'll be back as soon as I can." When he bent his head to kiss her good-bye, he received a look so cold it froze his blood. When he stared at her in confusion, her hand came up and rocked his head with the slap she delivered to his face.

"If you come near me again I'll shoot you, you no-good bastard," she grated out.

"But, Lark, I've got to go." Ace started after her as she hurried to the chuck wagon.

"Ace," the teenager called after him, "we'd better get started. Miss Roxy is anxious for you to get to Denver."

Ace stopped midway to the wagon, asking himself what to do. As angry as Lark was, it would take some time to find out what was wrong and to calm her down. He decided that it was best to wait until he had more time to talk her out of her snit.

It took him half an hour to catch up with the herd. Luckily, no one had been injured during the storm, and the men had managed to get the cattle back under control. It took another ten minutes to saddle Sam, find Jake Henry and tell him that he was leaving. He was astride Sam then, putting him to a gallop. The livery kid was soon left miles behind.

As the big horse thundered along, Ace's mind was a turmoil of thoughts. None of them was pleasant. What in the hell had gotten into Lark? Surely she understood that he had to go to Roxy. He had to find out why she had sent for him. Did Roxy's urgent message have anything to do with the boys? If so, how bad was it? Had they argued? Had Matt been thrown by a wild horse he was trying to tame?

The next afternoon Sam carried Ace into Denver. Ace turned the weary animal over to a livery man with orders to rub the horse down and to give him a feedbag of oats.

As he walked up the street to the Lady Chance, Ace prayed that Roxy would be in town and not out at her ranch. He didn't think he could ride another mile without a little rest.

When Ace walked into the saloon the first person he saw was his cousin. She stood at the end of the bar talking to the bartender. She stared at his whisker-stubbled face, his red-rimmed eyes and his weary body.

"Good heavens, Ace," she exclaimed, "you look awful."

"I feel awful. What's going on?" he said when she came to meet him.

"I'll tell you while you eat something." She took his arm and led him toward the kitchen. "You look ready to fall on your face."

Pee Wee, the cook, had seen Ace enter the establishment, and when the cousins walked into his domain he had a large steak sizzling in a frying pan. "You look like hell, Ace." He grinned his greeting as he filled a cup with coffee and placed it in front of Ace.

"Thanks." Ace grunted as he brought the strong brew to his mouth. When Roxy poured herself a cup and sat down, he looked at her and asked, "What's the bad news?"

"It's about the boys," she began; then, seeing the alarm that shot into Ace's eyes, she added, "They're all right as far as their health is concerned. But Drew is concerned that Matt is becoming too interested in that Mexican girl they have living with them. Drew said she is urging Matt to marry her."

"Oh, Lord." Ace rolled his eyes at the ceiling. "That idiot is dumb enough to do it too. She's his first, and he doesn't know the difference between love and lust. Hell, he wouldn't know if she was a virgin or not."

"I thought of something else," Roxy said quietly. "What if she is pregnant? With another man's child, I mean."

"Damn it!" Ace slammed his fist on the tabletop so hard his hot coffee splashed out of the cup and hit his hand. "I've got to get back there."

"Not until you've eaten, washed up and changed into some clean clothes," Roxy ordered.

Chapter Thirty-eight

From the top of a rocky slope Ace looked down at the unfinished house he hoped to share with Lark before long. His gaze moved to the corral where they kept the horses that had been broken. Seeing a dozen of them milling around in the pole enclosure, he thought with a wry twist of his lips that Matt hadn't been spending all his time in bed with the girl.

He looked next at the holding pen where ten unbroken horses nipped and kicked at each other as they waited to be brought under the control of man. His attention was caught then by a lone figure sitting on the top rail of the pen. Even from this distance he could see the shoulders slumped dejectedly. He recognized young Drew. He lifted the reins and started the horse down the hill. He had a pretty good idea where Matt was.

Drew jumped to the ground, relief on his face

when Ace rode up. "I've been waiting for you, Ace," he exclaimed.

"I know, son." Ace touched his shoulder affectionately. "Matt's been acting the fool, hasn't he?"

"He sure has. He spends half his time in bed with Maria. It's disgusting," the fifteen-year-old griped. "I can't even go in the house half the time because they're always at it."

Ace hid his amusement. Drew hadn't reached the age yet when he almost constantly thought of the opposite sex. He couldn't understand why his brother was making such a hog of himself.

Ace started walking toward the house. "You stay here, Drew," he said, "while I go jerk him out of bed and give him some home truths."

Ace heard the pair giggling when he stepped up on the finished porch. It was solidly built and had been put together in his absence. He saw Drew's hand in its construction. He was the carpenter. It had been he who framed the windows and hung the two doors.

Ace stepped inside the house and spotted the young lovers immediately. Naked as the day they were born, they lay sprawled on a mattress of gunnysacks sewn together and stuffed with hay. The pair was so engrossed with each other, they didn't know they had company until Ace stood over them and gave a gruff, attention-getting "harrumph." They jerked up on their elbows and gawked in stunned surprise at the thunderous-looking face staring down at them.

"Ace, you're back." Matt looked wildly around for his clothes, which lay in a pile out of his reach.

"And not a minute too soon, from the looks of things." Ace ran a contemptuous gaze over the pair.

Matt avoided his eyes, but the girl insolently returned Ace's stare.

"You"—Ace bored his eyes into her—"get dressed, gather up your duds and get the hell out of here. If I ever see you around here again, you'll regret it."

"I guess Matt will have something to say about that." Maria scrambled to her feet, her eyes flashing hate at him.

"Matt has nothing to say about it," Ace said coldly. He grabbed up her clothes and flung them at her. "If you don't want me to throw you out buck naked, you'd better get dressed right now."

Her face sullen, Maria pulled on the soiled petticoat, then the wrinkled dress with sweat stains in the armpits. She shoved her feet into a pair of worn boots. Before flouncing out of the house, she gave Matt a contemptuous look and said with a sneer, "I should be paid something for teaching this greenhorn a few tricks." It was obvious she cared nothing for him.

She was gone then, her head up in the air, leaving Matt embarrassed and ashamed. "Get dressed, son." Ace tossed a pair of wrinkled denims and a shirt into his lap. "I'll wait on the porch for you. We've got to talk."

It was a thoroughly abashed teenager who came out a few minutes later and sat down on the porch beside Ace. "Matt," Ace said quietly, "you're not the first man who has been fooled by a woman. If you're lucky, this will be your first and last time. Believe it or not, I was young once," Ace continued with a grin, "and I can remember what a seventeen-year-old always has on his mind. But you're going to have to learn some self-restraint and wait for visits to the pleasure house in Denver like the other cowboys.

"Now, if you have any clean clothes, go scrub yourself in the river. We're going to have supper with Ma, and right now you smell like hell."

Ace shook his head in amusement as he watched his mother bring a large platter of fried chicken to the table. Benny followed close behind her, a bowl of mashed potatoes in one hand, a bowl of string beans in the other. His brothers were looking askance at the youngster doing women's work.

Ace, however, saw no harm in Benny's helping his mother in the kitchen. He had done the same thing. He wondered if Benny also made up beds and helped tend the flower beds in the yard, as he had done.

But all that feminine work hadn't kept him from maturing into a full-fledged man when the time came. It would be the same with Benny. Betty Brandon would see to that. Besides, Benny was the intellect in the family. He might even become a lawyer or a doctor.

When Betty fondly asked Benny to please take the biscuits out of the oven, Ace knew that he couldn't take the boy away from her. He imagined her life had been pretty empty when he went off to pursue his career as a gambler. She needed the freckle-faced kid as much as Benny needed her.

It was best all around, he thought. Lark might not want the responsibility of a ten-year-old. It was different with the older brothers. They more or less took care of themselves.

Ace waited until supper was eaten and coffee was poured before making his announcement. "Ma, boys," he said, "I have something to tell you." When they had all lifted their heads and looked at him, he said, almost shyly, "I'm getting married."

Matt and Drew stared openmouthed at him, their expressions saying that they didn't like the idea at all. Benny didn't seem to care, but Betty smiled at him, her eyes saying that she was happy for her son.

"I sure never thought you'd do a fool thing like that." Matt pushed his cup of coffee away in disgust.

"Who is she? Do we know her?" Drew asked uneasily.

"Yes, son, tell us about her," Betty said softly.

"Her name is Lark Gibb. She's twenty-one years old and the most beautiful woman I have ever seen. She's sweet and gentle and a lady through and through. I met her last winter while working on her . . . her ranch." Ace didn't think this was the time to go into the details about how Lark was married at that time. He would only explain that if it became necessary.

"She sounds lovely, Ace." Betty placed her hand on his. "When will the wedding take place?"

"As soon as I can arrange it. I'm leaving for Denver in the morning." Ace saw the excitement that jumped into Matt's eyes and said, "No, Matt, you can't come with me this time. You can go later, when I've got my new wife settled in at the house." He gave the teenager a knowing grin.

Matt grinned back and squirmed a bit. He and Ace would be doing the same thing at different places.

It was time to leave Betty's house then and return to their own. Ace hugged his mother and kissed her cheek, then gave Benny an affectionate knuckle-rub on the head. "Make sure you look after Ma," he said, making his voice sound serious.

As Ace and his boys took the well-used trail home, he gave the brothers instructions about what to do while he was gone.

"I want you fellows to give all your attention to finishing the house while I'm gone. At least get the walls built in the bedroom Lark and I will be using. A married couple needs a little privacy, you know." He chuckled. When Matt and Drew laughed, he said, "See if Ma will loan me a bedstead and mattress. I can't expect my bride to sleep on the floor, on a straw pallet."

The unfinished house loomed up in the moonlight. When the boys dismounted, Ace said, "You fellows go on to bed. I'll put the horses up. I have to say good-bye to someone."

"Who?" Matt asked. "Do we know them?"

"No, you don't. I won't be gone long."

Betty had just thrown out a pan of soapy dishwater and was about to return to the kitchen when in the distance she recognized Ace riding toward the fenced-in gravesite of his first wife, Michelle. She smiled and nodded her head. Ace's marriage to the singer hadn't worked, but there had been respect between them, and she was pleased that he would say good-bye to her before he remarried.

Lark removed the bottle from her son's mouth and gazed down at his sleeping face. There was a melancholy look on her face that had never been there before. Her laughter no longer rang out, a quick smile no longer curved her lips. Those who loved her wondered and worried. What had happened to her in the short time she'd spent on the cattle drive?

But despite Lark's short temper and sharp tongue

these days, if one looked closely enough, deep sadness was evident in her eyes. No one seemed to notice this, however. So she suffered her heartache in silence. She didn't even want to share her misery with beloved Aunt Lucy.

She had been so sure that Ace loved her that day they were caught in the rain. She had been so sure that she had foolishly confessed her love for him. She directed a scornful laugh at herself. How he must have enjoyed breaking her down, making her say those hateful words. Had that been his intent all along? Was his arrogance so great that all women must love him?

Lark leaned her head on the chair back. It hadn't taken long to discover that his vows of love had meant nothing to Ace. As soon as he got the message that the woman Roxy wanted him back in Denver, he couldn't wait to run to her side.

At least I had the satisfaction of ordering him never to come near me again, she thought, then admitted that that had been cold comfort.

The rest of that day and night she had fought to vanquish her turbulent emotions. The next morning when the cook caught up with the herd and she was free to return home, she was empty of everything except her pride and love for her son.

Lark straightened up when Lucy walked out onto the porch and sat down in the chair beside her. "Lark, dear," she said softly, "why don't you take a walk, get some fresh air? You hardly ever leave the house anymore. You've became almost a recluse since you came home. Can't you tell me what's bothering you?"

"Maybe I will take a walk down to the river." Lark

carefully transferred the sleeping baby into her aunt's lap. She knew that Lucy would start asking questions, and she had no answers.

As Lark walked barefoot through the grass that was still wet from the drizzle of rain that had fallen all morning, a slight breeze felt good on her face. She breathed it deep into her lungs as she took the path to the willows.

Arriving at the swift-flowing river, she paced back and forth on the gravelly bank, searching in her mind for something, other than her son, to give her a focus in life. The ranch held no real interest for her. There were too many bad memories of her dead husband there. Nor did she feel any interest in city life, she thought. Was there any other choice in between? she asked herself.

"I guess I could go live with the Indians," she muttered with a sour laugh. That would certainly be a change for her.

A half hour later, feeling refreshed in body if not in mind, Lark walked back toward the house. She was within several yards of it when she stopped short and stared.

Sitting next to her aunt was a man who sent the blood racing through her veins. "What is he doing here?" she wailed as panic grabbed her. Aunt Lucy still held Aaron in her lap. Would Ace notice the little one? Would he see the strong resemblance to himself in the tiny features?

She ordered her face not to give away her fear as she tried to keep from running to the house.

Chapter Thirty-nine

Ace had never been so angry in all his life as he was right now at the sight of Lark rushing toward the house.

"Oh, dear." Aunt Lucy sighed. "Here comes Lark now."

When Lucy half rose as if to take the baby and go inside, Ace said with a growl, "Stay where you are, Aunt Lucy. If you're here I might not lay my hands on her."

Lark's heart plummeted when she stepped up on the porch. Ace had seen Aaron. Had he recognized his son? She glanced at Ace and saw by the fury in his eyes that he had. For the first time in her life she was afraid of him.

"What's this?" Ace growled with savage force.

"It's a baby," Lark answered evasively and took a step backward.

"I know it's a baby," Ace thundered. "It's my baby. Why didn't you tell me? I had a right to know. I loved you, woman."

Lark lost control at his words. "And you love that woman Roxy too," she yelled, her fingers clenched in fists.

"Yes, I love Roxy," Ace retorted, "but that has nothing to do with me and you, you jealous little cat. She's a wonderful person, and you're going to find that out."

Ace looked at Lucy and asked, "Will you look after the baby?"

Lucy nodded, afraid to say no.

"Good," Ace snapped, and, grabbing Lark by the wrist, he went down the steps, dragging her behind him.

"What do you think you're doing?" Lark screeched as Ace tossed her onto Sam's back. "I haven't got any shoes on and my dress is up past my knees."

"Good, I'll see how much brush I can ride through," Ace said as he swung up behind her.

There was no attempt at conversation as the gelding thundered along. It would be nearly impossible to hear each other above the noise of the great hooves striking the ground. Lark's hair was a banner, whipping Ace across the face. He swore and wound the heavy tresses around his left hand.

They arrived in Denver in record time. Ace pulled the weary horse to a halt and jumped from the saddle, swinging Lark down beside him. Before she could catch her breath, he was hustling her up the steps and into the Lady Chance.

"Good Lord, Ace, what are you doing?" Roxy demanded, coming from her office. "Why are you manhandling this young woman?" She ran her gaze over Lark's windblown hair, the furious glint in her eyes. Finally her eyes dropped to her slender bare feet. She glanced around at the few patrons in the saloon. They were all straining forward, listening and watching them. "Come in the office and explain yourself to me," she ordered Ace.

When they entered the small room, Ace pushed Lark into a chair, then went and stood in front of the door as if he was afraid she would try to run.

"All right, Ace, talk," Roxy said as she sat down on the edge of her desk.

"There's not much to say," Ace answered, his lips set in rigid lines. "This one had my baby a few months back and didn't think it necessary to tell me about it."

Roxy stared at her cousin. Never had she seen him so upset. He looked ready to kill, yet somehow hurt too. "Before you go on, Ace, who is this young woman?"

"What do you mean, who is she? You know who she is," Ace said.

"No, I don't. I've never met her."

Ace stared at Roxy, dumbfounded. Was it possible the two women didn't know each other? Why had he taken it for granted that they did? He moved away from the door and sat down in the chair next to Lark. He pushed his hat to the back of his head and looked at Lark, apology in his eyes and voice as he said meekly, "Lark, meet my cousin, Roxy. Roxy this is Lark. I guess I've ruined any chance I ever had of marrying her."

While Lark looked as if she'd been kicked by a horse, Roxy shook her head in disbelief. "Ace, how could you take it for granted that we knew each other?" she asked. "But it's not an unforgivable mistake," she added as she slid off the desk and walked to the door. "I'll leave you two together to talk about it."

When the door closed behind Roxy, there was an uneasy silence for a moment. Then Ace stood up and began to pace back and forth. "Look, Lark." He finally stopped and stood in front of her. "I know I've acted dumber than a post, but will you forgive me?"

"I shouldn't." Lark gazed up at him, her eyes softening. "You have put me through hell. But we have been star-crossed from the beginning."

"Why didn't you tell me you were expecting the night I left the ranch?"

"You had your heart set on starting your ranch, and I didn't want to jeopardize your dream."

"You could have told me when we saw each other again."

"No, I couldn't," Lark answered. "When I first saw you in town you were with a beautiful woman, Roxy, and a young boy that I took to be your son. Thad had told me he'd seen the three of you together before. We thought you were a family."

"My poor Lark." Ace took her by the arms and lifted her out of the chair. "I'm not the only one who has been suffering." He gazed down at her.

"I think we've both suffered enough," Lark whispered, and raised her lips for a kiss that melted away all the hurt and misunderstandings that had dogged their footsteps.

When the kiss ended, Ace said earnestly, "We're getting married tomorrow before some other kind of misunderstanding comes up."

"Yes, we must." Lark smiled up at him. "Your son Aaron needs a last name."

"So it's a son I have." Ace gave a whoop. "He sure looks like me, doesn't he?"

"He certainly does." Lark smiled at the beaming Ace. "There's no denying that you put your stamp on him."

Lark was silent a moment; then she asked, "What about your other three boys?"

Ace's laughter rang out. "Let's go to my room and I'll tell you all about them. I can't wait for you to meet them."

Lark thought that she could wait quite well as they left Roxy's office arm in arm.

Between heated lovemaking that lasted the rest of the day and part of the night, Ace brought Lark up to date about everything that had happened in his life since the night, so long ago, when he'd left her.

The next day at noon they were married in Denver's Methodist church. Ace wore his black gambler's suit and Lark stood up in finery borrowed from Roxy. It was a small ceremony with only Roxy, Lucy and Ben, who held baby Aaron, attending. Since Lark and Ace had each been married before, they didn't think it proper to make the wedding a big affair, so their only celebration was to eat lunch in Denver's fanciest restaurant. The only one attending who was not related to the happy couple was Ragged Feather. Ben had declared that if his best friend couldn't attend the festivities, then he would not be there either.

Ace barely tasted his tender steak. He couldn't wait to get back to his ranch, introduce Lark to the boys, then go to bed. He didn't care if the sun was high in

the sky and the boys gave him some knowing looks—
he would lead Lark into their bedroom, lock the door
and make love to her until they both were worn out.

And man, do I feel strong, he thought with a
crooked grin.

A toast to their happiness was finally made by Ben
and then everyone left for Utah. Lark and Ace rode
their horses ahead while Lucy and Ben took turns
holding baby Aaron in the wagon with Ragged
Feather.

It had been agreed that Mr. and Mrs. Elliot would
be making their home at the Brandon horse ranch,
and that, of course, Ragged Feather would live with
them. Ace and Lark had been riding for about half
an hour when Ace decided that the horses needed a
rest. Lark's pulse quickened and her lips curved in a
knowing smile. Her new husband wanted a little
lovemaking.

When she slid off her mare and into Ace's arms,
he kept her waist pinned to his. "Why, Mr. Brandon"—she gave him a coy look between her long
lashes—"what is that hard thing you have in your
pocket?"

"It could be most anything. Do you want to take a
look and find out?"

"Well, I am rather curious. Do you think I should?
It's nothing that will hurt me, is it? It feels awfully
long and hard."

"I know that it does, but it wouldn't hurt you for
the world. It only wants to bring you a wonderous
feeling. Something you'll never get tired of."

"Well, if you're sure . . ." Lark pretended doubt.
"I'll take a little peek."

"Good girl." Ace gazed into her eyes as he let her

slide down the length of him until her feet touched the ground. She stood and watched him unbutton his fly. She let loose a little squeak when his manhood sprang free like a live thing.

"It won't hurt you, Lark, you know that," Ace said softly. Taking her hand, he closed her fingers around his pulsating member. She automatically tightened her grip and began to stroke her hand up and down. Soon Ace was making growling noises deep in his throat. Taking himself from her hand, he scooped her up in his arms and laid her down in a patch of tall, tender grass under a tree. As he unbuttoned the Levi's she had changed into, she managed to tug off her boots.

Ace jerked off his own boots, and practically tore off his pants. Lark lifted her arms to receive him when he hung over her. "Lark," he whispered huskily, "I can't believe that I'm finally going to make love to you as my wife. I have waited so long for this day. I love you so much."

Lark cupped his lean face in her palms. "I feel like I have loved you forever, Ace Brandon," she whispered. "I was so miserable thinking that I could never have you."

"You have me, honey, and I hope that you never regret it," he said as he slid himself inside her. With a long sigh, Lark lifted her hips to meet his thrust.

They had barely gotten back into their clothes and mounted their horses when they heard the creaking of the wagon coming up behind them. Ace looked at Lark, a lazy, contented smile on his lips. "You're gonna cause me to get a bad name, you hussy," he drawled.

"I'm sure," Lark said, and freeing her foot, she gave him a sharp poke in the leg.

When they were almost home, the wagon turned off on a smaller road that would take its occupants to the Brandon ranch. It had been decided that Ben and Lucy and Ragged Feather would make their home there. Matt and Drew would live with Ace and Lark. At that thought, Ace realized he still had to explain about the boys to his wife.

I might as well tell her now, he decided, and slowed his horse to a walk. "Lark," he began, "I want to tell you about my three boys."

Lark wasn't sure she wanted to hear about them. She felt in such high spirits, she didn't want anything to spoil her pleasure. But when Ace finished the story of the three orphaned boys, she thought it was the best wedding gift she could receive. The teenagers weren't Ace's by blood.

"Will you mind letting them live with us?" Ace asked anxiously.

"Of course I wouldn't mind. I wouldn't have it any other way. I hope that they will like me."

"They will. They can't wait to meet you. You won't meet Benny, the youngest, yet. My mother is so taken with him, I don't have the heart to take him away from her."

Ace suddenly stood up in the stirrups and jerked off his Stetson. "Here come the boys now!" he exclaimed, wildly waving his hat.

What handsome teenagers, Lark thought when their horses pounded up beside them. The appreciative look Matt flashed at her told Lark that the older boy was of an age when the opposite sex interested him.

397

But Drew, even more handsome than his brother, was very shy. Her heart went out to him.

Ace swung to the ground and almost had his arm taken off as the boys energetically shook his hand. He helped Lark dismount then. "Meet Lark, boys." He grinned at them. Matt greeted her with a loud, smacking kiss on the cheek, but Drew's kiss was feather soft when he took his turn.

Matt gathered up the reins of the two horses and said, "I'll tend to the animals while Drew makes us some supper."

Ace awkwardly cleared his voice. "Don't make anything for us. We're beat from the long ride. I think we'll just go to bed."

Matt looked west where the sun had yet an hour before starting to sink behind the mountains. Ace wanted to give him a whack on the head when with a devilish grin Matt said, "Yeah, I guess a ride like that is tiring for a man your age."

Ace give him a black look and, taking Lark's arm, led her into the home where they would spend the rest of their lives.

Lacey
NORAH HESS

Norah Hess's historical romances are "delightful, tender and heartwarming reads from a special storyteller!"

—*Romantic Times*

Stranded on the Western frontier, Lacey Stewart suddenly has to depend on the kindness of strangers. And no one shows her more generosity than the rancher who offers to marry her. But shortly after Trey Saunders and Lacey are pronounced husband and wife, he is off to a cattle drive— and another woman's bed. Shocked to discover that the dashing groom wants her to be a pawn in a vicious game of revenge, the young firebrand refuses to obey her vows. Only when Trey proves that he loves, honors, and cherishes his blushing bride will Lacey forsake all others and unite with him in wedded bliss.

__3941-9 $5.99 US/$7.99 CAN